D1582767

SECOND TIME AROUND

Also by Patty Sleem

BACK IN TIME

Best wishes,
Patty Sleem

Patty Sleem

Second Time Around

PREP PUBLISHING

PREP Publishing
1110½ Hay Street
Fayetteville, NC 28305
(910) 483-6611

Library of Congress Cataloging-in-Publication Data
Sleem, Patty, 1948-
    Second time around : a novel / by Patty Sleem. — 1st ed.
    p. cm.
    ISBN 1-885288-00-X   ISBN 1-885288-05-0 (pbk.)
    1. Middle aged persons—United States—Fiction.
    2. Married people—United States—Fiction.
    3. Family—United States—Fiction. I. Title.
PS3569.L356S43 1995
813'.54—dc20   94-66481
                                                          CIP

Printed in the United States of America
First Edition

*This is a work of fiction. Characters and corporations in this novel are either
the product of the author's imagination or, if real, used fictitiously without
any intent to describe their actual conduct.*

In loving memory of

Louise Jarvis

Appreciation is expressed to the Reverend Billy Graham and to HarperCollins for allowing us to quote remarks he made about marriage to David Frost in the book *David Frost Talks With Billy Graham* published in 1971 by A.J. Holman Company, affiliated with J.B. Lippincott of Philadelphia.

Appreciation is also expressed to Viking and the Metropolitan Museum of Art for permission to use in chapter 2 some information about famous painters presented in the Met's trademark series *"What Makes a . . . a . . . ?"*

Graphic artist Kathi Quesenberry is the creator of both the hardcover book jacket and the trade paperback cover.

Part 1

$O\mathcal{NE}$

N ew York was covered with snow so the taxi drive from the airport was slower than usual. Kathryn felt mesmerized by the
sight of snow-covered buildings, cars, roads, bridges, people.
From the time she stepped off the plane, everything seemed different
from Macon. Of course, New York City *was* different in nearly every
way from Macon, Georgia, but on this particular trip, the differences
seemed more accentuated. Although it was January, Macon had been
in the middle of what felt like an Indian summer, with temperatures
in the eighties when she left. Her grandmother would have said they
were having a "spell" of hot weather. In theory, the hot weather should
have been a welcome break from their mild Southern winter, but
when you didn't have any summer clothes left in your closet, it was
plain inconvenient. Now she was in snow. She pulled her full-length
faux fur coat close to her body and realized it would feel delicious to
be out of warm weather for a week. She'd miss the kids, but it would
be nice to hang around New York as a businesswoman and not have
the usual merry-go-round of Cub Scouts, ballet, and all the other activities Stefan would be in charge of getting four children to and from.
A week from now, when she got home, she knew Stefan would be
glad to see her. She smiled to herself, recalling what a humbling experience it was for him when he had to do her "mommy" job for a
week.

When she checked into the Ritz-Carlton, a handwritten note was waiting for her at reception.

KATHRYN,

PLEASE CALL ME AT GALLERIA TOWERS WHEN YOU GET IN.

WELCOME TO NEW YORK!

MARCOS GALLERIA

She was stunned. How did Marcos know she would be in New York on a buying trip? She walked to the elevator as if in a trance, searching through her memory bank, trying to retrieve some conversation she must have had with him about David.

After she tipped the bellboy and heard the door close behind him, she picked up the phone and asked the switchboard operator to dial Galleria Towers and ask for Marcos Galleria.

"Hello?" said the thick Spanish accent her ear was becoming reaccustomed to. The sound of his voice on the phone could still make something thrill inside her. Amazing. After a weird and traumatic and hasty divorce, followed by fifteen years of silence, something inside her still, against her every wish, thrilled at the sound of his voice.

"Marcos?"

"Oh, hi," replied his voice, obviously glad to hear hers. "Welcome to New York. I happened to have a business trip to New York for a few days, and I remembered that you told me you'd be here to do some buying and you usually stayed at the Ritz. Do you have plans for dinner tonight?"

Kathryn paused before replying. Dinner with her ex-husband? From the time he'd called nine months ago, on David's fifteenth birthday, telling her he wanted to develop a relationship with his only son, whom he'd never seen, she'd told Marcos she wanted to have a warm relationship with him. Pure maternal instinct had taken over during and after that telephone call, and instinctively she'd known that she wanted to form a cordial relationship with Marcos so her son could venture into this relationship with his natural father with her blessing. And with Stefan's blessings, since Stefan had raised David with her since David was nearly four years old. By parental instinct, she and Stefan had both known that David must feel the love of his natural father to be emotionally intact.

Marcos listened to her silence and then added, "I know the absolutely best place in New York now. Some clients showed it to me the last time I was here . . . and you have to eat tonight, don't you, hmm?"

"Well, okay, why not? I mean, thank you, yes, I'd love to." They agreed to meet in the downstairs lobby of the Ritz a couple of hours later.

She saw his eyes catch sight of her as she got off the elevator on the second floor and walked the flight of circular stairs to the ground level where he was pacing the floor, elegantly adorned in a beautiful, full-length, tan camel-hair coat. His eyes focused on her as she walked toward him. Of medium height with an erect, aristocratic carriage, he had a build that was more solid at middle age, and he had the air of a man who had tasted of success and who was accustomed to the finer things in life. He still had the regal bearing and bold self-confidence that had attracted her years ago when they met as MBA graduate students at the Harvard Business School. Kathryn's super thin figure had changed over the years of childbirth and child rearing, but a combination of genes and a daily walking regimen had given her at middle age a voluptuous figure. She was no longer the size four she'd been when they were at Harvard. The thin, schoolgirl figure was gone and in its place was a fuller, more sensuous-looking shape on her 5-foot 5½-inch frame. In the fashion business, it wasn't a requirement that the retail barons be thin and beautiful, but it helped. And being in the fashion retailing business had been a strong motivating factor in keeping her figure disciplined and capable of showing off the fashions she came to New York to buy for the Chic Boutique. At least so far, middle-age spread had spread in the right places on her. Blessed from birth with a rosy Irish complexion and green eyes, she was a beauty at forty-five who looked more like thirty-five, and she could see the look of appreciation in his eyes as she walked toward him.

As she came nearer to him, an image flashed inside her mind. It had been a recurring image lately. It was "look number 87," he used to call it. That was the pet name he'd given years ago to the look on his face when he was admiring her physically and showing how aroused he was by looking at her. That's what his face looked like now, as she descended the circular staircase and walked toward him, except that his whole face wasn't composed into that particular expression he used to make when he was deliberately accentuating his desire for her. The look in his eyes was the same, though, and the same appetite was showing through the smile on his face.

"Hi," he said softly, looking into her large green eyes smiling at him.

"Hi," she answered cheerfully, looking him directly in the eyes at first and then feeling suddenly shier when she saw his eyes take a slow, lingering look at her body, from her shoulders to her shoes, and then back up again to her smiling face. She was dressed in a cable khaki sweater that made her look more buxom than she was and the matching khaki pants were slimming. The faux fur brown coat telegraphed her artistic, fun-loving personality and creative fashion sense. He put his arm around the outside of her coat as he guided her out of the glass doors of the hotel and into the night air where his driver waited in a long black car. When he saw them coming, the driver jumped out of the car to open the back door for them. The plush green leather interior smelled new. Spanish guitar music was playing softly on the radio.

"It's called Brandts," he said, smiling as he stared into her face, while the car sped off to the address he'd given the driver. She smiled back as she gently moved away to the other side of the car, trying to sit at a distance that felt comfortable and respectable. Even sitting at the other side of the car and looking out the window, she felt awkward and clumsy, like a freshman schoolgirl out for the first time with an upperclassman who was president of the student body and captain of the football team and leading man in the senior play. She couldn't believe how vulnerable she felt all of a sudden. She'd lived long enough to be able to sense when danger was near, and she sensed it now. Danger was near.

"What's got you so absorbed?" His voice seemed to come from far away, as though through a tunnel. It interrupted her train of thought, and she was transported back to the here and now.

"Oh, I was just looking at the tall buildings," she answered, looking at him with a smile. "Everything in New York is on such a grand scale, and I'm just a country girl, you know. It's almost like you start thinking differently when you're here. New York stimulates you and moves you up a few levels in intensity. At least, that's what seems to happen to me when I'm here."

The car stopped abruptly in front of a restaurant with an awning over it. After Marcos checked her coat, they were shown to their table by a handsome Italian man who recognized Marcos and seemed genuinely delighted to see him. Their table was in a corner of the room. Marcos helped her into her chair and then took the seat opposite her. He held up his hand to beckon a waiter, who was watching for his sign and appeared instantly. Marcos spoke in Spanish to the waiter and, after advising Kathryn of his recommendations, ordered for both of them. As she watched the aggressive and self-assured way he took charge, she felt simultaneously very uncomfortable and very comfortable. There was something that was uncomfortable about feeling so comfortable with him. She looked across the table into the large brown eyes of the man who had been her lover for two years, her husband for the eight months they lived together, and her ex-husband for fifteen years. The intellectual part of her was wondering what their relationship really was, anyway. She was the parent of their son, and he was the *in absentia* parent. That was the relationship. Very queer. He was an odd mix of someone in the family tree and a total stranger.

"So how are you doing?" he began, as the waiter disappeared to fetch their wine.

"Fine."

"How's Stefan?"

"Fine."

"How's David?"

"Fine."

He smiled at her. "So everyone's fine?"

"Yes, everyone is fine." *Except for me,* she was thinking. *I'm obviously not fine or I wouldn't be having dinner with you. I must be totally demented to even be here. What in the world am I doing having dinner with my ex-husband?* She considered walking out of the restaurant without saying a word. Just leaving. Actually, she felt like running out, getting far away, as though her safety were in jeopardy. But it seemed stupid. *Oh, for heaven's sake, it is only dinner, you nit brain,* she said to herself.

"And how's your family? How is Dolores doing?"

"Oh, she's fine. The girls are keeping her busy with their social engagements and after-school activities. But you know how that is, hmm?"

"Yes."

The wine steward appeared and filled their glasses.

"Well, I just want this dinner to be a kind of thank-you dinner, in a way."

"Thank-you?"

"Yes, thank-you. You've been really great about helping me establish the relationship with David after all those years, and I appreciate it. It was very kind of you."

She smiled.

"You've done a great job of raising him, you know."

She smiled again. *Oh, thank you, Marcos,* a voice inside her said as she stared at him. *Glad you like the way the crop turned out. Why, I'm sorry I didn't have five or six more for you!* It was nice of him to say so, though, and she liked hearing it. No one looking at them, sitting there enjoying a glass of wine together, looking like a married couple, would ever guess the stormy and destructive path their relationship had taken. Marcos and Kathryn had met during the first month they were at the Harvard Business School MBA Program, and they began dating almost immediately. For a year and a half, their relationship was on again, off again. Marcos was a brilliant, hot-tempered Mexican man, and she was a stubbornly independent American woman who was determined not to be dominated or possessed. They broke up several times after arguments that turned into heated outbursts and physical shoving matches. *Funny,* she thought to herself, *I can't remember anything we ever argued about. There was something once about crab terrine, but I can't remember what it was.*

"My grandmother used to tell me that a mother's love is the closest thing on earth to God's love, so I guess the strongest instinct we have is to do the best thing for our children, don't you think? I mean, even though our relationship ended, it's obviously in David's best interest to have a loving relationship with you." She paused, and a deep sigh came out of her. "Actually, I felt relieved after you called. For me, it meant that an old wound could heal. And for David, your call meant that he could be whole. Nothing I accomplish in life would ever mean anything if I even accidentally harmed one of my children emotionally." She paused again. "It never really entered my mind to stand in David's way of loving you and your family."

He smiled at her with obvious admiration and held his wine glass up to toast hers. She responded. "Here's to a cordial relationship between our families, Kathryn," he said. After they clinked glasses, the waiter appeared with their salad and bread.

"So you're in New York to do some business?" he asked as they began eating.

"Yes," she said, "I come every year in January to see the fall collections and to buy a few more things for summer for the shop. We're moving toward a very heated primary election in the spring in Macon, and I'm swamped with requests from candidates and candidates' wives who want to make fashion statements while they go through the campaign."

"It's funny, isn't it, that you've ended up in a business very similar to our family business. There's a twist of fate there, no?"

His voice was soft and gentle as he spoke. Kathryn looked into his face. She could see the pain and sadness under the smile. The reality dawned on her that they were trying to be friends now, although a whole battleground of a divorce and then a cold, cruel fifteen-year silence had once lain between them. They had never spoken of the divorce since his call on David's fifteenth birthday. Everything had been just polite conversation and social graces between them. They'd held many friendly phone conversations since his initial call, but the calls always had an underlying business purpose. Like arranging David's trip to see Marcos and his wife Dolores and their two daughters at their home in San Antonio last summer. And like arranging the week-long visit by David to see his Hispanic family right after Christmas. Suddenly, she was aware that sitting across from her in this elegant and romantic restaurant was the man she'd almost spent her life with, raised kids with, and loved until death. Sadness was what she felt, too. The kind of sadness that comes from personal failure and regret.

"Well, now that we're here," she said, with a smile on her face and a twinkle in her eyes, "I want to ask you some questions about what happened fifteen years ago." She paused to study the expression on his face before she continued in a serious tone. "I want to talk about what happened before we get too old to remember it."

A shocked look came over his face, as though he'd been caught by surprise by this request for a postmortem. He maintained his Latin dignity, however, and a stern look spread across his face. "Well, I guess you're right. We have to talk about it sometime. Go ahead." There was a starchiness in his voice that implied that, yes, she could go ahead, but she'd have to drag him along. He looked like his father now at middle age. Kathryn had tried to like his father but she'd felt intimidated in his presence. She'd always thought that his father didn't like her and didn't feel she measured up to the expectation he had for the woman his son would marry. Marcos never told her so, but she knew he'd married her over his father's objections. Despite the storminess of the relationship, they'd married in a fancy church wedding in Harvard Yard in the spring just before graduating with their MBAs. After graduation, they'd gone to Mexico City and had lived with his parents for a month or so before getting their own house.

"You know one thing I remember? When we were living with your parents, I was so intimidated by your father that I forgot how to set the table one day when I was helping your mother in the kitchen! I'd been setting the table since I was five years old and, suddenly, at age twenty-nine, I forgot how to set the table!"

He smiled a smile that had some pain in it. "Yes, he could seem rather hard at times."

"When did he die?" she asked.

"About ten years ago. It was a shock, actually, because he wasn't really old. He was just in his sixties, but he was very stubborn and refused to give up his smoking. I guess what they say about stubborn, hostile personalities being death-prone may be true."

"My gosh, I hope not," Kathryn replied, in a tone of mock exaggeration, "you and I are in serious trouble, if that's true."

He laughed heartily and spontaneously. Their eyes met as they grinned at each other.

"You know, Marcos, if I had it to do over again, I wouldn't do things the same way." Her tone was soft and mellow.

He smiled at her and looked . . . appreciative . . . grateful, sort of.

"Yes, well," he said, "that's what happens in life. After you get the experience, you know what you should have done. But it's too late then. There's an old saying in Spanish, you know, that that's what makes the devil the devil. It's not so much that he's mean or evil, but he's got the experience. You know?"

She nodded. "Who was it that said, 'Any fool can learn from his own mistakes. I want to learn from the mistakes of other people'?" A smile appeared on his face as he sipped his wine. She continued. "Middle-aged eyes do see some things more clearly."

"I agree with that," he replied stiffly.

She began again and spoke slowly and tentatively. "You know, I have to tell you this, Marcos, because I think there's been a misunderstanding all these years. I didn't exactly mean to leave you for good, you know."

"Oh, you didn't?" His tone was imperious, almost sarcastic, and he looked disbelieving. "Well, it certainly seemed like you did. I mean, you took your most precious things with you, all your poetry and all the things that meant the most to you."

"Yes, I know. But we had a baby on the way, a planned baby, and I think now, looking back on it, that I was very confused. We were having heavy marital problems, and I was scared by the escalating physical violence between us. I was living in a foreign country, not being able to speak the language, with in-laws everywhere, and you were always with them and never with me, and I got totally disoriented. I wanted a home that was peaceful and safe, and I think I was only trying to dramatize the point for you. Anyway, it wasn't my idea to leave."

"Oh?" He stared at her hard. There was a cold, suspicious look on his face.

"It was my mother's idea for me to leave Mexico. I thought I was coming home for a visit for Thanksgiving, and while I was home, I was going to try to reform you by telephone. Intelligent, huh?" Rueful was how she looked and how she sounded. She paused, then continued. "You know, I've learned one thing, Marcos, about being in trouble."

"What's that?"

"When you're in a lot of trouble, and you need someone to turn to, make sure the person you turn to has more sense than you do."

"That's a good principle," he responded, nodding once.

"Well, anyway, in the midst of my unhappiness in our eighth month of marriage, and when I was nearly five months pregnant, I turned to my mother for help, and she hatched a plan for me to leave my marriage. Only, I really didn't know what I was doing, Marcos. She suggested that I come home, and it sounded like a great idea to run away from my troubles for a while, from a husband who was acting like the devil, and from in-laws who didn't like me anyway. So I followed her advice and decided to visit Georgia. It's been a long time ago now, but in my confused state of thinking, I guess I imagined that I would give you a few ultimatums by telephone once I got home, after which you would act like a puppy and do whatever I commanded, and then I would return to Mexico and everything would be happy ever after. And, of course, everything would be all my way and just perfect."

He stared at her with no emotion showing in his face. He sat without moving, studying her with those large, liquid brown eyes of his.

"Real smart, huh?" she asked.

He cocked his head, nodded slowly, and swallowed a bite of food, still showing no emotion in his face while studying her expression.

"You didn't even call for two weeks after you left," he said matter-of-factly.

She shook her head and spoke slowly, as though the memory was painful. "I was physically exhausted. I was five months pregnant. I'd driven the whole way back to Georgia from Mexico City, and I was emotionally and physically drained." She paused and took a breath. "It's amazing how someone can graduate from the best business school in the world and be so completely ignorant about solving the teething troubles of a marriage." She sighed. "I guess that's why I never became a brain surgeon. Limited intelligence." She smiled at him. "Somehow what happened then reminds me of the slogan they printed on the back of the T-shirts they gave out at the last Harvard Business School reunion."

"What was that?" Marcos asked. He hadn't been to any of the HBS reunions since he and Kathryn had graduated as man and wife. Kathryn and Stefan had been to all of them.

"AGE AND TREACHERY WILL OVERCOME YOUTH AND INNOCENCE."

"Yes, that's usually the way it works," he sighed, as he nodded his head. "But," he continued slowly, "it *had* turned very sour between us, though, if you remember. I mean, my father saw the car right after you smashed the window in it when I left you alone that Sunday. Remember that? And remember when you threw the mayonnaise at the painting? Remember the violence between us?"

The violence between us? she thought to herself. *You always started it! I was just responding to your violence.*

"Well, anyway," she replied with a sigh, "I can see more clearly now, through middle-aged eyes, that marriage is very difficult in the first year." She paused and smiled impishly. "And sometimes in the other years!"

"You can say that again," he said, smiling broadly.

She smiled back. "Yep, I remember thinking shortly after I got married the second time, 'Oh, my gosh, I *was* right about marriage! This *is* a ball-busting experience!'"

Her candor caught him by surprise and he laughed out loud, almost choking on the sip of wine he'd just taken. Then he replied. "Oh, second marriages are different. You get married to stay married." He relaxed in his chair and smiled. "You know what a real estate broker told me once about second marriages?"

"What?"

"It's a friend of mine who's in real estate. Anyway, she was telling me that, in real estate, it's usually the third broker who becomes the hero with the seller of the house. Usually the seller thinks the first broker sets the selling price too low. Then the second broker doesn't please the seller for other reasons. Then along comes the third broker, after the attitudes become adjusted to reality, and the third broker—who actually performs much like the first and second—becomes the hero. So my friend was telling me that there's a saying in real estate circles that goes like this: 'If I can't be the first love or the second wife, then let me be the third broker.'" He shrugged and repositioned himself in his chair slightly. "Attitudes get adjusted over time. And the second wife benefits from the adjusting of attitudes just like the third broker benefits."

"I see." *So, it's just as I've come to believe in the last year,* she thought to herself. *We were going through an adjustment process when mommy dearest broke up our marriage.* "Well, looking back on it now, I know I must have been at a very low point, with no one to turn to, if I turned to my mother, because she and I have never gotten along."

"Is that right? I didn't know that."

"Oh, you and I never got that far in our relationship that I felt comfortable telling you that. Sometimes we want to pretend even to ourselves that our lives are better than they really are."

"What do you mean?"

Talking about this was going to be difficult. She felt like she might choke on the words, but she knew she had to have this conversation. If they were going to have a relationship as David's parents for the rest of their lives, there was a fundamental misunderstanding that had to be cleared up. She took a deep breath and plunged ahead. "I mean, I grew up in a home where there was always an argument going on. And a lot of other things going on." She shook her head as if to shake thoughts out of it, and Marcos could see she was embarrassed and uncomfortable. He stared as she struggled to get the words out. He could see a trace of the shyness and lack of confidence that had been key elements of her personality when he'd known her years ago. He looked into her eyes and saw a glimmer of sadness. "My father was very hot-tempered and would jump into a fight quicker than anyone I ever saw. He made his way through life by bullying people and pick-ing on people weaker than him. He demanded total obedience from me—I was the firstborn and was seven years older than my only sis-ter—and I had to endure harsh whippings for the slightest provoca-tion of him, even when I was a baby. My mother just stood by and let him do it. It was just ridiculous stuff, like not picking up something when he told me to, or something like that. Just the slightest thing would set him off." She paused and swallowed hard before she resumed. "As I got older it was usually something my mother did that angered him. It was something between them, but he never went after her directly. She was cold and domineering, to me and to him, and he was kind of afraid of her, I think. So he just took it out on me. I was his convenient scapegoat."

"That's terrible. I didn't know that." There was sympathy and compassion in his voice and on his face.

"I'm not telling you this to make you feel bad, or to make you feel better toward me, Marcos. It's just that I've done a lot of thinking since your phone call last year. It's sort of like that phone call was a watershed event in my life. It's forced me to look at so many things as they really are. Things I hadn't thought about in years. It feels like part of a dam broke and the water just starting gushing out. I . . . I . . . I don't know why I'm doing telling you all this, though . . . I really hadn't planned on it."

"No, please go on, I want to understand what happened between us, too."

She took a deep breath and looked embarrassed. "My father terrorized me physically, and they both terrorized me emotionally. Oh, I don't know. Maybe it was my fault, maybe I was just too sensitive to begin with. But my home with them was never a safe place. The whole time I was growing up, he was on the road most of the time building a business and living a very promiscuous life, and every time he was out of town and his back was turned, my mother was having an affair with one of the locals, and I was expected to be her confidante and the keeper of her secrets. And, of course, with my father's violent temper, I really did have to keep her secrets or he might have killed someone. That's what I thought, anyway. The whole burden of keeping the family intact was on my shoulders. I was more or less forced to become a parent when I was a little girl." She paused. "Of course, we went to church every Sunday like a model family." She shook her head and swallowed hard. "I think I flipped out when we went to Mexico. It felt like I was back in a hostile family like the one I'd tried to get away from all my life, and I just lost it. I panicked. I think some of that pain from childhood bubbled up and erupted like a volcano. Being pregnant probably made me a little crazier, because I guess I knew instinctively that I didn't want to raise a child in a family like the one I grew up in."

He stared at her in silence for a moment, and then spoke. "How about your sister?"

Kathryn looked uncomfortable but she continued. There was a sad look in her eyes. "She ended up a victim of their lifestyle. They flaunted their adulteries in front of her, too, but it made my sister glamorize that lifestyle, and she actually became a carbon copy of them. My sister started running around on her first husband as soon as she got married."

He shook his head. "That's too bad."

"Yes, it is. She didn't end up having a very good character, but she didn't have good role models, that's for sure." She paused. "I'll always feel guilty about Sally, but now that I have my own kids, I can't try to raise her, too. I was her surrogate mother while my mother was having her flings, so I feel like I half raised her, and I feel a little responsible for the way she turned out."

He swallowed and then spoke, as if choosing his words carefully. "Well, I did come to think over the years that maybe you were very disoriented from living in a foreign country, and learning a new language, and all that."

"And having relatives everywhere," she smiled.

He glared at her and looked gruff.

She continued with a smile. "Oh, I'm just teasing you a little, Marcos. Actually, I liked your family, I really did. I just got so overwhelmed by everything at the same time—marriage, pregnancy, in-laws, Spanish, Mexico, living in a big city, all of it was new to me, and I was so vulnerable to my mother's advice to run away. I was very weak emotionally, and you weren't treating me all that well either, of course." She paused, then smiled. "But, you know, to be honest, I never ended up liking a bunch of relatives in my face all the time. I think I would have made a good mistress if it weren't for the immorality of it, and for the fact that I wanted to have a litter of kids."

He laughed.

"I'm still too blunt for your tastes, you know," she grinned.

"Yes, that's probably true. That is what I used to tell you, isn't it?"

"Yes, you used to tell me that I needed to do more sweet-talking to get my way. And I guess I've learned through the years that you're right, to a degree. But, you know, I made a conscious decision when I was a young girl not to be a manipulator after watching my parents live such a dishonest lifestyle. I decided that I was going to grow up and be just like my grandmother, whom I spent every summer of my life with until I started working. So, you were right, there isn't enough sweet-talk in my style, because the one thing I don't want to do is use people. I guess I developed a style that's too blunt, and I know I intimidate people sometimes, but I never seduce them or trick them. And I think I'm finally out of that phase where I go around trying to please everybody, like I was trained to do."

"Yes, well, I guess we all spend a little time dealing with issues from childhood, don't we?"

"To tell you the truth, I'm still dealing with a lot of those issues, even at middle age. It's ridiculous, isn't it? But better late than never, don't you think?" She smiled. Then her face grew more serious. "I think I'm going through a new transition in my life. I don't want any relationships in my life that aren't honest anymore, and that includes my relationship with my parents. It's always been a pretend relationship, where we look like a healthy family on the outside but in private they step on me." She paused, then cocked her head and looked at him as though she were going to switch subjects. "Life has taught me some things in the last fifteen years, Marcos. And I think I know some things about marriage, too, now that I'm at middle age."

"What's that?"

"Well, I think marriage is a process. It's about two people coming together, usually when they're very immature, and finishing up the process of growing up together. I mean, to expect people to be grownups when they marry is not realistic. People get married, and then they deal with a lot of childhood pain and all kinds of other stuff while they're adjusting each other's attitudes and learning how to be married for the first time."

"Yes, it is mostly persistence that makes a marriage work, isn't it?" he asked. He paused and then continued in a tone of voice that sounded tentative. "I've had some regrets about our marriage breaking up."

She studied his expression as he sipped his wine. *If I'd only known fifteen years ago what I know now,* she thought, *maybe we could have made our marriage work. We had the love, and we shared a passion for life.*

"You know, I do resent my mother's meddling in our marriage." He could hear the anger in her voice. "I mean, I turned to someone who I thought knew something about fixing marital problems, who had experience, and I trusted her. And what she did was manipulate me when I was terribly unhappy into doing something that, I can see now, must have hurt and offended you horribly!"

"Yes, it did hurt." *How terribly sensitive of you to see that after all these years,* he thought. *Your mother flew to Mexico City to help you pack your things, and then you left like a thief in the night, lying to me that you were going home for a visit for Thanksgiving when, I discovered later, you'd taken your personal papers and all the stuff that meant the most to you. You humiliated me in public, in front of my family and my friends, and left me in agony wondering what your intentions were. And then you had the audacity to call me a couple of weeks later to give me some kind of ultimatum about my behavior and what I needed to change for you to come back to me. My behavior? What about your behavior? What about your sneaky, lying behavior?*

"But," she continued, "you know, I couldn't see it then. I couldn't see any of it. I was blinded by my anger and you were blinded by your pride. And I couldn't see your pain through my anger. All I saw were my own feelings and my own needs, and I couldn't see that my leaving you in such a devious way must have made you horrified at my character."

"Yes, that's right."

"Except . . . it wasn't my character you saw. It was hers. I was just a demoralized little pregnant lady who was her pawn, doing everything she told me to do and say." She paused. "I know that for a fact, Marcos. I kept a diary during those days, and I recently looked back at it for the first time and read about how she was sending me to see her lawyer about a divorce and how she was pushing me to sue you for pregnancy expenses and everything else. I really don't remember any of it, though. I was just pregnant and traumatized. I was out of my mind and emotionally numbed. Not quite at my fighting weight, you know?"

"Well, that's very sad," he replied, looking glum.

"But what I hadn't figured on, though," she said slowly, looking him in the eyes as he was finishing his meal, "was the way you just stopped talking to me. I mean, what I remember is that we had a conversation on the phone, and some angry words were exchanged, and then you absolutely refused to talk to me. I mean, you would only speak to me through your best friend, even though I begged him and begged him to let me talk to you. But you would only talk to me through him. That's right, isn't it? Isn't that what happened?"

"Yes, that's what happened." He looked embarrassed, uncomfortable.

"Then I finally called you anyway. Don't you remember that call I made to you late one night when you were having the party, when I was trying to talk with you and strike up some reconciliation?"

"Yes, I remember that call, but, no, I wasn't interested in talking to you about reconciling at that point."

There was a brief silence between them.

"I vividly remember saying to you, when you acted so cold to me on the phone, 'So you don't even care?' And you said, 'No, it's not that, it's just that I think it's better this way.' I remember your words exactly."

They sat in silence for what seemed like minutes, sipping wine and looking occasionally at each other as they sat preoccupied with memories.

"That must take a pair of balls, huh? I mean, not to take back your pregnant wife?" She was staring at him aggressively.

He hadn't anticipated her aggression. He looked uncomfortable and began to squirm in his seat.

She leaned across the table to stare boldly and directly into his eyes, as though she didn't want to miss the slightest bit of expression in his face when she asked the question. "So tell me, Marcos, what happened, exactly, that you wouldn't take me back? You know, I never understood that. Do you know, I just thought for years after David was born that it seemed so strange that I married a man who never loved me at all. I mean, I was twenty-nine years old when we married, and I'd been out with a lot of men who'd loved me a lot, so it just seemed strange that I ended up marrying someone who didn't love me."

"That wasn't it." There was an edge in his voice, as though he was guarding something.

"No, I know, I can see that now. I'm not an idiot. I've come to understand since your phone call to David that there are remnants of heavy feelings between us still, and I can see that you must have cared about me. So I don't understand. There I was, pregnant, feeling pretty unhappy but fairly secure when I left Mexico on what I thought would be a visit home for Thanksgiving. I mean, in spite of our troubles, I thought you loved me, and you *were* Catholic, and it *was* a planned pregnancy." She paused. There was an aggressive, defiant note in her voice when she spoke again. "So what happened after I left Mexico, Marcos?"

He did not reply but stared down at his plate, avoiding her gaze.

She continued. "Did a bunch of Mexican men get together in a back room somewhere and decide my fate? Is that what happened?" She paused, but he did not reply. She took the offensive again. "Isn't that how things are done in Mexico? A few men in the back room decide things?"

He still said nothing and continued sipping his wine.

"*That's* what happened, isn't it? And you went along with it. You went along with it because when I left Mexico City we were in the thick of adjusting each other's attitudes, and you didn't think that was a lot of fun. You were right when you said 'sour.' It wasn't fun having your attitudes adjusted by a headstrong gringa. And I'd been in Mexico City long enough to make some enemies, hadn't I? I know your father didn't like me, and his best friend didn't like me, either— and the feeling was mutual there, as you know." She rolled her large eyes and made a face showing disgust as she arched her eyebrows.

Marcos grinned boyishly, remembering. "Yes, you and Señor Garcia didn't like each other, did you?"

"No, we didn't," she replied angrily, irritated that he was amused by a memory that caused her pain. He could hear the passion in her voice, and he could see by the tautness in her face and neck that she was making an effort to restrain her emotions to a polite level. "I don't even remember why, but I guess I had a right to dislike a few people. Or did you and your father think you should have been able to pick my friends for me, too?" She paused. "So what did your father say after I left Mexico, Marcos? He didn't want you to be married to me, and you know it. He wanted you to be married to some pretty, upper-class, cultured Mexican girl, not some independent, sassy American."

Marcos looked uncomfortable and shrugged his shoulders, as though he were choosing his words carefully. "Well, he didn't say, 'Get a divorce.' He just said, 'Do what you have to do and don't drag it out.'"

"Oh, I see," Kathryn replied, with obvious contempt in her voice, "that's great advice to a man with a baby on the way. Very Catholic of him." She realized her sarcasm was showing but she didn't care. She could see clearly now what happened. Marcos's father had never accepted the opinionated, temperamental gringa into their upper-class Mexican family, and he had seized the opportunity when she left Mexico to convince his son that she hadn't been worth marrying in the first place. I mean, if you couldn't trust a pregnant woman to stay with you, when would you ever be able to trust her? The strong-willed woman from a professional business school just didn't fit with the picture he had of his firstborn son marrying a well-bred Mexican girl who would be a devoted wife and mother in the style they were accustomed to. It must have horrified him that Marcos had gone off to the world's most prestigious graduate school and brought back a working lady as a wife.

His voice turned soft as he replied, "I have had some regrets, though." He paused. "It must have been very hard for you."

"Yes, it *was* hard," she replied, matter-of-factly. "When I saw you weren't going to take me back, I disguised my pregnancy in a loose-fitting dress so I could answer an ad for a job as a college instructor at Wesleyan College. And then everything moved quickly toward divorce, didn't it? The marriage ruptured, I had a baby boy, and there was no contact between us for fifteen years, except when you called in November after David was born in April to tell me you were returning my things, getting an annulment, suing me for divorce on grounds of abandonment, and not challenging me for custody. And that was that, until your phone call last year. I couldn't really send you a baby picture or try to interest you in David after he was born, because the last thing I wanted to do was tempt you to kidnap him and take him from me."

"Yes, that's the way it turned out." He looked sad.

"Well, you know what I think now?"

"No, what do you think?"

"I think all the pain and unhappiness between us was for nothing. I think it was total bullshit. I think it's almost comical—"

"It's not comical!" he interrupted, sounding hostile and defensive.

"No, I don't really mean comical, I guess I mean pathetic and ironic. It looks, in hindsight, ridiculous and idiotic, and as though all of that pain and suffering and hurt could have been avoided. I mean, if I just hadn't left Mexico, I think we could have worked everything out. Or, if you'd just taken me back when I was finally coming to my senses . . . but just look at the comical part . . . there we were, right out of the Harvard Business School, and we didn't have the common sense that Mexican peasants have in keeping a marriage together."

"Yes, we both should have done things differently."

"No communication and no compromise, that's what killed the marriage, Marcos."

"You're right about that."

"It's weird how differently things look in hindsight. I can see it all now, I think. I can see that I hurt you, because like an idiot, I was doing everything my mother told me to do, and you were listening to your cultural advisors," she said, with a trace of sarcasm in her voice. She paused for a moment, then spoke again. "Your pride blinded you, and you threw it all away, you know that?" Her tone of voice was a mixture of accusatory and conciliatory. Then she said it again, this time without any conciliation, emphasizing every word as she stared at him. "*You* threw it all away," she said aggressively, bending her frame over the table slightly to make sure he could see the ferocity in her face and eyes.

"That's one way to look at it," he said, elegantly placing his arms on the chair arms as though he were a king holding court. He maintained that regal, almost defiant pose while he returned her stare. He looked stoic and inscrutable. He could still drive her crazy with that impenetrable Hispanic steel veneer. She felt like throwing something at him. A plate, food, anything.

She clasped the arms of her chair and leaned forward in her seat to glare at him. "You are an ass, Marcos."

"Well, frankly, I'm relieved," he replied coolly, with little emotion showing in his voice or face. Then he smiled. "I'd begun to think you'd lost that hot Irish temper you had when I last saw you."

Only the sound of her heavy breathing could be heard in the silence between them. She stared at him angrily. They continued to sit in silence while she glared at him.

"You're right, I am," he said, finally, in a confessional tone.

She took a deep breath and sighed a loud sigh. When she spoke again, there was a gentler, more reconciling tone in her voice.

"But I'm sure it must have hurt when I trampled on you and your family when I left that way."

"Yes. It was a cruel way to leave. And then all you wanted to talk about when you called was splitting up the wedding presents. Remember?"

A lingering silence fell between them before she spoke again.

"How can it be, Marcos, that I can see it so clearly now, but I couldn't see it then? I'm a mother now and, through the eyes of a mother, I can see how I'd be horrified if anyone treated one of my sons that way. But I didn't have any idea I was trashing the marriage when I left. I couldn't see how destructive my behavior was. I think I thought we were having an argument! You know, like we always did. Maybe being pregnant spooked me, like a colt. I knew I wanted to live in a peaceful home, and in a home where I didn't have to keep secrets about adultery or domestic violence, or pretend that things were a certain way when they weren't. I think I was experiencing a major reaction to my childhood, in a way, when I left . . . so much rage was spilling out . . . I didn't want to live in a house with meanness and aggression and phoniness, like the one I'd grown up in." She paused and shook her head. "So look what I did when I hit my marital problems. I turned to the person who'd stepped on me all my life emotionally, and she planned a way for me to trample on you publicly and destroy your ego and the marriage. Nice, huh?"

Again, there was silence between them. The waiter appeared during the silence to fetch their plates and ask if they wanted coffee, which they declined. Marcos asked him to bring the bill.

"Yes, dear old mommy did what she's always done best—she busted both of our egos. She traumatized me even further, and then she traumatized you and busted your ego, so that you had no ability yourself to think things through and provide any leadership. You were just nursing your own hurt ego and pride, and I was thousands of miles away, getting more pregnant every day and, all of a sudden, faced with the need to get a job and pay for pregnancy expenses."

"Well, I didn't know all that, about your childhood, I mean."

"No, I know you didn't. We didn't really know each other very well. We were just graduate students trying to earn a degree, and we never really meant to fall in love with each other anyway, did we?"

"No, we didn't."

"In fact, looking back now, I can see how that was part of your rage toward me."

"What do you mean?"

"You used to lash out at me because you really didn't want to love me. I wasn't at all the image you'd been programmed to love. We fell in love in spite of ourselves, Marcos, that's what happened, and so much of the turbulence in our relationship came from our not really wanting to be in love with each other. We were both terrified of being in love because that was, by definition, being out of control. We tried our best to trample on the feelings we had for each other, didn't we?"

"It looks that way."

"Just look at it, Marcos. The closer we grew and the more we fell in love, the more we felt dependent and scared and determined to prove that we didn't need each other."

"Maybe you should have been a psychologist."

"All wives learn to be psychologists, don't you know that? That's the only way we preserve our sanity."

They both broke into smiles.

"But I guess that's another thing I see now."

"What's that?" he asked.

"You can't control love. You can try, but you can't force yourself to love someone you don't love, and you can't force yourself to stop loving someone you do love. You can remove that person from your life, but you can't really control that feeling of love."

He signed the check, and she excused herself to go the ladies' room. He took out his cellular phone to call his driver as she left the table. She joined him in the lobby a few minutes later. His private car was waiting outside, and the driver jumped out to hold the door open for them as they walked toward the car. On the way back to her hotel, he asked if she wanted to stop off somewhere in midtown to have a drink.

"Probably not," she smiled.

"Probably not? What does that mean?" He smiled back.

"No, Marcos, I shouldn't. I have to go back to the hotel and get ready for Monday. I have a lot of paperwork, you know?"

"Well, it's only Saturday night. Monday's a long way away. What do you say about going to the Met tomorrow? You can't work all day."

There was silence in the car while he waited for her reply.

"You know I can be very persistent, don't you?" he added. He paused. Then he added softly, "Would you like me to walk you up to your room?"

"No! I mean, no, that's okay, don't worry, I can manage. I stay here all the time when I come to New York."

"You sound nervous," he said, as he leaned over to kiss her on the forehead before she disembarked. She felt his wet kiss on her forehead and something deep inside her stirred.

"Okay," she said, "let's go to the Met tomorrow. What time?"

"I'll pick you up in the lobby at eleven."

She waved goodbye as his car drove out of sight, and then the doorman helped her inside the double doors. She went up to her room feeling a little like a schoolgirl again.

She went to bed right away, determined to get a good night's sleep. As she laid her head on the pillow, her mind was still racing with questions. Would their turbulent relationship have settled down? Clearly, they had established homes similar in values. Would the volatility and immaturity have disappeared over time? What if the stormy relationship hadn't changed? What if the physical violence between them had continued? Escalating physical violence between two volatile, temperamental people—what nightmares might that have led to? Had she walked out of what ultimately would have been a good marriage at a particularly weak moment in time when she was learning a new language and trying to learn all the relatives' names? She'd been so afraid her marital home would be the kind of emotional torture chamber her childhood home had been. One person's castle shouldn't be another's prison. What she did know now, though, with twelve years experience in a second marriage, is that every marriage takes a lot of work and commitment and communication, that a lot of people who are immature when they marry just finish growing up together, that you don't solve marital problems by walking away from them physically or emotionally, and that, yes, relatives can be a real drag, whether it's the first marriage or the second marriage. At middle age, she felt some remorse and shame that she hadn't put into her first marriage even one percent of what she'd put into the second one. Now in a second marriage she cherished, she was more aware of how much relentless hard work goes into creating a stable relationship and happy home. Married the second time around to a man born and raised in Montreal, Canada, she could see how difficult cultural differences could be, especially when an American woman entered a strong patriarchal culture. Stefan's dad, who died before Kathryn and Stefan married, was a tough, autocratic Middle Easterner who would have been as hard on Kathryn as Marcos's father had been. Those old-world Spaniards and Middle Easterners were much alike in their attitude toward women. Women were, in their cultures, to be clearly subordinate to men and submissive to their husbands' will. But, over time, she had adjusted Stefan's chauvinistic attitudes, and she was now a middle-aged, happily married woman with four children and a successful business. At midlife, what she realized was that the things that matter most to you ultimately are the things you do for yourself and the things you accomplish yourself. That's why she liked making her own money and knowing she had economic independence and freedom, in case something happened between her and Stefan one day. After the divorce from Marcos, she'd vowed that never again would she put herself in the position of depending on a man to put food on her table. She'd make her own way in the world and pay her own bills and take care of her own children. Human experience isn't the same for everyone, but Kathryn's experience had taught her that people— men, parents, anyone—give favors and money as a means of controlling, and she'd made up her mind she'd never be dependent on anyone else for money. Not her parents. Not Marcos. Not Stefan. No one.

TWO

They met downstairs on Sunday morning at eleven o'clock. Normally this would be the time when she'd be cleaning up after teaching Veronica's Sunday school class and heading down to "big church" to meet Stefan. As Marcos guided her out of the elegant glass doors held open by the doorman, Kathryn realized it felt delicious to have a day off, just to kick back and enjoy New York. Family life was fun, but it was like a business itself, raising kids and making sure all four of them got the help and support they needed while providing the taxi service to and from their myriad activities.

"Let's hit a deli first," he said, steering her down the sidewalk holding her elbow. The city had been hit with six inches of snow the day before, but the sidewalks were clear. They both had on coats and boots, and they needed them. It was a sunny day, but the air was cold, and there was a breeze blowing. It was the kind of day that could chill the bones. Marcos seemed to know his way around that part of the city, and he guided her through the doorway of a warm, aromatic delicatessen a few blocks away. The smell of freshly brewed hazelnut coffee made her mouth water and, after they sat down, they ordered big breakfasts. Marcos bought a *New York Times* at the newsstand just outside the deli, and they sat reading the paper and basking in the sunshine pouring through the window next to their table. After a few minutes the waitress brought a fruit plate. Kathryn put her part of the newspaper down and became engrossed in watching the passersby and street life. There was a young fellow hawking his pen-and-ink drawings of cityscapes at the corner, near the newsstand. People who looked like tourists were stopping to gawk, but they didn't seem to be reaching for their wallets.

"That looks succulent."

"What does?" she asked.

"The fruit," he said, staring at her. "The mangoes." He wasn't smiling. He was staring at her, with that deadly serious look she remembered. He had something on his mind.

"Well, it'll be nice to visit a museum," she said, lightheartedly. "It takes all the time I have just to make sure everybody gets a bath and all that stuff, so culture is way far down on the list of things we get around to."

He didn't reply. He kept staring at her, looking reflective and relaxed, with his chin cupped in the hand held up by his elbow on the table. His hair was thinning on top, and his physique had changed from skinny and boyish into sturdy and masculine. On his frame were ten or fifteen pounds more than he needed, probably from too much time spent in airplanes and hotel rooms. He'd changed from a boy into a man since the last time they were in New York together.

"Remember the summer we spent here, between the first and second year of the business school?"

She looked at him. "Yes, I remember." She paused. "I remember taking Spanish lessons, and I vaguely remember arguing in a restaurant about crab terrine, and I remember your throwing me out of your apartment one night." They had sublet different apartments that summer, while he worked at a mortgage banking firm and she worked selling advertising for one of the publications at Harvard. Hers had been a flexible, entrepreneurial job, so mostly what she'd done that summer was take care of him when he wasn't working.

"So, what makes your relationship with Stefan work?"

"Oh," she said, smiling and heaving a sigh as she rolled her eyes toward the ceiling, "just hanging in there. Making peace with things, you know? I guess you learn to realistically face up to what marriage is. I saw a bumper sticker that captured it perfectly once. It said,

MARRIED TWENTY YEARS, TEN OF THEM HAPPILY." Marcos burst out laughing and nodded in agreement. She continued.

"Oh, Stefan agrees with me totally about marriage," she said, smiling. "We joke about it. He's always telling me he should have been a carefree bachelor. He says if anything ever happens to me, he's definitely not getting married again. He says if you do it once, you're ignorant. If you marry twice, you're a glutton for punishment."

They smiled knowingly at each other.

"You know how that is," she continued. "Marriage turns into a family business after a time and you have to run the family business after you have kids. Stefan and I have grown close over the last several years. But I can't say I enjoyed the first five or six years of married life much. For a while after I married him, I thought I just gave up one set of problems for another," she said, as she rolled her eyes. "Anyway, it seems that what happens in marriage is that you marry a boy and eventually he becomes a man."

"That's probably the way it is," he replied. "Girls are usually more mature."

"Over the long term, I think marriage can work, and it's satisfying to have a partner. But . . . marriage seems to bob and weave in and out of stress and turbulence. But I guess it's unrealistic to expect to be having fun all the time, in marriage or in anything else. I mean, we might be miserable half the time we're married, but we'd probably be just as miserable being single, wouldn't we?" She paused as their eyes met, and they smiled at each other. "I've learned that it's true, too, what the Scriptures say: that 'unless God builds the house, those who build it labor in vain.' And I guess my marriage has been best in the last several years as I've come to respect Stefan as a father. He's always had a congenial and fun-loving personality, but he's blossomed as a dad, and I respect the way he fathers the children. He's always helping one of them throw a ball, or study for an exam, or do math homework, or hanging out with them watching sports, or playing basketball or soccer in the backyard, or just being at their ball games." She paused again. "I guess what I'm beginning to think now is that marriage is like any other venture. We plant seeds that grow later. Who knows, maybe the fruits of a good marriage are in the last half of the relationship."

"You have to wait that long to get to the fruit, hmm?"

She smiled. "Actually, I have no idea what I'm talking about here. I'm in the fashion business, not the fortune-telling business, so don't make any bets or predictions based on my comments."

"Don't worry. I'm not placing any bets today."

"So, how's your family?" she asked. "Your mom and sisters and brother, I mean?"

"Ah, my mother's fine. She's in good health and travels some. My brother is still a wild bull, although he's settled down a bit. He's married to the same woman—you remember Helga, don't you? She puts up with a lot, I think, but she's from a very poor family and she likes the lifestyle and social standing and money she has now. She loves him, I think, but it's a marriage of convenience for both. He has girlfriends on the side and she pretends not to know, and that works for them."

"Funny, but that's what I never wanted . . . the pretense and doing things for show. Whatever I had, I wanted it to be real, not fake, not fiction. I went through my childhood pretending that my life was fine, and I didn't want that as an adult." She paused. "I'm sorry about your dad. Did you say he died ten years ago?"

"Yes. He began to get heart palpitations right after you left Mexico City. In fact, I sort of blamed you for his bad health for a while. Actually, when I look back on it now, I think he was a little manipulative about wanting my attention. The doctors told me they couldn't find anything wrong with him. But I convinced myself that you caused his bad health. I guess thinking that made it easier to turn my back on you and feel I was well rid of you. I mean, you must have been related to the devil, if you could even cause the bad health of my relatives!"

They both laughed.

"And how are your sisters?"

"They're okay," he answered. "They've both split from their husbands. They tried to bring their spouses into the family business, and it just didn't work. The business is large enough, it wasn't that, but Mexico is a very machismo-oriented culture, and there was always the feeling that they were working in their wives' business, even though the Galleria Corporation is a major international company. I think that caused their wives more mental trouble than it caused them. Anyway, it wasn't easy for them to come into our family and bond with everyone. Well, you know . . . don't you?"

"Yes, Mexico is tough," she said, matter-of-factly.

He took a deep breath and continued. "So, they're not married at the moment, but I think they'd like to be married. Mexico is a place where it's nice to have a husband to take you places. Better to be a señora, you know? They both seem a little lonely, but at least Luz had children, although hers are in college now. It looks as though Marianna is not going to have children, and I think she's sentimental about it. She would have been a good mother, but she married a Scandinavian fellow who was just too low-key for her strong, passionate, Spanish party-girl personality when she was in her twenties. He would have made a wonderful husband for her now, at this stage in her life, and he would have been a great father, but she thought he was too dull after they married. She used to tell me he always had his head in a book. They're good friends now, actually, but I wish they'd stayed married. I liked him. We went to their wedding, remember?"

"Yes, I remember." She sighed. "It seems that no matter who you are, or where you live, marriage is a tough thing to pull off, isn't it?"

"Yes, I think so," he said.

"There's just so much negotiation and compromise in it. Why, I would have walked out of my second marriage a dozen times if I could have, but once you have the kids," she smiled, "you're stuck like glue for a while, aren't you?" She smiled her fun-loving Irish smile. "And I guess that's part of growing up, too, isn't it? Realizing that you can't just do everything you feel like doing."

"Very true," he said, smiling appreciatively at her honesty.

"Oh, well, maybe you don't get what you want in life. Maybe you get what you need. Maybe that's the way it goes."

"Well, whatever you have in life is obviously agreeing with you. You look beautiful."

His compliment was unexpected and disarmed her. She blushed. "Not bad for an old lady," she answered impishly. She knew she did look beautiful. She'd aged well, her Irish complexion gave her a rosy glow, her body was taut and sexy at midlife, and she had the self-confidence she'd lacked in her twenties and thirties. Now in her midforties, she felt bold and beautiful, and that self-assurance oozed from every pore of her and communicated her dynamic, adventurous personality.

"Oh, I got the main thing in life I wanted, and that was my children. I'm just glad I was smart enough to wait until I was nearly thirty to get married the first time!"

A nostalgic look came over his face. "Maybe we shouldn't have moved to Mexico after we married."

"No, we had to move to Mexico, Marcos, you know that. That was your destiny, or so it seemed. You'd been programmed all your life to take over the family business. And you wanted to, Marcos. It wasn't realistic to think of your getting a job in someone else's company." A voice inside her counseled her privately. *But you know he's right, Kathryn. It would have been better if you'd had a chance to put your marriage together without all the relatives around. You know that it's hard for a man to grow up if he's living around his family and can go home to them anytime something in his own home doesn't go his way.*

"Are you finished?" he asked, changing the subject as he abruptly grabbed his cellular phone from his pocket and gave an order in Spanish.

He paid the bill, and they left. His private black car drove up just as they walked outside, and they climbed into the back seat. Driving in the city on Sunday was a pleasure, because there was none of the hustle-bustle of the workweek. Even the Met wasn't as crowded as she expected.

"Let's go see the Rembrandts," he said, steering her by holding onto her elbow as though it were a rudder. Suddenly they found themselves in front of *Storm on the Sea of Galilee.*

"This is the main thing I wanted to see today," Marcos said excitedly, as they stood in front of the masterpiece. "It's on loan from a Boston museum."

They stood there silently admiring the 63 x 50⅜ inch canvas illustrating the New Testament story of Jesus miraculously subduing a violent sea just by the sound of his voice saying, "Peace! Be still!"

"See that sailor there, holding the rigging stay and his own head?"

"Yes," she replied, admiring the canvas.

"Rembrandt painted himself into this picture," Marcos told her. "That's Rembrandt's face, right there," he said, pointing.

"Oh," she said, counting the people in the picture and finding what looked like twelve disciples and Jesus. "I guess Rembrandt was saying he was a disciple of Jesus, too, right?"

"Yes, I think so. He painted many religious paintings and was fond of painting the head of Jesus in his later years." Marcos paused. "He was happily married, you know."

"He was?"

"Yes, he married a lady named Saskia, who was from a prominent family in the Netherlands. He painted his wife as Flora, the Roman goddess of flowers, gardens, and spring. They say he gave her the gift of eternal youth by painting her as he did."

"Nice present to get from a husband," Kathryn grinned. He grinned back at her as he grabbed her elbow to steer her into another room.

"So, is Dolores from a prominent Mexican family?"

"Yes, yes, she's from an old family in Mexico City. Her family is quite respected and . . . wealthy, actually."

"Well, that was handy, wasn't it? . . . I mean, combining family resources . . . so what do you two do for fun? Stay up all night counting your money?"

"Meow," he said in a mock-feline tone, grinning in amusement at her unexpected catty remark. She smiled back.

"I guess she doesn't put mayonnaise on the table, does she?"

They smiled and their eyes met as they recalled an old argument about mayonnaise.

"No, she's not a silly gringa. She knows better than to put mayonnaise on the table. Yuck! But, unfortunately, since my girls are Americanized, they love ketchup. So I have to put up with that." Then a more serious look came over his face. "Actually, I travel a lot, Kathryn," he said, as they walked out of the room full of Rembrandts. "You know, you can't build a large national company into an international force by telephone, and even though I have a lot of people I can put on the road, I have to be in China, or Russia, or Japan, or wherever the major deal is made. I can't delegate the deal-making

part. No one else has the experience or takes the long-range view."
He paused. "Actually, my sister Marianna is good at that part of the
business, but a woman is still not accepted and respected in international business circles when it comes to making a tough deal. But she's
very shrewd, and I think over time she may wheel and deal as well as
I do. I have a theory that women probably get more accepted in business as they get older, but that's probably true of men, too. I mean,
people usually equate age with knowledge and vision."

"Well, you know what the Scriptures say about that, don't you?"

"No, what?"

"The Book of Job says that it's not necessarily the old who are
wise, and it's not always the geriatric set who understands what is right.
Old age doesn't necessarily bring wisdom, but it's what Job calls the
'breath of the Almighty' that gives a person understanding. I guess
that just means wisdom is a gift from God."

"What about 'there's no fool like an old fool'?"

"That's not in the Bible," she chided, as she punched him play-
fully on the arm. "Now you're just making fun of me." Then a serious
look appeared on her face. "But that is implied, though, in the story
of Solomon, when a man who'd been wise as a young king turned
foolish after he started marrying foreign wives and worshiping their
gods."

He turned to stare at her. She was still so much like that passionate, forthright young graduate student he'd loved years ago. "I didn't
know you were a biblical scholar. That must have happened in the
last fifteen years, no?"

She took a deep breath. "Yes, well, when David was a baby, we
were alone, you know." Their eyes met briefly, and then she turned
hers away to look down at the floor and then back up at him. "So I
used to sit at the kitchen table when he was sleeping in his crib and
read the Bible. I read it completely, from Genesis to Revelation, and,
in fact, I compiled a book of my favorite Bible verses. I used our computer at work to make a desktop version of it last year so I could give
a copy to each of the kids. Of course, they won't appreciate it until
they get older. And, then, the small college where I taught in Macon
is a Methodist college, so I ended up getting befriended by a bunch of

Methodist scholars." She paused. "But I do think the recipe for successful living is in the Scriptures. And I think the commandments were given to us because God understands his creation, and he knows what kind of lifestyle brings mental peace and emotional fulfillment to the human being."

"So he didn't give us the commandments to keep us from having fun, huh?" he teased, poking her in the ribs to accentuate the fact that he was teasing her.

"No, he didn't," she replied serenely, with a smile on her face. He looked at her radiant, beautiful face. She did look as though she had some of the answers in life.

"Let's go see the Bruegels," Marcos said, steering her elbow in another direction. They walked quickly as he guided her in a winding path, dodging other sightseers as though they were traveling an obstacle course, until they came to stand in front of another large oil painting, beside which was a sign indicating it was on loan from a Brussels museum.

"I love this painting," he said, sighing with obvious appreciation as he stared lovingly at it. "I saw it for the first time in Brussels. It's called *The Fall of the Rebel Angels*, and Bruegel painted it to warn people against one of the seven deadly sins, pride." He studied the painting. "See how the faithful angels look beautiful, and the rebellious angels look like monsters? Bruegel was trying to make people see the point of being humble." He grew silent as he stared at it. "It's very difficult."

She turned to look at his face. "What's difficult?"

He sighed. "Being humble. I mean, when I look at this painting, I understand intellectually the point he makes. But we have to live in a world that doesn't appreciate humility, that thinks kindness is weakness and humility is for sissies. It's very difficult." There was a melancholy look in his eyes. Kathryn felt tender toward him and yearned to reach out and take his arm, to give him a reassuring touch, but she restrained herself. It wasn't appropriate.

"This painting," she said, "reminds me of what Proverbs says about pride . . . that a proud and haughty spirit sets us up for a fall, but humility leads to honor."

"Yes," he answered flatly. His tone of voice was mellow and sounded brooding, as though he were weighted down by heavy thoughts.

"I think it was St. Augustine who called pride 'the mother of all sins,'" she continued. He did not respond. She decided to change the subject to try to make the mood less somber. "And what are the other seven deadly sins? Do you know?"

"Yes," he said, his face brightening with the confident look of a student who knows the answer, "I do know. We Catholics are schooled in all that stuff, you know."

"What are they then?" She smiled at him like a schoolmarm quizzing a young scholar.

He lifted his head erect and gave the answers confidently. "Envy, gluttony, wrath, sloth, avarice . . . and lust."

"So, those sins lead to death, huh?"

"Yes, that's what Catholicism teaches, although I don't think it has to mean literal death. It might be death spiritually. Maybe it's the death that comes when sin causes separation from the Father." He paused and then took her arm. "Let's go look at the Raphaels," he said suddenly, in a voice that sounded less moody. "Raphael is a little happier kind of painting," he said, as he steered her through the crowd. "He didn't try to scare people into doing the right thing, like Bruegel. He painted more than forty paintings of the Madonna, did you know that?"

"No, I didn't." As she replied, they stopped in the middle of a room containing more than a dozen paintings of Mary holding a chubby Jesus, sometimes with the infant John the Baptist by her side. He guided her to a circular painting with a sign underneath that said *The Alba Madonna*. A sign beside it said its permanent home was the National Gallery of Art in Washington, D.C.

"I love this one the best of all the Madonnas he painted," Marcos said.

"Why?"

"Oh, I don't know. I love the composition, and the way Jesus is holding the cross with John the Baptist looking up at him with those big, watery brown eyes. You can see the sorrow in Mary's face as she looks at the cross her son holds and thinks about the suffering in store for him. I guess I love their eyes. It reminds me of what the Spanish say about the eyes, that the eyes are the window of the soul."

"Yes. I love her face." As she stared at the painting, she became conscious of Marcos's stare. She ignored it at first, but then she felt her face blush.

"You still blush, do you?" he said, smiling as her eyes turned to look into his eyes. The smile left his face as he reached over to take one of her hands and place it gently between his two larger hands. "I never saw you as a mother. When you left you weren't in maternity clothes, so I never even really saw you pregnant." He spoke tenderly, but almost as though he were talking to himself, while shaking his head and looking alternately at her hand and then her face. She reached over to place her other hand, the one wearing the wedding band, on top of his hands.

She spoke softly. "I enjoyed being pregnant, and I always got pregnant easily. It was a very happy time in my life. I loved being pregnant with David, too, even though our relationship was disintegrating. I guess I really didn't have a chance to think much about our relationship then. You were so far away, and I was very quickly transforming into a totally different person—a mother. I just had to take care of myself and make sure I had a healthy baby."

He looked at her with a mournful expression in his eyes, and then his expression and tone of voice changed. When he spoke, the suddenly lighthearted tone in his voice sounded forced.

"Van Gogh is next," he said. "This way."

"You know your way around this museum, don't you?"

"Yes, I come here all the time when I'm in New York. I'm usually alone so it gives me some companionship."

A couple of rooms away they found themselves surrounded by the artist's spectacular sunflower paintings and famous French and Dutch countryside scenes.

"This is the one I like the most," Marcos said, standing in front of van Gogh's *The Starry Night*.

"What does it mean?" she asked, staring at the turbulent sky containing eleven magnified stars, two curling nebula, the moon partially eclipsing the sun, and a village below with a church spiral and cypress tree reaching up to the heavens.

"The artist never said what it meant, so art historians say that its meaning is obscure, but I think it's obvious that van Gogh was recalling the Old Testament story of Joseph, when Joseph saw the eleven stars representing his brothers and the sun and moon bowing down to him."

"Wow, it's beautiful," she said.

"You like it?"

"Yes, it's gorgeous."

"It's considered one of the great spiritual works of the nineteenth century."

"I can see why."

"Van Gogh was convinced that he was supposed to serve humanity through art."

"After you see the beauty of the painting, you think about the story itself, don't you? Remember?" Kathryn had taught that story to many Sunday school classes, so the painting inspired her. "Remember how Joseph told his brothers that he'd dreamed a dream that they would one day bow down to him, and so would his mother and father, and that made them even more jealous of him, and they conspired to kill him but sold him into slavery instead?"

"Yes, that story is bothersome," Marcos replied.

"I don't know if it's really bothersome. What I love most about the Bible is the way it tells the truth. I mean, it doesn't pretend that all family relationships are perfect. It reveals the way mothers have favorites, like how Rebekah favored Jacob, and how fathers have favorites, like the way Jacob loved Joseph best of all his children because he was his favorite son of his favorite wife born in his old age."

Marcos sighed. "Let's find less intellectual and sobering pastures, shall we?"

She felt him maneuver her body toward the archway near them and guide her into the next room.

"Monets," he announced, as they found themselves surrounded by paintings of seascapes and flower gardens.

"Flowers and water were two of his favorite things to paint,"

Marcos told her. "It was Monet who was the daddy of the Impressionists, you know. He liked to paint the same subject, like these grainstacks, at different hours of the day to capture his impressions of what a subject looked like under different circumstances."

"Interesting. It would be fun to read a novelist who did that with a person. You know, writing about a person leading one life under one set of circumstances, and then showing the person and how she would do in a totally different set of circumstances." They were standing in front of *Grainstacks (End of Summer)*.

"Ah, look at these," Kathryn said excitedly, pulling his arm so they came to stand in front of paintings of what the sign said was *Rouen Cathedral*. "These are the same cathedral, just painted at different times of the day and evening."

"Yes, interesting," he said. "But look at this," he added, pulling her toward a giant 39¾ x 78¾ inch canvas, which a sign said was on loan from the Collection of the Honorable and Mrs. Walter H. Annenberg. "*Water Lilies*," Marcos said. "In the last years of his life, Monet seldom left his home even though tourists flocked there to learn about Impressionism. He just stayed at home painting his lily pond, and he painted this beauty when he was seventy-nine years old."

"He mastered yellow, didn't he?"

"Yes. And he loved these water lilies. He painted them in the biggest project of his life, when he painted two huge murals six feet high and fifty-five feet long. They're in a museum in Paris. I saw them last year, when I went to France on business. They're breathtaking."

As he stood there, slightly to one side of her, enraptured by the water landscape, Kathryn turned to stare at him. *What would my life have been like if we'd stayed together?* She studied the masculine, angular features of his face and then looked closely at the lines put in his face by the years. *All that pain was for nothing. Why couldn't we have settled everything down, and stayed married, and raised David together, and had more children?*

He turned abruptly and caught her looking at him. He smiled a smile that was bold, and in his eyes she saw a desire and appetite for her. Suddenly, she felt awkward and out of place. She turned her face away.

"The Degas are coming up," he said, in a lower, calmer tone of voice. "Are you getting an appetite?" he asked, putting his arm around her waist as he guided her into the next room.

She felt her body weaken, then stiffen, and she said, "No, I don't think so."

"Degas's father was a banker. Did you know that?"

"No," she answered.

"Yes, and a very opinionated one, too. His father was half French and his mom American. His dad wanted to expose him to art and music but was very annoyed when Degas decided he wanted to be a painter after graduation. They had a falling out but they reconciled after he became convinced of his son's seriousness."

"I think it's obscene when people try to control other people's decisions about what to do with their lives," she said. "Oh, I like this," she said suddenly.

They were standing in front of *A Woman Seated Beside a Vase of Flowers.* "I guess everyone thinks about ballet when they think of Degas," Kathryn reflected.

"Yes, that's probably true." He didn't sound particularly interested in Degas. "I'll tell you what. We're going to be hungry again in an hour or so. Let's figure out where to eat and spend the afternoon doing something else."

"Like what?"

"We'll analyze it like a case study at the B-School, okay?" he said with a smile, turning her toward an archway so they were headed back toward the main entrance.

Walking through the museum with his arm around her in a proprietary way, Kathryn found herself comparing her second marriage to her first.

After her divorce from Marcos, Kathryn thought she'd escaped the cultural differences that had crippled her first marriage. What she found when she married Stefan was that she'd "jumped from the frying pan into the fire," as her grandmother used to say when someone left one bad situation for another just as bad. Although she and Stefan had developed a marriage that now had meaning and depth and warmth and love, she'd found marriage to be difficult. For the first few years, she'd felt that she'd given up cultural differences with Marcos only to encounter other kinds of cultural differences with Stefan. In fact, the second marriage seemed to differ from the first in only one major way: she worked harder at the second one. The second time around, she'd gotten married to stay married, too, like Marcos had. Oh, she'd felt like walking out at times, but it's not so easy to walk out once there are children. You just have to stick around and tolerate the discomfort while you're working on the problems. During the years of pregnancies and babies, while she was trying to make a home for her family and handle responsibilities at the office, Stefan had expected her to wait on him "hand and foot." If he'd given any of the kids a bath during those early years, she didn't remember it. But she'd knocked herself out taking care of him and trying to make the second marriage work for her and the children. And the marriage *had* worked in its way. At least motherhood had been fulfilling and everything she'd hoped for, even if the reality of being a wife hadn't lived up to the fantasy. Intellectually she knew, though, that sometimes in life it's not reality that fails but our expectations of reality, so maybe her dreams of marriage had been infantile and distorted. Certainly she hadn't had a model to go by in her parents' marriage, and Stefan hadn't had the greatest model himself. His Middle Eastern father had treated his wife with something like contempt although he'd treated Stefan, his only child, like a young prince, as had Stefan's mother. So Stefan was spoiled and selfish and expecting to be pampered by a wife as he had been by his parents when he and Kathryn married. Slowly but surely, though, through the years of working together in the business and tolerating each other's faults at home, she and Stefan had both matured and had become closer in their spiritual beliefs. In fact, in the last few years of their married life, Kathryn had begun to feel that she was in a marriage that was actually very valuable and special and full of promise for the future. There was something reassuring about having the four children turn out happy and well adjusted and, at least for the moment, not stealing anyone's hubcaps. She no longer felt like she was raising Stefan, and he probably felt the same toward her. And she'd always respected him for his decision to marry her when she was already a mom with a toddler.

Still, she had a history with Marcos, too. There had been an important relationship there, there had been a marriage, and there had been a son. And it felt comfortable to feel him by her side again. They'd had no experience in really being ex-spouses, and she didn't know how to behave like an ex-wife toward him. She was probably supposed to be in some essentially hostile relationship with this man, but she didn't feel hostile toward him. They had been soul mates at one point in their lives. They had come together at a point in time when they'd shared their dreams about the future and planned on accomplishing those dreams together. She couldn't help it; she felt close to him again now. They'd even slipped back into couple-like behavior patterns as they roamed the Met.

Kathryn felt her mind trying to focus on the actual relationship they now had as parents of a son they had not raised together. Truly, they *had* been skilled in working out a warm and gracious relationship so that their son would not be emotionally bruised by the sharing of his life with the Hispanic Catholic family he had only just met and the American Protestant family he had grown up in. Yes, they *had* worked out an amicable relationship, and yes, it was nice to pretend that Marcos would play "uncle" to her children, and that she could play "aunt" to his daughters, and that she and Marcos could have a warm relationship as adults, like good friends. But they were only in their forties, after all, not in their sixties, and there was a magnetism and animal attraction between them that might make it difficult to remain in the almost "sister-and-brother" state they were trying to settle into.

Marcos's favorite sport was, he had told her during a phone call recently, "going to wild places to hunt," like on safaris. Funny, but a "wild woman" was exactly what Stefan called her. Oh, she wasn't wild morally or ethically. In fact, she clung fast to very strongly rooted values of loyalty and fidelity and hard work. She was a "wild woman," though, she admitted, in terms of being an adventurer in life. Of all life's adventures, having children and raising a family had always been at the top of the list of things she'd wanted. But now, with no more babies at home, the hard physical part of raising children was over and the heavy adjustment period of their married life was behind them, too. Everyone in her house could now tie his shoes and wipe his nose and butt, and their marriage had come a long way. They lived in a beautiful house in an upscale neighborhood, and Stefan had become kinder and more considerate toward her. After "playing the market" as a hobby for a few years, Stefan had become a serious and success-ful investor, and together they were preparing to transform the bou-tique into a major fashion franchise along the lines of Liz Claiborne or the Limited. With Stefan's financial backing, Kathryn was ready to venture out into the world again and use her Harvard MBA to build a major fashion company. Her minister had once said from the pulpit, "Happiness is not getting what you want; it's wanting what you have." And wasn't that similar to what the Apostle Paul said about happi-ness in Philippians? "I've learned how to be content in whatever state I'm in. I've learned how to be content in situations when I have too little and in situations when I have too much. I've learned the secret of being content in any circumstance. I can do all things through God who strengthens me." Kathryn remembered thinking one day as she was taking a walk, just before Marcos reentered her life with his phone call, that life couldn't get much better.

Stefan had teased her in the last few years that she'd come out of her shell and, at middle age, she did feel like a butterfly getting ready to come out of a cocoon. Maybe there was something mental or hor-monal that happened at middle age, she'd thought lately, because middle age had given her new appetites, one of which was to become very successful in business. On one level, she and Stefan had evolved into a productive business partnership as they'd worked together to transform a mom-and-pop local retail shop into a respected regional business with a strong, affluent customer base. A risky repositioning strategy for the Chic Boutique had worked, and they were finally making some money and in a phase of their lives when they had no financial worries. She had more self-confidence at middle age than ever before, including the self-confidence to believe that they could, with her vision on the buying end and with Stefan's expertise as a comptroller, transform a robust single retail unit into a major fash-ion franchise. At midlife, she was determined to savor the next ten years and stretch her wings. The children were beyond the preschool "watch-me-Mom" age and already into those years where they all were aware of the importance of working toward college. Even the little one heard so much talk in the home about working hard to get into a great college that he was ready to dedicate himself to the task of mastering his studies. And "Mr. Dad," as Stefan's friends had nicknamed him because of his devotion as a father, was always ready to play tennis with the kids, throw a baseball with them, play touch football with them, and help them with homework. At middle age, Kathryn appreciated the fact that she'd married a smart guy who'd graduated Phi Beta Kappa from Princeton. He had a great brain and had received a great education in Montreal, so he could tutor the kids expertly in any subject. He was dumb like a fox about housework, but he was smart as a whip about anything to do with business and academics.

"Let's go to the Towers for lunch," he said, interrupting her train of thought. "I can have anything we want prepared by the restaurant," Marcos said, as he pulled his cellular phone out of his coat and summoned his driver in Spanish. Outside the Met, a rainy drizzle had begun, and they found themselves without an umbrella. Definitely not the kind of day to knock around New York window shopping. Mercifully, the private black car that catered to his needs in New York pulled up just as the drizzle picked up in intensity. In the car, their conversation turned to children.

"How are your children adjusting to David's having a whole other family?"

"Oh, they're fine with it. Adults seem to have less flexibility than children about such things, it seems. I'd always told Calvin that David had a natural father. He was nine years old when you called, and guess what he said when I told him that you'd called to invite David to San Antonio to meet his other family and do some sightseeing?"

"What?"

"He said, 'Oh, can I go, too?' Ever since Calvin was born, he's been trying to copy David in every way. Whatever David wants to do, Calvin is 'Me, too!' When I told him he couldn't go with David, all he said was, 'Boy, I bet he's going to have a lot of fun!'"

Marcos smiled appreciatively. One of his daughters was the same age as Calvin, so he could probably picture the scene.

"Calvin would have avarice as the deadly sin he's most prone to," she continued, as the car made its way more slowly through the slick streets of the city. The rain was coming down hard now. "I remember one day when the kids were looking through my jewelry box, Veronica said sweetly, 'Mom, when you die, can I have this locket?' So I said, 'Yes, dear, of course you can. How sweet of you to ask.' And the littlest one, Booth, said, 'Mommy, can I have this other piece of jewelry when you die?' So I said, 'Yes, of course, dear.' And then Calvin said, 'Mom, when you die . . . can I have the business, the house, and the cars?'"

Marcos burst out laughing. "He's a natural for the Harvard Business School," he said.

Kathryn continued. "But you're right. The youngest two children didn't know you existed until after you called. I decided to tell Veronica one day when we were alone in the car waiting for Calvin's soccer practice to end. I told her that, a long time ago, I'd been married to someone else, and that I'd had a baby, who was David, with that man, and that David's biological father wanted David to fly to Texas to meet his family. Veronica was seven years old at the time, and her response was, 'Oh, can I go, too, Mom? Please, Mom?' So I had to explain to her, too, that she couldn't go with David when he went to meet his other two sisters and stepmom. She kept begging me to let her go, and then she told me her final settlement offer: if I let David go at the beginning of the summer, then I *had* to let her go at the end of the summer."

Marcos smiled. Veronica was the age of his other daughter so he could probably appreciate the desire of a little girl to make sure she got her fair share. "And how about the little one?"

Kathryn sighed and rolled her eyes. "Booth was five, and I decided to tell him about David's other family one day when the kindergartners only had a half day at school. He breezed into the house and threw his lunch box on the table, and then I told him that I wanted to talk with him about something. I guess it sounded serious to him, so he sat on the kitchen table swinging his legs back and forth while I told him that David had a biological dad who was coming to visit us. At the end of my long speech he said, 'So you mean David's got *two* dads?' Yes, I said, but don't be talking about it all over the neighborhood.

Later that day, Calvin told me Booth came running up to meet his bus yelling, 'Hey, Calvin, I know something you don't know. Mom's been married before, and David's got two dads!'"

Marcos laughed heartily.

"And how about your daughters? Are they adjusting alright to the idea of having a brother?"

"Oh, yes, they love David, and so does Dolores. She and David get along very well."

"Well, I'm grateful to her for being so supportive of all this. I know it could never happen unless she helped it along."

Once inside Galleria Towers, a magnificent high-rise that contained numerous apartments as well as the New York offices of the Galleria Corporation, Marcos led her to the elevator.

"Is there a penthouse restaurant?"

"Sort of," he smiled.

"What kind of car are you driving now?" she asked him as the elevator continued its ascent.

"A green Lamborghini," he smiled, "and a Jag."

"So you still like cars, do you?"

He smiled, turning to look into her green eyes. "Don't you remember how you used to tease me that I liked pretty women and fast cars?"

She smiled back. "I think what I used to tease you about is that you liked pretty cars and fast women, didn't I?"

They laughed. When the elevator opened on the penthouse floor, he led her down the hall and unlocked a door that led to a beautiful and spacious apartment with breathtaking views of New York.

"Galleria Holdings owns the penthouse so this is where I stay when I'm in New York."

Once they were upstairs in his room, he bolted the door after putting a Do Not Disturb sign on the outside. The spacious apartment was beautifully decorated with lots of white fabric and chintz on French Provincial furniture, and the view of the city was spectacular.

"Let's have something to drink," he said, as he went to the back of the elegant bar to bartend for them.

THREE

"I've wanted to ask you this for a while," he said, as he handed her a glass of white wine and sat down on the couch beside her. "How did you tell David about my call on his birthday last year?"

"I'd always told David about you, ever since he was a little boy. On the day Stefan and I got married, I took him aside and said, 'David, Stefan and I are married now, and that means he's going to be my husband, and he's going to be your dad.' And David asked, 'Well, where's my regular dad?' And I just told him that you lived far away from us. Then he ran off to play like any four-year-old. And through the years, I showed him the paragraphs of news about you in the *Harvard Business School Bulletin*, like when you took over as CEO of the Galleria Corporation. I put them in a large brown envelope that I keep for each of the children. But, it's funny, Marcos, he never asked me a single question about you, even though I spoke highly about you from time to time. And so did Stefan."

Kathryn was referring to her habit of maintaining a huge manila envelope for each of the children containing bits and pieces from their childhood—articles they wrote for the school newspaper, snack cookbooks compiled by their first-grade classes, newspaper photographs they happened to be in, poems they wrote for school contests, and so forth. Included in David's envelope were magazine and newspaper articles she'd stumbled across through the years that referred to Marcos.

There was pain and regret clearly etched on Marcos's face when he replied. "I might not have handled it right by staying away from him, but I felt through the years that he was growing up in a happy home, and I didn't want to confuse the little boy and put him through the usual stuff kids have to go through in divorces." He paused. "But you kept his heart tender toward me through all those years. He was ready to love me when I came into his life. That was good of you, Kathryn. I respect you for that."

She smiled and repositioned herself on the couch to assume a more relaxed sitting posture. "I'm a realist, Marcos. You know that. I know there's a place in his heart that only the love of his natural father can fill. Stefan's been a great father to him, too, and he's been a gentleman about David's developing this relationship with you."

"Yes, I know, he's been great. I'm very lucky he took that attitude."

"When I told Stefan you'd called to say you wanted to develop a relationship with David, he thought about it and said, 'Well, I suppose as many people in your life who can love you, the better.' He's a gentleman."

The rain was pelting against the apartment windows now, and they both seemed in a nostalgic mood. Marcos excused himself to go to the bathroom, and Kathryn found herself drifting back in time, remembering the trauma of their marital breakup. She hadn't thought about it for a long time, and she'd never really dealt with it as a reality in her life. It was as though she'd been in an accident and had experienced a kind of memory loss. Suddenly though, sitting here in Marcos's apartment, old memories came rushing back.

Dumped back in her hometown as a single parent, Kathryn had scrambled to figure out what she would do to make a living. She had to think quickly. At Thanksgiving she was arguing by telephone with Marcos. By Christmas, it seemed clear the marriage was over. Expecting her first child in April, she was trying to pay the wedding photography bills angrily handed to her by her mother, focusing on how she'd pay rent to her parents while she lived with them during her

pregnancy, and worrying about how to cover the maternity expenses
and hospital bills. Looking back now, she could see that she'd instinctively numbed herself emotionally just to get through the trauma. Her
childhood had taught her how to do that, anyway. She'd grown up in
a family where it was like living in an explosives factory, so she'd
learned how to lie low and walk on eggshells and numb herself from
pain. Then a newspaper ad appeared over Christmas for a college instructor at Wesleyan College, a Methodist university. She got the job,
and college teaching on a religious campus had provided a wonderful
lifestyle while David was a baby. With a teaching load of only twelve
classroom hours a week, she had plenty of time off to take care of her
little son, and she and David had moved into their own house when
David was six months old. She and Stefan had been friends at the
Harvard Business School, so she'd written him a note after the divorce was final, telling him the marriage with Marcos had come to an
end. A note had come back from Stefan, who was living in New England at the time and working as a commodity broker, saying he
wanted to visit her and pay his respects to her little son.

Stefan told her once that he fell in love with her after seeing her as
a mother. His father died when he was at Princeton, and his mother
died unexpectedly in her forties a couple of years later, so Stefan was
alone in the world when he traveled to Macon to pay his respects to
Kathryn and her little boy. Stefan's Middle Eastern father had emigrated from Lebanon as a child when his father decided to take the
Haddad family to the United States for a better life. In those days
people paid their fare by bits and pieces, often stopping along the
way to work and save money for the next increment of the trip. The
Haddad family landed in the Caribbean with the plan of working in
Barbados for a while until they had enough money to make the final
leg of the journey to America. Stefan didn't know why the Haddads
abandoned their dream of getting to the United States, but they did.
When he was a teenager, Stefan's autocratic father had a falling out
with his equally autocratic dad, and Stefan's father left Barbados at
fifteen to go to Canada. He ended up in Montreal, where a few years
later he met and married a young woman who'd grown up in an or-
phanage. Because of the family acrimony on the Haddad side and the

fact that his mother had been abandoned at birth and never knew her relatives, Stefan had no family after his parents died and was probably yearning for one when his path in life crossed Kathryn's path at the time she was a single parent.

While he was drawn to her because of the strong Christian home she was building for herself and her child, Kathryn had been drawn to him because of his gentle, easygoing, kind disposition, which meshed with the tone of tranquility and good-naturedness of the home she'd built for herself with young David. After starting life over at age thirty as a single parent, Kathryn went into the decade of her thirties with a clearer vision of what she wanted out of life. Above all, she knew she wanted a different kind of home than the one she'd grown up in. Dramatic flares of temper by her father and extended periods of chronic, persistent moodiness by her mother had been common in her home, and Kathryn was determined to have something different. Over her parents' objections, she had married Stefan about a year and a half after his initial visit.

Marcos came back into the room, smiling at her. He'd changed into a more casual sweater and looked ready to relax for the afternoon.

"What was David's reaction when you told him I wanted to develop a relationship with him?"

"The day you called, on his fifteenth birthday, I went to pick him up from a science club meeting after school. We were planning to take him to dinner that night to celebrate his birthday and give him some presents. When he got into the car, I looked at him and said, 'David, your biological dad called today, and he said he'd like to develop a relationship with you and invite you to visit him in Texas.'"

"What did he say?"

"He just looked happy and said, 'He did?'" She paused. "And then we just took it from there, didn't we?"

Kathryn and Marcos sat in silence, remembering the scenario of the last nine months. By the time Kathryn and Marcos had spoken on the phone a few times, it was decided how David's first meeting with his biological dad would take place. Marcos would fly from San Antonio, where he lived with his wife and daughters, to Macon, Georgia, where David lived with his two brothers, Calvin and Booth, his sister, Veronica, and his parents. Marcos would come to their house for breakfast on Saturday morning. Then he and David would head off in a rented car to Atlanta, for the three-day Memorial Day Weekend to get to know each other while sightseeing. Stefan was in agreement.

Memorial Day Weekend came and went as planned. David and Kathryn met Marcos at the airport. Kathryn and David followed as Marcos checked into the hotel and then followed him upstairs to his room. For more than an hour, David sat in a chair and watched as Kathryn and Marcos sat talking and catching up on mutual friends and family. That night in the hotel room was the first time in his life David had seen his natural parents together as they talked and laughed. The next morning Marcos came to breakfast at their house and, like an uncle, brought San Antonio Spurs hats for the boys and a cowgirl hat for Veronica.

When Kathryn picked David up three days later from the airport at ten o'clock Monday evening, he said he'd had a great time with his "other dad." They'd visited Underground Atlanta, Six Flags Over Georgia, gone to see an Atlanta Braves game, eaten in nice restaurants, and enjoyed getting to know each other. David told Kathryn in the car ride home from the airport they had "a lot in common. We both like the outdoors, and we both like to tell jokes."

That summer, David flew to San Antonio to see Marcos and to meet his other two sisters and their mother. He returned from his three-week stay excited about his other family and glad he had two other sisters and a nice stepmother who wanted him to call her "Mom" when he visited their home. At first, Kathryn hadn't been thrilled about David's calling Marcos's wife "Mom," but she wrestled with her reaction to it and decided it was silly to get hung up on something so trivial. Still, his San Antonio family seemed to love him instantly and to want to spend as much time with him as possible, and Kathryn realized she'd have to let go of her firstborn a few years earlier than she'd expected. Intellectually, she knew he'd be leaving home for college one day, and then the day would come when a beautiful young woman would catch his eye, and his first family would just be a pit stop in his life after that. She'd have to let go one day soon anyway, she counseled herself during her long walks in the neighborhood. Letting go just came a little earlier than she expected, and in a different form. But it was letting him go to be loved by his other family, and she had to do it for him.

"Yes, thank God, it has worked out better than I imagined," Marcos said, with a tone in his voice that sounded grateful and reverent. "We both have a lot to be thankful for, Kathryn. We have wonderful families, and we should be very thankful to God that our lives have turned out so well."

"Yes, that's how I feel, too. That's been the best thing about the last fifteen years for me. Luckily, my grandmother taught me about God, and I turned to God when David was a baby and began to develop a deeper spiritual relationship. And you know what I've discovered, Marcos?"

"What's that?"

"I've discovered that my grandmother was right when she said that God puts something very special inside each of us, that no one can ever mistreat or abuse or ridicule or humiliate. It's the Spirit. That's what connects us to God, and it's what no human being can ever take from us. The people around you may trample on your feelings, they can abuse you emotionally, they can step on your ego and squash you until you have the lowest opinion of yourself. But the Spirit is like a light burning inside you that no person can ever extinguish. It connects you to God and permits you to be born again, to be made new again, over and over if need be, no matter what you do to yourself or what other people do to you. It's a permanent lifeline to God that can never be taken from us. It's like a spiritual umbilical cord."

Marcos squirmed and looked uncomfortable at this evangelical turn in the conversation.

"It's a good thing to know," he replied awkwardly, sipping his drink, "but it sounds like you had to figure that out through some pain."

"Yes, but what is it they say? 'No pain, no gain'? I think pain and struggle are just part of the learning process in life. I mean, we struggled at the Harvard Business School, too, to play that game and get through, didn't we?"

"Yes."

"So, the game of life is like that, too. We have to endure some hard lessons to learn how to play the game well."

"And are you enjoying the game now?" He seemed to be deliberately steering the conversation in another direction.

Her eyes brightened as she smiled at him. "Actually, I'm enjoying life very much now. There's something that happens at middle age, I think. I don't know what it is, but there's a kind of refocusing that goes on. At least that's what happened to me, just lately. I've entered a new phase in my life, and I can feel it."

"Oh?"

"Yes," she replied, nodding her head vigorously. "I'm moving out of the phase of life that's filled up with PTA and scouts and volunteer work and moving back into my professional phase."

"You mean the fashion business?"

"Yes, that's what I mean. The kiddie phase of my life is nearing its end. Oh, I loved doing kiddie stuff when my kids were little, but I like it that they're old enough so I can jump-start my career. I think women and men have different career cycles, don't you?"

"Well, I don't know about that. Dolores stays home and takes care of the kids. That's her job."

"Yes, well, that's been my job, too, while I've been trying to grow the business. But a professional woman has to put her career on ice, or at least in slow gear, if she sits on the nest for a few years."

"And what about Stefan? Does he like the business?"

She cocked her head and shrugged her shoulders. "We've built the business together, and he likes it alright. Oh, he complains sometimes, but don't all men?" She smiled to show she was teasing, then she continued slowly, as though she were choosing her words carefully. "Stefan didn't have one particular thing he wanted to do, that he was really passionate about, like you were with the import-export business, so he's adapted to a small Southern town and a small business."

"You could have moved to Canada, no?"

She shook her head vigorously. "No, he doesn't have any family there. His parents are dead, and he has no relatives in Canada who could lend him a helping hand in business. The French Canadians are an odd lot, anyway. It seems that Canada is a country of immigrants, and Stefan doesn't really feel his roots are in Montreal. In a way, he's a man without a country. His dad wanted him to get to America one day to make his fortune, so he made sure he got to an Ivy League school. He went to Princeton before the Harvard Business School, you know."

Marcos nodded. He and Stefan had met on several occasions socially while the three of them were at Harvard. "So you two have built a retail fashion business together, haven't you?"

"Yes. We sort of stumbled into it, I guess. Neither of us knew anything about retailing when we learned one day through someone at church that one of the town's oldest dress shops was for sale because the owner was dying of cancer. I was pregnant at the time we bought it, but we both thought we could eventually turn it into a cash cow." She paused. "Remember that concept at the Business School? I figured out later that I wanted one of those cash cows!"

Marcos laughed.

"We struggled to make ends meet during the early years of our marriage," she continued. "We thought we'd made a mistake buying the shop about a thousand times. After a few years of managing it, we were both pretty disgusted. It just didn't seem like it was capable of producing enough income. But we were in a small Southern town, with few other prospects for making a reasonable living, and we were spoiled by the flexible lifestyle of the entrepreneur. So we decided we'd better 'go for it' in a really bold way. It became clear that hard work wasn't going to be enough. We figured out we'd have to reposition the business from a store selling ugly clothes to old ladies into a chic, upscale boutique catering to affluent women throughout the Sun Belt. So, we took a risk, and off the racks came the dowdy little dresses for older women and onto the racks went the glamorous, designer creations I buy in New York, or Los Angeles, or Atlanta, or Dallas."

"So the repositioning of the store has been successful?"

"Yes, thank God, it has. Apparently, there was an underlying strong consumer demand for this kind of boutique. I have to travel more now, but the children are at the right ages for me to do more traveling. Stefan is a great Mr. Dad, and the regular employees run the office while I'm gone. He's made some smart investments in the stock market lately, and we're going to use the money he's made in the market to franchise the boutique."

"Sounds like you have a nice life."

"Yes. And you saw our house when you came to Macon."

"It's beautiful," he said, remembering the impressive two-story, five-bedroom brick home he'd seen when he had breakfast with them on that Memorial Day Weekend he came to see David.

"We built it a few years ago and finally moved out of the little house we lived in during the years we were building the business. So, yes, I'd have to say that life at middle age is better for me than life has ever been, Marcos." *Yes, Marcos, life has turned out alright for me,* she thought to herself. *Like any ex-husband, I guess you thought my life would be over when you ditched me, and you probably thought when you came back into my life that I'd be living on welfare in a tenement with my illiterate, alcoholic husband and my seven starving children. You dumped me, Marcos, but I have survived without you.*

"Well, I'm glad for you. You richly deserve to be happy."

She smiled and felt her face flush with color. "We don't have the usual type of ex-wife–ex-husband relationship, do we?"

"No, we don't."

"And how 'bout you, Marcos? Has your career been everything you hoped it would be?"

"Yes, it's lived up to my expectations. Pappy started it from scratch as a garment sweatshop in a rat-infested building in a commercial part of Mexico City. It was already a respected national business when I graduated with my MBA, but I've brought it into the twentieth century in terms of its accounting practices and management approach. I've transformed it into an international giant. I promised him before his death that I'd do my best to build it into a company of international stature, and I've done that."

Kathryn nodded and stared at him. She knew he wasn't bragging. He was merely stating the facts. From what a few people had whispered into her ear at the Harvard Business School reunions, Marcos had become quite wealthy, as she'd expected. Actually, he was already wealthy when they were at Harvard, since he was the heir apparent to a vast family fortune and business.

"What made you leave Mexico City? I thought you'd always live there. I know how you love Mexico."

"Dolores doesn't really like Mexico."

Serves you right, Marcos! she thought. *It serves your father right, too, even if he has gone to his grave. You dumped your troublesome gringa who was at least willing to move to Mexico City so that you could marry a cultured, upper-class, beautiful Mexican wife who didn't even share your love of Mexico!*

"But Dolores and I like San Antonio very much. The girls are in the third and fifth grades and attend San Antonio's best Catholic private school."

"Well, it seems you've gotten everything you wanted out of life."

He nodded. "I'm comfortable." He stared at her.

There was a melancholy sound in her voice when she spoke. "We were too much alike, you and I. Too bold and headstrong and stubborn." She paused. "You know, I've learned, in the last fifteen years, that demands and ultimatums don't work very well in marriage. But I didn't know it then."

"Well, as I told you, I've had some regrets, but there's no going back in time, unfortunately."

"No. You know, I read once that the hardest thing in life is to know when to burn a bridge and when to walk over it. It's funny, isn't it, what we know after it's too late to use the knowledge?"

They stared across the couch into each other's eyes.

"You know what Billy Graham says about marriage?"

"No, what does he say?" asked Marcos.

"I heard him say once that what a successful marriage needs is two very good forgivers. He said that people have to learn to forgive one another, and he said the hardest time for a marriage is the first five years. He said that after people learn to forgive each other and accept each other's faults, they can really establish a marriage that's built on friendship and based on the reality that no one is perfect, and that we all have our little faults. And he said there has to be a spiritual harmony in a marriage so that people can face a problem and pray about it in a kind of spiritual unity. He said the kind of puppy love you start out a marriage with eventually pales in comparison to the deep love that can grow between two married people. But that kind of love takes a lot of work and persistence, he said."

"Yes," Marcos answered in a tone of voice that sounded flat and unemotional. His face, however, was taut and his look intense, and Kathryn could see that underneath the controlled mask, there was pain and sadness for him over this discussion of marriage. Kathryn felt it, too. It was like flunking a test and then sitting down with the answer key and looking at all the choices you should have made but didn't. She decided to change the subject to something a little more lighthearted.

"How did we get together, anyway? I mean, a hillbilly country girl like me, raised by my grandmother from Tennessee, with a sophisticated city slicker from Mexico City like you?"

His smile broadened as he answered. "I guess maybe city boys like country girls." Then a serious look came over his face. "Well, I know we should both thank God for our families and for our blessings, because we've both been blessed, haven't we?"

She could see in his face he was struggling with self-control. She wanted to reach over, to put her hand on his, in an almost maternal way, but it wasn't appropriate. One of the many Spanish sayings he'd taught her flashed through her mind: *No hagas cosas buenas que parecen malas. (Don't do good things that look bad.) Then what was she doing here, in her ex-husband's penthouse?*

"And how is Macon?" he asked, changing the subject. "Are you and Stefan enjoying living there?"

"It's been alright while the kids were growing up, but I don't think we'll live there a lot longer. It's been a real struggle living around my parents."

"Oh?"

"Yes, between my father's bullying us and my mother's manipulating us, we've been pounded by them the whole time we've been in town. Oh, it's a lot of silly little things that sound trivial when you say them out loud, but they aggravate you on a daily basis. Things like dropping in on us anytime they want to, even though I've asked them to call before they come over. They love to drop in on us at dinner time, unannounced, bringing fried chicken and donuts. Of course, the kids love that, but I have to put aside the beef stew or whatever else I've cooked that night because they've dropped in and brought something else. Of course, they feel outraged when I ask them to call before they come over." She shook her head slowly and seemed lost in thought. "It just never seems to end. They're wealthy, you know, so they give us presents from time to time, but the presents always have strings attached, and there's always an emotional or psychological debt we owe. They'll do nice things out of the blue that surprise us, but the relationship is so volatile, it's like cruelty mixed with kindness in an unpredictable way, and it's net negative." She sighed.

"Well, I feel terrible that I put you back into that situation when our marriage failed."

"No, don't feel bad," she said, shaking her head. "It may be good in the end when life toughens you up. Who knows? Maybe there was a kind of fate there. I'm not sure. Perhaps I had to actually bring all this to some kind of conclusion. And I don't think they would ever have left us alone if we'd stayed married. No matter where you and I would have been, they would have preyed on me somehow."

"So what's the situation with your parents now?"

"Actually there's hardly any relationship there at all, unless you call hostility and distrust a relationship. Since my grandmother's funeral a few months ago, there's been a kind of sinister silence. It seems like the relationship is coming to a point of no return soon. I can almost feel it, in an ominous kind of way."

"Ominous? Ominous means evil. Isn't that a little strong?" He stared at her. *She's still the same dramatic, theatrical person she used to be,* he thought to himself.

"Oh, maybe it is," she said, shrugging her shoulders. There was a weary look on her face. "I struggle with my desire to be obedient to the commandment that says, 'Honor your father and your mother.' But I can't let them beat me up emotionally. And I don't think I'm required to take their abuse just because they're my parents. Maybe that's what Jesus was talking about when he said in Matthew something about how he didn't come to bring peace on earth, but a sword, and that a man would be set against his father, and a daughter against her mother, and a man's enemies would be those of his own house-hold."

"What does that mean?"

"I don't know for sure, but I think Jesus knew that even within the family, there's conflict between evil and good, and you're going to provoke people's hatred if you refuse to call evil good, and if you refuse to compromise with immorality. My parents have become very bitter in their old age because they saw their baby, their favorite daugh-ter, follow in their footsteps. I mean the adultery, the deceit, the lying, and all that. It's as though they look at her life now and see their own life, and they've become very hostile. I know Sally's disappointed them, but there's been an unfair transference of their hostility and negativ-ism toward me. Mother really resents my having a great life while her baby daughter lives in the fast lane. But I don't care anymore what they think, I really don't. I've become more and more determined not to compromise with evil since I've been a mother. I won't let my children be trained into thinking that immorality is acceptable. I want my kids to know how to distinguish between right and wrong, if it's the last thing I do as a mother. That's what the Bible says made Jesus ready to begin his ministry, you know—that he was able to distin-guish between the good and the evil. It isn't easy to stand up for good in this world, Marcos. It isn't."

"You sound full of judgment. Where's the forgiveness like you were talking about a few minutes ago?"

She shrugged. "Oh, it's there. It's the heart of Jesus' message about love. But forgiveness isn't letting people mistreat you. I once heard a minister explain it when he said, 'Servanthood isn't shithood.' Jesus never said to let people mistreat you. In fact, the more you under-stand that God loves you and values you, the more you understand that he wants you to value yourself, and he would never want one of his children, one of his adopted heirs, mistreated." She paused, then spoke in a softer voice. "I know it's a sickness when parents pick on one of their children, so I forgive them. But I don't want a relationship with people who mistreat me, and I don't want anything to do with religion that's lacking in reverence or morality."

Marcos looked into her face. She was clearly in distress over some internal struggle, but she'd always had an artistic nature. He remembered suddenly how he used to tease her that she was a "drama queen."

"Well, not every relationship works out, does it? You know what the Spanish say about family? 'Your friends you pick; your family falls out of the tree like monkeys.'"

She smiled. "Yes, I remember you told me that. But parents are in a commandment, so that makes it harder to know how to act."

"Well, what Jesus said was he wanted to free man from bondage, so I guess that means any kind of bondage. He wanted to free people from whatever enslaved them, and he wanted them to be free to find and enjoy a relationship with God and with God's creation. To feel good about themselves, and to be able to see God in themselves and in other people, too."

Kathryn stared at him with surprise clearly etched on her face. "You don't sound like a Catholic!"

Now it was his turn to look and sound theatrical. "I don't? What does a Catholic sound like?" From the mock-serious expression on his face and the Shakespearean tone in his voice, she could see he was teasing her.

"Well, Catholics are more hung up on the rituals of religion, aren't they?"

"More hung up than who? As compared to what?" His tone was playful, and he was pretending to be offended.

They both laughed. It was beginning to sound vaguely like a case analysis from the Harvard Business School.

"More hung up than Protestants," she smiled. "You're sounding more like a Protestant than a Catholic. I mean, don't the Catholics follow the letter of the law and try to stick literally with the commandments?"

"Oh, no, don't say that! You can say anything about me, but just please don't say that I sound like a Protestant!" He was obviously poking fun. "Oh, I guess *some* Catholics eventually learn to think for themselves," he smiled. Then his face became serious. "Obviously Jesus never meant for someone to accept mistreatment under the guise of honoring one of the commandments. That would be blasphemy, if a commandment led to the victimizing of anyone. We know that something evil is at work if someone is being forced to accept something bad and call it good, or if someone is forced to honor something dishonorable. Anyway, there's probably a classic way out of that one. You can love the sinner and hate the sin, can't you? So, what you do is honor the parent but detest the evil behavior. I guess what that means, though, is that there is no enduring human relationship with people who want to rule and tyrannize you. You need to forgive them because it frees you from bitterness and hatred, but you don't have to have a relationship with them. Ah, I guess we really do reap what we sow, don't we?"

"Yes, it's true, like everything else the Bible says," she said, suddenly feeling better about things and feeling that she had a slightly altered way to look at her relationship with her parents. She felt strangely transported back in time. She and Marcos had always been able to hold the most fascinating conversations, conversations that were rich because they had the wisdom of two cultures to draw on. Suddenly, she missed the high level of conversation they used to have, and she missed hearing his brain work and listening to the procession of his thoughts. She stared at him, overwhelmed by the thought that she'd been robbed of his companionship over the last fifteen years. They had once shared a special kinship. That she understood. But what she couldn't understand was the eccentric relationship developing between them now.

The conversation turned back to the children. Kathryn had never seen a situation where the ex-spouses behaved in such a civilized and caring way toward each other's children, but it felt right. She was operating on pure instinct when she thought about his children, and she couldn't help but think of them in affectionate ways. I mean, they were just little girls, and she could remember how vulnerable and frail and helpless and how much in need of acceptance she'd been when she was a little girl. There was no way Kathryn would ever intentionally cause any trouble for a child, not for her children and not for his children. His children were in a special category. It was as though she was their aunt and Stefan was their uncle, in a way. Anyway, in her religious frame of reference, she more or less felt that it was the responsibility of all the adults to look after all the children. It didn't necessarily work like that in real life, but that kind of caring by one generation for another was the way it should work, in her view.

"Are you getting hungry?" he asked, interrupting her train of thought.

"A little bit," she replied.

"It will be more comfortable to eat here than anywhere in the city tonight. It's so wet and miserable outside. I can have anything sent up we want. You might even want some crab terrine." They both laughed.

Kathryn excused herself to go to the bathroom and, when she returned, he was standing beside one of the huge picture windows watching the rain. She went over and stood beside him. He turned to look at her and then walked around to stand behind her. He put his arms around her and clasped his hands in front of her as they both stood there, watching the rain. She could smell the scent of his cologne and feel his breath on her neck. Then he turned her around so that he was facing her. Standing arms length from her, with his hands holding onto her shoulder bones, he looked into her eyes, and she looked back at him. It was a bold stare, and his eyes were searching for some sign of encouragement. After looking into her eyes for what seemed like minutes, he lowered his eyes. For some reason, she didn't feel awkward at all as she seemed to be almost standing on the sidelines watching him study her angles. As she stared at him looking at her, she looked up into his eyes and saw the lust and passion he felt for her. She knew she should look away, walk away, run away, but she didn't. She felt his mouth on hers, and against her will she responded.

"Come with me," he said softly, gently taking her hand and leading her into a room down the hall. She followed him and then she stood facing the king-size bed as he helped her take off her sweater and pants. He pulled down the bedspread and sheets so she could climb into the bed, and he pulled the sheet over her gently. Then he took his own clothes off and climbed into the bed beside her.

Once under the sheets, he took her in his arms and passionate kisses inflamed the desire they had for each other. The yearning she felt for him came from the deepest part of her, and she felt overpowered by sensuality.

"Do you have a condom, Marcos?" Kathryn whispered in his ear as the heat intensified.

He started to nuzzle her cheek and ear. She could remember that, too. How she used to love the way he snuggled with her in bed and nuzzled her cheek and ear.

"We need a condom? You mean, you haven't closed the factory?"

"No, the factory's still operating, and I always got pregnant so easily." She paused. A memory buried deep suddenly flashed back, and she remembered the scare she'd had that summer in New York between their first and second years in graduate school when she thought she was pregnant.

He didn't have a condom with him. And why would a married Catholic man carry condoms on a business trip without his wife, anyway? After some conversation, it was decided that he would dress and go outside the room to find condoms. They might have a dispenser in one of the men's bathrooms downstairs, he told her. That made sense, she thought. I mean, you probably couldn't just order them through room service.

During the fifteen minutes he was gone, the phone rang once and the caller didn't seem to want to believe he wasn't in. The rings went on, and on, and on, and on, it seemed. Probably his wife, Kathryn thought.

She sat up in the bed and began thinking about what she was doing. Suddenly appalled at herself, she decided to put her clothes back on and go into the living room. She began thinking logically. Yes, that's what Stefan would want her to do. Think logically. Here she was, apparently getting ready to have an affair—or at least a brief infidelity—with her ex-husband! She was getting ready to cheat on her husband and betray the trust he had in her. She was going to become an adulterer while she was a mother with children who looked up to her as their moral example. She had transgressed God's law one time, by breaking her marriage vows. "For better or for worse," the marriage vows stipulate. "What God has joined together, let no man break apart," the warning is given. Nevertheless, for whatever reason, she had participated fully in the trashing of her first marriage. Now would she break another of God's laws? "Thou shalt not commit adultery," it is written in the Ten Commandments. Would she commit an offense now, on perhaps an even higher level?

Kathryn had vowed that the one thing she would never do in her life was commit adultery. All her life she'd watched her parents have extramarital affairs. Dysfunctional as her parents' marriage had been, however, Vera and Miles Faison had remained married. Born poor, they'd risen into the ranks of the upper middle class through guile and hard work. Miles and his Tennessee wife married when they were teenagers, and Miles often joked about how they "ran out of gas and money" in Macon, Georgia. To them, Macon looked like the big city, and it sure seemed better than the one-horse town they were trying to escape from, so they decided to stay for a while. For the first few years they lived in Macon, they didn't live as though they intended to put down roots. Although a baby named Kathryn came along ten months after they married, they were too young to be parents. They were just children themselves, away from home for the first time and eager to taste some of the fruits in the big city.

Miles Faison was a self-made man. A strong person physically and a hard worker, Miles began working in a salvage yard and, after learning the business, the thrifty and resourceful Miles Faison took the first few thousand dollars he saved and bought his first salvage yard. By the time Kathryn was an adult, Miles and Vera Faison owned salvage yards all over Georgia, Virginia, Tennessee, North and South Carolina, Florida, and Alabama. Vera Faison liked the money her country-boy husband made, but she looked down on him for the way he had to make it. She used to confide in her daughter when Kathryn was five or six years old that she hated the smelliness of her father when he came home showing her girlie calendars he'd picked up at the salvage yards, and Vera told her daughter she loved the soft business suits and the smell of cologne on the men who came to visit her when Miles Faison was out of town setting up a new operation. Kathryn's mother had confided about her affairs and discussed her boyfriends with her young daughter, and Kathryn had been expected to "feel special" because she was the one whom her mother took into her confidence. In a subtle version of child abuse, Vera Faison had taken her young daughter and manipulated her into a position where she had to keep her mother's secrets from her volatile and belligerent father. She'd flaunted her affairs, and giggled about the affairs her friends were having, in front of both her daughters, but the girls had experienced very different reactions. Kathryn had grown up feeling ashamed and guilty and dirty herself for knowing the secrets, whereas Kathryn's sister had grown up to be secretive and seductive and dishonest like her mother. One of Kathryn's strongest memories from childhood was going into her bedroom and closing the door with a sad feeling in the pit of her stomach when one of her mom's gentlemen friends came calling during Miles's frequent business trips to salvage yards in other states. She could remember the music playing in the family room, it was usually Tony Bennett or Nat King Cole or someone like that, and she could remember the sound of her mom and her friend for the evening dancing and laughing.

Married at seventeen and a mother by eighteen, Vera Faison certainly had ample opportunities to engage in adulteries. Miles Faison had traveled extensively throughout the Sun Belt in the process of acquiring and building his salvage yard empire, making no secret of the female companionship he enjoyed on the road. In his travels, he left behind a drop-dead beautiful young wife who craved sex and affection. A Rita Hayworth look-alike, the redheaded Vera Faison had been a movie-star-beautiful woman in her twenties and thirties, so there had never been a shortage of men ready to "visit" when Miles Faison was out of town. Kathryn tended to think that her father suspected his wife's infidelities but made certain that he never knew for sure. Like somebody told Kathryn once, there are a lot of things you don't have to do if you just don't know for sure. There was one scene etched into Kathryn's memory that made her think her father eventually didn't care what Vera Faison did because he was in love with someone else. One night when she was a teenager, Kathryn remembered hearing her parents arguing about another woman. The way her mother screamed at her father made Kathryn think that her dad had fallen in love with another woman during his frequent road trips and had been having a prolonged affair. Vera Faison had threatened to take him to the cleaners and rob him of everything—his business and his two daughters—if he didn't give up his "whore," as Vera

Faison had referred to her in the loud and vulgar conversation behind their bedroom doors that Kathryn had easily overheard.

There seemed to be an unspoken understanding between Vera and Miles that making as much money as possible was the shared goal of their relationship. They were determined to put their rural hillbilly past behind them. That's what his road trips were about, and Vera was the one left behind at home to take care of the social climbing and social networking for the family. Vera ended up enjoying her job in life. She left her young daughters at home with a succession of maids and housekeepers while she became involved in charity work and church activities. She quickly fell prey to the charms of the doctors and lawyers she came in contact with, and they fell prey themselves to the hot-natured, passionate, promiscuous young transplant from Tennessee who enjoyed them in earthy ways their wives never could. The professional men who visited Vera when Miles was gone would impress the beautiful young hillbilly with stories of their petty power plays in courtrooms and boardrooms and initiate her into the local intrigues, and Vera was captivated with the coercive and power-broking lifestyle of the smooth talkers who visited her.

As soon as Miles had "made it" in the salvage yard business, he bought his way into the country club in Macon. Over time, the beautiful and self-centered Vera became convinced that she had married beneath herself by marrying the poor boy from Tennessee who became "the millionaire king of the salvage yards," as he'd been dubbed by some jealous businessmen in town who envied the business savvy of the Tennessee country boy without any education. The old-money families clearly looked down on the brash new millionaire who had made his money "in grease pits," as Kathryn had once heard two old biddies describing her father. Perhaps that was how Kathryn's mother got even with the arrogant, fat old bitches who talked about her behind her back—she bedded their husbands when they weren't looking. Vera dreamed of being married to the sweet-smelling doctors and honey-tongued lawyers in the aristocratic Southern town where they lived, but she was a smart woman and figured out that no one in Georgia seemed to be better than her hillbilly husband at making money.

As a little girl, Kathryn had grown weary of the weak attempts the men made to justify their visits to her mother's house. I mean, how many "house calls" from doctors could one woman need? How many "financial matters" could her mother have to discuss? By outward appearances, her mother needed private medical treatment almost continuously and had to be engaged in endless discussions of real estate opportunities with the town's leading agents! By the time Kathryn was entering puberty, Vera Faison had graduated from her string of one "friend" after another to a monogamous adultery with a man in town who was now a powerful local official. In her mind, Vera had somehow rationalized the fact that, since the adultery was with one man, it was more or less okay. Kathryn knew that many people in town knew about her mother's enduring affair with the man, but no one would have dared tell the hotheaded Miles Faison about it, for fear that Miles would hate the message and kill the messenger. After her mother settled into the relationship with her friend, Kathryn had almost wished for the "good old days" of her mother's one-night stands because her relationship with her new friend had come at a time when the girl was becoming a woman, and he used to make suggestive remarks about her body and tell dirty jokes to her when her mother wasn't around. Even when her mother was around, he would compliment her on occasion in a lecherous way. When she told her mother that he made inappropriate remarks to her, Vera's only response was to get jealous of Kathryn, as though Kathryn was at fault for inviting his attention. As Kathryn grew into womanhood, her relationship with Vera seemed to mirror the relationship between Snow White and the disapproving stepmother. "Pretty is as pretty *does*," Vera would reply sarcastically when someone would compliment the young girl on inheriting her mother's good looks. After more than a decade of having her mother flagrantly throw her infidelities in her face, Kathryn had revolted against the concept of adultery by her teenage years, but the younger girl—and the apple of her mother's eye—had become trained to be an adulterer herself. Kathryn's sister Sally had begun her long descent into drugs and meaningless sex shortly after she got married for the first time to a promising young attorney who was wild about her. When he first learned of his young wife's infidelity, he blamed himself for neglecting her, but she laughed in his face when he begged her to go to marriage counseling with him. After that, he'd bitterly divorced her, while Vera and Miles helped Sally negotiate a large lump-sum payment as part of the divorce settlement.

Kathryn hated being the keeper of her mother's secrets. But her mother always warned her that she could never, never, never tell her father about the "friends" who came to see Mommy when Daddy was gone. Keeping those secrets as a child had given Kathryn a dirty feeling inside that never seemed to go away.

Somewhere along the way to getting rich, while juggling their promiscuity with their growing church and civic involvement, Vera and Miles convinced themselves that the way they were living was fine. The fact that they prospered financially made them think that their success must be a blessing from God, and as they grew richer, they outgrew any willingness to be corrected or judged in any way. It had been hard for Kathryn as a little girl to try to reconcile going to church on Sunday with what she saw in her home the other six days of the week. But at least her parents did take her to church, because that put her in touch with the gentle and loving Savior whose life she would one day study and from whose life she would learn that morality can be your choice, even if your parents choose something else.

Suddenly her memory shut down, and Kathryn remembered where she was, in Marcos's penthouse, and she remembered that he would be back momentarily with the condom. She yearned to experience with him, just one more time, the ultimate intimacy that sex is. Just once more. But she knew she couldn't.

When Marcos opened the door, he smiled sheepishly as he found her dressed and sitting in the living room part of the hotel suite.

"Well, it's obvious none of this was planned," he announced, smiling boyishly at her as he sat down on the couch beside her. "The only thing they had was psychedelic-colored condoms," he said, smiling. They both laughed at the ludicrous situation they found themselves in. He twisted his body towards her on the couch before he spoke, this time with a serious tone. "I have a lot of strong feelings for you still, Kathryn." There was a melancholy sound in his voice.

"I know," she said, in a tone of voice that was almost a whisper, as she looked into his large brown eyes and reached over to gently place her hand on his. "Perhaps you can destroy a marriage without destroying the . . . feeling. But I can't go to bed with you, Marcos, as much as I want to. It just compromises so many things I believe in, and I just can't live with the guilt and hypocrisy and emotional conflicts."

"I know, I understand, I totally agree," he said. She could hear the sadness in his voice.

"I have to go, Marcos, I really do." There was a definiteness in her voice that implied she wasn't going to change her mind.

"Are you sure?" he asked, searching her face and eyes as he took one of her hands and held it between both of his.

"Yes, I'm very sure," she said.

"I'll call my driver for you," he said, as he picked up the phone near the couch. He dialed a number and gave a command in Spanish to someone. He walked her to the door.

"Let me at least see you for lunch here on Wednesday before I go home," he said, putting his arms around her and embracing her gently. His touch was strong and passionate and loving. "Just come, please. We'll talk."

"Lunch would be nice," she replied, pulling herself away from him.

"I'll see you Wednesday at twelve noon here, alright? I have to go back to San Antonio on an afternoon flight, so I might be doing some packing while we have lunch." He opened the front door for her and waved goodbye as she walked to the elevator. His driver was waiting downstairs.

"Ritz-Carlton, right?" asked the driver as she entered the car.

FOUR

Monday turned out to be the kind of day that has given Monday a bad reputation, and Kathryn felt pulled in a dozen directions at the same time, seeing new designers and catching the fashion shows in the large hotel banquet room. This was a semiannual fashion show, over a four-day period, in which the lines of numerous designers were shown or spotlighted. She'd proven to be extraordinarily talented at selecting fashion that would sell at a markup of at least ten times, but she'd found that buying trips were the one thing she couldn't delegate. Her own buying decisions and judgment calls, made at fashion shows like this, were the key to their profitability. When the children were younger, Kathryn had tried sending key employees to make the buys, but profitability suffered. Now that they were positioned aggressively in expensive *haute couture*, she had only one person—herself—who could buy so that they would maximize profit. Anyway, she didn't mind the traveling now that the kids were older. She had peace of mind knowing Stefan was playing Mr. Dad almost as well as she would play Mrs. Mom. The kids were at the age when she could travel unencumbered by guilt.

On Monday night, she had dinner with some other boutique owners and buyers from around the country, and then she fell into bed exhausted about ten-thirty. It was too late to call Stefan by that time, and the kids were probably in bed. At least, she wanted to think they were in bed. She knew there was a good possibility the kids were up having an all-night party with Dad, playing Crazy Eights and Hearts and eating ice cream and popcorn and waiting for *SportsCenter* to come on. Stefan didn't play Mr. Dad the way Mom might write the script for the part.

Tuesday began with a knock on her door at seven-thirty. As she opened the door, a young messenger thrust some fabulous-looking flowers into her hands. The card on the flowers said:

LOOKING FORWARD TO SEE YOU WEDNESDAY AT NOON.
MARCOS.

At eleven-thirty on Wednesday, she was still in the thick of working out the details of purchasing some evening wear from one of the most exciting new designers she'd seen in a long time. Once the details of packing the dresses were arranged, she broke away and focused on finding a taxi to Marcos's apartment.

On the taxi ride to his hotel, Kathryn reflected on her relationship with Marcos. Looking out the taxi window, she realized how alike she and Marcos were. Both aggressive, hard-charging, temperamental, impatient go-getters. Both totally lacking in patience when they were younger. Both hungry for challenge and adventure. She remembered how Marcos's mother used to advise her *"poco a poco"* when she was trying to tell Kathryn to simmer down and be more patient, but Kathryn hadn't been interested in bit by bit, slowly but surely. An instant marriage and an instant relationship was what she'd wanted. Now, more than fifteen years later, both she and Marcos had been mellowed by life and by the challenge and adventure that parenting is. It was a sad, melancholy, nostalgic thought to realize that, if only they'd stuck it out, focusing their love on a child might have brought a mellowness to their relationship long ago. Maybe everything would have settled down. Maybe they would have sorted through the cultural differences. Maybe the supercharged intensity that had defined their relationship would have been channeled into the bedroom and into their careers. Maybe they would have had a peaceful, loving marriage over the long haul. She hadn't stayed long enough to find out, and it was like a riddle she'd never know the answer to, like looking back at the fork in the road and wondering what the journey would have been like on the road not taken.

The front desk called to tell him Mrs. Haddad was downstairs, and he asked the desk clerk to send her up to the penthouse. Kathryn straightened her clothes in the elevator. Underneath her coat, she was wearing an outfit she'd bought in New York, and the blouse was a thin, see-through material with fuchsia and orange and red shapes of all sizes on the fabric. The blouse was made to be worn without a brassiere, with geometric shapes well positioned where the breasts would protrude. She had on a bra, but it was still a sexy top. She'd coordinated it with a short red leather skirt that came above her knees and showed off her long, thin legs. Over the blouse, she was wearing a matching red vest that clung to her breasts. She wished she'd worn something less hot and sexy, but she always liked to work the shows in impeccable fashion herself, and in the hustle-bustle she hadn't thought about changing clothes until this moment. She had a figure like a model, and she had found she could more easily arouse the eye and ear of a designer when she was hot looking herself. At least, the designers she worked with seemed to have a little respect for her and seemed to remember her name better when she looked like she could be one of their models. She was always trying to buy unique creations of highest quality for a great price, and designers seemed to enjoy dealing with the voluptuous-looking Southern woman who looked so arousing in their creations.

"Wow," Marcos said, as he opened the door to find her long French-braided auburn hair set off by her tantalizing outfit with the hot electric colors.

"Let's order the food first so we can talk, Kathryn," he suggested, as he helped her take off her coat. After she nodded her approval, she saw a smile appear on his face, and she watched his eyes examine her in slow motion as his eyes began at the top of her head and slowly moved down her body, studying her in silence.

After they looked over the menu together, he picked up the phone and ordered. While they were waiting for the food to arrive, Marcos showed her a photo album of press clippings about the Galleria Corporation that chronicled his success in building the company into an international giant. Pictures of Dolores Galleria appeared throughout the album as she stood beside him at formal ceremonies and ribbon-cutting events. She looked happy, pretty, and refined. The food came quickly, and they ate on serving trays while he continued to show her memorabilia and paraphernalia from the past.

"I want to come to Georgia for a hunting trip with David soon," Marcos said, in a suddenly more businesslike tone. "Can you talk Stefan into letting David go? I know he doesn't hunt himself, but I have all the required certifications. It'll be in about three months. All that's in season that time of year are turkeys and wild boar, but they don't have wild boar in Georgia. There's a lot of skill in turkey hunting, though. I think David will enjoy it."

"Sure, I can talk to Stefan. And, you know, there's an old Vanderbilt estate in Macon where a lot of the good ol' boys go hunting. I know the man who manages it. He goes to our church. I could ask him if you and David could hunt there, if you want me to."

"Oh," he said, smiling appreciatively, "I'd be very grateful if you'd check on that. I really don't know the area in Georgia, so if you can find us a place close by, that would be wonderful. I'm sure it must have a lodge, and David and I can stay there together for a few nights, or he could go home at night to sleep, whichever way he wants to do it. But, yes, Kathryn, that would be very kind of you to check on that."

"Oh," she said, as she walked over to pick up her red leather tote bag, "I wrote a poem last night. Remember you asked me if I still did any writing?"

"Yes, yes, let me read it." He walked over to the coffee table to retrieve his glasses. Then he read the legal-size piece of paper she'd placed in his hand. She watched him as he read it. He looked older with his glasses on. She felt a pang of pain somewhere deep inside as she realized that this might be the last time she'd ever see him alone like this. Oh, probably there would be parties, weddings, graduations, reunions, maybe even funerals, and all kinds of other functions in the future, way down the road, where they'd be thrown together, but they'd probably never again be alone like this. She'd enjoyed the few hours they'd been together in New York. That time would always seem a treasure. She wanted to cling to the last few moments of it. Some healing of that old wound had occurred, she could feel it, but the wound was still tender. Tenderness toward him wasn't what she wanted to feel, but that was definitely the emotion surging through her. There hadn't been a proper parting fifteen years ago. This time, the second time around, she could see that a closure, a goodbye, was coming up, and it made her sad.

"Being Human Is Hard"

Being human is hard.
I see in others
The faults I cannot see in myself.
I preach patience and tolerance
But I cannot forgive
The human weakness in those I love.
It is so tempting
To choose the shallow course over the rough.
Sometimes I feel
Life should not require me
To choose the hard way.
Still, I thank God
For the times of tireless toil and devotion.
I once fell to the bottom of my soul,
Into that swirling, bottomless depth of myself,
Into the arms of God.
I felt the protection of my Maker,
And I rededicated my life to God.
I still am a miserable mortal.
I regret my frailties
But I no longer loathe them.
Swirling in that bottomless abyss
That is the soul of me
Are the actions I have taken
Toward others.
That soul inside me,
My spiritual computer,
Has calculated the choices I have made
And knows my character.

It is comforting
To look into the well of my soul
And see God's influence in it.
I see his tests
Of my strength
And I have often been a good soldier.
The agony of doing what is right
Is the most intense human passion.

"It's beautiful, Kathryn," he said, enthusiastically.

"No, you don't have to say that. I know I'm not a real poet, but I guess everyone has some poetry in him."

He walked over and put his arms around her and hugged her tight. She hugged him back, tightly, the way you hug a relative you care about but haven't seen in a long time.

Then he put his hands on her shoulders and pushed her back gently so he could look into her eyes. "Fifteen years, huh?" he said, as his brown eyes looked into her green ones. "Still waters run deep, don't they?" He looked into her eyes, but she could tell by his face and his voice that it wasn't really a question he expected an answer to. "I've missed you, Kathryn. Sometimes you just don't know what you have until you lose it." He took her into his arms and held her close against him. "I don't know what's next," he said, holding her head in his arms and stroking her head and hair. "But I know I feel happy with you in my life again. And I regret that I have to leave you now. We never really got to say goodbye fifteen years ago, and now we're always going to be saying a quick hello and goodbye to each other. We've drawn close again emotionally, just like before, but there are so many barriers between us now."

She didn't mean to burst out crying, but that's what happened. Maybe it was the sadness in his voice. Maybe it was the way he articulated her feelings exactly. But spontaneously, immediately, and uncontrollably, she cried as he held her in his arms. He was right. They were going to say goodbye now, like the goodbye they never said fifteen years before. It hurt.

"Your war paint is messed up," he said, looking into her watery eyes.

"That's not all that's messed up," she answered, weeping.

Then, he took her hand and she followed as he led her into the bedroom. They laid down together, her head resting on his shoulder as both of them looked up at the ceiling trying to see where exactly they'd taken the wrong turn in the road. She felt the sting of hot tears on her face, and she could taste their saltiness. He reached over to pull a tissue from the container beside his bed and, after he wiped her tears, he bent down to kiss her. It was a soft, tentative kiss that felt more like a caress. She returned his affection. Then, something ignited, and tenderness became passion as he took her in his arms and began to make love to her the way a man makes love to a woman he cherishes and honors. It wasn't right to accept the love from him, she knew it, but the desire to feel loved by him once more overpowered the sentiment that it was an illicit love that couldn't belong to her again. Why couldn't it belong to her again, just for a moment?

After they made love, she laid against his chest with one of his arms around her shoulders and his other arm across her stomach, holding one of her hands in his hand. They laid together, breathing heavily, for what seemed like a long time. Maybe it was the silence between them that made the moments of time stretch out. Then, she pushed herself away from him. Aggressively, he pulled her back toward him and put his arms around her, locking his hands together to hold her tight inside his arms. She looked over at the bedside table and saw the box of condoms still unopened.

"You forgot to put the condom on!" she said anxiously.

"I know, I just thought of it myself, just now. But don't worry, the laws of probability will make everything fine, I'm sure."

"Oh, Marcos, I get pregnant so easily. Stefan says all he has to do is look at me and I'm pregnant. I wish you'd put it on."

"I'm sorry. I really am. But just lie here with me for a while. I've missed you so much, Kathryn," he said, in a voice that sounded tender and husbandly. She quit stirring and lay beside him, in silence, for what must have been half an hour as he stroked her hair. She loved listening to the sound of his breathing.

Oh, what have I done? a remorseful voice inside her asked after the feeling of sexual stupor ebbed and consciousness returned. "I can't do this again," she said, breaking the silence and turning over to sit up in bed. Once the feeling of guilt kicked in, it seemed to multiply geometrically and instantly, and Kathryn's mind raced to unconnected thoughts in the guilt genre. "We pay a price for everything," a prominent theologian had once said. "Take what you want, and pay for it," God is reported in Spanish folklore to have warned. At Kathryn's grandmother's church, a Baptist minister once made this point after telling the story of Elvis and his struggle with drugs: "You can take what you want, and lose what you have." As soon as she sat up in bed, she felt weak, and she laid back down beside him, her head on his shoulder.

"Oh, hell," he said, as he glanced at the clock beside his bed. "Time is getting on, and planes don't wait, unfortunately." Marcos would soon be checking out of the hotel and flying to San Antonio to his family, and Kathryn would be returning to her family on Friday.

Marcos said it would be best if she left by the elevator a few minutes before he left. They could rejoin in the lobby after he let the front desk know he was leaving, in case messages arrived that needed to be forwarded to the San Antonio headquarters. He walked her to the front door of the penthouse.

"Well, I'd better give you your goodbye kiss now, since I won't see you alone again," he said, taking her two hands in his hands and kissing them one after the other before he took her into his arms and kissed her first tenderly, then passionately. "I can't wait until I see you again," he whispered.

In the elevator she smoothed her clothes and examined herself in the elevator mirror. A little frumpy looking and disheveled, she looked like she'd been some "businessman's special" for lunch, she decided, as she stared at her curvy body and displaced clothing. She straightened the vest that had fallen away from her breasts, making her look like someone had just savored every inch of her and forgot to put her clothes back on right. She pulled her hair back into the scrunch she'd brought along and tried to look like a school teacher.

She opened her eyes wide and tried to bring reality into focus as the elevator door opened into a flower-filled lobby of tropical elegance. In the lobby, she admired the red ginger, pusstail, crotons, and orchids. Soon, she spotted Marcos at the front desk. He put on his sunglasses as he walked away from the desk carrying two bags. He made a slight head gesture that let her know she was to follow him outside the hotel. She did.

Outside the hotel waiting for his car to drive up from the basement garage, they chatted at a distance from each other, as though they were business acquaintances.

"You take care of yourself, Kathryn," he began. "I want to see you looking very well rested and energetic when I see you next."

"And you take care of yourself. If you want to talk with David, it's best to call him on Saturday nights or on Sunday evenings after church."

He looked at her, not as a man looks at an ex-wife, but as a husband looks at a wife, as a man looks at a woman who interests him. She could tell that he yearned to reach out and touch her, caress her. Fifteen years hadn't eliminated the feeling they had for each other, and it hadn't dulled the passion they felt. It was curious that the passion would burn so hot after so many years and after they had caused each other so much hurt and pain.

They stood there together, at a respectable distance from each other, looking out at New York. He seemed to be thinking the same kinds of unspoken thoughts as she was thinking. From the look on his face, she felt that she could read his mind and overhear the conversation he was having with himself.

Could this really be happening? Was he really having an affair— or an infidelity—with his ex-wife who had left him and humiliated him publicly so long ago? It had hurt so much when she left. He hadn't known how to deal with it. He'd wanted her back, but he'd been in a tough spot. If he'd taken her back he would have seemed weak and spineless. If he hadn't taken her back, he would have seemed hard and masculine. So, immature and hotheaded on top of hurt and humiliated, he'd thrown away his relationship with Kathryn and David because of pride. In her presence again, he could feel that she was his intended one. He loved her brain, her adventurous approach to life, and the positive way she dealt with problems. He'd been a bull with her during their courtship, and she'd behaved badly herself at times in Mexico. But the qualities he fell in love with years ago were in full measure displayed the second time around. When he'd first placed the call to Kathryn on David's fifteenth birthday, it had seemed like a long shot that he'd be able to form a bond with David since they hadn't met until after the boy's fifteenth birthday. All his friends who had ex-wives had educated him on what a mortal enemy the ex-wife can be, so he'd expected Kathryn to be pissed off and looking for revenge, for good reason, because he'd stayed away from her and David for fifteen years after she left. There were a lot of reasons why he'd stayed away, none of them particularly noble. Pride, pain, hurt, fear of rejection. Through the years, he'd been glad his son was being raised in a happy home. He'd seen many children emotionally brutalized and terrorized by divorce, and he hadn't wanted that for his son. So he'd decided to leave the boy in Kathryn's nest and in her care until his son got old enough to understand the fact that relationships sometimes, make that often, fail. Oh, it hadn't exactly been that calculated a decision. Inertia set in after a while and the trauma of her leaving just never went away. He had to give her credit, though; she hadn't acted like a petulant ex-wife when he called. She'd put the boy's needs for love and acceptance above her own need for retaliation and revenge. She'd done her best to make sure it went well for both of them, and they'd gone into this thinking it would be best for David if his natural parents could maintain a cordial relationship. But a cordial relationship wasn't what he wanted with her, now that he'd been with her again. He wanted to watch her smile and hear her talk. Apparently, she still had an appetite for him, too. She would be vulnerable to him now, as she always had been. If he couldn't have a life with her, maybe a part of her every now and then would be enough. He could see now that they could have settled into an exciting and balanced life together sharing many mutual interests. She apparently loved to travel, and he made the kind of money that would have satisfied her gypsy blood. She'd gone to college in London and had worked there after graduation, and now she was apparently looking forward to more travel in her later years. Only, it would be with Stefan now, and not with him. She would have been his ideal companion after the stage of bearing and raising children. What a loss that they had not had many children together, as he'd hoped when they married. We don't look far enough ahead in youth when we slam doors shut.

As his car drove into the circle driveway, Marcos helped her into the backseat as the driver placed his bags in the trunk. When he climbed into the car beside her he spoke rapidly in Spanish to the driver. "Ritz-Carlton," was all she could understand of what he said. As the car picked up speed, he said, "I'll call you in the next few weeks, just to see how everyone is doing," he said, placing his hand on hers as it lay on the back seat. The melancholy look on Marcos's face made Kathryn sense that he felt sadness for the years of missed intimacy.

The car pulled in front of her hotel and the driver announced, "Ritz-Carlton." Kathryn turned to face Marcos before she disembarked, and at the same time he leaned over and kissed her gently on the lips, holding her chin in his cupped hand.

"Take care of yourself," he said, kissing her forehead quickly and then taking one of her hands in both of his and bringing his head down to kiss her hand gently. She exited and waved until she could no longer see his car in the distance.

After waving goodbye, she felt in no mood to deal with frenzied designers, so she decided to walk for a few blocks around New York. In spite of the cold, it was a sunny day, and she thought a walk might shake this nostalgic mood. She thought of the summer they'd spent in New York. It had been a stormy experience. Arguments just seemed to erupt when they were together, and they had a way of taking a violent turn once they got started. But he'd always come back to her with an apology and an excuse, and she would bond every time to that softer side of him that asked her to put the bad scene out of her mind. She always could, because her childhood had trained her to be a forgiver.

Now here she was, years later, compromising some of her most fundamental values and beliefs, and playing potentially fatal games with her marriage. If their prior relationship had been a stage for their destructive tendencies, then, the second time around, it seemed they both still had that ability to self-destruct. At least, it felt like there was something very destructive about what they were doing. But why did she still have these strong feelings for him? How, after all these years, could she still care for him so much? It seemed like an unusually cruel joke for life to play. Could she still be in love with her ex-husband after all that time—what a human farce! Surely, that would be the ultimate irony in life! Like the old saying that "hindsight is 20/20," she could see clearly now: she'd loved Marcos, and she should have stayed to work it out. Maybe it wouldn't have been a happy marriage. Maybe it would have ended in divorce, anyway. But she should have tried, and it should have been left up to her alone to screw up her marriage. She'd never been a quitter, and she didn't like looking back at the shallow, capricious way she'd run away from her first marriage and at the deceitful and deceptive way she'd done it.

Everything in her life had made perfect sense nine months ago. Marcos's call a decade and a half after David's birth was like a pebble being thrown into smooth and tranquil water. Then, so many things that had settled at the bottom of the water had gravitated to the top. And now that those things were disturbed and exposed, Kathryn looked at them in a different way through middle-aged eyes. In a way, it was like a sorrow from the past had been reborn and, like her grandmother used to say, "There's no sorrow like a living sorrow."

This resurfacing of her feelings for Marcos was coming at a time when she was really falling in love on a deeper level with her own husband. She'd made her peace with a lot of dissatisfactions about marriage during the early years of married life. During those hard years of building the business and having babies, she'd yearned for just a little romance every now and then, and she'd craved an escape from the tedium and humdrum of life. But work, work, work, and taking care of people was what married life had been, and she'd felt like she had to do all the giving. Maybe it was the way males were programmed genetically or environmentally, but they seemed to need a mother more than a wife, a maid more than a lover, an underling more than an equal. For the first three years they were married, Stefan hadn't even bothered to get her a Christmas present after she knocked herself out doing all the shopping for him and the kids and the extended family. Fatherhood was what had ultimately changed Stefan and forced him to blossom out of his state of arrested development into manhood. He'd responded with love to the demands placed by the children on his time, and he was a devoted and affectionate father. Now Stefan, too, worked all day in the business and then all night at home, tutoring one kid in algebra, helping another study for a social studies test, listening to a speech prepared by another, checking homework, and preparing them for exams. He was the one who attended the school ceremonies when the kids made the honor roll, and he was the one who coached two soccer teams a season and who made sure he attended every game they played in. As her respect for him had increased, love had grown, too.

Ultimately, it is probably the qualities in others that we most admire and not so much what they achieve, and Kathryn admired Stefan's devotion and tenderness as a father. He'd blossomed in character in the last year or so. He was more considerate of her, and he'd grown appreciative of her good qualities. They'd grown spiritually together through those years, too. He hadn't gone to church as a child and didn't go very often the first few years they were married, even though Kathryn took the children every Sunday and always taught one of their Sunday school classes. When the children were babies, Stefan had begun meeting her occasionally at "big church" but now he came faithfully to the eleven o'clock worship service so they could sit together and worship as a family. He told her once he wasn't sure if he had faith, but he had hope. He'd been willing to make a personal sacrifice every Sunday morning so they could become strong spiritually as a family unit. The children had developed a foundation of religious beliefs and values, and they always prayed as a family at the dinner table and talked about God at home. Not getting the romance and attention from him she'd craved in her thirties seemed a shallow problem now when she thought about the spiritual depth and family network they'd built into their relationship over the years.

Through the shared experiences of raising children, building a business, and enjoying the adventure of life, Kathryn and Stefan had built a relationship that now included love, companionship, and a family that thrived on their being together. His laid-back personality gave way to her headstrong, intense, emotional nature, and she had a very wide space in which to operate. After twelve years of married life, they'd come through a lot together, including learning how to stay out of each other's functional area at work, since working in the same business placed them in nearly continuous contact twenty-four hours a day. And now, they were getting ready to embark on yet another business adventure together when they attempted to franchise the Chic Boutique. Stefan almost had the franchise documents drawn up and the money he'd made in the stock market in the last few years would provide the seed capital they needed in order to kick the ball in the air.

So, she asked herself as she walked down Fifth Avenue and wandered past Tiffany's, *if I'm enjoying my marriage so much, What am I doing having an affair?*

FIVE

It was after eleven on Friday when she was flicking the garage opener. She opened the back door into the house slowly. *SportsCenter* was on. She walked into the family room. Stefan was playing solitaire on her lap desk and watching television on their fifty-inch screen from his La-Z-Boy recliner.

"Hi, honey," he said, immediately rising to walk toward her. He put his arms around her and gave her a big hug. "I missed you. We all missed you." She felt his affection as he put his arms around her and held her tight, as though he didn't want to let her go.

"I missed you, too," Kathryn said, returning his affection.

"Did you get some great stuff, honey?" he said, as he followed her into their bedroom adjoining the family room. She loved coming home to the gorgeous new five-bedroom house they'd built a few years ago. Building an upscale executive home had seemed a gamble at the time, since they were in the middle of repositioning the boutique, but they had figured and figured and finally decided they'd take the risk. Besides, they had reasoned, they could always sell the house if the repositioning didn't work. During the year it took to build it, Kathryn had run the business while Stefan supervised the builders in every detail of construction. Kathryn decorated the first floor with lots of colorful paint and wallpaper, and they positioned their bedroom downstairs while the four kids each had a bedroom upstairs. Their large master bedroom suite included a luxurious bathroom containing a sunken Jacuzzi and adjoining a huge walk-in closet.

"When did the kids go to bed?" she asked as she was unbuttoning her blouse and walking toward the walk-in closet.

Suddenly she heard "Surprise!" and four children, ranging in age from Booth at six to David at fifteen, jumped out from her closet.

"I knew something was funny if you were already in bed! I was just going to ask Dad if you were sick," she laughed, as she held out her arms to her children.

Nearly an hour of talking and watching television followed. When the children were sent up to bed, she and Stefan went into the bathroom to brush their teeth and get ready for bed.

Kathryn began unpacking and putting her clothes on the shelves in their walk-in closet. She loved unpacking after one of her buying trips, because her closet became even more full of beautiful things. She always had gorgeous clothes because of the boutique. She was becoming known around town as a fashion barometer, so she tried to look well dressed. "It's a hard job, but somebody's got to do it," she used to tell Stefan when he teased her about having so many svelte clothes. In their small Southern town, wearing her products was the best way to promote her business. Well dressed, especially with her trim and curvy body, she was a walking advertisement for the boutique, and as the business became more successful, she became aware that people noticed what she had on. At first she'd felt robbed of the privilege of grunging around town in a scruffy-looking outfit. But she'd faced realistically the need to be "in uniform" at all times, and she'd made it one of her missions every time she was in New York to find chic casual clothes so she could be a fashion plate and yet still feel comfortable even as a volunteer at the children's schools or at scout meetings. It was good propaganda for the store, and she didn't mind being a living billboard for one of the South's most exclusive ladies' boutiques.

Most of her classmates from Harvard Business School were in major corporations or financial services, and they probably looked with disdain on the decision of a fellow MBA to own and run a retail shop. Actually, Kathryn had combined her entrepreneurial instincts and creativity while applying the wisdom taught at the B-School when she identified the niche for a high-fashion regional boutique. She finally had a cash cow of her very own! Thanks to Stefan's rugged bargaining skills, they'd bought the store, including land and building, for an excellent price when its founder, an older woman whom Kathryn knew through the church, discovered she had cancer and decided her health was too poor to continue managing the business she'd founded many years previously. Shortly after Kathryn and Stefan bought the shop, they saw that most of its customers were the age of the lady who founded the store, and that the store was basically a break-even proposition after paying the bills and payroll. They began to see the problem when they realized that they were losing dozens of customers yearly not to the competition but to funerals. So, after a few disgruntled years of owning it, they'd decided to take the risk of changing the business concept from dowdy and cheap to exciting and expensive. The repositioning had worked. Cash flow was so good, in fact, that she and Stefan were able to live in comfort while putting aside money for college educations. So many things had become easier in the last few years. The risk of building the house had been worth the gamble. They were free of the financial worries they had in the early years of their married life. And the children were such a joy and a pleasure to both of them. Life was good.

She walked out of the master bathroom into the bedroom. Stefan was propped up in bed watching an interview with a University of Georgia football player. In Macon, as well as in most other Southern towns, high school football games on Friday nights and college football games on Saturday were their own kind of religion, and sports mania was one Southern tradition that Stefan had no trouble embracing. Miles Faison was a big Bulldog Club supporter at the University of Georgia and had season tickets to the Georgia Bulldog games. Vera had no interest in football, so Miles always wanted to take David and Calvin with him to the games ninety miles away in Athens on Saturday. Miles claimed he didn't understand what Kathryn meant when she tried to explain to him why the boys couldn't go off every weekend, and he pretended not to know what she meant when she said she wanted to have a family life with the kids home on the weekend. There had been frequent scenes in the Chic Boutique when Miles had appeared on

Friday to ask if the two older boys could go see the Bulldogs on Saturday. When Kathryn tried to politely decline his invitation, he would become belligerent and storm out of the shop like a teenager, cursing her and rattling the composure of the customers and employees. Miles accused her repeatedly of being selfish and self-centered, and he'd tried to program her two oldest sons to pout and complain about not being able to go. It seemed as though Miles was trying to act like a father to her two oldest boys. What Kathryn tried to do was to put Stefan first and make sure the children knew and loved their father while they were growing up. Stefan wanted his children home on the weekend, too, so he took Kathryn's side when she refused to let the boys be taken away for the fancy trips their grandparents dangled in front of them. She felt weary just thinking about it, as she went over to her side of the bed and lay down beside Stefan, putting her head on his stomach. He began to massage her shoulder.

"I bet you're tired, aren't you, honey?" he asked softly.

"I sure am, but I think we're going to find this buying trip very profitable. I found some wonderful fabrics and tantalizing colors. There are fabulous new designers doing wonderful things that I know will sell great. I found a lot of casual chic clothes for day and night that will be extremely popular. There's really been a trend lately for our customers to want a slightly casual feel even when they're in *haute couture* or in something very dressy and tailored. It's as though they want to look beautiful but give the impression that it took no effort. Anyway, I found some great young designers who are expressing that beautifully. All I have to do is send out a postcard to our regulars." The Chic Boutique now enjoyed quite a reputation regionally, and affluent women from all over the South were willing to make the trek to Macon to shop there. Loyal customers in Georgia traveled from Athens, Atlanta, Augusta, Savannah, Albany, Valdosta, and Columbus. Word of mouth had kicked in and women also drove from Jacksonville, Tallahassee, and Panama City in Florida, from Birmingham and Montgomery in Alabama, from Chattanooga in Tennessee, and from Columbia and Greenville and lots of other little towns in South Carolina. Every bit of that new inventory would turn over in less than a month. She could just feel it.

She snuggled up beside him in bed and he put his arm around her.

"Welcome home, honey," he said, as he bent down to kiss her and begin their love-making process. She responded but felt guilty.

"I know you're tired," he said, after a few minutes. "I just wanted to love you a little."

They went to church, as usual, on Sunday morning, and Kathryn taught Veronica's third-grade Sunday school class. Something gnawed at her when Dr. Kotler preached the sermon about putting morality into action. She and Stefan laughed when he told the joke about a lady who criticized her minister for preaching a sermon that went over her head. The minister looked at the lady, Dr. Kotler said, and told her the problem was that she was ducking. He also told a joke about a lady who informed her minister after his Sunday sermon, "I didn't get fed today." The minister replied, "Well, isn't it good that the symbol for this religion is a cross, not a trough?"

On Monday morning, there was the organized hustle-bustle it usually was at their house. Children dressed themselves now that the youngest was six, but there were still shoes to find, socks to locate, lunches to fix, and breakfast dishes to put away. They walked through their morning routine without incident. The three oldest children caught the bus to school, and then Kathryn dropped Booth at his first-grade class at a quarter of eight, since his school was only three blocks from her office. She liked getting to work early, before anyone else. The employees didn't get there until nine o'clock, and Kathryn enjoyed having time alone to refine a display or check the racks or do some planning. The new garments she'd bought in New York might begin to arrive today. Stefan would be in around eleven o'clock to show her the franchising documents. He'd told her that morning that he had a new concept in mind: franchising the Chic Boutique units not only to retail exclusive ladies' clothing selected by Kathryn and a central buying team, but also to sell home design and interior decorating items. He'd said excitedly at breakfast that morning that he thought such a concept would cushion their risky dependence on ladies' fashion and cater to the tastes of their upscale clients, most of whom were Southern women who took pride not only in their clothes but also in the presentation of their homes. As she drove the few blocks to work after dropping off Booth, she felt excited about the new designs that would be arriving from New York, and she couldn't wait to hear what Stefan had been thinking in the last week about their franchising plan.

Once she got to work, she felt in a nostalgic mood. She crossed her feet on the desk and reclined in the Williamsburg-blue swivel armchair. Life had definitely been easier lately, not just at home with Stefan but at the office too. Luckily, she'd found an employee who could run the store while she was on buying trips. Tracy would be in soon, after picking up the mail, to fill Kathryn in on what had happened during the week she was away.

Kathryn and Stefan had butted heads frequently in the early days of running the store together, probably because they'd been in a situation where there were two strong chiefs and too few Indians. About three years ago, Stefan had announced that he wanted to do something on his own and was going to try his hand at investing in the stock market. Although Kathryn hadn't been happy about the idea at first, as it turned out, he'd been smart not to let himself get buried in the day-to-day details of managing a ladies' clothing store, and the time he'd spent investing in the stock market had paid off handsomely. As the repositioning became successful and the Chic Boutique became well known regionally, he'd encouraged Kathryn, too, to get out of the "daily grind" of operations and focus her creative energies on the buying end of their fashion business, and that had proved to be excellent strategic advice. Their cash flow was now considerable, and the cash cow was producing ample milk. That's what Kathryn's buying trips were all about—making sure the cow had the necessary nutrients. The family business now permitted them an exotic summer vacation of three weeks or so, usually in the Caribbean. After Stefan fathered three children of his own, he'd felt the yearning to return to his roots and try to locate the family members who'd settled in the Caribbean islands years ago. So they'd embarked on adventures with the children every summer and had located lots of "lost relatives" on the islands of Barbados and Jamaica. Even when they were in Macon, the business afforded them a leisurely lifestyle with lots of flexibility. Owning a business allowed Kathryn the flexibility to be involved in the kids' school, church, scouts, and other extracurricular activities, and the shop was acclimated to the fact that she turned into a mommy at two forty-five daily so she could be waiting at the front door when the kids burst in at three. Stefan used the flexibility the business gave him to be involved in the children's activities and coach their sports teams while he handled the finances of the business and made time for church and Rotary Club.

For the last couple of years, she and Stefan had been discussing lifestyle plans for the time down the road when the last child was in college. Their hope was to go to Jamaica to live nearly year round, perhaps in Ocho Rios, although the pretty mountains of Kingston had their allure. Kingston was a city set on hills, and the views from Jack's Hill and Beverly Hills and Stony Hill were spectacular. Because Stefan had located Haddad cousins and other Middle Eastern relatives in the capital city, Kingston was more alive than Ocho Rios for them in terms of parties and social life. Kingston was a bustling hub of commerce, where it would be possible to set up a garment sweatshop and have fashion stitched cheaply, if they wanted to have clothing manufactured there. On the other hand, "Ochy," as the locals called Ocho Rios, was a relaxed, touristy environment planted on the white sandy beaches of the north coast. At Fisherman's Point overlooking the bay, where they stayed in Ocho Rios, they could catch the sea breeze and hear the music undulating across the water from the Jamaica Grande on the far tip of the bay. She loved listening to the sounds of the big bands across the bay drifting into her bedroom at night, serenading her. In the years of taking the children to the Caribbean for a summer family vacation, she'd fallen in love with the tropics and the islands.

Macon as a place to retire held no fascination for either Stefan or Kathryn, even though Stefan, a transplant, had become accepted, even loved, by the "ol' boy network" in the community because he was an old-fashioned gentleman and a "man's man." His father had been a Canadian civil servant married to a French-speaking orphan brought up by nuns in a convent, and they had been determined to make every sacrifice so that their only son could have all the advantages in life.

Before he went off to Princeton on a full academic scholarship, Stefan
knew three languages, had studied under the best tutors and scholars
in Montreal, was a skilled pianist, and was a champion sportsman who
could play ice hockey, soccer, and tennis at nearly professional levels.
By temperament as well as by training, Stefan was an elegant, kind
man with impeccable manners, and the community had watched as
he adopted David and raised him as a son while he and Kathryn had
three more children. Elected president of Macon's Rotary Club, Stefan
was admired for his gentle leadership and rock-solid character. But,
as Kathryn and Stefan often discussed, they were living in "redneck
country" and Stefan was not really one of the good ol' boys. He'd always be an outsider, he told Kathryn, in a small Southern town that
would accept people for large community service jobs without including them in the inner circle. He and Kathryn did nothing to climb the
social ladder in Macon, anyway, and they had no desire to join the
country club. The only organization they were members of was the
Methodist church, but they'd joined the church to worship God, which
was not always the primary motivation of church members. In a Southern town, church membership provided important business and political connections, so going to church in the South was often a social
duty and obligation. "Beware of making a show of your piety," the
Scriptures warned, but that warning didn't keep many churchgoers
from making vows on Sunday that they had no intention of acting on.
The reality was that it was virtually a business necessity in a small
Southern town to belong to a Baptist, Presbyterian, or Methodist
church, and the larger the church you belonged to, the more contacts
you could make. Religion without morality, and religion without humility, was the style of many churchgoers in the South.

   Kathryn never had felt that she fit in, in Macon, Georgia. Funny
how you can grow up in a place and never really belong. Her grandparents' house had been her real home, and rural Tennessee seemed
more like her home state. Living at her grandparents' small frame
house in Tennessee every summer, she'd had the freedom to climb
trees, pick apples and blueberries, and play with her second and third
cousins while acting like a fun-loving hillbilly tomboy. Her Tennessee relatives adored her unconditionally and regarded her as "one of

them," more like her grandmother's daughter than granddaughter, and she felt more at home in the unassuming, spartan shacks of those coal miners from Tennessee than in the elegant Southern homes of Georgia. Kathryn used to love it when summer would roll around, and her parents would take her to Tennessee for the whole summer. Not that her grandparents' home was a perfect one. They argued a lot, mostly because he was a stubborn old goat who wanted everything his way. Her grandmother once told her how Vera got her name. Kathryn's grandmother wanted to name her new baby Jenny, but her husband wouldn't even discuss it. "You call her whatever you want. I'm naming her Vera," he'd told his wife arrogantly after she'd been through a tough, twenty-hour labor. But, even though those two old people had their disagreements with each other, they both agreed on one thing: they loved their oldest grandchild and told her repeatedly that she would make something of her life one day. To Kathryn, that little shack in Tennessee without running water or inside toilets was home, and it was a safe place where she was loved and respected.

Just as cultural differences had been largely responsible for the failure of her marriage to Marcos, so, too, cultural differences existed for her in Macon, Georgia. Maybe there were just too many things you had to fit into in a small Southern town, but it had always been a tug of war living there. She could remember vividly how she'd dreaded the journey through the mountains back to her parents' house after her summers in Tennessee. She remembered looking back at her grandmother crying on the porch, waving goodbye to her with her handkerchief as Kathryn waved back through the rear window of the car. It was like going from unassuming to overbearing, from comfortable overalls to stiff and expensive starched dresses, from love to hostility, from acceptance to disapproval, from safety to danger, from simplicity to complexity, from happiness to sadness, from being free of burdens to shouldering heavy responsibilities, from being a child to being a parent. Thrust back into her "pretend family" after summer ended, Kathryn felt like she was the alien in the house. Suddenly, she remembered the scene when she'd told Miles in her junior year of high school that she didn't want to go off to the University of Georgia after graduating from Macon High School.

"And why the hell not? You're one of the top three graduating students. You can easily get in. It's what all your friends want to do."

"No, I'm going to apply to the London School of Economics. One of the counselors at school told me she thought I could get in."

"London? Why in the hell would anybody want to go to London when you could live in Bulldog country? Why, the toilets don't even flush in London. The plumbing and housing all over England are from World War II."

"I want to study in London and then go get a Ph.D. or go to a graduate business school."

"It's a damned communist school, and I'm not paying for it," Miles had barked.

"I'm applying for a scholarship, Daddy, and I'm going, even if I have to borrow the money or get a job while I'm there to pay my way."

"But," Miles had whined, "you could go off to Athens and maybe be Homecoming Queen. You've got the looks and the brains."

"Daddy, I don't want to be Homecoming Queen," Kathryn had replied firmly. They'd already had battles a few years earlier about cheerleading. She hadn't wanted to be a cheerleader. Vera had wanted her to be one. Kathryn had won the battle, but they'd played their usual control game of withholding love and kindness because of her disobedience.

And then there had been the virulent argument when she'd come home at Christmas during her freshman year at the London School of Economics. Miles and Vera had been playing politics while she was away, and they had a special Christmas present for her that year, they said.

"Guess what?" Miles had asked, when she came home in early December for Christmas break. "I've arranged for you to be invited to be a debutante!" She could still remember the proud smile on his face and almost feel the lump in her throat when she replied.

"Daddy, I don't want to be a debutante."

"Oh, so you don't want to be a debutante?" he'd replied sarcastically and belligerently. "After your mother and I have done months of work, and after we've kissed enough asses in this state, and contributed to enough reelection campaigns, you don't want to be a debutante."

The hostility in his voice had scared her. "It's not easy," he'd continued, "to buy your way into these old family circles, you know. And they're willing to let you in because you're a distinguished young scholar on the rise and because I've made more money than they can count. This would be your way to get connected into the best social circles, and you look down your damned nose at it!" She could remember the violent look on his face, and she'd been right to feel afraid.

"You bitch," he'd screamed at her, while Vera and Sally sat quietly in the next room. Then, he'd slapped her across the face and hit her on the back. She'd escaped his temper by running into a back bedroom and locking herself in. Although Vera and Sally overheard the argument, they didn't respond to the disturbance. In their view, it was just Kathryn acting up again and being disobedient, and if Kathryn didn't do it, then Sally might not have a chance to do it later. It was selfish of Kathryn not to blaze the trail for Sally.

Although Kathryn always wanted her mother to rescue her from Miles's violent temper when it erupted, Vera never did. "That's *his* thing," Vera Faison would say haughtily when Kathryn tried to seek her mother's sympathy and compassion later. Miles could do "his thing" and Vera could do "her thing" in the family, and Kathryn's role was to behave and obey and forgive. Several years later, Sally, who wasn't a bit bothered by their order to grow up and be a Georgia Peach, would come home from the University of Georgia with barely passing grades but with boundless enthusiasm for the expensive debutante parties Vera and Miles would shower on her in order to showcase their importance in society. Sally appreciated them, Kathryn didn't, it was as simple as that in Vera's and Miles's eyes.

Anyway, living in Macon had been an accidental by-product of being dumped by Marcos, and she had no desire to stay in Macon after their youngest child, Booth, was in college. Although born there, she was different from most of the women she knew. There were few women entrepreneurs, except for a handful of doctors and lawyers. The women she worked with on children's activities at the kids' schools were a gossipy and snobbish lot overall, although Southern women did place a premium on raising their kids well, and Kathryn respected that orientation. They also placed importance on dressing well, which Kathryn was able to cash in on. With some exceptions, most of those Southern women she knew were vain and provincial social climbers with a narrow frame of reference that included obsessive participation in "the League," garden clubs, and country club. What Kathryn found particularly dull about those women was that they focused on such trivial and self-centered issues. They knew who was running around on whom, and the terms of so-and-so's divorce settlement, but they had no idea where Haiti was. The ones from old-money families were in therapy and were what psychologists called the "worried well." The "middle-class neurotic" is how Kathryn thought of them, and their main problem seemed to be their idleness and self-absorption. Over the last few years, Kathryn had realized she didn't fit in with them, and she didn't want to. After living in a town most of your life, you know whether you fit in or not, and Kathryn and Stefan simply did not have close friendships or bonds with many people in town. Her best friend Mary, from junior high school, was the exception.

So Kathryn was as ready as Stefan to find a home in the Caribbean one day when the kids were in college. If they could franchise the business in the next few years, they might be able to have a lifestyle that would allow them to live on a tropical island, and that's what they were working toward.

Being at middle age had its comforts and advantages. She could feel herself at a juncture in the road, with the diapers and kiddie viruses behind her. It was exhilarating to be looking ahead to capping off years of hard work by franchising a successful concept, and she treasured the family life she had with Stefan and the children. Having a family with a mellow man who'd turned out to be a devoted father had provided the most love she'd known in life.

An involuntary shudder came over her body as her mind flashed back to the "house of secrets" where she grew up. God, had she been glad to escape that. Adulthood with all its complications had been a playground compared to the battlefield of childhood. Vera Faison had been too preoccupied with social climbing in the church and country club, and Miles Faison had been too busy making money and building a successful business to take the time to get to know the girl who was their accidental firstborn. By the time their baby daughter, Sally, came along, seven years after Kathryn's birth, the Faisons had money and were ready for a child, so they'd pampered and spoiled Sally. Actually, their doting on Sally hadn't turned out very well for their baby. Kathryn was born smart, and she'd inherited Miles Faison's hardworking instincts, so she'd reacted to the cold moodiness of her mother and the violent temper of her father by burying her head in her books and excelling academically, knowing even as a child that making good grades would be the means of escape from her childhood prison. On the other hand, Sally had no demands placed on her, so she grew into a beautiful, rich playgirl.

In the last few years, Kathryn's relationship with her mother had worsened steadily. Vera's confident, bold approach to life seemed to twist into a brittle and bitter outlook after she recognized Sally's self-destructive behavior as the product of her parents' marital infidelities. Whatever remorse Vera felt, however, was unleashed as hostility toward Kathryn in some strange transference of emotion. It was as though all the shame and animosity Vera and Miles felt over Sally was redirected at Kathryn, as though Kathryn was responsible for Sally's immorality and infidelity or at least wasn't doing anything to fix the problem. Kathryn shuddered suddenly, involuntarily, as she reclined in the chair. Feeling her parents' hatred was a terrifying feeling that chilled her to the bone.

In the years she and Stefan had lived in Macon, Kathryn had grown weary of her mother's manipulation and her father's bullying. Everything had to be done just like they wanted it done. Vera acted like she'd been betrayed when Stefan and Kathryn changed churches and denominations because they felt more at home in the Methodist Church than in the Baptist Church. Vera had taken it personally, accusing Kathryn of maliciously "taking the children from their grandparents." And Vera made it clear she thought it was treasonous when Kathryn and Stefan decided, for reasons of privacy, not to use the Faison's real estate agent when they were trying to decide whether to buy an existing house or build a new one. Kathryn knew the agent was one of her mother's old boyfriends, and she didn't want Vera snooping in their business. No matter how hard she tried to get along with her parents, it seemed they made one demand after another and, on top of juggling the often stressful responsibilities of raising four children and making a business perform, Kathryn had tired of her mother's selfishness and narcissism and her father's violent temper.

Maybe it was something to do with being at middle age, but Kathryn felt unwilling to try much longer to have a relationship with her parents. She'd done her best to be a dutiful daughter and to accept their harsh, overbearing behavior—after all, they were her parents so they had a right, didn't they?—but her kindness only fueled their aggression. The straw that broke the camel's back, though, was the way Vera and Miles treated Stefan. Domineering Vera and insulting Miles tried their best to emasculate the kindhearted Stefan and ridiculed his laid-back, low-key personality that was so supportive of Kathryn. Miles and Vera snickered and poked fun at his willingness to work in a ladies' clothing store, and Miles ridiculed Stefan in public, whenever he got a chance, as "one of the girls" who worked in the store. The soft-spoken Stefan always reacted in a gracious way, with a smile, and he would tell Kathryn later, when they were alone, that they were her parents and that he was strong enough to withstand their verbal abuse, so she should just ignore it.

"They are your parents," Stefan would tell her, "and they're not going to change. My parents are dead now, but you still have yours, Kathryn, and you should value them." Slow to anger, and always amiable and courteous with them, Stefan never retaliated when they verbally insulted him and insinuated that he was an opportunist for marrying Kathryn.

Before Kathryn married Stefan, Vera and Miles had done their best to persuade Kathryn that Stefan didn't give a damn about her and was interested only in her family's money and in becoming a citizen of the United States. They threatened to take her out of their will if she became his wife. Kathryn knew that the real reason they were opposed to the marriage was that they could more easily dominate a single parent than a married woman. They were accustomed to dropping in on Kathryn anytime they wanted to and, if she married, they feared they might be denied unlimited access to the grandson, David, whom they'd come to idolize as a son.

"He's only after your money," Miles had savagely protested when she told him she and Stefan were going to be married.

"I don't have any money, Daddy," Kathryn had replied.

"Don't be such a smart-ass, Kathryn," Miles had retorted. "You know I'm talking about your family's money. This man is a damned immigrant. I don't even know what in the hell he is. Some kind of French Canadian or Arab or something. He doesn't even have any family, and he's not really from anywhere. Why, he told me he was working here on a green card. He's probably just trying to become a citizen of the United States."

"He loves me and David, Daddy," she'd replied.

"Love, my ass," Miles had sneered. "You know that Hamilton Hughes IV is interested in you, but you won't give him the time of day. You don't need to get married again, but if you do, at least marry somebody with some social connections in this town. Get out of your selfishness and at least do it for your son. Why do you have to marry a damned foreigner like you did the last time?"

"I can't stand Hamilton Hughes. Anyway, I don't want to marry somebody with two last names, Daddy," she had teased. Miles hadn't been amused.

"But this Stefan hasn't been raised in the church," Vera had protested.

Raised in the church? Maybe he hadn't been dragged to church every Sunday with starched clothes on, but neither had he been tormented by the hypocrisy of watching the artful combination of visible church work with passionate adulteries.

Offended that Kathryn didn't take their advice and married Stefan anyway in a small church wedding to which only a handful of Stefan's and Kathryn's friends were invited, the Faisons did their best to ruin the day. They kept Kathryn and Stefan waiting for them to show up at the church, and, then, a messenger appeared saying that Miles and Vera had a virus and wouldn't be able to come. So a friend of Stefan's who'd come from New York acted as the stand-in father and "gave her away." Kathryn smiled as she remembered what Dr. Kotler said once about the practice of "giving the bride away." He said it's bad enough that you have to give the bride away, but you have to gift wrap her, too! After the wedding, the Faisons took a condescending attitude toward Stefan and refused to accept his new relationship as the father of the grandson whom they felt belonged to them. Kathryn was determined to make the second marriage work, but it seemed as though Vera and Miles were on the sidelines doing everything they could to help the marriage fail. Stefan was a nobody, in their eyes.

The fact that Stefan returned their overbearing attitude with respect and affection further convinced them that he was a spineless idiot. At Stefan's urging, Kathryn subdued her hot Irish temper and tried to love and honor her parents, but year by year, insult by insult, sarcastic remark by sarcastic remark, the relationship deteriorated into rancor. Their possessive attitude toward David, and their contemptuous behavior toward Kathryn and Stefan, grew worse over the years. As Kathryn and Stefan blossomed into financially successful and well-respected people in the community, the obsessive and self-centered Vera resented their economic independence and envied Kathryn's self-made wealth and fine reputation because, in her twisted perspective, it diminished the younger daughter. Kathryn was showing up Sally, just like Kathryn had always done. Kathryn just had to be the smartest, the nicest, the best liked. Goody-goody Kathryn. In Vera's eyes, whatever Kathryn did with her life was designed to make poor little Sally look even more weak and defective. If Kathryn had never come back to Macon pregnant and dumped by her first husband, Sally might have blossomed in a different way. In Vera's eyes, Kathryn was responsible for the character flaws of her baby girl. It had been painful to face up to but, slowly, over the years, it became clear to Kathryn that her mother had a deep-seated jealousy and hatred toward her for being the "miss know-it-all" who overshadowed her baby sister.

It was Kathryn's grandmother's death, several months after Marcos's call on David's fifteenth birthday, that brought about the death of Kathryn's relationship with her parents. At least she'd had a chance to tell her grandmother about Marcos's call before she died. On their way to Mexico City after graduating from Harvard, she and Marcos had visited her grandmother, so Marcos had known the special lady whom Kathryn called "Mama." David had been close to Mama when he was a baby, too, because Kathryn had visited her grandmother with David during the summers before she married Stefan and became involved in having kids and running a business. When she'd told her grandmother by telephone that Marcos called, her grandma had simply said, "Well, you've got to forgive, don't you?" The woman who loved and raised her died a few weeks after that call.

Miles Faison didn't attend his mother-in-law's funeral. Kathryn and her mother traveled to Tennessee separately, Vera by plane and Kathryn by car. After the funeral, Vera decided to ride back to Macon with Kathryn. In the seven-hour trip from Tennessee to Georgia, they didn't exchange a word of conversation. The hostility in the car was almost tactile. Clearly, there was an absence of any feeling such as normally exists between a mother and daughter. Sad as that reality was, sadness wouldn't change the reality, wishful thinking wouldn't change the reality, hope wouldn't change the reality. As they rolled back into Macon at the end of the trip, Vera broke the silence. "You're a good driver, Kathryn. I hope you'll let the children come over to our house for the weekend. We want to take them to Atlanta to do some shopping." Although the deterioration of their relationship had taken more than forty years, that was the moment in time when Kathryn saw clearly the moribund state of the relationship and decided the pretense had to end. So the funeral for her grandmother had been a funeral for the relationship between her and her parents. It takes so much energy to have a hostile relationship, and Kathryn just didn't have any more energy to put into shielding herself from their hatred and anger. Looking at it another way, that trip back from her grandmother's funeral had been the birth of an honest relationship with her parents. From now on, no pretenses, no secrets, no hypocrisy, no deceit, no bullying and manipulation. No more. The combination of her grandmother's death and Marcos's reappearance in her life had dislodged some emotions and memories that had been buried deep somewhere. Strangely, the sad realization that her relationship with her parents was ending had been accompanied by an almost euphoric feeling that she was "coming out of the closet" and finally released of the burden to please them.

A week after the funeral, Vera called the boutique to tell Kathryn they wanted to take the four children to their beach house in Savannah that weekend. "You know how much they love the beach, Kathryn," Vera had said. It was classic Vera, hoping she could instill a little guilt by insinuating that Kathryn was depriving the children of an advantage in life if she didn't let them go off with their grandparents for the weekend.

"No, they can't go. We want the children home with us for the weekend. You know we like to do things as a family on the weekend." Kathryn paused. "And from now on, Mother, you and I are going to have an honest relationship."

"Fine," Vera replied angrily, slamming down the phone.

Two days later, Vera called the boutique to ask Kathryn for the children's social security numbers. "Your father and I are going to redo our will," she said, in that saccharine and seductive, yet deceptive and threatening tone Kathryn had come to despise over the years.

In the months following her grandmother's funeral, all Kathryn knew was that she was much happier not having her parents in her life. More out of guilt than out of wanting to, Kathryn had invited Miles and Vera to come for Christmas dinner with her and Stefan and the family but Vera had declined.

"No, thank you," Vera had replied angrily. "We're going to Sally's house for Christmas dinner. At least we feel welcome there."

Kathryn wished she didn't have to see her parents again anytime soon, but the whole family would be together in three months, when Sally married the doctor. Her relatives from Tennessee wouldn't be at the wedding, of course, because their hillbilly manners and country upbringing embarrassed Miles and Vera and were a reminder of the poverty-stricken past they'd risen above. Kathryn found the doctor who'd soon be Sally's fourth husband disgusting, a "dirty old man." It was quite the talk of the town, his leaving his wife and marrying a woman younger than one of his children. Vera was planning a lavish wedding reception at the country club, and many of the women would be wearing creations from the Chic Boutique. Kathryn had made it a point to find gorgeous wedding attire for just that purpose when she was in New York.

"Hi, boss lady," Tracy said, peeking her head inside Kathryn's office.

"Oh, hi. Is it nine o'clock already?" Kathryn replied. "Come on in. Did anything arrive this morning?"

"Actually, it's after nine. And several huge packages just came by UPS. I assume it's what you bought in New York, right?"

"Probably. We'll open them up in a few minutes. Tell me what happened while I was gone."

"Okay," said Tracy, taking out her notepad. Kathryn studied her young assistant as she looked over the notes she'd made while her boss was gone. Tracy was a twenty-four-year-old woman who'd been sent on a job interview through PREP Personnel when Kathryn was looking for a management trainee. She'd been in Macon only a few days when Kathryn met her, just after she'd arrived from Germany with her father, an Air Force officer reassigned to Warner Robins Air Force Base near Macon. Tracy had become a valuable asset to the business. She had a head full of common sense, and military life had taught her how to handle a wide variety of people. Her youthful exuberance was refreshing, and she was totally honest, as far as Kathryn could tell, in the way she handled money and in the way she evaluated people. Tracy loved her job at the Chic Boutique because she was addicted to shopping and got a natural high from being around fabulous designer creations. When she wasn't at work, she was shopping, and that habit kept Kathryn informed about what the competition was doing. Tracy enjoyed her reputation and boasted about how she had her "black belt" in shopping.

"Okay," Tracy said, "the Daughters of the American Revolution called and want you to donate fifty dollars and be listed as a patron in the junior high citizenship essay contest they sponsor."

"Go ahead and send it to them."

Tracy looked surprised. "I didn't think you'd do it. I thought they were one of those snooty organizations you don't like."

"The DAR does a lot of good things. I won an essay competition they sponsored when I was in junior high."

Tracy made a note on her pad and nodded. "The president of the Junior League called to ask if everything's all set for the spring fashion show."

"Have they decided on the location?"

"Macon Country Club on the first Friday in March."

"Fine. Call the regular models, and then call the League president and ask her if any League ladies want to model. They usually do."

Tracy rolled her eyes and made a face.

"What's the matter, Tracy? Don't you like Junior League ladies?"

"Oh, they just strike me as vain and pretentious, that's all. But I guess Southern women are a culture shock for me, anyway. I was raised in the North. I've just never seen vanity and snobbery raised to such high levels as they are down here." She paused, then continued. "The Historical Society called and wants you to act as a sponsor for their fall scholarship awards banquet."

"Call them and find out exactly what they mean."

"Okay." Tracy paused to study her notes. "Oh, your high school wants you to be a sponsor for the senior prom. They need a contribution. They're suggesting a hundred dollars, and they'll print your name in the program." Tracy grimaced. "You'll never guess what the theme is this year."

"What is it?"

"They say they're going to sell bumper stickers and produce posters that say, BORN AMERICAN. SOUTHERN BY THE GRACE OF GOD." Tracy made a face and shook her head as she delivered the information.

Kathryn smiled. "Okay. Send them a hundred dollars. And make a window display using some of the promotional materials, can you?"

"If I hold my nose, I can. I can take only so much of this Confederate crap, excuse my language."

Kathryn smiled at her young assistant. She liked Tracy's directness, and she enjoyed the irreverent way the young transplant looked at the venerable institutions of the South.

"Just don't talk like that around the customers, Tracy. Anything else?"

"Two more things. You'll like this one," Tracy said, with a smile and a pause that was designed to tease her impatient boss. She pushed it to the limit and didn't say what she meant until she saw Kathryn twist in her chair and wrinkle her brow. "*Southern Living* called and said they're doing a story on prominent families from Macon, Athens, and Savannah who came over on the *Mayflower*. They've picked out the ladies in Macon they're going to use and part of the story will show them shopping at the Chic Boutique. It's sort of a 'Lifestyles of the Rich and Southern' piece, I think. Anyway, the editor left her name and asked you to call when you got back from the Big Apple."

"Sounds like great propaganda for us. Put the name on my desk, and I'll call today. What else?"

Tracy had left the worst news for last. "Your mother called and said she's sending some friends of hers by and wants us to treat them real well." Vera expected Kathryn to sell to her friends at close to cost, and she frequently called to announce the imminent visit to the Chic Boutique of new acquaintances and visiting relatives. It gave Vera a sense of power that she could make a phone call to a glamorous business and command special prices for her cronies. All the women who came recommended by Vera had plenty of money, but what Kathryn had learned about the wealthy since she'd been in business is that rich people tend to be stingier than poor people. "Tight as a tick," her grandmother used to say when she was describing somebody with a big bankroll who was tightfisted.

"Okay, Miss Shop-'Til-You-Drop, let's open up the boxes. You're going to go wild over the things I bought in New York this time!"

SIX

Marcos telephoned Kathryn's office a couple of weeks after she returned from the New York trip. He was businesslike and warm and said his wife would be sending some Valentine's Day presents for the kids.

"I'm going to mail the packages from the office so I can send you something special from me," Marcos said.

"That's very kind of you," Kathryn replied. It was awkward talking to him in the office. After their intimacy in New York in January, speaking politely and in a businesslike manner seemed stiff, but no other way of speaking to him was appropriate.

It was nice of Marcos's wife to send Valentine's Day presents, Kathryn thought after they hung up. From what David said, Marcos's wife had opened up her heart to David when he went to San Antonio for his visit in the summer and then for a week after Christmas. Dolores told David she wanted to pretend that he was the handsome and gentlemanly son she'd always yearned for but whom God never gave her. Once in a while, Kathryn liked imagining her ex-husband being married to a woman who was cold to him but a nymphomaniac with everybody in the neighborhood as soon as he went to work, but when it came to David's visiting their home, she was grateful her ex was married to someone like Dolores Galleria, a warm and loving Mexican woman who would be willing to "adopt" her son and be his other mom. Kathryn felt appreciative for Dolores Galleria's warmth toward the boy.

The children were delighted when the presents arrived. Veronica got an adorable outfit, Calvin and Booth got sweatshirts with official Spurs logos on them, and David got several presents including a boom box. They sent Stefan some monogrammed handkerchiefs, and Kathryn received an expensive-looking gold watch with what looked like diamonds in it.

"Isn't that an unusual present for them to send an ex-wife?" Stefan asked, as she opened it in the bedroom when they were alone.

"Well, it is pretty," Kathryn admitted, not meeting his eyes as he stared at her.

Stefan made a quizzical expression with his large, bushy eyebrows and then said "Wafa do," a Caribbean expression he'd picked up from his relatives that meant, "Oh well, what can you do?" In his characteristic laid-back style, he wasn't going to worry about it. Stefan didn't worry about much, anyway.

When Marcos called David that evening, he said he was arranging a spring hunting trip for the two of them to coincide with David's next school holidays, which would fall around Easter.

The next day was Saturday. The boutique closed at three on Saturdays and, although she didn't work on the weekend, Kathryn was in the habit of checking the shop sometime between three and five to make sure everything was locked up and to take the cash out of the store. She didn't like to leave money in the building overnight, and it only took a few minutes, since the store was less than two miles from their home. Kathryn had just retrieved the money from the registers and had sprinted to her office in the back of the store to grab something off her desk when the phone rang. She looked at her watch. Three-fifteen. She considered not answering it but she picked it up, expecting to hear the voice of one of the children asking her to get something at the convenience store before coming home.

"Hello, Kathryn?" It was Marcos's voice.

"Yes. Hello. How are you?"

"I thought I might find you there, escaping from your responsibilities. And how do you like your watch?"

"Oh, it's beautiful," she replied, holding it up to admire it as she spoke. "It's a jewel. You shouldn't have been so generous."

"I have something else I want to give you when I come to Macon in April to take David hunting." He paused, and she kept listening. "I wish I could give it to you right now, but I guess I'll just have to save it up until I can see you."

It made her feel nervous and anxious to hear him talking like that. She could feel her heart pounding and hear herself breathing more heavily. "Marcos, please don't say that. I've been feeling so guilty and conflicted. I just can't live like this, in some pretend state," Kathryn answered, with anguish in her voice. Perhaps he was ready to pamper his lust, but she wasn't. All their brief encounter had done was rob her of inner peace and pierce her heart with guilt. He was trying to have a conversation with the person she'd been in New York, but she was back home now, trying to be her old self, and not feeling very successful at it. Middle age had seemed so nice and comfortable until Marcos reappeared. Now, everything that had felt certain seemed questionable, and she didn't feel good about herself at the core anymore. Where there had been satisfaction and assurance, there now were conflicts and doubt. She felt flawed and compromised and defective. Intellectually, she knew there is no inconsistency like moral inconsistency, and that was suddenly the essence of her. She'd gone from feeling morally clean and strong one day, to morally dirty and weak the next. There's no strength like the strength that comes from moral purity, and she could not claim that strength anymore. She didn't like the weak and impure person she'd become. What an irony. She'd turned into an adulterer when it was exactly the thing she'd vowed never to do. But why wasn't she comfortable with it? Hadn't she been trained during childhood to feel comfortable keeping dirty little secrets?

"Well, I feel conflicted, too, but I can't help these feelings I have. I feel drawn to you, and I can't hold myself back. You're a part of me, and there's a part of me that's alive only when I'm with you."

"Don't say that. I know now that what happened in New York was wrong, and I regret it. You told me one time that you'd had some regrets about us, but all we're doing is just adding regrets to regrets. I can't betray my children and my husband. This is eating me alive. You have to leave me alone now. I just can't handle having a relationship with you that's secret and sexual. What we did was wrong, and I don't want to add wrong to wrong."

"Oh, I don't think we should ever split up our families. I know you have your family, and I have mine."

"So, you want to have a relationship on the side? I can't handle that, that's what I'm saying. I grew up in a home where things were morally gray, and I can't do it that way. It's moral or immoral for me, it's right or wrong, one way or the other, or I can't handle life." There was terror as well as anguish in her voice.

His voice was soft and tender when he spoke. "I can say that I'll leave you alone, but when I see you again, all these feelings come back to me, and I know you feel that way, too. Whatever I say I'll do or try to do, I know I'll be overcome by the emotion I feel for you."

"Please don't say that. You know you could always outsmart me and drive me crazy if you wanted to, and I can't handle it. I'm telling you, this is making me crazy. I just can't handle the hypocrisy and deception."

He could hear the fear and stress in her words and in her breathing. "Now, just relax, I don't want you to get all upset. We'll sort this out when I come over Easter to take David hunting."

"Just don't come here expecting it to be the way it was in New York. I'm not going to compromise myself and abandon everything I believe in. This is just plain wrong and I know it, and I just can't do this."

"There's no need to talk about it now. Put it out of your mind. We'll talk again sometime next month about the hunting trip."

After they hung up, Kathryn wilted in her oversized leather chair. The back room was dark, and she felt glad to be totally alone for a few minutes. She reclined in the chair with her head back, eyes shut, arms stretched out on the chair arms and legs crossed on the desk top. She hadn't been able to regain her balance emotionally since New York. She hadn't gone there to cheat on her husband, but that's what had happened and now she was thoroughly conflicted and guilty. As if what happened in New York hadn't been bad enough, her life was becoming a big lie. She could see what lay ahead. She'd lived through that while she was growing up, all the lies, deceptions, and phoniness. Back to keeping secrets. She couldn't do it, she just couldn't do it. She picked up the phone and dialed a number.

"Hello?" It gave Kathryn a feeling of relief to hear Mary's warm and familiar voice.

"Oh, Mary, I'm so glad you're home. I need to talk to you if you have some time today," said Kathryn.

"Kathryn! I'm glad you called! Greg's out playing golf, and I'm home alone. Please come by, and let's catch up," Mary replied.

After a quick phone call letting Stefan know she'd be stopping at Mary's house for a few minutes, Kathryn locked the store and headed over to the fashionable neighborhood where her best friend since junior high school lived. They'd talked of going to the University of Georgia and rooming together after graduating from Macon High School but Kathryn had decided to get as far away from home as possible and had gone off to the London School of Economics. After Mary graduated Phi Beta Kappa from college, she and her high school sweetheart had married. Their marriage had endured some bumps and storms. Mary's husband had been emasculated by a domineering aunt who'd raised him after his mother died, and his personality had been bruised. Coming into marriage with a rage instilled in him during childhood, he'd taken his insecurities out on Mary in the privacy of their home during bitter arguments in their early married years, and his cruel words had wounded Mary's spirit. Until his marriage to Mary, he'd never been in a situation where he felt safe, and without being aware of what he was doing, he emotionally abused his wife when all the repressed anger from childhood broke loose. "You always hurt the one you love," so the old saying goes, and that had been true of his relationship with Mary. He had a damaged sense of self coming into the marriage and, in the safety net of being married to a wonderful and supportive wife, he'd expressed his internal rage as anger toward her. Mary had come to Kathryn, and Kathryn had, on many occasions, counseled her about how to break the cycle of verbal abuse. Mary had been smart and had recognized the symptoms of a damaged child in her husband that she'd seen in her best friend. Kathryn had intuitively understood the rage he felt and had been helpful to Mary. Too bad, Kathryn thought on the way over to her friend's house, there hadn't been a Mary to help her sort out her marital problems with Marcos during that turbulent first year of married life that had erupted into divorce so quickly. Greg and Mary had weathered their storms, though, and finished growing up together, and they had, in the process, developed a relationship that was faithful and loving and based on respect and kindness.

After Mary and Kathryn hugged a brief hello, Mary showed her friend to the family room where a roaring gas-log fire was heating the room and creating a homey atmosphere. Mary's cozy yet elegant home was beautifully decorated and revealed the sense of style and good taste Southern women are known for.

"What's up?" Mary asked, as she poured them a cup of coffee from the coffee set she'd set up on the table in front of the couch facing the fire. February was the coldest month of the year in Macon, and on that particular day, it was a crisp thirty degrees outside. To Southerners, that felt like subzero. The fire felt tranquilizing and reassuring.

"I'm in trouble, Mary," Kathryn began, in her characteristically direct way, as she searched Mary's eyes for the green light to share her troubles. Kathryn's best friend since the sixth grade, Mary had seen Kathryn make it through a turbulent childhood, she'd watched her go off to a prestigious international university and then to Harvard Business School, and she'd observed her struggle to rebuild her life after her first marriage failed. Kathryn had not revealed much to Mary about her first marriage, so Mary never knew what really happened. All she knew was that Kathryn never went back to Mexico City after her Thanksgiving visit home. Keeping silent about such an important life event would have been out of character for most people, but not for Kathryn. Kathryn had been taught in childhood to hold her pain in, so although she was a sensitive person, she was unaccustomed to expressing her own hurt. She'd grown up in a mine field, and the experience had trained her to keep her emotions bottled up inside. Mary had watched Kathryn get buffeted all her life by the emotionally abusive relationship with her parents. Kathryn never knew from one minute to the next whether she'd be treated with contempt or

kindness, cruelty or affection, disgust or acceptance, and the vacillating nature of the relationship had created an inner core of uncertainty,
anxiety, fear, and distrust in Kathryn. Maybe that insecurity had been
part of what destroyed her first marriage, Mary thought, as she sat on
the couch looking at her friend.

"What's the matter? Is everything going alright at the store?"

"It's not the store. The business is doing fine, better than it ever
has. It's me, Mary. I'm becoming something I always said I never
would."

Mary had never seen Kathryn look so agitated, and it scared her.
She appeared distraught, at the edge emotionally, and Mary could
hear the terror in her voice.

"I'm having an affair, Mary, I'm having an affair," Kathryn
groaned. "And I can't help myself. I ran into Marcos in New York
when I was there on business, and it started up all over again between
us." Her voice cracked, and she took a moment to compose herself.
"I'm in despair over what I've done. I can't stand myself." She began
to cry and dabbed tears from her eyes with a tissue she had in one
hand. "My mother meddled in our relationship, Mary," Kathryn continued, with a defiant and bitter tone in her voice.

"What do you mean?"

"She shouldn't have suggested that I leave him when I was five
months pregnant!" Kathryn's tone was angry now. "It's like it always
is with her. She meddles in the most malicious way, and then she steps
away from the scene so that no one can see the part she played. How
could anyone help someone five months pregnant leave her husband?"

Mary felt blown away by Kathryn's news. Why, it had been less
than a year ago that she'd been totally surprised when Kathryn had
dropped by to tell her about Marcos's telephone call saying he wanted
to develop a relationship with David. That had been a surprise, but
now this? She really didn't know what to say. "But weren't you having problems in your first marriage?"

"Yes, we were having problems, but who doesn't in the first year
of married life? I was twenty-nine years old, married for the first time,
and pregnant. Yes, I'm sure I was miserable and vulnerable. But she
shouldn't have talked me into leaving him. If she'd wanted to help,

she would have helped by talking to us, not breaking us apart. I can't believe I even turned to her. Looking back, I can see what happened. I was so desperate . . ." Kathryn's voice was seething with a mixture of anger and despair. She took a few deep breaths and then continued, sounding more sad than angry. "Marriage is hard enough the first year, Mary, and we were putting a marriage together between cultures and with me not speaking the language. Why did I turn to her?"

Mary tried to choose her words carefully. She'd never seen her friend so vexed and so close to the edge. She wanted to be compassionate, but she wanted to be firm, too. "Well, what's done is done. You can't go back on that road again," Mary declared somberly. She paused for a few seconds before continuing and then spoke slowly and deliberately. "Listen, Kathryn, you've worked hard to have a family, and you have the greatest family in the world. God has really blessed you. It's too bad about your first marriage. You know, you never told me until now what happened. But that's a bridge you burned a long time ago, and you have to live in the present. Why, don't you remember all those sermons you've preached to me over the years about living in the present?" Mary was smiling, trying to inject a more lighthearted mood into the conversation, but Kathryn did not return her upbeat look. "You have a great life now with Stefan and the kids. You have everything you ever wanted out of life, and you've worked really hard to have it. I don't want you to destroy anything."

"But it causes me so much pain that I did it the way I did—completely secretive and deceptive and conniving. I didn't know what I was doing. I was pregnant and confused and lonely and angry, and I trusted her, and she led me in the wrong direction, like she always did. *She* made the decision that I should not be married to him, do you know that? *She* decided! And she engineered my leaving him in a way that was designed to step on him in public and alienate his whole family, not just from me but from David too. And it could have turned out even worse, you know. What if Marcos had kidnapped my baby, and I'd never seen him again? She was just playing games with my life and didn't give a damn about me." She paused. "You know what's funny, Mary?"

"What?"

Kathryn stood up to pace the floor in front of the fire, and Mary could hear the resentment and anger in her voice when she spoke. "You know, during all those years after our divorce I just figured that Marcos never cared about me in the first place. When David was a baby, I used to think how odd it was that, after so many opportunities to get married, I married someone who never loved me. And then, last year, when Marcos came back into David's life, it hit me what I did to him, and how I did it. It was like throwing gasoline in his face to leave the way I did. But that was her style, Mary, not mine. She took a volatile situation and made it worse, that's what she did, and she led me to trash my marriage. And you know, I didn't think about any of it at the time. One minute I was married and pregnant, and the next minute I was separated and trying to find a job. I just can't stand looking back on it and seeing how she broke it apart." Kathryn stopped pacing and turned with her back to the fire, looking directly into her friend's eyes. "I loved him, Mary. I guess I still love him in a way. And I can see how I humiliated him publicly and trampled on him."

She walked to the couch and then, sitting sideways next to her friend, started sobbing with her head against her arm. The sound was like the sobbing at a funeral, when someone is grieving over a loss too deep to express in words.

Mary started to speak, but Kathryn shook her head vigorously. She made a visible effort to compose herself, and there was a forlorn, melancholy sound in her voice when she spoke again.

"Middle-aged eyes see some things more clearly, Mary. If I'd only known then what I know now . . . when Marcos called, Mary, I thought he'd be coming back into David's life full of middle-aged regrets. But what I've found . . . is that I have my own share of regrets at middle age, too." Her voice became impassioned, and an angry look appeared in her eyes. "But I'll tell you what I'll never again have regrets about! I'm not going to put up with any more garbage from my parents, Mary. They've treated Stefan like a dog, and I'm not putting up with it anymore. I know we're supposed to honor our parents, but I can't handle it anymore. I'm just at the end of my rope."

"Well, that's probably a good decision." Mary paused, trying to choose her words carefully. She knew she had to be cautious about criticizing the Faisons. Everything Kathryn said was true, but families have a way of kissing and making up, and Mary didn't want to make disparaging remarks about Kathryn's aging parents that Kathryn might later remember and resent when she patched up things with them. "All they've ever tried to do is control and dominate you. You're not supposed to be destroyed by the relationships you want to honor. We all want to make our relationships real and honest, but we can't make every relationship a normal one. Unfortunately." She paused. "But that's a separate issue from your relationship with Marcos." Mary took a deep breath and then spoke again tentatively. "Have you ever thought that maybe you grew up in an abusive home and that's why you ended up in a troubled relationship? Didn't you tell me that some of your friends in grad school wouldn't go to your wedding because they didn't like the way he treated you?"

"Yes," Kathryn replied defiantly, "but I took a vow 'for better or for worse,' and I should have stayed to keep that promise. You know as well as I do that marriage is a tough situation where two people who love each other get together and finish growing up together. The wedding ritual tells people they shouldn't do anything to break the marriage up. Your parents should try to strengthen your marriage, not break it up, Mary!" She paused and a wry smile came across Kathryn's face as she shook her head. "Interesting, isn't it, Mary, that with all their marital problems and adultery, those two stayed together. They deserved each other, those two." Kathryn stopped, as though trying to compose herself. When she spoke again, her tone was reflective and bitter. "You know, after she helped me lie and sneak away, she charted our path by car so she could take me around like a freak show to show me off to relatives in Texas and Mississippi and Alabama on our way back to Georgia. She took me to see relatives I hadn't seen since I was a baby, so I could tell them all about my marital troubles. That's a nice picture, isn't it? A little pregnant lady being paraded around the country so the relatives could see what a pathetic creature I was and what a good mommy she was for helping me out. Mommy dearest didn't take me to see my grandmother, though. She would have put me straight." She was seething with anger.

"Well, that's too bad, but it doesn't change the fact that it can't be right for you to have an affair with Marcos. I know you, Kathryn. You're not going to be able to handle it. You've always defined your-self by your moral standards. And think about your kids. What can come of this that could be good for you? Just think about what you're walking into here, and don't forget that, whatever his reasons were, however hurt he felt, Marcos turned his back on you. He trashed you and his child. That's a fact. You were his first family, and he trashed you. He tried to ruin your life. Don't you remember? He didn't even send your things back for a long time, and when he did send every-thing back, he'd destroyed your personal papers. I don't trust him."

"He was hurt." She began shaking her head vigorously. "I know, I know, I might be getting drawn back into a very destructive rela-tionship. I just don't know what's happening. I'm out of control, just like I was around him before. It's like he's my weakness in life."

Mary remembered how she and Kathryn had talked when they were younger about how a true friend doesn't tell another friend what she wants to hear. As teenagers they'd agreed that a real friend risks displeasure by telling the truth rather than taking a "yes-sir-you're-right-boss" attitude. They had almost bonded in blood on that con-cept in junior high. Mary took a deep breath. She knew Kathryn had come to her because she expected to hear the truth as Mary saw it.

"Look, Kathryn," Mary began slowly, as she turned her body to-ward her friend sitting next to her on the couch, "a lot of things have happened in your life in the last year. Marcos reappeared, David has another family, you still have that nasty relationship with your par-ents, and now this, on top of the fact that you're at middle age. And then, you have the regular stress of running a business, and being married, and raising four kids. Most people our age seem like they're in some sort of midlife crisis, Kathryn, assessing everything in their lives, trying to make sense of the past and figure out what's ahead. Maybe Marcos is going through that, too. Maybe that's why he came back after all these years. Maybe you've both gone a little 'middle-age crazy.' And how do you know what kind of relationship he's in now, anyway? Maybe he realizes at middle age what he gave up when he let you go. Men are famous for looking in the mirror and seeing their baldness and then suddenly going out and getting a girlfriend just to feel youthful again." She paused and a firm tone was in her voice when she spoke again. "But you *have* to pull yourself together before you destroy your marriage and your children's lives and your own happiness. Don't you remember how hard it was on you when your parents had affairs? I think you've begun to feel guilty about what happened a long time ago between you and Marcos, and somehow that guilt is keeping you from thinking clearly. I don't know all the answers here, Kathryn, but I do know that this is destructive, and it's going to hurt you if you don't stop."

"I don't know if I can stop, Mary. I mean, I told him today that it had to stop, but I feel confused about my feelings and ashamed of what I've done to Stefan, how I've betrayed him. I feel like I've lost my way, like I can't help being drawn back into this relationship with him." Kathryn paused, then looked at Mary directly in the eyes, and there was a softness and tenderness in her voice when she spoke. "We have a son, Mary. There's a bond between us. Whether we've lived together or not, we're a family, the three of us. There's a sense I have when we're together that we're a family."

"You're talking like a crazy lady, Kathryn! You are *not* 'a family' with Marcos! You're a devoted mother of four children and a loyal wife to Stefan. You're a successful businesswoman. You're a Sunday school teacher. You're a scouting leader. You're a respected person in this community. You would *never* be happy if you allowed Marcos to break up your family and separate you from your husband and children. You would never be able to build happiness for you and Marcos on the unhappiness of your husband and children. You know what you've always told me, about how children deserve a happy childhood."

Mary stared at Kathryn's wet eyes and sad, forlorn expression as her friend sat with her head nearly bowed, eyes looking down at the couch. Kathryn looked weak and uncertain and depressed. Mary decided to continue, changing the subject slightly.

"I do think you're on the right track minimizing contact with your parents, Kathryn. You need to eliminate any relationships of stress right now and try to regain your emotional balance. All Vera and Miles ever do is put pressure on you to perform for them in some way, and if you don't do exactly what they want, they make sure you feel bad about yourself. It's like they think you're one of their possessions, and they think you owe them whatever they want. But maybe this is where the cycle ends." She stared hard at Kathryn. "I don't think Vera and Miles would ever stop picking on you, Kathryn. They're the kind of people who have to have a scapegoat, and if you're not their scapegoat, they'll find another one . . . and it might be one of your own children."

"I know," Kathryn answered sadly. "That's what I finally realized. It's weird, Mary, but I get the feeling lately that Vera thinks she's finished with me and Sally, and she's ready to pounce on the next generation. We've both disappointed her. I won't do whatever she wants me to, and even though she loves Sally, she hates her weakness and dependence." Kathryn's body suddenly stiffened, and her voice became passionate and intense. "Over my dead body will she ever do to my kids what she did to me, all that affection in public and the meanness behind the scenes that really screws you up."

Mary looked at her friend as she sat on the couch, clearly in agony. Words seemed inadequate to ease her pain. In Mary's formal education as a psychologist and, after that, in her practical experience as a school psychologist and in a limited private practice, she'd become acquainted with the symptoms of post-traumatic stress disorder, and that's what was popping into her head as she studied her abject friend and listened to the repressed rage in her voice.

"That's a healthy move, but it seems like you're reexperiencing an old stress now, Kathryn, and you need to be careful about making decisions when you're in a vulnerable emotional state. You know, you were trained as a child to forgive people for anything. But your parents taught you a wrong definition of forgiveness. They trained you to think that forgiveness is submitting yourself for abuse anytime the abuser wishes you to do so. Forgiveness really is more about the abuser repenting and changing his ways. And your parents even used religion to subdue you into obedience to their whims. 'Honor your father and mother.' They used that one really well, didn't they?" There was cold anger in Mary's voice now. "They coached you—

actually they let the church coach you—about the obedience a child owes his parents, and you've spent your life trying to be a dutiful daughter and letting them batter you emotionally. Your background, which you'll never escape from or erase, has conditioned you to accept mistreatment. You're more willing to accept it than other people." Mary paused, swallowed hard, and then continued. "It's not a rule, you know, that everyone gets a good mother or a good father, and it's not a rule that everybody becomes a good parent. You didn't start out with the best family, but you can't get on a destructive binge here. Look at yourself now. You've rebuilt your life, and now you're putting everything at risk. Don't forget how hard you've worked to have a good marriage, and Stefan really loves you. I just couldn't stand to see you throw it all away in some destructive gesture." She paused, and her tone was firm when she spoke again. "I don't care if you do still love Marcos, or think you do, and it doesn't matter if your mother messed your first marriage up. None of that matters in the here and now. You know you could never have happiness with Marcos if you tried to build that happiness over the pain of the unhappiness you caused Stefan and your children. It would never, never lead to happiness, Kathryn. You burned that bridge a long time ago. You can't walk over it. It's not there."

"I know, I know, I want it to end, and I told him that on the phone today just before I came to see you. He's coming here to take David hunting while the kids are out for spring break, and I'm going to stop it. I have to do it in person, I know I won't be able to make him understand on the phone."

"But doesn't he have a terrible temper? Maybe you should do it on the phone, before he comes. Look, every day that you don't settle it, that you let it go on, you're playing head games with yourself, and you're playing Russian roulette with your life and the lives of the people you love. You don't need to let yourself be drawn into something that degrades you." She paused. "And destroys you."

Kathryn was sitting on the couch, with her hands clasped together on her knees. Her face appeared disoriented, almost tortured. She was shaking her head slowly, absorbed in thought about something. The rage that had been in her voice moments earlier had been replaced by something that sounded like grief and hopelessness. As a psychologist, Mary knew that most people can get to their emotional breaking point by having just one important relationship disintegrate. Kathryn had several important relationships crumbling at the same time. It was already too much pressure for one person to handle, but if anything else went wrong, if Stefan found out about the affair and her marriage fell apart, she wouldn't be able to keep it together mentally and emotionally.

"I just can't get a handle on all this," Kathryn said slowly. She was clearly under emotional pressure.

"Well, let me give you one perspective on it," Mary said gently. "My private practice has really picked up lately in terms of the middle-aged crowd. People our age, Kathryn. People seem to go a little nuts in middle age. I've seen people do the craziest things in the last few months! I've seen respectable middle-aged people with young families have blazing affairs with people with whom they have nothing in common. In other words, it isn't real or lasting: it's a groping for excitement. It's a yearning to be back in carefree, romantic days, and it's a desire to have it all, when we know that to have it all isn't possible. We'd probably just get the gout anyway, if we had it all. There seems to be some wild hormonal rush people get at middle age that makes them go mad. You're on a suicide track here, Kathryn. I don't want you to destroy everything you care about just because Marcos has you off balance. Don't forget, he destroyed your life one time, and you had to rethink and rebuild. You were in your thirties then. Now, you have it all—the husband, the family, the business, the reputation. Remember that men come out of an affair better than women. Sometimes a man can have a second woman, but you'd be disgracing your children and your husband and yourself in the crudest way, and this would never make you happy." She paused. "You'd never be able to live with yourself if you continue this affair, you know that."

There was something in Kathryn's eyes that made Mary feel like she should keep talking, say more, make another point, argue more convincingly. She knew she'd been saying the same thing over and over, repeating herself, but she didn't want to leave unsaid anything that might give Kathryn a reality shock. There was a void in Kathryn's eyes, something like a wall that was impenetrable, that made Mary feel like she'd need a battering ram to get through. The more she talked, the less Kathryn seemed to be listening. She was thinking of something else, focusing on someone else, probably Marcos. But whatever she was focusing on, it didn't seem to make her happy.

"Kathryn, let me suggest this. Don't you trust your minister?"

"Yes."

"Go talk to him. I think you need to sit down with someone who's a professional counselor. Of course, you can come to see me professionally, too, if you want to, but you might prefer talking with a minister."

"Actually I'm going to make an appointment with my doctor soon if I don't feel better. I haven't been sleeping very well lately. I keep having the same dream, over and over again, and it terrifies me and wakes me up at all hours of the night."

"What's the dream?"

"It's a crazy dream. I dream that Mother and Daddy move out of their house because they want to downsize and simplify their life, so they give us their house. And after we move in—Stefan and me and the kids—they come over all the time with their friends and with Sally and her friends, anytime they want. They always bring food with them, so I have to put up chairs and tables and make room for a crowd of people nearly every night. And they bring me presents. They bring paintings and pictures, and they come into my house and take the pictures off the walls that I've hung and replace them with pictures they're giving me. And because their pictures are presents, I can't refuse. It wouldn't be good manners. So it's never my home. We never get to sit down as a family and say the grace and have a quiet, reverent home. It turns into a kind of headquarters for Vera and Sally and Miles and their buddies."

"Ugh," Mary replied, making a disgusted face.

"Yes, it's a frightening dream. I dream it over and over, almost every night now. I don't know why. I feel so worn-out from everything, Mary."

"Kathryn, go talk to your minister, or come and see me professionally, like I said. I've told you for a long time you could benefit from therapy. You always act like therapy is only for the mentally insane. It's not. It can help anybody, you know."

After Kathryn left, Mary had a sinking feeling that all would not be well. She made Kathryn promise to call her soon, but as Kathryn was waving goodbye, Mary doubted she would hear from her confused and unhappy friend anytime soon. As she watched her friend drive away, the Bible verse warning that "the sins of the parents will be visited on the children" popped into her brain. That phrase had always been a mystery until now. But, as Kathryn was driving out of sight, Mary had a fresh insight into it. She'd always doubted that it had anything to do with God punishing children for their parents' sins. Mary didn't believe in a God who went around punishing and zapping people for other people's sins. Now, she could see that what that Bible verse was saying is that parents teach their children to sin, and then children suffer because they've learned the sins of their parents. So, the sins of the parents do visit the children, not because God does it, but because he gives the human being freedom of choice.

Mary went back into the breakfast nook adjoining the kitchen and sat down to have a cup of coffee as she watched the birds play "catch me if you can" with the cat in the backyard. She hadn't been kidding Kathryn. She'd seen many of her friends go nuts in middle age. What was it about middle age that suddenly made so many people want to make a bold and dramatic lifestyle change that was usually incompatible with their moral values and religious principles? Oh, Mary had known people who'd had affairs throughout their marriage that their spouses seemed to tolerate or ignore. They were people whose lives had a pattern of moral inconsistency, and they appeared comfortable with it. But what seemed to happen at middle age is that some of the pillars of the community just fell down with no warning. People who seemed to have it all, and who seemed to have it all together, fell apart in the most surprising and impulsive ways. It made no sense. It was as though some strange, repressed neediness came raging to the surface and overpowered every sensible feeling.

In Kathryn's case, it seemed that an old vulnerability had crept back into her life. As a psychologist, Mary felt sure she'd identified several serious warning signs in Kathryn's behavior. People in

Kathryn's frame of mind sometimes got worse and made really terrible decisions. She'd gently recommended to her friend on several occasions that she get involved in some kind of therapy, and she hoped Kathryn would talk to a professional in her current crisis. An old wound that had never healed had been reopened, and the rest of Kathryn's life seemed in danger of rupturing while the wound healed. What an oddity that there were so many middle-aged teenagers. What was it about middle age that induced madness? Or was it blindness?

"Oh, hi, honey," Mary greeted her husband as he came suddenly into the kitchen.

"Hi," her husband smiled. "Any possibility of getting an early dinner around here?"

"There's a possibility, but sit down for a minute, would you?" He glanced at her as he grabbed a soft drink out of the refrigerator and went back to sit down next to her at the kitchen table.

"I'm worried about Kathryn, Greg," Mary began.

"Why?"

"She seemed really distraught when she came to see me this afternoon."

"Call Stefan, and tell him. He's a sensitive type."

"No. I can't call Stefan. What she told me is confidential, and I can't talk to him about it."

"Well, how did she seem?"

"I don't know . . . I don't want to think she's suicidal, but I'm worried about her."

"Did she say anything about suicide?"

"No."

"Well, isn't that a stretch, then? I thought you told me that people usually telegraph their intentions and mention suicide if they have it on their mind."

"Yes, that's true most of the time. It's just that she's had a lot of trauma and stress lately."

"Like what?"

"Oh, you know Marcos came back into her life last year to develop a relationship with David. She handled it well, but it had to be hard emotionally. And then her grandmother died last year, which was basically like her mother dying. And her parents are always producing stress. I just don't think she can handle much more pressure or trauma without exceeding her physical and mental limits."

"Well, maybe she should talk to you or to someone else professionally."

"Yeah, I told her that." Mary paused and shook her head. "Oh, I don't know, this is probably silly. She's a tough woman who's survived a lot, but she's got a lot of serious things she's trying to handle right now, and she's definitely near her maximum stress limit. I'm not even sure she realizes it, though." Mary stared at Greg and seemed lost in thought. "Oh, she'll probably be okay. She always comes out of this stuff. Let me fix you some dinner."

SEVEN

A stewardess with tawny skin and black wavy hair demonstrated the flotation devices that would appear if the plane malfunctioned over the Caribbean Sea. Most of the passengers were dozing or reading as she delivered the canned presentation.

The two-and-a-half-hour trip from Atlanta over the Atlantic and into Caribbean waters was smooth, and Kathryn rested until the captain's voice announced their descent into Montego Bay. She opened her eyes and watched as the border of the deep, choppy, blue Atlantic Ocean met the blues and greens of the sparkling Caribbean Sea just before the plane settled onto the "Mo Bay" runway. The aircraft landed just long enough to allow some passengers to disembark and a few others to board for the short flight over the Jamaican mountains to Kingston. The engines sounded as though they were still running as luggage was extracted and replenished.

When the plane took off from Montego Bay, it headed toward the sea and then quickly turned back toward land. The lush green countryside below was dotted with houses and crisscrossed by roads. Small planes were flying beneath them. Within two minutes, there were no signs of civilization. Only dense, lush, green mountains, seemingly untamed by human hands, lay beneath them. After a few minutes, civilization began to reappear in the form of winding roads carved through the jungle foliage. Then, huge, gleaming white clouds hung beside the plane and eclipsed their view as the captain notified them that Kingston was just fifteen minutes away. Suddenly, they were flying in a cloudless sky. The farming countryside below was cut into geometric patterns by white sandy roads. The sea appeared again suddenly in front of them, and the signs of a big city came into view in the form of squares of land dotted by what looked like Monopoly-sized houses. The peninsula-like Palisadoes that contained Norman Manley Airport appeared in their view.

"Fasten your seat belts, ladies and gentlemen," the captain announced in a voice that sounded cheerful, "we're starting our descent into Kingston, Jamaica."

Kathryn reached over to place her hand on Stefan's hand and, looking at his face as he gazed out the window excitedly to catch a glimpse of what had become his favorite city, she realized how understanding and gentle he'd been with her lately. It had been his idea to come on this second honeymoon and, although she hadn't wanted to leave the kids with her parents, she'd felt too frail emotionally and physically to protest. Stefan didn't know what was wrong with her, but he knew something was terribly off. For weeks, Kathryn hadn't been able to sleep, ate fitfully, and was unable to concentrate on important things at work that usually excited her and kept her attention totally. He'd come into the boutique one day about eleven o'clock and announced, "Guess what, honey? I'm taking you to Jamaica for a holiday. Your birthday's coming up and you need to get away and relax. I'm going to treat you to a second honeymoon."

Five days later, they were on a flight. It was the middle of March, the coldest and rainiest part of the year in Georgia, and it would be good to feel the sea breeze and see the colors of the tropics. Although she wanted to relax, she knew she was bringing with her to Kingston the remorse and guilt that seemed to be growing inside her and keeping her on edge in Macon. Still, going to Jamaica seemed like a good idea. Sally's wedding was coming up in less than three weeks, and Marcos would be flying into town that same weekend to take David hunting over spring break. It would be a family reunion of sorts at Sally's wedding, and those were always stressful. The poorer relatives from Tennessee, the ones Kathryn liked the most, hadn't been invited.

They wouldn't have felt at home in a country club, and the thought that someone could be on her fourth wedding wouldn't have made sense to them. The relatives living in Florida and Alabama who'd made it financially and who disdained their country background, like Vera and Miles, would be there. Most of them had kids who were screwed up, too, so they felt a bond with Vera and Miles. Then, she had to face the conversation that would be coming up between her and Marcos. How had things gotten so screwed up?

"Honey, we're having dinner tonight with Kahlil and Pearl. Did you know that Pearl was a psychiatrist when she married Kahlil?"

"No, I didn't."

"She was. She stopped practicing after she married to be a full-time mommy, but she went back to work after her kids got older. She's a smart lady, and I thought it might be a good idea if you talked with her privately while we're here. I already spoke with Kahlil by phone, and he wants to take me to play golf tomorrow at his club, so you can just spend the day with Pearl if you want to. You like her a lot, don't you?"

Kathryn nodded. She did like Pearl a lot. Pearl was a beautiful white Jamaican lady with a British accent. She and Kahlil, who had emigrated to Jamaica from Barbados years ago so that he could pursue law studies at the University of the West Indies, were very much in love after thirty years of married life. It was always nice to be around them. They had a wonderfully genteel island lifestyle and were very family oriented. The highlight of their year was their six-week trip to England to see their grown boys, both lawyers, married, and living in London. Kathryn and Stefan had met Pearl and Kahlil when they took the children to the Caribbean on a relatives-hunting trip one summer. In Barbados, they'd met a doctor who'd told them about a young man named Kahlil Haddad who'd emigrated from Barbados to Jamaica. Stefan had placed a phone call to Kahlil introducing himself and wondering if there was, indeed, a family connection, and then Pearl and Kahlil had invited the six of them to dinner. A warm relationship had developed after they discovered that Stefan and Kahlil were third cousins, sharing the same last name. Now, a summer vacation to the Caribbean wouldn't seem complete without looking up Pearl and Kahlil.

There was something that felt like home away from home about the Courtleigh Manor, where they always stayed when they were in Kingston. A beautiful, spread-out hotel in the center of Kingston with two restaurants and a couple of pools, the Courtleigh had dozens of apartments surrounded by immaculately manicured courtyards. As they checked into their one-bedroom apartment, Kathryn looked at the courtyards and remembered how the three boys liked to throw the baseball to practice their catching during the summers when they brought them here. It seemed strange not having the kids with them, but Stefan hadn't suggested bringing them along this trip. He knew Kathryn was too drained of physical energy and emotional strength to be looking after anyone. Anyway, who needs kids on a second honeymoon?

After she and Stefan checked into the Courtleigh, they made love gently, and then she fell asleep. When she awoke, she realized it was dusk, and she heard Stefan's voice talking on the phone. She listened for a moment and then realized he'd called the children to see how they were doing and to give them their number in case they needed to get hold of them. She heard him hang up, dial another number, and begin speaking with someone else, arranging a time for dinner. It had to be Pearl.

An hour later, as they were driving at dusk on the winding island roads up into the mountains where Kahlil and Pearl lived, Kathryn felt some energy return as she listened to the familiar sound of men playing dominoes. She turned to stare at Stefan. He always loved driving on those island roads that reminded her of the country roads where her grandmother used to live. Stefan looked happy. A guilt pang shot through her as she realized how little he deserved her unfaithfulness. The bad feeling just wouldn't go away. Every time she felt herself pulling out of this depression, she remembered vividly what she'd done and sank back into despair. It just seemed like she was facing a wall that couldn't be scaled. It felt like she was in a prison of self-hate and self-recrimination that appeared to be a lifelong sentence without any chance of pardon or parole.

"Darling Kathryn, you look lovely, dear," Pearl said, "but you need a little of this fresh island air to bring that rosy complexion back to life." Pearl hugged her warmly and so did Kahlil. Pearl had organized a dinner party for the four of them, and they spent the next few hours having dinner and talking afterwards about international politics and island gossip. Kahlil was upset with the vacillating policy of the United States toward the refugees from Haiti and Cuba, but he was always berating U.S. foreign policy for one thing or another. It just happened to be the refugee issue this year.

"The Yankees talk about human rights, but they want Jamaica and the other Caribbean islands to take in the refugees when we're having enough trouble in Jamaica finding employment for our three million people." Kahlil was a brilliant and respected lawyer who detested what he thought were the hypocritical political positions taken by the major industrialized nations.

"So, you're coming tomorrow, darling, to spend the day with me, are you?" Pearl said, as she stood beside the car door after Stefan helped Kathryn in.

"Are you sure it's alright?"

"Of course, dear. I'd love to have the company. And I've been planning on it. I want to hear more about what you're doing with the boutique. I've told Kahlil that he absolutely must take me to Georgia next year so I can buy some things. We have several fancy balls to attend next year, and I want some smashing new clothes."

"Well, if you're sure I'm not imposing," Kathryn said. In her voice was a weakness that wasn't characteristic of her usually vibrant personality. "Stefan can drop me here when he meets Kahlil for golf in the morning, if that's alright."

"Bye! See you in the morning!" Kahlil and Pearl continued to wave as Stefan backed the car out of the driveway and headed down the steep mountain road leading back to the city.

The next three days Kathryn spent with Pearl while Kahlil and Stefan played golf. The day began when Stefan and Kathryn arrived for breakfast at seven. The four of them were served the egglike ackee, sausage, sweet rolls, and fruit outside on the patio by uniformed helpers, and by eight, Kahlil and Stefan were leaving for the golf course for the day while the two women stayed home. By the time she'd spent an hour talking with Pearl, Kathryn felt confident she was in the company of an exceptionally intelligent and insightful person. By the time she'd spent two hours with Pearl, she suspected that Pearl just might have the ability to exorcise demons.

For the first couple of hours, Pearl did the talking, telling Kathryn about her theories as a psychiatrist. Pearl said she was a deeply religious person and thought psychiatry had to do with meeting spiritual needs. A devotee of Freud, Pearl told her Freud was terribly misunderstood because of the crude translations of his writings.

"You know what Freud said about psychoanalysis? He said it was a form of love. He actually called it 'a cure through love,' and he thought the goal of psychoanalysis was to help people discover secrets buried in the unconscious that were tormenting them and causing them to lead unhappy and tormented lives."

"But Freud wasn't religious, was he?"

"Maybe not in the usual way, but he talked a lot about the soul. That's where the translations of his thoughts really fail the most miserably," Pearl replied. "In fact, I've been writing a book about Freud's life and intend to look for a publisher next year. The Greek word 'psyche' is translated as 'soul' in German. Freud thought his work was about the treatment of the morbid dysfunction of the soul. In fact, a poet named Hilda Doolittle once called Freud 'the midwife of the soul.'"

Kathryn warmed to the idea of psychoanalysis after she learned that Pearl's orientation was to free the soul of inner torment and turmoil.

"So, it's like a spiritual process then?"

"Done the right way, yes, I definitely think so. Of course, in our profession, as in every profession, there are charlatans and fakes who prey on people's weakness. But, yes, psychoanalysis done the right way is intended to make the soul aware of itself and set it free from the dark forces that enslave it."

"But it sounds confrontational. It's scary, then . . . isn't it?"

Pearl looked into the eyes of the frail middle-aged woman sitting in the chair across from her. Pearl was convinced there was something Kathryn needed to confront. Something inside Kathryn was intimidating her and disturbing her peace.

"Yes, you're right. The journey of self-discovery is scary and threatening. But what Freud discovered in treating people is that too much repression over a lifetime has crippling consequences."

Pearl stared at her friend as Kathryn looked at the floor. That's how Kathryn looked. Crippled mentally by something.

"And I guess," Pearl continued, "that's where psychiatry and religion can intersect. I believe psychiatry can be a tool people can use in claiming the 'abundant life' that Jesus said God wants us to have."

It took Kathryn a few hours to get comfortable with the idea of revealing herself to Pearl, but once Kathryn started talking, she told Pearl everything. It was like a floodgate opening, and Kathryn was surprised at how freely she exposed her most private self to that strong, resourceful, loving woman. She didn't get any negative judgments from Pearl, although she'd expected plenty of them when she unloaded the truth of her adultery with Marcos. Pearl remained professional, compassionate, and objective during the three-day catharsis she guided Kathryn through. At the end of those three days, Kathryn could feel the remarkable transformation and renewal that had taken place inside her. She had a renewed understanding of the unconscious pressures that were leading her to act detrimentally. The process was one of confrontation, and there were lots of tears during the three days, but there was a special prize at the end of the road. An exhilarating strength like she'd never known before resulted from getting through that painful process of confronting those dark forces and hopefully freeing herself of their ability to harm her again.

The last hour or so she spent with Pearl seemed like a deeply religious experience. At the end of their conversation on the third day, Pearl asked her if she wanted to end their session with some scripture from the Bible. Kathryn replied that she wanted to pray the prayer King David had composed after he'd committed adultery with Bathsheba. In a time of idleness and boredom, David had committed adultery with Bathsheba when her husband was away at war. She'd become pregnant. When her husband Uriah, a gentleman soldier, wouldn't go home to sleep with his wife so that David could conceal his paternity, King David had Uriah sent to the front line of a fierce battle in which he was killed. David married Bathsheba after her period of mourning passed, and then the baby fathered by David was

born and died a few days later. Later, Bathsheba became the mother
of Solomon. David had transgressed one of the Ten Commandments,
just as Kathryn had. And just as the gratification of David's sinful
desire had led to moral havoc in his own home, Kathryn's dallying
with sin and her adultery with Marcos had led to bitter suffering.
David's prayer of repentance was the Fifty-first Psalm, and Kathryn
had always loved it because of the abject way a king, reminded of his
sin against God, humbled himself and asked for forgiveness. It captured the torment of her soul, and when she read the words she could
see in her mind an image of a strong, loving king who'd offended his
Creator and who had the wisdom to plead for forgiveness.

> *Have mercy on me, God, through your steadfast love,*
> *Through your unlimited mercy pardon my sins.*
> *Wash me thoroughly and clean me up, O God.*
> *For I understand the bad thing I've done*
> *And I see clearly how wrong I was.*
> *I've sinned against the laws of God*
> *And I've done something that's evil in your eyes, Father.*
> *So you would be justified to judge and sentence me*
> *For my crime against you.*
> *Like every human being, I was born into a sinful world*
> *And I've learned to sin.*
> *But I know that you, God, desire truth to be our guide*
> *So I've come asking that you will teach me wisdom.*
> *Purge me of my evil thoughts and evil intentions,*
> *Wash me, cure me, and make me clean and pure.*
> *I want to be whiter than snow.*
> *Fill me with joy and gladness*
> *And let my brokenness be healed.*
> *Turn your face away from looking at my sins*
> *And remember no more the evil things I've done.*
> *Create in me a clean heart, O God,*
> *And put in me a new spirit that wants to do right.*
> *Please don't cast me aside like a reject,*
> *And please don't withhold your holy Spirit from me.*

Restore me through your ability to save
And hold me up with a willing spirit.
Then I will be able to teach others about you
And I will help other sinners return to you.
O God, open my lips and mouth to praise you.
I know the rituals of religion are not what you want.
I know that the only sacrifice you find acceptable
Is the true yearning to be in a right relationship with you
That comes from a humble heart.

After their four nights in Kingston came to an end, they still had six days left of the ten-day excursion that was their second honeymoon. They decided they didn't want to do the things they normally did when they brought the kids because they'd start missing them too much. When they had the kids with them, they usually spent a few days in Kingston and then traveled the island by car, exploring whatever they came across, from the primitive caves that had once been the hangout of pirates in the seventeenth and eighteenth centuries, to the fancy homes formerly owned by the likes of Errol Flynn and Noel Coward. When they were having dinner with Pearl and Kahlil the last evening before leaving Kingston the next day, they picked Kahlil's and Pearl's brains about what might be fun to do on a second honeymoon.

The Trident in Port Antonio was Pearl's idea. They'd never stayed in Port Antonio before, although it was widely regarded as the most beautiful and least commercial part of the island. Pearl knew Edward, the hotel manager at the Trident, because Edward's Middle Eastern family lived in Kingston, and Kahlil was a good friend of the Jamaican architect who'd built the Trident thirty years ago. Over those years, the Trident had grown into a famous watering hole of the rich and famous, and its $550-a-night rooms were said to be lavish and well attended to by a professional and discreet staff.

Port Antonio was a two-hour drive by car from Kingston, half through the mountains and half along the coast road. Pearl had called ahead the night before to ask Edward to get villa 12 ready for them.

When they pulled into the sculpted entranceway of the Trident,

Stefan and Kathryn could see it was going to be a special experience. This was not the typically Jamaican place they normally stayed when they came with the kids. It looked fancier. Being in Jamaica without children did seem strange, but one day they'd be at college, and it would just be the two of them, anyway.

Pearl had told them about Port Antonio's reputation for being the playground of the rich and famous. According to her, the wealthy of European descent frequented Port Antonio, whereas Negril was the playpen of the jet set who wanted to go topless and party all night. The Trident, they learned from an old newspaper article on the wall as they checked in, had been built to cater to the moneyed and pedigreed who wanted to feel like they were at home while they were relaxing in the Caribbean.

They were shown to villa 12, a two-bedroom "double villa" with a black-and-white marble patio overlooking the sea. On their way, they walked past the croquet court next to the oversized swimming pool and near the canopied restaurant with its army of solicitous waiters vigilantly overseeing the food-and-beverage needs of guests. The grounds were breathtakingly beautiful. Pine shrubs on both sides of the walkway had been sculpted into interesting shapes of animals and geometric designs, and Stefan especially liked seeing the fuzzy red pusstail hanging on a bush outside their villa. He didn't see any birds of paradise or red ginger on the grounds, but the bellboy said he could take Kathryn down the road to Somerset Falls to see exotic sci-fi foliage. And the Blue Lagoon, the famous "blue hole" with a prism of blue shades, was right down the road from the Trident. A guide had told him that scuba divers estimated its depth to be 186 feet but weren't sure, because there seemed to be a dark tunnel at the bottom that looked like a place where the sea might swallow up anyone who ventured in.

Villa 12 seemed perfect for them. The furniture looked new, and it probably was new, they realized, after the bellboy told them that the Trident had been brutalized by two hurricanes in the last five years. There was a rich, deep-pink patterned fabric on the couch and matching chairs, and the patio furniture cushions were of the same material. Just a few steps from their marble terrace and across a grassy lawn lay the Caribbean. Where the sea met the rocks, there was a steep drop into a rocky terrain, below which danced the mossy green, cobalt blue, and aquamarine colors of the sea.

After Kathryn put their clothes in the dresser drawers, they decided to fetch the map from the glove compartment to develop their plans for sightseeing the following day. Looking on the detailed drawing of Jamaica, they saw that Port Antonio was made up of bay after bay along the coast. Within the bays were cove after cove, and there were several coves, including the cove containing the Trident's beach, nestled up against the Trident's villas and hotel that followed the line of the sea. Rising behind the Trident, but not visible from their villa, were the famous Blue Mountains where Jamaican coffee grows, so it was no wonder that pines and firs abounded on the Trident property. As they walked around the grounds to explore further, they saw firs that had been grown in clusters or bunches and then shaped into balls, squares, Christmas trees, cylinders, ice cream cones, and undulating roller-coaster patterns. Almond trees and palms were the soil mates of the pines and firs. Near the edge of the Caribbean were porous white rocks forming the barrier to the sea.

They discovered a gazebo high up on the rocks above the pool and, sitting in it, they could see the tips of two bays visible on the right. The Caribbean lay without end to the left. It was something close to a religious experience, sitting in the gazebo in late afternoon, looking out at the sea that was a swirl of green and navy blue waters. From that vantage point, they could see what the rich and powerful liked about the Trident. With the sea lapping at the rocks, they were filled with a sense of power and wonder watching the ocean genuflecting obediently beneath them. After exploring the Trident for a few days, it became even clearer what the wealthy and powerful liked about the place. There was a tranquility and serenity there, and it had been built to put nature on display and to give man the illusion that he was in control of the world.

As one stood looking toward the sea, the Blue Mountains lush with coffee beans were to the right of the Trident, so there was always a breeze blowing, from the mountains if not from the sea. The mountains around Portland, the parish Port Antonio was in, were

not the dense jungle of some of Jamaica's interior but were rich farm-
land on which cows and other livestock pastured.

The changing moods of the Caribbean were on display during
the six days they spent at the Trident. They went to sleep each night
listening to the sound of the waves lapping against the rocks outside
the villa. To the left of the patio was a long curved finger of rocks that
stretched out into the sea, creating a tiny inlet, and they sat during the
evenings after dinner looking out at the ocean, watching the sea charge
into the inlet and then, as though furious at making a wrong turn,
roar in anger and communicate passionately its dismay. Some nights
the sea would turn stormy, and the waves would crash against the
rocks near their lawn chairs, as though mocking the notion that the
human had any control in the universe. In the mornings, they awak-
ened to a sea that was frisky and playful, like a child, and they would
have breakfast on the patio watching the sea spit the waves against
the rocks with a childlike playfulness. At the moment of impact with
the rocks, beads of white spray splattered in the air while the sky blue
underbelly of the wave was revealed momentarily, like a woman's dress
unexpectedly lifted by the wind to display her underwear.

The days at the Trident went by quickly and were therapeutic.
They were content to spend most of the day at the Trident, enjoying
its luxury and beauty, but they got out a few hours a day to explore
Port Antonio's famous coves. The one they liked best was Frenchman's
Cove, an intimate beach in a cove into which a mountain stream fed.
Swimming in the cove's water was a sensual experience because the
cold stream water near the rocks met the balmy water baked by the
sun in the middle of the cove.

As they boarded the airplane in Kingston Airport at the end of
their trip, Kathryn felt like a new woman. This had been an unusual
trip. They'd missed the kids, but on their day trips they'd found some
villas, not quite as fancy as the Trident but equipped with kitchens,
that would be perfect places to stay with the kids next summer. In
fact, Stefan had booked them into two places. One was Goblin Hill, a
steep and lush property perched so high up on a mountain that you
could stand on the edge of the property and actually see the main
island road directly below. It would be a great place to lose a soccer

ball, so they made a mental note to bring several balls with them next summer. The tennis courts at Goblin Hill would be a hit with the kids. Stefan also booked a villa for a week at Dragon Bay, a sprawling estate with gingerbread-looking row houses. Both Goblin Hill and Dragon Bay were filled with lush tropical vegetation including the purple lignum vitae tree, the red poinciana tree, crotons, palms, coconuts, hibiscus, breadfruit, mangoes, oranges, bananas, bamboo, sugarcane, and orchids.

This trip to Jamaica had been planned by Stefan as a quiet, recuperative, therapeutic holiday. And it had worked. The conversations with Pearl, followed by the days of tropical rest and relaxation, had helped her move to a new level of self-awareness, and she was returning to Georgia with a deeply committed sense of who she was and what she needed to do.

She was also returning to Macon with a sense that she had repented and that she had been forgiven. Forgiving herself had been part of the forgiveness process, too. She had a new awareness of who God was in her life, and she had a renewed understanding of the reality that no other person and no other thing could be the god of her life. Her business couldn't be her god, her husband couldn't be her god, and her children couldn't be her god. Only God himself could be the thing she loved most and worshiped. Only God himself could be first in her life, and it was only in being known by God and in being loved by him that a human being could become truly fulfilled and blossom in every other area of life. First things first. She was returning to Georgia with a sense that she was in a renewed covenant relationship, a relationship of love and obedience, with her Maker. On the plane ride back to Macon, she found herself lost in thought as she renewed her understanding of what the Ten Commandments meant to her personally.

> *I will put God first in my life. I will have no other gods except the one true God.*
> *I will remain vigilant so that no idols creep into my life. This means that I cannot worship or put first in my life anything except God. My husband cannot be my idol,*

my children cannot be my idol, and my business cannot be my idol or the thing that I am most passionate about.

I will not misuse God's name in language, and I will not mock his name by making a show of worshiping him in public while participating in all kinds of sins in private. God sees our private sins and often exposes them.

I will take time off to rest, to worship God, and to spiritually renew myself.

I will honor my mother and father. For me this means that, although we will probably never have a normal parent-child relationship, I will remember my parents' good qualities and make a conscious effort to remember that everyone has both bad and good in them. I will try to honor the good things about them, even as I steadfastly refuse to let them mistreat me in any way, ever again. I will also try to lead my life in such a way that this commandment will not be as hard for my children to obey as it is for me.

Although I have never murdered anyone, I will try to control my anger and rage so that I never murder anyone.

I will not commit adultery again. I realize that God wants us to be faithful to the vows we take in marriage, and I want to honor and hold marriage sacred. I will love my husband and cherish the covenant relationship I have entered into with him.

I will not cheat people in business or steal anything from anyone.

I will not lie. Honesty in everything will be my motto in life.

I will not desire the talents, abilities, skills, material possessions, or lot in life of others. I will make every effort to be content with what I have and thank God for the blessings he has given me. I will resist greed and envy in every form.

EIGHT

"Mommy, are the men Aunt Sally used to be married to still our uncles?" Booth asked the question as they backed out of the driveway on their way to the country club. Kathryn cast a look at Stefan, and their eyes met.

"I don't honestly know, honey," she replied. "It's a good question, though. I don't know what the relationship is when someone who was your uncle is no longer married to your aunt."

"Well, I don't like our new uncle. He's an old man," said Veronica in her sauciest voice.

"Yeah, he looks older than Granddaddy," added Calvin.

Kathryn cast a look into the back seat at her children. They looked adorable. Their grandmother had insisted on dressing them in new outfits, the boys in ties and jackets and Veronica in a dress the color of the bridesmaids' dresses. Kathryn remembered how Vera used to dress her in a fine Sunday dress to show her off when she was little. Everything had to look perfect in public, Vera told her daughters. Actually, Kathryn had been terrified of wearing those fancy dresses designed to show off Vera's money and good taste, because if she ever got a spot on them, it meant a spanking with the belt from her father. Always hot-tempered, Miles took out his immaturity on Kathryn by harsh physical whippings when she was a child and then by slappings that got close to beatings when she was a teenager. Eventually, she got

too big to hit and that's when the more subtle emotional abuse began. Her "pretend family" had always been a family in camouflage
with an external facade that covered up the internal dysfunction. She
couldn't wait to get this wedding over with.

Vera had grown livid with rage when Kathryn told her a few weeks
earlier that she and Stefan didn't want Veronica to be the flower girl.
This would have been the third wedding in which Veronica was Sally's
flower girl, and Kathryn and Stefan thought it would be giving their
children the wrong signal. They tried to explain to Vera that they didn't
want the children to think marriage was as disposable as Sally's frequent weddings made it appear. They'd told Vera in the nicest way
they could, but Vera had no interest in their reasoning, and she'd
blasted Kathryn for trying to destroy everything Sally ever did.

"Well, at least let me dress the children for the wedding," Vera
had sneered, "so they don't look like the ragged little country bumpkins they look like when you take them to church. This is going to be
at the club, and all our friends will be there."

"God doesn't judge the way people dress in church," Kathryn had
replied. Vera had simply glared at her in cold hostility, unable to com-
prehend why her firstborn was so contrary.

"Hey, Mom," Booth said again. "So David isn't really our brother,
is he?"

Kathryn turned around to look into Booth's eyes as she replied.
Her eyes caught David's eyes, and he smiled at her self-confidently,
unconcerned at his baby brother's question. "Why, yes, he's your
brother, honey."

"Yeah, but he has a different dad, doesn't he?"

"Yes, you're right, Mr. Galleria is his dad, but all of you have the
same mom, so he's your brother." She glanced quickly at Stefan. He
was staring straight ahead at the road, showing no emotion.

"So, if you were still married to Mr. Galleria, would I have been
his son?" Booth continued.

"If Dad and I hadn't gotten married, Booth, you wouldn't have
been born at all," she replied cheerfully, briefly touching Stefan's pants
leg to show support. Mercifully, an argument erupted between Booth
and Calvin in the back seat, and their wrestling ended the discussion.

Kathryn looked out the car window, reflecting on how difficult it is for children to understand the nuances of broken relationships.

Her thoughts returned to Vera, who'd been especially cold and hostile to her since she'd picked up the children from their house after they returned from the second honeymoon. Kathryn was used to that, though. Her relationship with her parents went from frigid, to thawed, back to frigid again, depending on her ability to perform according to their desires. Vera was focusing on Veronica's not being in the wedding as a major embarrassment, but that was classic Vera, picking something trivial and turning it into a soap opera for months. When they didn't think she was being a good girl and doing what they wanted her to do, they didn't speak to her. There was never any part of the relationship with them anymore that wasn't traumatic. In the last couple of years, when it began to look like Sally wasn't going to have children, the thing they'd made a major issue of was their right to spend time with Kathryn's children. They'd become abnormally possessive and demanding and took the attitude that their grandchildren should be available to them at any time. Kathryn and Stefan had grown weary of their pushiness in insisting that the children come to visit them on the weekends "to fill up the void in our lives," as Miles once put it to Kathryn. What Kathryn and Stefan tried to tell them in a nice way was that if the children were at their grandparents' house, that robbed the children of the experience of family life with their parents. As usual, when Miles and Vera couldn't get something they wanted, they twisted the truth to their point of view. They'd given Kathryn and Stefan the cold shoulder recently, knowing that Kathryn, encouraged by Stefan, would eventually try to soothe their hurt feelings and bandage their egos. Not this time, though, Kathryn decided. She felt worn-out from the roller-coaster relationship with them. Their withholding love and respect because she didn't cater to their whims had diminished her love for them over the years. She was tired of the emotional blackmail and their deliberate attempts to damage her ego and self-concept through guile, bullying, and intimidation. If something couldn't be on Vera's terms, it wouldn't be on any terms, and Miles went along with whatever minimized Vera's hostility. She and her mother had exchanged angry words when she'd picked up the kids after Jamaica because Vera insisted that they stay another night. Vera had taken offense at her determination to take them home, and the venom in her mother's eyes let Kathryn know she felt her older daughter was treacherous and disobedient. Vera and Miles seemed to have an unusual amount of anger and hostility lately, probably because of the scandal Sally's fourth marriage had stirred. Every time an angry episode came into their lives, they seemed to displace their rage on Kathryn. Lately, Vera and Miles seemed to be fixated on the notion that Kathryn and Stefan were maliciously keeping their grandchildren away from them. As usual, the slight was in Vera's mind. There had been no deliberate antagonism of Vera and Miles by Kathryn and Stefan.

Vera and Miles seemed to have the desire to do it all over again, this time the right way, with their grandchildren. Their daughters hadn't turned out very well, in their view. They had a cold relationship with Kathryn and, although they loved Sally, they wished she would just get married and stay married and stay out of trouble. They'd bailed her out of jail several times on drunken driving and drug charges, and they were tired of overhearing the whispering at the country club about who she was sleeping with now. Their bitchy older daughter snubbed them, and the younger girl they truly loved was an embarrassment. Their money kept them in the social circle they wanted to belong to, so they just made a family out of their friends at the club and church.

The wedding ceremony was held outside in the beautiful garden adjoining the golf course. The minister from Vera's church conducted the brief ceremony, which was attended by nearly a hundred people. As Kathryn looked around while they sat and waited for the ceremony to begin, she caught Mrs. Crosland and Mrs. Beaut staring at her. Actually, they were glaring at her. Her mother's friends always glared at her, as though they had been told some horrible fact about her. Their glare was so cold and mean, it chilled Kathryn to the bone. Both of them shopped at the Chic Boutique occasionally, on what always seemed like "spy missions" organized by Vera. They were her mother's closest friends, and they always acted as though they hated Kathryn. She remembered them from her mother's younger days. They were the two women who used to show up at her house when her father was out of town, so they could party with her mother and the men who would join them. On those occasions, Kathryn was expected to go into her bedroom and take care of her baby sister while they partied. Mrs. Crosland's husband had left her long ago, and Mrs. Beaut was a widow. They both seemed to have a lot of hostility and anger in them, just like Vera.

"Darling Kathryn, you look beautiful," said Mrs. McCormick, the sheriff's wife, as she and her husband took a seat behind Kathryn and Stefan and their family. Kathryn liked Mrs. McCormick. She was a beautiful, buxom, intelligent woman with short, cropped hair who always had a big smile on her face. In her early sixties, she'd gone to the College of William and Mary and married Matt McCormick shortly afterward. They had four children just like Kathryn, and Doris McCormick had always been very supportive of Kathryn and Stefan. A loving mother and wife, Doris McCormick sensed those same qualities in Kathryn, so she'd more or less adopted Kathryn in terms of proposing her for membership in the most prominent garden club in town and in the Women's Club. In a small Southern town, proper ladies belong to a garden club and a women's club. Flattered at Mrs. McCormick's support, Kathryn nevertheless had to tell Doris that she couldn't be active in those organizations while her children were small, and Doris had understood her reasons right away.

"Oh, honey, I think you're right," Doris had said when Kathryn told her about eight years ago she couldn't join either club. "You can't neglect the good you need to do inside your home in order to do good outside. I understand, honey. You've got plenty of time to be in old ladies' clubs like I am," she'd laughed. "I always stayed home with my kids, too. I didn't leave them at night either, even for that Junior League stuff."

Kathryn wondered if Doris McCormick knew that her husband had been involved in a long-term affair with Vera. Since she saw her mother as infrequently as possible now, Kathryn didn't honestly know if Vera and Matt McCormick were still involved, but she knew her mother was still active in his reelection campaigns and in fund-raising activities of the sheriff's department. Vera's relationship with

McCormick had begun when Kathryn was eleven or twelve years old, and the affair had lasted for years. That was way before he was sheriff, and Mr. McCormick had pretended he was coming to the house to talk about real estate, since he managed a real estate company started by his father. He used to come prowling around at night, pretending to be there on business. Kathryn remembered wondering why adults think kids are so dumb and why adults think they can fool kids. Kids always see through adults.

McCormick had run for sheriff for the first time almost twenty years ago, and he'd soon be coming up for reelection for the fifth time. In an odd twist of fate, Miles Faison, who'd never suspected Vera's adultery with McCormick and who had actually been delighted that her social climbing had snared a real sheriff, was now apparently one of the biggest contributors to McCormick's campaign. In the South, sheriff was a powerful position, and it made sense for anyone who had money as well as a son or daughter in frequent trouble with the law to make sizable campaign contributions. Like most places in the world, in a small Southern town, people got the justice they could afford, and having connections to McCormick helped Miles and Vera get their salvage yards on the outskirts of town watched by the cops and permitted them to bail Sally out of trouble quickly and quietly. The city police chief had jurisdiction over law enforcement problems in the city, but the sheriff's department was responsible for law and order outside city limits.

The music began, and everyone stood as the bride came down the aisle. Kathryn heard whispering. She looked at her sister. Sally was a beautiful redhead, and she was wearing an off-white ivory dress that must have cost a fortune. As she walked down the aisle on her father's arm, Sally looked tired and thin. It almost broke her heart to look at the sister she'd helped to mother. Kathryn wondered why she was getting married to Dr. Pegast. He was disgusting looking. Her sister was marrying a "dirty old man." More than twenty years her senior, he'd left his wife of many years, with whom he had grown children, to go through this new marital adventure with Sally. It was pure lust on his part and who knows what on Sally's part. Kathryn glanced at the section where Sally's friends were sitting. All of them were cocaine-thin looking. Most of them were the ne'er-do-wells from the country club set she'd grown up with. Sally had adapted to country club life like a fish to water, whereas Kathryn had rebelled against it and rejected it. Suddenly, she remembered how angry Vera had gotten when Kathryn and Stefan refused to let Vera pay their country club entrance fee.

"But your father and I can get you into the club," Vera had protested angrily.

"We don't want into the club, mother," Kathryn had told Vera. "We're just hardworking, busy, simple people, and we don't want to be part of the country club scene. That's not the way we want to raise our children."

Vera had glared at her as though Kathryn had personally attacked her. "You're a damned reject from the sixties, Kathryn. Wake up and at least give your children some advantages and stop being so selfish," she had said. "And what do you mean, that's not the way you want to raise them? You mean, with some advantages and social contacts?"

Kathryn and Stefan had briefly discussed accepting Vera and Miles's offer to pay the fifteen-thousand-dollar entrance fee and their monthly dues for one year, but they just didn't want to. "Beware of Greeks bearing gifts" was the phrase that came to mind whenever her parents wanted to do a "favor" for her. Their favors were always designed to produce a debt or to leave Kathryn burdened with guilt for having been so undeserving. The narcissistic Vera enjoyed giving Kathryn gifts because she enjoyed the generous image it gave her in front of others. If Kathryn and Stefan had joined the club, the club would have become a second home to the grandchildren. Membership costs and dues were so high that, once a family joined, the club became its hangout and its place to swim, eat dinner, play pool, have parties, and so forth. Vera and Miles would have had open hunting season on their grandchildren at all times. Unlimited access to their grandchildren without having to ask Kathryn's permission for anything was what they wanted, and club membership would have accomplished that. Vera and Miles seemed to take the view that they could emotionally spit on Kathryn and Stefan and still have an independent relationship with their grandchildren. It enraged the Faisons when Kathryn told them they couldn't accept their generous offer, and they retaliated as they always did, by an attempt at character assassination of Kathryn with some of the relatives and with selected people in Macon. Vera had even gotten into the habit in the last couple of years of writing notes to some of Kathryn's best friends out of town crying the blues about her mean daughter, hoping her friends would reform Kathryn or, if they couldn't reform her, at least think less of her.

While many of the guests were enjoying the lavish spread and open bar after the ceremony, Kathryn squeezed Stefan's hand and said she'd be back after a brief trip to the ladies' room. The door leading into the fancy ladies' bathroom closed behind her, and she walked through the small corridor leading to the second door, which opened up into the beautifully decorated ladies' room. As soon as she opened the second door, she saw her mother. Why did such a cold chill come over her every time she saw her own mother?

"Hi," Kathryn said, taking a position next to her mother to check her makeup in the mirror. Vera did not speak. She didn't look at her. She simply continued to check her makeup and push at her hairdo. She guessed her mother was still pouting over Stefan and Kathryn's not wanting Veronica to be in the wedding. Same old Vera. Always pissed about something. Kathryn heard a door open, and she saw the smiling face of Mabel Schmidt appear in the mirror. Suddenly, Vera's face broke into her socialite smile. Kathryn had always detested that fake smile of hers.

"Mabel, you look gorgeous, honey," gushed Vera.

"Well, you can thank your beautiful daughter for that, Vera. If it weren't for the Chic Boutique, I wouldn't have any clothes to wear! Oh, Kathryn brought me back the most beautiful dress from New York recently, and I can't wait to wear it to the Spring Folly." Spring Folly was an annual country club event held on the eve of the Dogwood Festival, and it was the occasion when the country club women dressed in their finest. It was proving to be a real boondoggle sales time for Kathryn, because some of the women who used to go to New York to find something for the occasion now trusted Kathryn to select beautiful garments for them.

"You're so lucky to have this sweet girl for a daughter," Mabel said, putting her arms around Kathryn from behind and giving her a big hug.

"And didn't Sally just look fabulous?" responded Vera.

Mabel's face grew serious. "Yes, Vera, she did look nice, but she's so thin. I hope she's alright. I think she looks better when she's got a little more meat on her bones. She's such a beautiful girl, though. I just hope she'll be happy . . ."

"Her dress came from Priscilla's in Boston, you know," continued Vera, cutting her off, as though she hadn't heard what Mabel was saying.

The door opened again, and Mrs. Crosland poked her head inside. "Vera dear, we need you outside for a moment. We're talking about the cruise this summer." She shot Kathryn a cold look as she spoke to Vera.

As Vera left the ladies' room, Kathryn excused herself and went into one of the lavatories. "Cheerio, Kathryn," she heard Mabel say as she heard the door open and close. A few seconds later, Kathryn heard the door open again, and then, she heard two voices.

"It's just a crime that he left his wife for that little tramp," a voice said.

"She's not much, is she?" another voice replied.

"Margaret is devastated, you know. And the children aren't speaking to him anymore. They can't believe Arthur Pegast could do this to his wife and their mother. I mean, his kids grew up in this club, and now he just walks away from his real life with a well-known runaround girl."

"Well, what can you expect, given the family she grew up in?"

"That may be true, but enough is enough. How could she walk down the aisle in a white dress on her fourth go-round?"

As Kathryn stood in the toilet cubicle, waiting for the ladies to leave so she could rejoin Stefan, she was overcome by a feeling of compassion for her sister. She'd clearly lost her way. She'd followed in her parents' footsteps, that was for sure. Kathryn felt sad and guilty for the way Sally had turned out, since she'd sort of been Sally's "little mother" when Sally was a baby and toddler. Certainly, Vera had tried to instill guilt in Kathryn about Sally. Vera had come to Kathryn on the eve of all three of Sally's divorces to try to get Kathryn to apply her Harvard-trained intellect to the business of helping Sally extract a large lump-sum payment from each former husband. Coached by Vera, Sally made it her goal to make sure each husband paid more than the last one had. It was a game. Alimony didn't interest Sally. She seemed to know that alimony would be a fleeting thing until the next husband came along, and she was more interested in building net worth than in getting temporary cash flow. When Kathryn refused to use her brains to develop "maximum payout strategies" for her baby sister, Vera took the view that Kathryn was a snot, and she acted mortally wounded when Kathryn had the audacity to suggest that the failure of those marriages had been Sally's fault. Vera came up with a lot of creative excuses to explain why her baby's marriages had failed, like one of the men drank too much, another was physically abusive, and one was just too immature ("not man enough," Vera pronounced) to handle Sally. Kathryn wondered if she could have done more to help her baby sister, but then she remembered how Vera always tried to make sure she and Sally never had a good relationship. Vera had to control that, too. They probably wouldn't have had a good relationship anyway, because Sally thought relationships were just a framework for using people. Kathryn loved her sister but she didn't trust her. She'd turned into a beautiful, manipulative, promiscuous woman like her mother.

After the two women left the ladies' room, Kathryn came out of the cubicle. She reapplied her lipstick and joined Stefan in the ballroom.

"Hi," she smiled, as she rejoined her slim, handsome husband with the salt-and-pepper hair and chiseled good looks.

"Hi, honey," Stefan said, his eyes lighting up when he saw her.

"Sold any ladies' underwear lately?" chortled the voice of Miles Faison, as he came up behind Stefan and thumped him on the back so hard that he bumped into Kathryn.

"Hello, Mr. Faison. Nice party. Congratulations, sir," Stefan replied with a smile, extending his hand for a handshake. Stefan could always be counted on to act like a gentleman while Miles Faison acted like an overgrown punk. Kathryn bristled when she looked at her father. Their relationship had grown colder and more hostile over the years, as he'd given in to Vera's ornery disposition and taken her side on every issue that came up between her and her mother. Vera controlled him totally now that he was older. With a full head of gray hair, he had a muscular physique and was extremely handsome, even in his sixties. But he still had the same punkish and often lewd sense of humor that he expressed in the coarse and crude language of the salvage yard set. Actually, what he passed off as a sense of humor were sarcastic remarks designed to belittle and embarrass other people, especially Kathryn and Stefan. Kathryn had come to see him in a more detached way in the last few years. She'd come to look at him objectively, not as a daughter looks at a father, but as a middle-aged woman looks at an older relative. And she realized when she looked at him that she didn't like at all the loud way he talked, and the vulgar, off-color jokes he made in front of her, and the rude and insensitive way he treated Stefan. She glared at him, wanting to tell him that he wasn't fit to tie Stefan's shoes.

As soon as he moved on, Kathryn felt Stefan squeeze her hand.

"Don't worry, honey, it'll soon be over. They are your parents, you know, and you just need to be nice to them. We don't have to see them much, so let's just be polite and get through this, okay? You know I love you, and we can handle this. It'll soon be over."

"Yes, well, speaking of that, I probably need to make a call to see if Marcos got into town and find out what time they're going hunting tomorrow." It was Friday evening, actually it was Good Friday, and Marcos was scheduled to arrive in town that evening to take David hunting over the Easter holidays. How Vera had gotten her minister to conduct a wedding service on Good Friday was a mystery. Easter was the busiest time of year for ministers. But whatever Vera wanted, she seemed to get, even when it came to men of the cloth.

"You go ahead, honey. Then we won't have to bother with it when we get home. I'll stay here with my baby," he said, looking down affectionately at Veronica, who was staring up equally adoringly into her father's eyes.

Kathryn walked down the corridor to the general manager's

office where the club members often went to make their private
calls during parties. As she opened the door, she caught a whiff of
marijuana. She opened the door all the way to discover Sally, another woman, and two men sitting on the couch and chairs. One of
the men made a weak attempt to put his hands over a mirror on
which Kathryn saw two lines of white powder.

"Well, hi there, sis," beckoned a blond, preppy-looking man who
had his arm around Sally. Sally looked disheveled, and her wedding
dress had been pulled down on one arm. "I'm just warming up the
bride, getting her ready for hubby," cackled the man, as he leered toward Sally.

"What you ought to do," replied the other man in the foursome,
"is take care of her before she gets to hubby, because I don't know if
hubby can handle what she's got." The three friends of Sally's laughed,
and then Sally put her face down toward the mirror to take a line of
cocaine. Sally looked "out of it."

"Sally, don't you think you should get out of here?" asked Kathryn.

"Sally," one of the men echoed in a high-pitched voice mocking
her, "don't you think you should get out of here?" The three com-
panions of Sally all laughed again loudly, and Sally kept snorting.

"Come on over here, sister, I'll warm you up, too," beckoned the
blond man, gesturing her over with his arm. His face was red and
ruddy, like he'd been drinking all day, and Kathryn could smell his
alcoholic breath from across the room. "I like doing it with sisters.
Why, we can even make it a threesome. Remember how we did that
once at the beach, Sally? Or was it twice?" Then, he reached over to
put his hand into the bra of her wedding dress on the side where it
was off her shoulder. "Oh, I just love wedding girls. They're just so
hot, aren't they, honey?" Sally let him paw her. She just sat there, seeming to be in some kind of catatonic state. She was obviously drunk
and cocaine high and oblivious to what was going on around her.

Kathryn closed the door and walked back down the corridor to
join Stefan. She was ready to round up the children and go home.

After they got home, the kids went upstairs to the game room to
watch a movie while Kathryn and Stefan decided to watch television
in their bedroom.

"Did you see Dr. Lambert? He was looking for you."

"Yes. He found me."

"What did he want?"

She didn't answer for a moment. "I went for a checkup this week."

"Oh, you did? Good, I'm glad. You hadn't been for a physical in a long time. Is your blood pressure alright?

"Yes. My blood pressure is alright," she answered unemotionally.

"I'm glad. We want to make sure we keep our mommy in excellent working order," he said, as he walked toward her and put his arms around her and hugged her. Then he sat down on the bed to begin undressing.

"I can't take any more of this," Kathryn whimpered in a voice that sounded distraught and full of fatigue, as Stefan sat on the bed, unbuttoning the buttons of his tuxedo shirt.

"I know, I know," Stefan replied, looking at her. He could see the tension in her eyes and on her face. Every time they were around the relatives, Kathryn came home stressed out. It never failed.

"I mean it, Stefan, I can't handle any more of it," Kathryn continued. He stared at her as she undressed and put on her negligee. The sight of her aroused him.

"Well, let's lie down, honey. You'll feel better in the morning." Then his tone of voice changed. "By the way, what's going on with David tomorrow?"

"I didn't use the phone at the club, but we had a message on our answering machine when we got home that Marcos is in town, and I had David call him at the Marriott to ask him what time he should be there tomorrow. David said I'm supposed to drop him off real early at the Marriott, at about four-thirty, and then I'm going to the mall to do some early-bird shopping. Most of the stores are opening before dawn with Easter early-bird specials, and I might see about doing some early Christmas shopping. I may even get Veronica a new dress if I see something at a good price."

"Okay."

"Are you going running tomorrow?"

"Probably."

"I might go by the lodge at lunch to see how David has done in his first day of hunting and to thank Tom for letting them hunt for a few days."

"Sounds good."

Kathryn went over to the bed and sat beside Stefan. He put one arm around her shoulders to embrace and comfort her.

"I know what I have to do," she said in a soft voice, as she stared down at the plush carpeting on the floor. "You know," she said, looking up at him, "I do love you so much."

He turned to her with a smile and with surprise etched on his face as he gave her a squeeze with the arm that was around her shoulders. "Well, I'm glad, honey, but I wish you didn't feel so sad about it," he teased, making a reference to her plaintive tone of voice. "I love you, too," he continued, as he dropped his arm to her waist. "Look, don't worry about anything. Let's have a nice Easter weekend. All we need to think about is David's going on this hunting trip. I want to talk to him before he goes to bed. I want to make sure he stays with Marcos at all times. I don't want the boy wandering off in the woods by himself."

Only partially undressed, Stefan then disappeared upstairs to find David. Kathryn knew Stefan wasn't wild about this hunting trip, but he'd agreed to let it happen. Marcos had assured Kathryn that he was a skilled hunter with all the credentials and considerable first-aid knowledge, and David seemed thrilled that his father was coming into town, giving up his Easter vacation with his own family, to take him hunting for the first time. Hunting was actually pretty big around Macon, and, through church, Kathryn knew Tom Lefert, the manager of the prestigious hunting lodge that was on a beautiful piece of property outside the city. Lefert's daughter was the same age as Veronica and was in Veronica's Sunday school class, which Kathryn taught. Tom had graciously agreed to let David and Marcos hunt during the Easter week on the members-only property known around town as "the Estate." The five-hundred-acre property had been an estate owned at one time by the Vanderbilts, who used to come to Macon for a few months a year to escape the harsh New England winters while turkey hunting. The Vanderbilt heirs had sold the estate ten years previously to some wealthy local businessmen, who'd turned it into a private hunting club and party lodge. Kathryn and Stefan had been to a couple of parties at the lodge, including her own high school reunion parties. Several of the homes on the estate were rented out regularly as party houses for events like family reunions, church retreats, business meetings, and group getaways. Kathryn and Stefan had recently discussed taking a family weekend retreat to a cabin on the property. The cabins had belonged to wealthy families in the Vanderbilt clan and were beautifully decorated and elegantly furnished. She and Stefan thought it would be fun for the whole family to escape together one weekend.

Part 2

NINE

S tefan saw the patrol car outside through the sidelites as he walked toward the front door. That's odd, he thought. He felt his heart beating faster as he fiddled with his key chain, trying to find the key to the front door. God forbid there'd been an accident with David. He certainly hadn't been enthusiastic about David's going hunting with Marcos. He and Kathryn had no guns in their house, and he wasn't happy that an inexperienced young Boy Scout was going turkey hunting for the first time. David was a son to Stefan in every way, and Stefan felt protective of the boy he'd known since he was two years old. They'd never had a stepfather-stepson relationship. He'd entered David's life when he was a toddler and became the boy's father a couple of years later when he married Kathryn. Another son, Calvin, joined their family when David was five years old, then Veronica came along when David was seven, then Booth was born when David was nine. He'd always thought of David as his first son and treated him like one of his own children. He'd tutored him in math, trained him to do household chores such as locking the doors at night as his own father had trained him to do, scolded him for making Bs instead of As, and taught him table manners. He and Kathryn both felt strongly that all the children should be treated the same and there should be no favorites. Stefan's father had grown up as his father's favorite until he left home at fifteen, and he had told Stefan stories of how the resulting jealousy had alienated him from his siblings.

From the moment Kathryn had told him about Marcos's calling on David's fifteenth birthday, it never seriously entered his mind to stand in the way of the boy's relationship with his natural father. Not that it had been thoroughly comfortable for him since David's relationship with Marcos started. To be honest, he wasn't comfortable with one of his children having two homes while he was still a youth, and he wondered if this arrangement didn't glamorize divorce for all the children involved. But he had to admit it was working with no real problems. Kathryn and Marcos seemed to have worked out amicably the arrangements for David's visits to San Antonio, and Marcos appeared to have married a beautiful and loving woman who made David feel very much like he had a home with his natural father and his other family. So far, so good. Actually, this hunting trip was the main thing so far that had made Stefan feel extremely uncomfortable. But Marcos was a skilled hunter and wanted to introduce the boy to the sport and groom him as a hunting buddy. Stefan wouldn't have allowed the boy to go hunting with anyone else, but in this case, it was a parent pulling rank on another parent. Kathryn thought it was okay, Marcos obviously thought it was okay, so who was he to object? Anyway, the boy was nearly sixteen, so he was old enough, sort of. In fact, he would celebrate his sixteenth birthday while Marcos was in town over his Easter break from school. *What had Kathryn seen in Marcos anyway?* Stefan wondered as he opened the door to find two men on his front porch.

"Mr. Stefan Haddad?"

"Yes, sir," answered Stefan respectfully.

"Sir," began the taller gentleman, holding identification in one hand for Stefan to see, "I'm Detective Sullivan and this is Detective Robbey. May we come inside for a moment? We have something we need to talk with you about."

As he closed the front door behind the officers, Stefan saw a couple of neighbors peering out of their garages at the patrol car in the front of his house. He led the officers into the family room.

"Could we talk to you alone, sir?" said Sullivan, looking at eight-year-old Veronica and six-year-old Booth playing games at two of the computers in the room.

Stefan asked Veronica and Booth to go upstairs to the game room to play for a while, and they ran upstairs obediently, challenging each other to a game of table tennis. Then he motioned for the two detectives to sit down on the couch.

"What can I help you two gentlemen with?" asked Stefan, as he seated himself facing them.

"Mr. Haddad, we have some bad news for you, sir. We need to ask you to come with us. We have reason to believe that the body of a woman found in a parked car is that of your wife."

"Body? My wife? No, my wife is out shopping. She went out early this morning. There were some sales at the mall beginning at five o'clock. I don't understand . . . what do you mean?"

"Just come with us, sir, if you would. Can you leave your kids here, or ask a neighbor to stay with them?"

"My oldest son is on a hunting trip, but my next oldest son can supervise the others while I'm gone."

Stefan felt himself going quite numb, as though he were beginning to go into shock. Surely these officers were wrong.

"Calvin," he said to his son as the boy came into the family room from the kitchen, "please ride herd on your sister and brother while I go with these officers for a few minutes."

"When is Mom coming home?" Veronica was their little scaredy-cat, and she'd run down the stairs to check on her dad after she saw the patrol car in front of the house through the game room window. She never liked staying in the house unless David or one of her parents was there. She and Calvin were too close in age for her to think of him as an appropriate supervisor for her. Tyrant was a better word for Calvin, in her opinion.

"I'm not sure, honey," Stefan answered her. "I won't be gone long, though. Just be a good girl and stay here until I get back."

Sitting on the back seat of the patrol car, Stefan felt too stunned to ask where they were going. He could see the neighbors watching as the patrol car left the neighborhood and then sped along Greystone Boulevard, past the city limits of Macon. The car turned off to the left down a dirt road and, almost immediately after that, Stefan saw Kathryn's red Lincoln. At least it looked like her red Lincoln. Unfortunately. They pulled up behind the car. From another patrol car in front of the Lincoln, two officers disembarked and walked back to greet Stefan's escorts.

"Mr. Haddad?" asked one of the officers approaching the car.

"Yes." He heard himself affirm his identity in a flat, unemotional tone of voice that seemed unconnected to him. It felt like he was having an out-of-body experience. The officer opened the back door of the car to permit Stefan to get out.

"Sir, I know this is hard for you, but would you walk with me to the car in front of us and tell us if the lady inside is your wife? We found identification in the car which leads us to believe she is."

Stefan knew it was Kathryn when he saw the wild-looking permed auburn hair against the back of the front seat. He felt sick to his stomach as he walked more slowly to the front door window of the car to stare into the face of the woman attached to the familiar-looking hair. It was Kathryn.

He hadn't meant to cry. The last time he'd cried was at his father's funeral, nearly twenty years earlier. But somewhere from the depth of him a primal scream broke through as a muted sob, and Stefan felt hot tears coming from his eyes as he laid his head down on his arms and collapsed against the car.

"No, no, it can't be," he cried. He pulled himself together after a couple of moments. "When did you find her here? What happened to her?"

"Sir, a food service worker from the nearby hunting lodge was on a cigarette break and saw the car with a lady inside and thought it looked odd. So he called the police. Can we ask you a few questions, sir?"

Stefan nodded, feeling unable to utter a sound.

"I'm real sorry about your wife, sir," the detective named Sullivan said, with obvious pity in his voice. "Are you familiar with this road, Mr. Haddad?" the detective asked, in a more businesslike tone.

"Yes, it's next to the track where I run sometimes. This is part of the old Vanderbilt property. The hunting lodge is just through those trees over there."

"Sir, did your wife have a drug habit?"

"What? No, no. She never used drugs. What do you mean?"

"You may not have noticed, sir, but there's a hypodermic needle and a rubber armband in the front seat beside her, and there's a bag of what appears to be cocaine lying next to her. It looks like a drug overdose."

"That's impossible! She went shopping, for God's sake."

"Well, sir, we're going to order an autopsy to be performed," Sullivan continued. "It's more or less standard procedure when the death doesn't appear to be from natural causes."

Stefan shook his head slowly in disbelief. Autopsy. This couldn't be. The children ... God in heaven, What would he possibly say to the children? This couldn't be happening. It had to be a bad dream he'd wake up from.

"Do you want us to take you home now, sir?"

"What? Yes, yes, I guess so. What do you do now? What happens to her?"

"We've called the appropriate hospital personnel and a vehicle is on its way. She'll be taken to Mercy Hospital and then they'll either perform the autopsy here or have her body transferred to the Chief Medical Examiner's Office in Athens. Our medical examiner in Macon is only part time, and it's a holiday weekend, so we may have her body taken to Athens. Since it's Saturday, I doubt if an autopsy will be performed before Monday, and I think we'll have to push to get it done even then, since that's Easter Monday. You probably won't be able to have the funeral before Wednesday. Here comes the ambulance."

Stefan felt in a state of shock as he watched emergency rescue personnel retrieve Kathryn's body from the car under the watchful eyes of the detectives and transport it on a stretcher to the ambulance. Autopsy? Body? Funeral? It made no sense, and it couldn't be happening. As the ambulance drove off, he felt the strong arm of one of the officers helping him climb into the back of the patrol car. He stared out the car window and wondered how he would tell his children that their mother was dead.

When he got home, David and Marcos were there, sitting in the family room with Calvin, laughing and talking. Stefan looked at his watch. Four-thirty.

"Hi, Dad! We just got home a few minutes ago," said David, standing courteously and waving his arm enthusiastically as he greeted Stefan with a smile. He called him "Dad" and he called Marcos "Dad," and the duality didn't seem to be confusing the kid a bit.

"Hi, son," answered Stefan. There was a conspicuous absence of cheerfulness in his normally good-natured voice that David picked up on immediately.

"What's the matter, Dad?" David asked, as Booth and Veronica joined them in the family room. Marcos walked over and extended his hand to Stefan.

"Hello, Stefan," Marcos said, extending his hand. "I just brought David home and was helping him put his gear in the garage. Thanks for letting him go. We had a great time."

"Hi, Marcos," Stefan said, clasping his hand. "How was the hunting trip? Did you find any turkey?"

"No, we didn't have much luck, unfortunately. It's too bad we missed dove season by a few weeks. I really want to take him squirrel and dove hunting, and maybe one day on a safari, but turkey season is all there is right now, and of course this is when we had to do the hunting, when David's out of school."

"Would you please sit down, all of you?" Stefan began. "Marcos, you might want to sit down with us, too. This is something you need to know about."

The children knew their father didn't look normal, and they followed his instructions immediately, without their usual litany of protests about why it wasn't a convenient time.

Once they were seated, Stefan sighed deeply, then deeply again, then shook his head slowly. "I have something very sad to tell you. I'm sorry," he said, looking at each one of his children in the eyes. He paused before beginning again. "I just went with some detectives who had found your mother's car with her in the front seat slumped over. We're not sure what happened or how it happened, but she was not alive when they found her."

None of the kids said anything at first, but a look of horror and terror spread over Veronica's eight-year-old face. Then Booth, the youngest, spoke.

"Did she have blood on her, Dad?"

"No, son. She didn't have blood on her."

"What happened to her, Dad?" asked ten-year-old Calvin.

Stefan tried to swallow the lump in his throat so he could speak. He had a lot of questions himself, but fate had put him in the position of fielding everybody else's questions. "We're not sure, son. It may have been a heart attack or something like that. There'll be an investigation and we'll find out what happened."

Marcos was listening intently, but he showed no emotion and asked no questions, as though he were trying not to intrude on their privacy as a family. He did reach over, though, and put his arm around David's shoulders as they sat next to each other on the couch. Veronica and Booth got up from where they were sitting and went over to sit next to their dad. Calvin remained on the couch where he was, sitting alone, looking abandoned and forlorn. Then, like a floodgate opening, the children began to weep, each in his or her own way. Veronica sobbed like a baby with her head on one of Stefan's legs while she held her rag of a "blankey" and tried to suck her thumb at the same time. David put his head against Marcos's shoulder while Calvin was trying to stifle tears that came faster and faster. Stefan heard their tears and felt his pants legs getting wet where Booth and Veronica had laid their heads against his legs, and he reached over Booth and Veronica as they sat on either side of him to grab a Kleenex from the coffee table. No one spoke. There were so many questions to ask, but there was no clear place to begin. And, whatever answers there would eventually be to all their questions, those answers would not change the tragic reality that four children and their father had lost their matriarch and guardian, mother and wife, confidante and friend, helper and companion. Permeating the room was a gloominess that came from their shared feeling of loss, futility, frailty, grief, sorrow, and fear.

A moment or two later their wet silence was interrupted by the telephone. An official from the sheriff's department identified himself and informed Stefan that, on the local station's six o'clock news, and then on special television bulletins that evening, there would be a picture of Kathryn, along with a description of the location where the body was found, accompanied by a request for any leads, clues, or information from the public related to the crime. The voice on the phone said it was a possible suicide, but they didn't rule out homicide. He suggested that Stefan call appropriate family members in town so they wouldn't hear about her death for the first time on the evening news. Stefan thanked him and then turned on the channel where the bulletin would be appearing. The caller mentioned that they'd decided to use the photograph on her driver's license. Suddenly, out of nowhere, the most ridiculous thought cut through his grief. Kathryn would approve of their using that picture. Taken four years ago, it was flattering, and he'd recently teased her that she'd have to glamorize herself the next time she renewed it so she could maintain that youthful look on her driver's license.

Stefan told the children and Marcos there would be a news story as part of the investigation into the cause of death. Then he got on the phone to their minister, Kathryn's parents and sister, her best friend Mary, and a dozen or more family members and friends. He also called the two women who'd been her best friends at the Harvard Business School. Kathryn was extremely well organized so he found the numbers easily in her Rolodex.

Mercifully, the special bulletin did not mention the needle and armband and drug-use suspicion. Thank God the children didn't have to handle the shock and shame of that publicity, at least not for the moment. After the bulletin aired, the phone rang off the hook, and Marcos stayed around to help the children get cereal and milk. An hour later the house began to be flooded with people bringing food and sympathy. A few visitors were surprised to be introduced to Marcos, David's "other dad," but their curiosity about him was muted by their grief and shock over the tragedy. After the house started filling up with people, David located Stefan to tell him that Marcos had gone back to the hotel to give them some privacy with their friends but said he'd call David tomorrow.

Dr. Kotler, the minister from the Methodist church that Stefan and Kathryn belonged to, was one of the first people to show up. He whispered to Stefan after he'd been in the house for a few moments that he wanted to talk with him alone, outside, after he spoke to the children and shook hands with a few neighbors and church members floating through the house. The night air could be chilly in early April in the South, so Stefan donned his jacket before joining Dr. Kotler on the back brick patio. Together they descended the steps leading from the patio into the backyard, so they could talk in confidence near the back wooden fence enclosing the long, grassy, rectangular, flat backyard shaped like a football field.

"I know this is the worst experience of your life, Stefan. And words can do little now. I know that, too," Dr. Kotler said in a soft, sorrowful voice. "But I want to pray with you. And I also must confide in you about a conversation I had with Kathryn nearly three weeks ago."

"Oh?"

"Yes, she called and asked my secretary if she could make an appointment with me. Usually when she has a committee matter she wants to discuss, she'll just pick up the phone and talk to me about it briefly. That was the only time she'd ever called to make an appointment, so I knew she had something on her mind that was important." Dr. Kotler took a deep breath, then swallowed hard, as though the words were hard to speak.

"I don't know how to tell you this, but I'm certain I must tell you. I'd rather you hear this from me than from another source. This may be the gentlest way for you." He paused again and turned to look away from Stefan into the undeveloped lot beyond the fence. It was dark outside, but the street lights and patio lights illuminated his face. He took another deep breath and then looked Stefan in the eyes.

"Kathryn came to see me just before you two went to Jamaica." He cleared his throat. "She was struggling with some moral dilemmas when she came to my office."

"Moral dilemmas?" asked Stefan, looking studiously at him, searching his bushy eyebrows and serious face. He was a respected minister and, at fifty-five, he was a handsome, virile man with a stocky build and a warm, social personality.

"Yes. Moral dilemmas. She was in turmoil mentally and feeling a terrible amount of guilt. She told me she'd recently fallen into a relationship with her ex-husband."

"Relationship? What do you mean, relationship?"

"She told me they were having an affair and that she wanted desperately to break it off. She was very remorseful. I don't think in all my years in the ministry I've seen anyone who felt more compromised and conflicted. I'd always known her to be a very strong lady, but she broke down in tears in my office, and she was in really bad shape when she left. I tried to help her. I gave her all the encouragement I could. Mostly what was bothering her was how she'd betrayed you . . . and her principles. She was really bad off, very depressed." He stopped and paused again and took a deep breath. "I would have her go to her grave with my keeping this confidence if I thought it would be best for her and for you, but I think there may be talk behind the scenes as time goes on. I'm not sure of that, but I know questions will be asked as they attempt to find out if this is a suicide or homicide. I've already gotten a call from some detectives who wanted to set up an appointment with me, but I told them it'll have to wait until I get Easter over with. I didn't want you to hear about this from anyone else except me, because I love you and your family."

Dr. Kotler reached over and embraced Stefan in what felt like a bear hug from a daddy. The hug at once weakened him and strengthened him. He hadn't realized how much he needed physical warmth from another human being. But, ah, what hurtful words were those from Dr. Kotler. Hurt kept getting added to hurt, pain to pain, insult to tragedy. How much more pain could a broken heart take? Still, Dr. Kotler was not just a minister. He was also a scholarly and erudite man who'd taught at some leading academic institutions. So Stefan wanted to hear what he knew and what he thought. Getting some insight into her state of mind might not help, but it couldn't make reality worse.

"I just can't believe that. I mean, I know it must be true if you tell me so. But . . . we had a happy marriage, I . . . I don't know why. I mean, I don't know why she had an affair, and with him, of all people. You know, her moral consistency always meant so much to her. I just can't see her throwing that away."

He nodded his head vigorously. "Yes, I know. She was in deep despair when she talked to me. She felt flawed and defective. She kept talking about not wanting to be a hypocrite. She was fully aware of how little sense it made, and she was miserable. I think she felt like a failure at her core."

"So why'd she do it? Why'd she abandon all the moral principles that glued her together?"

"I don't know. If I knew the answer to that, I probably wouldn't be a minister, I'd be God. I wish I had an answer for you. As a pastor I've watched people over the years follow a momentary stimulation— I've watched them become blinded by something and totally lose perspective. I've watched some people become blinded by anger and make a decision that ruins their whole life. I've watched other people become blinded by love, and lose perspective on everything they value. Sometimes it's not even love, it's lust that blinds them. The blinding usually takes place when they're in a weak situation. Maybe they're feeling old, or middle-aged, or very young. Sometimes there's pain, or unresolved anger, or some deep hurt from the past that they haven't dealt with. And whatever comes along to blind them may not heal the hurt or ease the trauma from the past, but it dulls the pain for a while. You know, the daily grind wears most of us down, and it wears our resistance down, too. We all yearn, at least a little, for the stimulations of earlier times. We want to feel alive. We want intimacy and passion. We want to feel loved and attractive and heroic and vital, and that yearning creates a vulnerability. Usually there's something inside us that needs to be dealt with but, instead of changing the thing inside, we change something outside because it's easier. We can feel like a new person by doing that, and we want to feel renewed."

"Why Marcos? And when did this happen? I don't know of any time when they were together."

"I think she said she was on a buying trip in New York."

"Oh, I see," Stefan said, nodding. "In January, when she went to New York." He paused. "So that's why she was so despondent for the last few months." Stefan's voice was flat and unemotional. He stared into the vacant lot. When he spoke again, his voice had a cynical tone. "That's great. I took her on a second honeymoon to Jamaica to help her get over her affair with her ex-husband. Great."

Kotler sighed and continued. "I know this hurts you. I guess there were loose ends, maybe unresolved issues, between them, even after all those years. Anyway, an opportunity presented itself when she went on a business trip, and they had an encounter. I honestly believe she was trying to break it off, but she couldn't undo the sin, she kept telling me. And when she faced up to what she'd done—to you, to the children, to herself—she felt repugnant. She was very distressed when she left my office."

"I don't think she'd kill herself, though, Dr. Kotler, do you? You knew her for eight years. Can you see Kathryn killing herself with cocaine and letting herself be found in a car like she was? She wouldn't have done that to the children." Stefan shook his head. "I won't accept suicide as the cause of her death."

"No, I don't think so myself," Dr. Kotler replied tentatively. "But she *was* very depressed when she talked with me."

There was a touch of bitterness and anger in Stefan's voice when he spoke. "So what does this say about morality and the power of Christianity when people like Kathryn can't be counted on? I mean, I thought her Christianity was pretty solid. And I know she felt strongly about not being a hypocrite."

"Well, I think it certainly says that the power of sin and evil is very strong. You know, the Bible is a book of truth and wisdom, and what it says is that the devil is prowling around in the world like a lion, trying to devour us. And nothing makes a better meal than a person who seems to have a solid faith and moral system. It also says that 'bad company ruins good morals.' I don't know how it happened exactly, Stefan, but it's easy for anyone to sin when temptation, weakness, and opportunity intersect. That's what happened. A strong temptation overcame her at the same time she was weak and when opportunity presented itself. And she suffered bitterly for it. Believe me, she paid a heavy price for what she did, in terms of the guilt and remorse she suffered."

"But can't people avoid temptation? It's a choice you make, isn't it?"

Dr. Kotler shrugged. "A lot of times it takes more than our personal resources to resist temptation. We try to do it all ourselves when what we should do is turn to God and put the matter in his hands. But no, Stefan, no one can avoid temptation totally. No one. Not even ministers. And I feel a little responsible myself, I must admit."

"You, responsible? Why?"

"Oh, I'm getting near the end of a long career in ministry, so I'm in a reflective mode in my life. I worry that the 'good news' of Christianity—the love of God, the forgiveness of sins, all that good news—has become a drug for people. They come to Christianity, and to most religions, for the blessings, sometimes even for the emotional high they get, but we're not training them sufficiently in the tools and techniques of their faith. We ministers are like anyone else, I guess. We like to talk about the good news, but we might be failing to teach people that, even though God will forgive their sins if they're repentant, they may not forgive themselves, and their fellow men will almost never forgive them. I don't think Kathryn meant to cheat on you. I think the temptation was strong, and she tried to overcome the temptation on her own rather than relying on the power of God through prayer. That's what we mean by taking our burdens to God and leaving them with him. But we try to do it all ourselves, when we're only weak and defective creatures who, in moments of weakness, won't be able to resist temptation on our own. We can get connected to God's power through prayer, and that's what Jesus said we should do, is draw near to God in prayer in times of heavy temptation and grief. He says in Matthew, 'Come to me, all who labor under heavy burdens, and I will give you rest.'" Dr. Kotler's face was lighting up as he spoke. "Can you feel the power of that? That's the invitation to pull close to God in prayer. But we try to face our greatest temptations alone and we fail ourselves, and the sins we sin do destroy us, just like the Scriptures say. I know we haven't done a good job in this century of teaching people how to maintain the discipline of the Christian life." He paused and sounded wistful when he spoke again. "We pay a price for everything we do. There really isn't any cheap grace, or cheap forgiveness, and I'm not sure we're getting that point across. I guess the church needs to do what the health care industry is doing—spend more time on prevention rather than waiting for sin to happen and then curing it. We need to let folks know that you really do reap what you sow, even though divine forgiveness is possible."

"I still don't believe Kathryn killed herself; there's just no way I'm going to believe that. She wouldn't have done that to the children. I'm absolutely positive. She wouldn't have abandoned them and taken her life in a way that disgraced and shamed them." Stefan sounded agitated and seemed to be talking to himself as much as to Dr. Kotler, as he stood at the back fence and looked out into the lot behind their house.

"Stefan, I wasn't implying that I thought she took her own life. That's hard for me to believe, too, although I'd have to say that, when I look back on it, she might have been borderline suicidal when she last talked to me. But what I'm seeing in her death is how wimpy the church is, and what a poor defense against sin the good news by itself is. We have to help Christians mature in their faith and become skilled in using tools like prayer to defend themselves against temptations. Because the temptations can destroy even the best of us. We're all vulnerable."

Pain and turmoil were etched on Stefan's face as he placed his hands on the fence and stared in silence into the undeveloped property next to the fence. All of a sudden he felt two arms around his waist and, jostled, he looked down to see the swollen eyes of his littlest child, Booth. Stefan turned his body to return the hug.

"I'm tired, Daddy," his six-year-old said.

"I know, son. I'll come in and help you get your bath."

It was lucky he and Kathryn had built four bedrooms upstairs and the master bedroom down, Stefan thought to himself as he took his boy's hand. That plan would now grant them some privacy from the mass of people who'd come to pay their respects. The children, especially Booth, needed to be able to get away from the pressing crowd. Assembled neighbors and friends let him pass quickly when he said he needed to get Booth upstairs to the bathroom.

After he helped Booth get a change of clothes from his drawers, he stayed with him as the boy undressed in the bathroom he shared with two brothers. Then the little tyke climbed into the warm bath Stefan had drawn. There was a quick knock, and then the door of the bathroom was pushed open abruptly.

"Oh, there you are, I was wondering how I could help you. Let me give Booth his bath and you go downstairs to your guests, Stefan," a woman's voice commanded.

Normally Stefan was able to dismiss the pushiness of his mother-in-law. In fact, he'd encouraged Kathryn to just let go of the anger and friction produced by her parents' domineering mannerisms. Although he'd counseled Kathryn to be tolerant of their pushiness because they were her parents, privately he'd come to dislike them. He'd watched their cunning, contemptuous, and meddlesome style of dealing with her, and it never made sense to him. There was Kathryn, the more accomplished of their two daughters, yet she was the one they picked on continually and belittled emotionally. What angered them, he thought, was their inability to control Kathryn. They'd brought her up to be their "good little girl," and they thought she should do anything her parents wanted her to do and think whatever they wanted her to think. In their minds, they seemed to have some permanent, privileged ability to require her to do their will. Stefan had watched as they'd tried to brand her as a family traitor for not taking an aggressive role in working out the details of Sally's divorce settlements. In the on-again, off-again relationship they had with Kathryn, they'd give her the cold shoulder and the silent treatment intermittently until they decided they wanted to see the grandchildren again. They were hot and cold, back and forth, up and down, never in any pattern except a capricious one. Always picking fights with her over one thing or another, they'd snub her one week and then shower presents on the children the next week, creating something new for her to feel grateful for and guilty about. The reality is that they never gave her anything that they didn't throw in her face and expect her to be in debt to them for in some way. Kathryn never seemed to be able to do enough to please them, enough to stay in their good graces, enough to receive their blessing and love. As Kathryn grew into a competent and self-confident career woman, her parents resented her independence from them, and her mother seemed jealous and resentful of her happiness in life, even of her happy marriage. Always comparing the two daughters, it seemed to stick in Vera's craw that Kathryn had a happy life with four children and a husband while Sally bounced from one marriage to another. Nevertheless, Stefan had counseled Kathryn to ignore their insults, and he'd overlooked their discourtesies and unkindnesses to him, too. In the years that followed their marriage, his in-laws had been condescending and critical of him and had taken every opportunity to ridicule him for working in a ladies' fashion boutique. That hadn't endeared them to him, but he had the type of personality that could shrug it off, and he'd advised Kathryn to do the same. He knew they were just country people, hillbillies actually, and he could dismiss their rudeness as ignorance and lack of manners.

Now that Kathryn was not around, though, Stefan could see he'd have to take a more aggressive posture toward his pushy in-laws. He wouldn't tolerate them trying to control his actions or meddle with the children. Now that he was on the front line instead of being a sideline coach, he saw the position Kathryn had been in. She'd been the family bouncer. Now he'd have to assume that job.

"Please get out of here, Mrs. Faison," he said, without any attempt to disguise his displeasure at her barging into the bathroom and interrupting his private time with his son.

"Oh, of course, dear," she said, surprised. "I just thought I'd do you a favor and help you out. You must get down to your guests, you know. They came over here to see you. Don't you think you should mingle for a while?"

"Mrs. Faison, I'm going to come downstairs in just a few minutes and ask you and the other guests to go home so that I can be with my children. Now, please, leave the bathroom so that I can bathe my son. Thank you."

After she closed the door behind her, Stefan felt good about his firm style with her. Kathryn would approve. The last thing she would want on the day of her death was her mother taking over everything in her house. There was a knock on the bathroom door and then he heard her voice again, although she did not enter the bathroom.

"Stefan, Veronica wants to go home and spend the night with her grandfather and me tonight, is that okay?"

Stefan jumped up off the floor where he was sitting next to the tub and opened the door quickly. Outside the bathroom door he saw his daughter with her arm around her grandmother's waist and the grandmother's arm around her shoulder.

"No, it is *not* alright for Veronica to spend the night with you tonight, Mrs. Faison. She needs to stay home with her family, and we need her here with us. Now, if you want to do something useful, you can take Veronica into her room and help her find her bed clothes." He looked at Veronica. "I'll see you in a minute, honey. I just need to help Booth out of the bath and let the guests know we want to be alone as a family."

He'd never spoken to Vera like that before. Like a human shock absorber, Kathryn had absorbed the full brunt of Vera's arrogance and bossiness while he sat on the bench. Now it would be his job to protect the children from attempts to drive a wedge between the four of them and him. Kathryn's loyalty to him personally had been the thing that had finally driven her away from her parents for good. It irritated her that they were patronizing and demeaning toward him. Kathryn used to tell him that they mistook his kindness for weakness, and that's why they treated him like he was a wimp. Now he wouldn't be able to stand by and let them push him around, and he wouldn't let them come and fetch the children anytime they wished in the guise of doing him a favor. Kathryn hadn't been on good terms with her parents for months when she died, but that wasn't unusual. Their relationship frequently went through long periods of silence during which even more petulance, anger, resentment, and hostility seemed to breed. Vera and Miles always broke the silence at some point and called, because they wanted to see the grandchildren, but their hostility toward Kathryn seemed to be heightened each time they called because of their perception that Kathryn was controlling their relationship with their grandchildren. Actually, Kathryn hadn't been trying to control anything. A busy wife, mother, and professional woman, she had her hands full every day, and catering to the whims of relatives had become less and less of a priority with her. Kathryn had tried her whole life to get the relationship with them "right." She'd never been able to, though, no matter how hard she tried. Manipulation was a way of life with Vera, and she coldly and deliberately set up a family system in which Kathryn could never manage to earn their affection. In the last year or so, though, and probably because of Kathryn's deep spirituality, Stefan had noticed a change in his wife.

Kathryn seemed to have outgrown the necessity to earn their love and win their approval. And they didn't like her refusal to play their power-and-control games anymore. In their eyes, she was an ingrate and a family traitor.

As he dressed Booth, he knew what he had to do with the Faisons. The less relationship he had with them, the better, he knew that. But, tonight, he didn't need to be thinking about them. He had four children who had lost their mother and who would be needing all the love and sympathy he could give them.

After he dressed Booth and escorted him into his room, he went downstairs. He whispered into the ears of Dr. Kotler and a few of his wife's women friends that he would appreciate their easing everyone out so he could be alone with the children. He knew they'd handle it tastefully and tactfully. Most of the guests left within twenty minutes after learning that Stefan felt the children needed to be alone with him. Only two ladies from Kathryn's church circle remained downstairs, and they stayed to answer the phone and door so Stefan's quiet time with his children would not be disturbed.

"Dad, did Mom kill herself?" Calvin asked when the five of them gathered in Booth's room as the guests were departing.

"Son, I don't think so, but the detectives are investigating. We don't need to think about that right now. All we can do now is wonder about it, and that might make us feel worse. I don't think she did. But I know that what she'd want us to do now is to think about helping each other and try to love each other."

"But I'm going to miss her," wailed Veronica with a piercing, agonizing cry that seemed to originate from the deepest part of her. As she began to bawl, she crawled over to where Stefan was stretched out on the plush carpet near Booth's bed. David was sitting near them Indian style while both Calvin and Booth were stretched out on Booth's bed.

"I know, honey," he said, suddenly recalling how Kathryn and Veronica used to give each other a "high five" and say, "Two girls!" when they were celebrating some momentary triumph over the four males with whom they shared a residence. Yes, that little girl would miss her mother.

"Who's going to take me to school?" whined Booth.

"I will, don't worry," Stefan said. "And don't forget, David can get his driver's license on his birthday, so he can help me with the driving."

"Dad, I don't understand why she was in a car on that dirt road near the hunting lodge. Mom never went there. I don't get it." There was restrained despair in David's tense voice as he expressed his disbelief.

"Does a person go to heaven if she commits suicide?" It was Calvin's voice. A straight-A student, he was a thoughtful child who always could be counted on to approach any problem with an intelligent question.

Stefan took a deep breath before responding. He was getting outside his comfort zone when it came to talking about anything in the afterlife. "Son, I think good people like your mother always go to heaven to live with God when they die. So we can feel good, knowing that she's with God right now."

David cut in quickly, sounding as though he was lashing out at them all. "I don't believe for one minute that Mom killed herself. She wouldn't have done that to us. She wouldn't have left us alone." A laid-back child with a mellow temperament, he sounded unusually angry and defensive.

"I agree with you, son," Stefan responded, smiling at his oldest boy. David had grown up into a handsome young gentleman, and his mother had loved him very much. When he looked at his eldest boy, he could see the resemblance to Marcos.

There was a gentle knock on the door, and Victoria, the kind, elderly Christian lady with the British accent who'd been in Kathryn's church circle, popped her bespectacled, smiling face inside the room. Although she and Kathryn were three decades apart in age, they'd developed great affection and respect for each other. Kathryn would have approved of Victoria's being in the house on the evening of her death. Victoria was a person of quiet refinement and simple elegance. You could tell she wasn't a person who had grown up around great wealth, but she lived the principles and values that Kathryn believed in. Victoria was a lady.

"Stefan, I'm sorry to be a bother, but there's a gentleman downstairs who insists that he talk with you now."

"Oh, okay, Victoria, I'll be right down," he replied. "Hey, why don't you two big guys take your bath and get all that stuff done while I'm downstairs. Then we'll play some Crazy Eights or watch a movie or something to take our mind off things. Tomorrow is Easter Sunday, you know."

"Do we have to go to church?" asked Veronica and Booth in chorus. Life or death, rain or shine, cold or hot, they could always be counted on to ask that question every Saturday night, even though they knew that, without fail, Kathryn would be taking them to Sunday school. Not tomorrow, though.

Stefan felt he was operating outside space and time as he walked the fifteen or so carpeted steps that led down from the second floor to the foyer of their house. Was it really Easter Sunday tomorrow? The kids' spring break had begun on Good Friday, and they'd be out of school the whole next week. Good. They wouldn't have to miss any school. And they wouldn't have to face their friends until they had some time to grieve and begin healing.

"Just a few messages for you, Stefan, before you sit down with these two gentlemen," Victoria said, as he walked into the family room. He saw the backs of the two detectives staring through the windows of the French doors into the lighted patio. "Mr. Marcos called for David and wants him to call back. He left his number. Several people called from out of town asking when the funeral will be. I wrote their names and numbers down on the pad near the phone. And your mother-in-law called and said she's going ahead with the funeral arrangements for her daughter. She said she knows you're busy and she'll check with you later to finalize the details."

As weary as he felt, he felt a surge of anger at Vera's arrogant usurpation of his privilege of planning his wife's funeral. Typical Vera. Doing him a favor he didn't want. He wanted to think carefully about every detail associated with her funeral service, but he'd see to that in a few minutes. Right now he had to see what the officers wanted.

"Sir," one of them said, as they heard him coming and turned around to extend their hands for a handshake, "you remember us, I think. I'm Detective Sullivan and this is Detective Robbey. We're investigating your wife's death, sir. The body can't be autopsied until Monday, and there's been some speculation about suicide, but we have to pursue this as though it's a regular homicide for now and investigate various angles."

"Well, thank God," Stefan blurted out. "What I mean, Detectives, is that I don't think my wife killed herself. It just wouldn't have been her style. It was against her religious beliefs. And she wouldn't have done that to herself—for one thing, she was too vain to die in a car with drug paraphernalia next to her. And she didn't use drugs, anyway! But, please. Please sit down." The detectives took a seat on the long couch, and Stefan sat on the love seat perpendicular to them. "What do you need from me, Detectives?"

"We'd like to ask you some questions, sir."

The younger detective took out a notepad while the older one asked the questions. "Sir, we just need to ask you a series of questions, all related to finding out more about her in general. Did your wife keep a diary?"

"No," Stefan answered, shaking his head emphatically.

"Can you tell us something about her life recently? Was there anything unusual going on? And can we ask, how had the two of you been getting along lately?"

"Getting along? Why, yes, we get along; I mean, we got along. We had a good marriage. Why are you asking me that?"

"Mr. Haddad, you need to understand that we're going to have to check out every possible angle of a homicide here. We have to determine whether or not someone killed your wife and what her mental state was."

"Are you wondering if I killed my wife? Am I a suspect?"

"Mr. Haddad, please don't take our questions too personally. We need your cooperation if we're going to find your wife's killer, if such a person exists."

Stefan took a deep breath, and looking up at the nine-foot ceiling, he suddenly remembered how he and Kathryn had argued when they built the house over which rooms should have smooth ceilings and which ceilings should be blown in. Eventually he'd won, and all the ceilings in their house had smooth ceilings, even the garage. In the year he'd taken off work to supervise construction, he'd figured out how he could spend very little extra and get formal smooth ceilings everywhere in the house. Reality suddenly intruded as he wondered why he was lost in space thinking about smooth ceilings when there were detectives in the room discussing Kathryn's death.

"I'm sorry, Detectives, I'm here, but I'm feeling like I'm not here. This hasn't really sunk in yet for me."

"I know, sir. We just need to ask you to tell us the names of all the people your wife spent any time with in the last six months. We need to take some notes about her whereabouts and activities so we can make inquiries."

They spent about thirty minutes with Stefan, taking notes on the people and places he told them about. They encouraged him to use her calendar from the previous year and from the current year in relaying information about her goings on. The detectives thanked him and left with extensive notes containing the names of Marcos, Mary, New York retail and fashion acquaintances, and others who fit into Kathryn's life in various ways such as Dr. Kotler and church people. He'd always enjoyed discussing Kathryn with people because he was proud of her. But, as he began to talk about her in past tense, he came closer to the realization that she was in the past, too. She was permanently gone.

"One last question, sir. How did you and your wife feel about the baby?"

"The baby?"

The detective stared at him, studying his demeanor and expression. "Sir, you knew your wife was pregnant, didn't you?"

"Pregnant?"

Sullivan stared into Haddad's eyes. "Didn't you know your wife was three months pregnant, sir?"

"No, I didn't," he said, swallowing hard. "Are you sure?"

"Yes, Mr. Haddad. There was a three-month fetus inside her. They did a brief examination of the body at Mercy Hospital, and that turned up."

Stefan shook his head as he answered. "Well, this is my day for surprises, Detective Sullivan. That comes as news to me. If Kathryn knew, she didn't tell me."

"So you two hadn't planned on another child?"

"No. We have four children already and Kathryn just turned forty-six years old a couple of weeks ago, so we weren't planning on more." He paused. "But I would have been happy about it."

"Do you think she would have been happy about it?"

Stefan looked thoughtful and then smiled slightly as he replied. "She would have adjusted to it, I think. We often talked about having one more after our last baby was born. But we sort of figured we had enough little guys to take care of and pay attention to. We hadn't talked about it in the last couple of years, so it would have been an unplanned pregnancy."

"Well, I think that's all for now, sir. We appreciate your time."

He closed the door behind them, pressed his back and head against the door, and heaved a deep breath. The breathtaking tangerine color of the foyer caught his eye in a new way. Kathryn had been a colorful person, and she'd splashed color gaily throughout their house. Yellow and tangerine on the walls, purple and green and red and brown in the wallpaper, color everywhere. The colors had always looked brilliant and beautiful to him before. But all of a sudden, they seemed like colors going wild and coming at him from every direction. Three months pregnant? So she'd gotten pregnant in January. They certainly hadn't had any unprotected sex, not that he knew about, anyway. And Kathryn had been careful about that. So could she have been carrying Marcos's child? He'd never taken a sleeping pill in his life, but he felt like he'd do anything to get his hands on one right now. How in the hell was he going to keep himself together for the children?

TEN

Her funeral was on the Wednesday after Easter Monday. What an irony that the saddest days in his life and in his children's lives were during the happiest season of the Christian calendar. The days after Jesus' resurrection when Christ reunited with his disciples.

The official autopsy had been performed on Easter Monday, so they hadn't been able to get the body to the funeral home until Tuesday. Stefan had noticed some bruising near her left cheek when the casket was opened in the funeral home. The morticians had camouflaged it well, and it was barely noticeable because her body was positioned with the left side farthest away from viewers, but Stefan had detected the bluish-blackish bruises underneath the makeup.

The church was packed, with people standing outside the eight-hundred-person capacity sanctuary, and her funeral had an especially somber tone. There was never a funeral sadder than one for a mother who left young children, and the church was overflowing with people whose hearts were full of sorrow for the children she left behind. David, Calvin, Veronica, and Booth sat on the front row next to their dad in the church Kathryn had attended faithfully, worked in diligently, and loved so much. She and Dr. Kotler had grown to be good friends, so she would have been pleased with his preaching her funeral service. A refined, experienced Methodist minister who had been on the faculty of Yale Divinity School before taking over the senior minister's job at this one-thousand-member church in the South, Dr. Kotler had an engaging combination of down-to-earth farm-boy charm and city-educated preacher knowledge that Kathryn respected. Stefan knew Dr. Kotler had admired Kathryn's gifts of leadership and creativity and her willingness to use them in church work, especially in teaching and in children's ministries. As Stefan listened to the words, it seemed that Dr. Kotler was having a hard time preaching this particular funeral service.

Stefan tried to listen intently to every word spoken from the pulpit. He knew Dr. Kotler would have intentionally and lovingly crafted this service and would be trying to make it special for the children. But Stefan kept getting distracted, recalling events of the last two days. It had been four days ago that the detectives had come to his house to take some notes about Kathryn's recent activities, and they'd indicated they would be getting in contact with Marcos, Mary, the staff at the Chic Boutique, church friends, people at her grocery store, their insurance agent, her parents, Sally, friends from Harvard Business School, and others.

The crowd at the house after the funeral was a crowd Kathryn would have enjoyed. Since the autopsy had delayed the funeral by at least a couple of days, many of her closest friends and acquaintances from out of town had had enough time to take a day off work and make plane connections. A lot of her best friends were there, and it was interesting to see the people who really cared about her. Her four best girlfriends from high school, including Mary, were there, all from out of town except Mary. Hardly anyone from Kathryn's college days was there. From what he remembered, she had a Christmas card relationship with quite a few college buddies, but they didn't talk by phone or see each other from time to time like she did with friends from Macon High School. There were quite a few friends from the Harvard Business School, and lots of people sent telegrams or flowers. Stefan didn't know how so many of them could have learned of her death so soon. Many of Stefan's friends from his college days at Princeton were there, too—people who'd become their mutual friends in married life. And there were people from the community, and church, and people they knew through business—suppliers, customers, and competitors with whom Kathryn often traded predictions. It was comforting to have them around. Sort of.

Stefan ambled through the living room, dining room, kitchen, and family room, trying to thank people who'd come from long distances and responding to the frequent summons of the doorbell. He realized he was locomoting around the house without any particular destination, as though he were only half there mentally. That's how his whole life felt now. He had no anchor. He was drifting. He'd been catapulted without warning into a totally new life. Single parent of four children. Wow! He felt vacant, numb, empty, as he moved aimlessly through the house, catching bits and pieces of conversation and wandering past friends and acquaintances absorbed in conversation.

It was mostly a forty-something crowd, full of people with common concerns, no matter what part of the country they came from, and there seemed to be something close to a party mood in the house after an hour or so. Old friends were bumping into each other, and many people were meeting each other for the first time. It was a secure place to meet someone, inside the home of a person they'd loved and respected and admired. Joanna, Kathryn's writer friend from New York whom she talked to frequently but hadn't seen in years, was talking with Ned, who lived in Boston, about her aborted writing career and the need to find her "voice." Ned had lost his job with a computer company in New York and relocated to Boston for the third time since he'd graduated from Harvard Business School.

He saw Marcos talking with some investment bankers they'd gone to HBS with. Marcos had stayed in town to attend the funeral, since he'd already made arrangements to spend the week with David before the sad event altered their plans. Perhaps their mutual friends from Harvard Business School accepted his being there as a gracious courtesy and Latin chivalry toward David's family. Most people who knew that Kathryn and Marcos had been married briefly and had a son probably imagined that Marcos had always been a part of their lives. He overheard Marcos chatting about trade sanctions affecting the import-export business. Stefan felt a surge of anger as he observed Marcos laughing and talking with their mutual friends. Suddenly, he realized in a new way that he was a cuckold. Here was the man who had bedded his wife behind his back. If Kathryn had committed suicide, which he still couldn't accept, it had to have been mostly due to her feeling like a moral failure and being pregnant with Marcos's baby. When he looked at Marcos now, he looked at him as an adulterer and as the instrument of her death. Stefan knew he shouldn't make a scene, and that wasn't his style anyway, but if Marcos didn't leave soon, he'd ask him to go. It was surreal having Marcos there, but it was surreal to have Kathryn dead, too. Nothing seemed real. Everything was off. He didn't feel remotely in touch with reality anymore.

Walking in circles around the house, Stefan was glad to have banter and laughter bouncing off the walls. The space would be filled with silence soon enough, and he'd just get lost in the crowd for now. He overheard fragments of conversations in which people were discussing dislocations in their lives that had occurred since Business School graduation. Job losses were the main topic of discussion—and the distress caused by the loss of compensation of one hundred thousand dollars or more. Most of the people he overheard sang the same tune: when they graduated from HBS, they hadn't expected to lose their jobs if they were doing everything right. But that's what had happened, they were telling each other. Stefan overheard Ned telling Joanna that it had happened to him twice.

"That'll change your personality in a hurry," Ned told Joanna. At least Ned, a friend of Stefan's from Princeton, was single with a wealthy mother to fall back on. That was not the case with Turner Palmer, who'd recently lost his second job during the epidemic middle-management massacre. "Downsizing" was the current excuse companies gave with the "pink slip," he was telling his circle of friends. Turner had been accepted at the B-School right after Princeton, as Ned and Stefan had been, an unusual accomplishment since Harvard typically wanted its MBA students to have worked for a couple of years. The theory was that work experience enriched the case study analysis process. He worked as a stockbroker in New York after he got his MBA, and that's when he experienced his first job loss. His long-established company was wracked by charges of security fraud and insider trading, and the company's employees were reduced by

20 percent to adjust to a loss in customer base. He found himself out of work for six months after his first job loss. Finally, he found a job at a Fortune 500 company but at a salary cut of several thousand dollars. By that time, he'd married a fellow broker and they had a small family. Then, when their children were four and two, Turner found himself without a job again. This time his company's story was that it was heavily into defense contracts and, with the military "downsizing," the company was "adjusting to changing market conditions." He was adjusted, too.

"I felt so emasculated and devastated. There's just no loyalty in business anymore," Turner was telling his Business School buddy Matthew, who'd spent ten years climbing the corporate ladder into a comfortable executive position before he decided to quit his job and go the entrepreneurial route by starting a funds management company. Matthew had not been canned from his Fortune 500 company employer; in fact, they'd begged him to stay.

"At first," Stefan heard Matthew saying, "I missed the power, perks, and social life that went with an executive job, but I sure don't miss the travel. I wouldn't trade the flexibility and autonomy I have now as an entrepreneur. What I like most is having more time to spend with my kids. But, you know," Matthew was telling Turner as Stefan walked past them in the crowded dining room that looked and sounded like a cocktail party, "Maslow was right. There are social needs that get satisfied through work."

"Yeah," responded Turner, with a touch of cynicism in his voice, "there are financial needs that get satisfied, too."

"So what was the company's problem when you lost your last job?" Matthew asked Turner.

"It was the same ugly problem rearing its head. Corporate mismanagement plus short-term shareholder greed equals companies with no direction. There are so many companies like that out there, like ships drifting at sea. Even if you're doing a good job, things can change in an instant if there's a takeover, or if majority shareholders decide to squeeze out more productivity through layoffs. They're like ships without a rudder, and they have no economic purpose except to feed the shareholders. And when companies find themselves bought and sold by different corporate parents, there's even less loyalty to a central focus. Profit is the only focus, and the long-term gets sacrificed to the short-term. There's really no job security anymore for the middle manager in the major corporations."

If the Business School crowd has no job security, Stefan thought to himself as he walked past them, patting Matthew's shoulder to acknowledge the presence of his friends, the rest of the working population is in a ton of trouble. Sure, the corporation could look at ten B-Schoolers and think, "Wow, we could get rid of these guys and save a million dollars for the shareholders!" But the corporation would be ridding itself of the experience that is the "pixie dust" of creative opportunity finding. Stefan had a lot of respect for the intellect, creativity, and dedication of these Harvard Business School grads. Even laying creativity and dedication aside, those HBS'ers seemed to work damned hard. When he compared them to the people he'd gone to school with at Princeton, he saw that, while Princeton attracted bright students, the Princetonians were more provincial, less worldly, and less suited to assuming control of the world's major companies than the Harvard Business School crowd. A few of the people he and Kathryn had graduated with had become entangled in financial foul play, and a few had been involved in the greedy feeding frenzy of the savings and loan fiasco, but, overall, the B-School crowd was an almost wholesome group of high achievers who seemed to live by high principles. They certainly were the "best and brightest" people he'd ever known. A Latin teacher he'd had in Montreal in high school told him once that Harvard Business School had a knack for picking top talents. He said it wasn't so much the training they got at HBS but the fact that Harvard had a crystal ball about who was going to make it big.

"They're just ships without a rudder," Turner was repeating, obviously enjoying his metaphor, to the small group of eight standing around him in the dining room, helping themselves to the goodies. The dining table was piled high with food as though they were having a party. Kathryn would have approved. She was always talented at creating a great-looking table of party food. As he helped himself to cheese and crackers, Stefan overheard some outspoken baby boomers discussing their midlife crises. Margaret was telling Kimberly about the three separate entrepreneurial ventures she'd been through. Philip was telling Hall that he and his wife of twenty years had recently separated. Everyone he overheard in the dining room seemed to be surviving a midlife dislocation of some sort.

Without warning, out of nowhere, he felt stung by anger. He suddenly realized that none of these people were discussing Kathryn. It was a pay-your-respects party after her funeral, and no one was mentioning her name! He felt overcome by a feeling of helpless anger that stemmed from his fierce loyalty toward her. Then it dawned on him that what he actually felt was some electric mix of love and hate, sympathy and anger, and what he really wanted to do was to tell Kathryn off, just one last time. Feeling his mind drift into an almost catatonic state, he visualized the scene between him and Kathryn in his mind's eye.

Hi, darling, she would say.

Hi, darling, yourself, he would answer sarcastically.

What's wrong? she would respond, acting surprised at his hostile tone.

What's wrong? Well, let me start with a few things. First of all, congratulations. You did, after all, turn into an adulterer. You turned into the lying and cheating and manipulating person you always swore you'd never become.

Why, whatever do you mean? Kathryn would answer in that Southern accent that had always charmed him.

What do I mean? I mean, you did a real number on me, Kathryn, dear. Here I am, the grieving husband, left here alone with four children and a business that you insisted we buy and do together, in this Southern redneck town where I relocated to marry you and change you from single parent to married woman. That's what I mean, Kathryn. And here's something else. How could you leave in such a tacky way? How could you disgrace your children, and their family name, by dying with drug paraphernalia around you and a cloud of suspicion hanging over the whole scene? And there's one more thing, Kathryn, dear.

And what's that? Kathryn would say, sounding shocked at what he was saying.

How could you go behind my back and have an affair with your ex-husband? How could you make an idiot of me like that? All I ever did was come along in your life when you needed a gentleman, and I made you a wife, and adopted your son, and supported you in everything you ever wanted to do, like buying that chickenshit ladies' clothing store you wanted. I could have done a hell of a lot better with my life than getting stuck in a stupid woman's business, which I don't have any interest in running anyway.

Ah, but Stefan knew what Kathryn would say to that. She'd say just what she always said every time they argued about the shop. She'd open her large eyes and give him one of her intimidating looks, and then she'd say, *Why, I worked hard in that store to make it a success. I'm the one who made the boutique successful and profitable so that you could lead the life of a gentleman in this town. You worked there, but you didn't shoulder the main responsibility. I had to make sure the shop made money at the same time that I was doing everything at home. So I don't think you should complain about what you got out of life!*

Some things never change, Stefan thought. Here we are, in a communication between life and death, still arguing about the same crap.

Don't try to change the focus of what I'm talking about, Kathryn.

What are *you talking about?* she would say in that condescending way she had of communicating that she thought he was talking about trivial and insignificant details that were of no interest to a big shot like her.

I'm talking about the sleazy way you cheated on me with that ex-husband of yours. What in the hell did you ever see in him, anyway? How could you screw me over like that as your last act in life, Kathryn? And how could you do it to yourself? How could you leave the earth with so little dignity? How could you bring to shame everything you tried to stand for, everything you said you believed in? What happened to all those Christian values, to all that morality you claimed to hold so dear? What happened to your view of hypocrisy? You used to tell me there was nothing you hated more than a damned hypocrite. You used to tell me you'd rather be a whore than a Christian hypocrite. What you said you hated was when someone sat on the front pew pretending to live in a state of righteousness with God when she was living like a tramp. Well, Kathryn, it looks like you settled for hypocrisy big time in the end, didn't you? You made a fool out of me, you made an adulterer and hypocrite out of yourself, and you made your children bear up under mockery and shame. You gave your own children a bad reputation, Kathryn. How does that feel, Kathryn?

Her beautiful face disappeared and the scene faded from view as Dr. Kotler put his brawny arm around his shoulder.

"Would you like to go upstairs into your bedroom to talk privately for a few moments, Stefan?" Dr. Kotler seemed to sense his agony.

Actually, he felt more like going to a cockfight or a boxing match. There was so much aggression and anger churning inside him, and there seemed no obvious way to ventilate it.

"Maybe in a few minutes, Dr. Kotler," Stefan replied. "There's something I need to do first, though." Stefan realized as he spoke the words that it wasn't Kathryn he wanted to tell off, it was Marcos. He made his way back to the room where Marcos was talking with friends and tapped him on the shoulder.

"Oh, Stefan, join us, please," Marcos said with a smile, making room for him in the circle of men who were discussing finance and investments.

Stefan smiled back. "I wonder if I could borrow you for just a moment, Marcos."

"Oh, of course," Marcos replied. Marcos followed him upstairs to Veronica's bedroom, where they could talk privately. It was out of the way of the crowd. The master bedroom was full of people talking. As he walked up the stairs, Stefan's thoughts drifted back to the time when he and Kathryn had planned every detail of their gorgeous master bedroom with the sunken Jacuzzi. They'd planned the layout so that they'd have a suite downstairs that included bedroom, family room, and kitchen for the time in their future when the kids would all be off at college and they'd be alone in the house. So much for planning out the rest of one's life. He and Kathryn had lived in that suite at night after the kids went to bed. Kathryn would stay in the bedroom reading or watching the public broadcasting station while he would remain in the family room watching sports. They had been an odd couple. Before they married, he'd been a carefree bachelor in a casual job as a commodity broker, which he'd taken mostly to make sure he got his green card since he was a Canadian citizen residing in the U.S. She'd been a single parent of a two-and-a-half-year-old boy and a college teacher when they renewed their friendship after HBS. After they began dating steadily, she'd pressed him to get married. He hadn't particularly wanted to rush into anything in life. His laid-back personality would have been content to wait a lot longer. In terms of their interests, they didn't have many in common when they married. He loved sports. She was ignorant of sports, although she never complained about his passion for watching television sports. It was only over the course of their marriage that they began to acquire common interests—their kids, primarily. But what they seemed to have in common all along, though, were their values. They both held to traditional family values. Or at least he thought they both did, until he learned from Dr. Kotler a few days ago that she was going to bed with her ex-husband behind his back.

"What's up?" Marcos asked, as the two men eyed each other standing together near the front window in the upstairs bedroom.

"I'm not comfortable with your being here any longer, Marcos."

"Oh?"

"I know about you and Kathryn," Stefan stated flatly, as he stared at Marcos. "I think you have a nerve acting like a family friend when you were going to bed with my wife behind my back."

Marcos looked stunned. "I see," he sighed. "Yes. It wasn't what you think, though."

"It wasn't? She was three months pregnant. Did you know that? That sounds like a New York baby to me."

"Yes, I know," he replied morosely, looking Stefan in the eyes and then staring out the window. "She told me she thought she was pregnant when she brought David to see me Saturday morning. I walked her out to the car after she brought David to my room, and she told me. She seemed quite upset. It wasn't supposed to happen this way, Stefan. It was an accident."

"An accident? My four children don't have a mother anymore, and you're talking about an accident?" Stefan shook his head. "I'm down to the no-bullshit level in my life now, Marcos. You and I aren't going to be friends. Don't think we are. As far as I'm concerned, you killed my wife. You broke up my family and destroyed my happiness. I don't want you in my house." He paused. "Where was Kathryn going after she saw you?"

"Shopping, I think."

"You need to leave my house. I'm filled with grief, and seeing you makes it worse. I don't want you here. I'm sorry."

"Okay, I'll leave. I understand," Marcos said, walking toward the door. He turned around to face Stefan as he put his hand on the door knob. "But we are in each other's lives, Stefan. We share a son, you know. And I love David very much. He's my only son, and I'm going to make it up to him for the years we weren't together during his childhood."

"What are you talking about?" Stefan replied, clearly emotional. "I want you out of my life, that's what I'm telling you."

Marcos cleared his throat. "I don't want to add to your grief, Stefan, but I'm not going to get out of David's life. Now that his mother is gone, he needs his father more than ever."

"I'm his father."

"I'm his father, too."

As the two men glared at each other, there was a knock at the door.

"Come in," Stefan replied, expecting to see his daughter's face.

"Oh, I'm sorry to bother you," Dr. Kotler said, as he pushed the door open gently. "I thought you said to meet you upstairs."

"Yes, yes, I did," Stefan answered.

"I was just leaving," Marcos said, shaking Dr. Kotler's hand on his way out. "It was very nice to meet you, sir."

Feeling mentally drained and emotionally exhausted, Stefan sat down on the bed and Dr. Kotler sat in the rocking chair that Kathryn used to sit in when she rocked their babies to sleep.

"We can say a prayer together, Stefan, if you want to. Let's do that. I know you're hurting."

"Dr. Kotler, I don't know what to pray. Instead of grieving over a faithful and loving wife tonight, I'm beginning to face the reality that

I've been left by a woman who betrayed me and her own children and who left us in the middle of a scandal in this small Southern town." He paused. Dr. Kotler could hear the anger and confusion and tension in his voice. "I don't know what to pray."

"Let's pray for forgiveness."

"Forgiveness?"

"Yes, let's pray that God will open a door for you so that you can find a way to forgive the wrongs that have been done to you."

Stefan bowed his head, more in despair than in hope, more in desperation and futility and dejection than in praise or worship.

"Father," Dr. Kotler began, "take this heart so tender and keep it from bitterness. May the Holy Spirit minister to this soul, so that the healing that can come only from forgiveness will take place. May the spirit of peace and love descend upon this family, so bereaved without their mother and wife, and may the loving arms of the Father enfold these helpless mortals in their sorrow and in their hour of greatest need. In the name of Jesus we pray. Amen."

Stefan looked up dumbly, to signal his recognition that the prayer was ended. There was a thick silence in the room. Neither of them spoke for a few moments. Stefan had never felt so depressed as he did at that moment.

"Does everyone know?"

"Does everyone know?" Dr. Kotler echoed kindly and gently, without a trace of judgment. He sighed a deep sigh before answering. "Do you mean, does everyone know about Kathryn's infidelity? No. I think she only told me and her best friend Mary. You know, Stefan, Kathryn was a wonderful woman and a truly special wife and mother. It isn't fair that she should somehow be showcased in the darkest hour of her life and breathe her last breath in a silhouette that makes her appear less than what she was. But, you know, that's the work of the devil."

"Is that the devil with the red tail?" Dr. Kotler looked surprised at his contemptuous response, but he also seemed appreciative of his candor.

Dr. Kotler smiled a wise-looking smile. "That's one of the problems with this world, Stefan. You can't tell who the bad guys are from the way they look. And I've never seen a devil with a red tail. But I do know there's no playing with sin in this world. The devil is really out there, prowling around like a lion, like the Scriptures say, ready to devour us. And I think that's what happened to Kathryn. She got caught and devoured. We still don't know all the details, but somehow the forces of evil were at work here, ensnaring her, and using her own weaknesses to entrap her."

"I'm sorry, I didn't mean to be rude to you a moment ago. But tell me, why a prayer for forgiveness?"

"Because, Stefan, that devil is still at work, trying to weaken you by preying on your pride and anger. He'll try to turn your righteous pride and anger into hatred and bitterness and, if that happens, that hatred and bitterness will destroy you and your family. It will eat you up like a cancer and break your family apart from the inside. The only thing that can free you is forgiveness. But it's beyond your power personally to get to that level of forgiveness by yourself. You have to turn to God in your grief and despair and ask him to give you the strength to forgive whatever you may ultimately need to forgive. We're all human, all in need of forgiveness, and we have to see forgiveness as freeing. Forgiveness frees us to love and to let go of all the hurt and pain that try to enslave us as memories."

"I can't focus on anything that's going on right now, Dr. Kotler, much less on forgiveness. I'm sorry. I feel too weak and empty."

"But that's just when anger and bitterness take hold, when you're at your weakest moment. That's when many of us make our worst decisions in life, right after some misfortune occurs. We often have to make critical decisions when we're in our weakest condition. That's what I think happened to Kathryn, too. She wasn't really having an affair as much as a tumultuous inner conflict. Good was battling evil, right was waging war with wrong, and she was completely powerless to fight it off by herself."

"Powerless?" Stefan's voice was angry and intense. "Isn't that what Christianity is supposed to do? To give people the power to resist temptation? You know, Dr. Kotler, I never went to church as a child. I began going to church as an adult when Kathryn took the kids, and I started to join them for the eleven o'clock service. But I thought that's what going to church was supposed to do, to strengthen you so you know the difference between right and wrong and can make moral choices."

"That's partly true, but a higher truth is that only by turning to God in our weakest moment can we receive the power to resist the evil. We can't do it on our own power. Remember that miracle that Jesus performed in the ninth chapter of Mark? Jesus had given his disciples power to heal, and they tried in vain to heal a boy possessed by a demon. Anyway, the disciples finally brought him to Jesus and he cured the boy, and then they asked him how he'd been able to heal him. Jesus simply told them, 'The only thing that works in a case like this is prayer.' You know, Stefan, prayer is our lifeline to God, to the source of our strength and life, but we try to handle the toughest situations in life on our own strength, and we alone are just no match for the forces of evil and destruction. I think it's very sad what happened to Kathryn, because I think she was sincerely battling evil and wanted with all her being to do the right thing. She just couldn't do it by herself."

"Dr. Kotler, I have to be honest and tell you that I resent her leaving us this way. I'll tell you something you don't know, but please don't tell anyone else. Kathryn was three months pregnant. And I don't think there's any way it was our child. So maybe she did commit suicide. All I know is that the children are pitiful without a mother, and on top of that, they'll have to put up with a lot of gossip about her reputation. And their family name will always be tarnished."

"Don't be too hard on her right now, Stefan. We don't know anything except that a tragedy occurred. Random violence is a distinct possibility. I heard on television that the sheriff's department is evaluating whether or not this could be a copycat killing like the ones in Texas and California last month. Remember when those young mothers were abducted as they were leaving shopping malls and then forced into their cars and injected with enough cocaine to kill a horse? They haven't caught that killer yet, and it may be that serial killer. Perhaps you're thinking too selfishly at the moment. You're tortured by how other people will think about you and the children because of the way she died, and that's too much for you to speculate about. You know,

Stefan, I'm in the middle of my sixth decade in life, and one thing I've learned is that the things you spend your life worrying about rarely happen. Something else happens. It's like the Bible says, 'Don't spend your time worrying about what trouble might happen tomorrow. Let the day's own trouble be sufficient for the day.' You'll have no peace or rest if you allow your mind to get lost worrying about tomorrow's idle talk." He smiled knowingly. "Most people are selfish and would rather spend their time talking about themselves, anyway."

"Dr. Kotler, I appreciate your love and concern for our family. I'm so stressed out right now, I don't know what to think. I want to be there for my kids, but I don't have much to give them right now. I feel lost and alone and afraid, and I know I'll just communicate that if I'm alone with them."

"I'll tell you what. I can have my wife stay with you tonight, if you wish, to help with the children. She can read them stories while you rest and get some sleep. I know you have to deal with policemen and insurance people tomorrow, so we can help you get a good night's sleep."

His offer seemed like the best thing, and he'd have a way of resisting his pushy mother-in-law who would no doubt be manipulating to get the children over to her house. He really didn't have the physical or mental resources to do battle with that woman tonight. He'd go down and make sure he spoke to all the people who'd come from out of town for the funeral, and he'd try to handle his social obligations as well as he could, given his physically weary and mentally worn-out state. Then he'd let Dr. and Mrs. Kotler take over for the evening, and he'd try to sleep.

ELEVEN

A sleeping pill provided by a doctor who lived in the neighborhood put Stefan to sleep quickly on the extra bed in Booth's room on the night of the funeral. Mrs. Kotler attended to the children, and some ladies from Kathryn's circle looked after the lingering guests, mostly out-of-towners staying at nearby hotels, and cleaned up the downstairs after they left. As he fell asleep under the influence of heavy sedation, all their faces seemed to blur together when he tried to remember who'd been at the funeral and who came to the house afterwards.

Stefan woke at seven-thirty, feeling groggy, and went downstairs to the breakfast nook. Before he went downstairs, he looked in on all the children sleeping in their beds. It was good to know he wasn't alone in that big house, but it still felt empty and quiet. There was no coffee brewing as there normally was. Kathryn used to get the coffee ready the night before so she could just click it on when she got up, and it had always been there when he awoke. On a normal Thursday, Kathryn would already have seen the kids onto their school buses and left with Booth to drop him at his classroom. She liked taking the children to school when they were in kindergarten and first grade. She said it gave her a chance to see the teacher every day and catch a problem early if one was brewing.

He sat down at the kitchen nook. How she had loved that bay

window. That had been the main architectural feature she'd wanted in the new house. There was also a bay window in the bathroom near the sunken Jacuzzi, but the exaggerated bay window in the elongated kitchen nook contained the rug, table, and chairs that constituted their informal dining room, study hall, and all-purpose hangout. It was where the children did homework and where Kathryn used to read the newspaper, write thank-you letters, and cut coupons. There he was, sitting in her favorite place in the house, a place where she'd never again sit. It felt as though she'd been ripped from him. If he could just have her back now, he'd forgive her for everything. Life had taught him that things aren't always what they seem, so maybe there was something he hadn't considered. As he read the directions for making coffee, he realized how much he would miss her. He was a total klutz in the kitchen and had generally been slack about helping around the house. At least his oldest son, who was a Boy Scout, could make soup and cookies and hot dogs. He could see a lot of cookies and soup and hot dogs in their future.

Staring out the window listening to the birds chirp, he realized in a new way that his and Kathryn's relationship had bloomed in the last year or so. After they'd been married a few years, it had dawned on him what a smart and talented woman he was married to. A friend of his father had told him once that big breasts are nice and shapely legs are exciting, but what a man really wants ultimately is the company of an intelligent woman. And Stefan had found that to be true in his relationship with Kathryn. Long after other women would have bored him, Kathryn kept him interested and guessing with her business savvy, ambition, drive, zest for life, and zany sense of humor. She had excelled as a wife in every way. Sure, their married life had been rough-and-tumble during the childbearing years when they were also building the business. But things had become easier in the last few years: more money, more time, more in common, more patience between them, and more love and understanding.

His life now would be like starting over, with a broken heart and four kids to raise by himself in a Southern redneck town surrounded by meddlesome in-laws. Ah, in the bright sunshine of the morning, it didn't much seem to matter why she was dead, or how she died. The fact that she was gone for good and never coming back was all that mattered. He'd just poured his first cup of coffee when he heard the doorbell ring. Who could it be at this early hour?

"Mr. Haddad?" said one of the detectives, as Stefan opened the door to find the same two law enforcement officers on his front porch.

"Yes, Detective Sullivan," he said. "Hello, Detective Robbey."

"Sir, we'd like to come in, if you don't mind," replied Detective Sullivan, with proper Southern courtesy.

Stefan showed them into the kitchen nook area.

"Coffee?"

"Yes, sir, if you don't mind," Sullivan replied. He prepared their coffee as they requested and brought it to the table and sat down next to them.

"Nice house, sir," Robbey said.

"Thanks," Stefan said, forcing a smile. "We built it together, Kathryn and me. We were going to get old together in this house." His smile faded as he added, "Plans don't always work out."

"Sir, we know this is a terrible time for you," Sullivan began, "but we need to ask you a few questions, and we apologize in advance for invading your privacy."

"Go ahead, Detective." Stefan felt numb. The ordeal continued.

"Sir, we'd like to ask you what time your wife left the house on the morning of her death."

"She left early, about four-thirty or a little before, I think. I was still in bed. The main reason for leaving so early was to drop David off at the Marriott near the mall so he could go hunting with his other dad." He paused and looked Sullivan in the eyes. "Kathryn was married briefly before, and her ex-husband was in town to take our son hunting. She said since she was going so early, she'd catch the Easter early-bird specials at the mall, which began at five o'clock, I think."

"Okay, sir. So she left the house at four-thirty on Saturday. Then when did you miss her?"

"Miss her? I never missed her. You came to my house that after-noon and told me you thought you'd found her, didn't you?"

"Sir, we need you to remember anything you can about that morn-ing. Until the medical examiner publishes the official autopsy, we have to work on the assumption that this is a regular homicide, and we have to suspect foul play."

"What do you mean?" Stefan interrupted.

"It's just routine stuff at this point, sir. Right now we need you to remember the details as specifically as you can. When she left, where she was going, what state she was in. Try to remember as precisely as you can."

"I think I've told you everything, Detective. I remember her leaving early in the morning to go to the mall." Stefan shrugged his shoulders, frustrated that he couldn't supply more details. "I'm sorry. I took a sleeping pill last night, and I still feel a little groggy."

"Try to remember as best you can. Did she seem distracted or preoccupied or worried about anything?"

"No, not really," he said, shaking his head.

"What does that mean?"

Stefan sighed. "We'd attended her sister's wedding the night before, so it had been a pretty emotional weekend for her. She was a little upset the night before, but it wasn't anything except jangled nerves." Then Stefan changed the subject, and this time he asked the question. "Why don't you already have the autopsy results, anyway? It was performed on Monday, wasn't it?"

"Yes, it was. Maybe there's something the experts are disagreeing about. That's usually what it is when the autopsy results are held up like this." Then Sullivan changed the subject. "Sir, we have to ask you something else, too. We've learned that you purchased a key-person insurance policy on your wife about two years ago. And there's a two-million-dollar payoff in the event of her death."

"Yes. That's true," Stefan replied, looking surprised. "We bought that policy at my wife's suggestion. Kathryn was a few years older than I am and she wanted to make sure that, if one of us died, the other one would be able to pay off the house and put the kids through college. One of her friends in the insurance industry strongly recommended it, and we trust her advice, so we contacted our local agent and arranged it. It's a standard policy in business when there might be a substantial loss of income if one partner dies. Without Kathryn buying for the business, we figured we'd have no business. She was a valid insurable interest and our underwriter was satisfied that, given our business volume and her talent for buying, two million dollars was appropriate as insurance payable upon her death."

"There is a two-year contestability period, according to your agent, when the insurance company can reexamine the application," Sullivan said flatly.

"Yes, I know that, but what are you getting at?"

"Your insurance agent will be talking to you about it, but he gave me to understand that they're checking on the purchase date details of the policy. If the insured commits suicide within the two-year period, the policy won't pay. Or if the insured dies suspiciously within two years of the purchase date, the company can conduct its own investigation and make sure the deceased had no known health problems, including alcohol or drug addiction, that should have been revealed."

"She didn't have any health problems we didn't reveal."

"No drug problems, either?"

"She didn't use drugs."

"How do you account for the needle and armband next to her body?"

"I don't account for that at all. It makes no sense, just like her death makes no sense. Frankly, I'm still hoping this morning that this has all been a tasteless joke, and she's not really dead, and someone's going to come over to my house soon to tell me that I've just had a major bad dream. Because I certainly can't explain any of it, Detective." Stefan put his hands in front of him on the table and locked his fingers together. He looked like a man who wanted the earth to swallow him up in one bite and put an end to the horror and pain.

"Yes, sir, I think I understand," replied Sullivan unemotionally. "Sir, who is the beneficiary of the policy?"

"The business is the beneficiary," Stefan sighed. "The Chic Boutique is a corporation. We changed it from a proprietorship to a corporation a few years ago, and when we took out the policy we decided the business should pay the premiums and the business should be the beneficiary. Of course, I am the company now, so I'm the beneficiary, in a way."

"Did you and your wife have a business continuation plan that specifies what will happen in the event of either of your deaths?"

"No," Stefan said, shaking his head slowly. "We were advised by Kathryn's insurance friend, the one who told us to buy the key-person policy, that we should, but we never got around to making one."

"But you have a will, don't you?"

Haddad shook his head. "I was in the process of drafting our will but, no, we don't have a formal one drawn up by a lawyer. It's funny, but we'd been working on it for the past couple of months and debating who to ask to be guardians of the kids if anything happened to both of us. Kathryn did have a handwritten will she used to keep in a drawer when we went away, just the two of us, that said what would happen to the children if both of us were killed."

"And what does it specify, that paper that might be in a drawer somewhere?"

"I think it says that she wanted the kids to be raised by their grandparents, so they could all be together, if both of us were dead."

"So she had a pretty good relationship with her parents?"

"I wouldn't say that, Detective, no. Relatives meddle sometimes, you know how that is. It was probably nothing more than happens in most families. They're just a little overbearing, that's all."

"Sir, I have to ask you this again. What time did your wife leave the house, and did you leave with her, or did you stay here, or did you go somewhere else?"

Stefan's response revealed his agitation.

"Why are you asking me that? I told you she left the house early, about four-thirty, and I stayed here, in bed."

"Did you have any witnesses that saw you here, sir?

"Witnesses? My kids got up later, I don't know what time. Oh, I did go out to get some milk after I saw there was none. The kids need milk for their cereal. And I went running for an hour or so later that morning. I usually go running on Saturday."

"So, you did leave the house that morning after she left?"

"Yes, to get milk. And to go running."

"Can anyone verify where you were on Saturday, sir? Did any of the kids go with you? Where did you go running?"

"Well, I went out early to get milk and a *USA Today.* No one saw me, that I know of. It might have been around seven-thirty. And then . . . I don't remember seeing anyone when I went running. That was about half past eight. I usually go running alone, unless David or Calvin wants to come with me, and I always go to the same place. I park my car near the old Vanderbilt property—you know, the place where people go hunting—and I run on that track that surrounds the property. In fact, the track where I run goes past the road where you found her car. But why do I have to verify anything here, Detective? I don't see the point."

"Sir, as a matter of routine in homicides, we have to suspect foul play, as I told you before, and that's why we need you to remember the details as best you can."

"Well, that's what I can remember, Detectives. It was just a regular morning, or at least I thought it was going to be a regular day, and I didn't keep an eye on the time, although I might have gone running about nine-thirty. But tell me, what do you mean exactly by foul play?"

"Sir, you know there was a needle near your wife in the car where we found her. You saw that when you walked up to her car and identified her. And the bag on the seat next to her did contain cocaine. Now, she might have administered the drug to herself, or the drugs may have been administered to her, possibly by a companion."

"A companion?"

"Yes, sir, a companion. That companion might have been someone she knew, or it may have been someone she didn't know. We're trying to identify some tire tracks near the car. It's rained since we started zeroing in on this part of the investigation, so we're trying to analyze the tracks near your wife's car that might have come from another vehicle. They look like tire tracks that could have come from a BMW. What kind of car do you drive, Mr. Haddad?"

"I drive a BMW, like a lot of other people, Detective Sullivan. You know yourself the BMW dealership is one of the biggest in town."

"Do you know anyone who would have wanted to kill your wife, sir?"

"No, Detective, my wife was very respected and very loved in this community."

"One thing I've learned from years in law enforcement, sir, is that everyone has enemies. We need your help in figuring out who hers were and who might have been happy to see her disappear."

Stefan thought about what they said. Who were her enemies? She was a bold, outspoken woman with a generous and kind disposition, and people did admire her. Actually, though, not everyone did like Kathryn, and pandering to everyone's tastes had never interested his opinionated wife. You could always tell where she was coming from. She was blunt and plainspoken, to a fault, some said. She never did anything with special effects and mirrors. There was a total honesty about her, and she had a revulsion for anything manipulative, secretive, or controlling.

"You might talk to her parents," Stefan finally said.

"Her parents? You think they might know someone who had it in for her?"

"Well," Stefan replied tentatively, "they were certainly antagonistic toward her." Stefan shook his head as though he were waking himself up. "Oh, I can hear how ridiculous I sound, Detective. I'm not really very clearheaded. It must be the results of this sleeping pill. I'm rambling on about silly things. This is in poor taste of me to even talk about this. I mean, it's just family stuff and doesn't amount to anything. And it's over with now, anyway," he added, with obvious sadness in his voice.

"Just not the best family relationship, right, sir?" asked Sullivan, in a tone that sounded compassionate.

"Yes, yes, that's right. Lots of families are probably like that."

"Who else, sir?" said Sullivan, taking notes.

"I can't think of any real enemies. The only other relationship she had lately was a relationship with her ex-husband, who was in town visiting his son, their son from Kathryn's first marriage."

"How old is their son?"

"Nearly sixteen. This week he'll be sixteen."

"Who has custody of the boy?"

"Kathryn did. We did. I adopted him and we raised him together. She and her ex-husband weren't even married a year, and Kathryn was pregnant alone and had a baby alone and then raised David by herself until we got married. Marcos didn't become a part of David's life 'til last year."

"And that was alright with your wife, that he initiate a relationship with the boy after a disconnect of fifteen years?"

"My wife was an optimist, and she was always trying to do the best thing for her children. She used to tell me that every problem was an opportunity, and she tried to look on the bright side of everything. She thought we should encourage the relationship between David and his natural father and his other family. She felt David might have a hurt place somewhere deep inside, sometime down the road in his life, if we didn't encourage love to grow between him and his natural father. And she felt it would enrich the boy's life. So we encouraged the relationship and helped to nurture it. And I guess we did the right thing."

"You guess you did the right thing?" Detective Sullivan probed.

"Well, I always had some reservations about whether or not it was good for a child to have two homes. But Marcos *is* his natural father, and Kathryn thought it was the right thing to do, so I couldn't stand in the way."

"Do you think her ex-husband was her enemy for any reason?" asked Detective Sullivan. "Ex-wives and ex-husbands traditionally have a reputation for disliking each other. Was there any 'bad blood' between your wife and her ex-husband?"

Stefan swallowed hard. "No, I don't think there was any bad feeling."

"What about the custody issue? What about control?"

"My wife didn't believe that human beings controlled other human beings. She believed that the best thing you could do for your kids was to help them become self-confident and independent. She used to tell me that she wanted to make sure they could flap their wings and fly out of the nest at the appropriate time, even if she cried watching them fly away. She and her ex had a verbal agreement that David would live with us until he got out of high school, so, no, there weren't really any issues of control. She just wanted to make sure David had all the help and love he needed to be able to take control of his own life one day. My wife loved her children."

"It sounds a little like a fairy tale. I mean, the ex-husband enters the picture after a fifteen-year absence and two families sort of blend happily ever after? Isn't that a little hard to believe?"

"You didn't know my wife, Detective. She didn't do anything for show or for revenge. And especially with her children, she always had their best interests in mind. She wouldn't have done anything that was hurtful or harmful to them. And she was a very strong person who was good at putting her personal feelings aside and taking the long-range view. That's part of why she was so great as a buyer, too, and why we were able to get the key-person insurance on her."

"But she may have killed herself, sir, right? I mean, suicide is a possibility we're still exploring, and wouldn't that have been harmful to them?"

"Detective Sullivan, I know people can 'lose it' sometimes, and I guess my wife could have been as much a candidate for 'losing it' as anyone else. She had it all, in a way, and I think she was happy, but she may have hit a hard moment in her life when things were just too complex. That's obviously a possibility. But I don't believe that happened. She felt that life was a gift from God, and she was more determined than anyone I ever met to savor every moment of it and not to trivialize it in any way. I don't think she took her own life. It just wouldn't have been in character."

"Well, sir, if she didn't take her own life, someone took it from her. And we have to find out who would have done that."

TWELVE

On the way to the home of the Faisons, Sullivan and Robbey discussed the case. A prominent lady in the community with four children and a husband had been found dead on a country road on the outskirts of town near the hunting preserve with drug paraphernalia around her. Official autopsy results would be available any day, but a preliminary exam at Mercy Hospital on the day of her death had discovered her pregnancy and had also revealed that she'd been struck on the head at some point. The lab had analyzed the contents of the hypodermic needle and reported that it contained a lethal mix of cocaine and a new strain of heroin called "China Cat." Not your typical yuppie recreational drug. Maybe her death had followed a quarrel. But who would have done that? Why? It also looked like a copycat killing of those weird murders of mothers in California and Texas, so death at the hands of another serial killer produced by a sick society was a possibility. On the other hand, it was a possibility that, regardless of how the blow to the head occurred, Mrs. Haddad had killed herself. But why? A lot of insurance money was on the line, and a slick adjuster from the insurance company had told them that the purchase date of Haddad's key-person policy was in a gray area, and that they were going to play hardball and contest the payoff if the suicide theory proved valid. The case had a strange smell to it.

Mrs. Faison answered the doorbell smiling. "Come in, officers, what can we do for you?" A slim, attractive, well-dressed woman in her mid-sixties who looked ten years younger, she showed them into her living room, a clean and neatly arranged room with minishutters on the windows. It looked like a living room no one used. There were no knickknacks on the end tables, and there was no clutter. "Miles," she called to her husband, who was apparently in another room, "some nice officers have come to see us."

"Detectives, ma'am," Sullivan said. "I think we've met before, Mrs. Faison, at some political fund-raisers. I'm Detective John Sullivan and this is Detective Robbey." Sullivan extended his hand to shake hers, but she reached out and hugged him.

"Why, that's way too formal, John. I've watched you grow up, you know, and I knew your dad."

Sullivan stiffened when she embraced him and pulled away. Miles came into the room with a handshake for each of the detectives. He smiled somewhat sheepishly.

"What can we do for you gentlemen?" asked Miles, motioning for them to sit down. About six feet tall, Miles Faison looked sixtyish in the face but his athletic body could have belonged to a much younger fellow.

"Mr. and Mrs. Faison, I know this might be hard for you to talk about, but we're investigating your daughter's death."

"Yes," she sighed, "this is very hard for us. Thank heavens we have our friends from church and the club to support us at a time like this. The suicide of a family member is really hard, Detectives," said Vera Faison.

"Well, let's start with that, ma'am. Do you think your daughter committed suicide?"

"Well," she answered, looking somber, "it certainly looks that way. And I'm afraid suicide would have fit into her general pattern."

"Oh? Could you explain what her general pattern was, Mrs. Faison?"

"Well, Detective Sullivan," Mrs. Faison began, "let me get you something to drink first. You might think I've forgotten my Southern hospitality." She had a friendly, almost seductive look on her face, the look a woman has when she's trying to come on to a man. It looked like she was flirting with him. Sullivan glanced at her husband. Mr. Faison sat in the easy chair near the couch, unfazed, as though he was accustomed to it.

"We're not hungry or thirsty, ma'am," Detective Sullivan said, in a polite tone of voice that sounded very definite. It was clear one had to be firm with this woman. He looked at her directly in the face. She was somewhat tall—maybe five-foot-seven—and thin with angular features. Younger, she would have been pretty and her looks would have given her a lot of control over men and situations. Now, she was just an older lady trying a little too hard to control the situation.

"Miles, did you hear that? The detectives just asked me if I thought Kathryn could have killed herself. And I said I thought she could have. She had her good qualities, Detective, but she was in her own world. She just didn't think about other people. I hate to say that, but she hadn't remembered her father's birthday or my birthday in the last ten years. Frankly, her father and I have wondered in the last few years if she wasn't a little off mentally." She paused and shook her head sadly. "This has just been so hard on us. Of course, we're going to miss her and we're sad about it, but I know you're looking for the truth."

"Mrs. Faison, I've interviewed people who have given me the impression that your daughter was a generous and loving person always involved in doing things for others."

"Well, she probably treated her friends better than she did us." Mrs. Faison's tone was imperious, but there was a hint of sad resignation in her voice, too. "Who did you talk to?"

"That's confidential, ma'am, but what I'd like to ask you is why your daughter would have committed suicide."

Mrs. Faison shrugged her shoulders and looked at her husband, as though seeking support, as she replied. "Well, she was having an affair with her ex-husband. Maybe that triggered something."

"Was she?" asked Detective Sullivan.

"Yes, she was. I hate telling you this. It's so embarrassing to our family. But maybe that made her take her life. And, of course, her father and I feel so bad. Parents always end up feeling guilty about things like this, because they think there's something they should have done to prevent it. But, I guess she more or less made her own bed when she started having an affair, and she drove herself to this tragic end. That's what our minister has been counseling us about lately. That we shouldn't feel responsible. But it's hard, Detective. Parents always feel guilty about things like this and wonder if there's something they could have done better."

"So you think your daughter committed suicide because she was having an affair with her ex-husband?"

"Yes," she said, shaking her head slowly, "I think so. I am her mother, and I knew her better than anyone else."

"But her husband and other people seem to think she cared too much for her children to take her own life, that she loved them too much to leave them without a mother."

Mrs. Faison smiled a smile that exuded smugness. She rolled her eyes at the ceiling before she responded. "She didn't care about anything except herself, Detective Sullivan. I hate to say that, since she was my flesh and blood. But she wouldn't have put her children's concerns above her own. Why, she wouldn't even let the children come over here to see their grandparents very often, even though they wanted to. I hate to say it, but the truth is that she was a very selfish woman, and she didn't give a moment's thought to what was best for the children."

"When was the last time you saw your daughter, Mrs. Faison?" Sullivan asked.

"Hmm, when was it, honey?" Mrs. Faison asked her husband.

As the detectives and Mrs. Faison stared at him, Mr. Faison shook his head slowly as though he couldn't recall.

There was silence, followed by more silence.

"Mrs. Faison, when was the last time you saw your daughter?" asked Sullivan, this time more insistently.

As Sullivan stared at her waiting for an answer, he could almost hear her brain working, calculating her options. A clever woman, she seemed to sense that she would not be able to evade his question.

"We saw her on the morning of her death," she replied matter-of-factly.

"You did?" Sullivan looked surprised and Robbey, like a schoolboy, made a note in the small notebook he always had with him.

"Yes, she came here, to visit her dad and me."

"She did? I thought you said she was selfish and inconsiderate and didn't pay much attention to her parents."

Mrs. Faison shot him a hard look and then the hard look melted under the force of a smile. "You're right, John. You understand her personality totally. She didn't come here to pay her respects to her parents. Actually, she came here whining about her affair with her ex-husband and accusing us of meddling in her first marriage and separating her from him in the first place."

"Oh? That must have been an emotional discussion. What happened exactly, and how long was she here?"

"Well, she came early in the morning, and I fixed her some breakfast. She said she was going to catch some sales that morning at the mall." Mrs. Faison looked at Sullivan and lowered her voice, as though she were confiding in him. "Maybe she was going to meet her boyfriend, I don't know."

"It must be terrible to have your child die from committing suicide, Mrs. Faison," Sullivan said, studying her.

"Yes, it is, Detective," Mrs. Faison sobbed unexpectedly, putting her hand on her forehead to shield her face from view as she composed herself and dabbed at her nose with a handkerchief. "And, of course, there are those poor kids. We love them all, but we're especially fond of David. He's like our own child. Why, we practically raised him when he was a baby. But we're going to do everything we can for those children, aren't we, Miles?"

If Miles had been a dog, he would have wagged his tail.

"When did your daughter arrive, and when did she leave that morning?" Sullivan asked her.

"Oh, I don't know. Honey, what time was it when she came?"

Miles Faison stared straight ahead. He sighed, then spoke. "I don't remember."

"Try to make a rough stab at what time she came over. If there's a grand jury investigation of this, you'll be asked what time she came and left."

Mr. Faison broke the silence. "She came about five-thirty in the morning."

"Isn't that early for someone to come by?"

"We always get up early. She knew that. We were up having coffee," Mrs. Faison replied.

"And what time did she leave, sir?" asked Detective Sullivan.

Mr. Faison stared at them when he answered, but he sounded like a man confused by grief when he spoke. "I don't remember."

"Try to remember, sir. What time did your daughter leave, Mr. Faison?"

"I think she left about eight-fifteen or so," interjected Mrs. Faison.

"So she stayed quite a while, didn't she?"

"Yes, we had a great time. We had breakfast and talked," said Mrs. Faison. "Her sister dropped by, too, and we all talked. Her sister just got married last weekend, so it was mostly girl talk, you know how that is," Mrs. Faison said, smiling sweetly. "And she wanted to get some of her old trophies from the attic to take home to show Veronica."

"I thought you said she came over in a bad mood, whining about her affair and blaming you for things."

"Yes, but we were used to that. Her father and I put up with a lot from her, you know. We were used to her complaining and blaming us for things, so we didn't make anything of it. Her bad mood improved after I cooked breakfast," Mrs. Faison said, smiling.

"Was Mrs. Haddad driving?" asked Detective Sullivan.

"Yes, of course, she was driving," replied Mrs. Faison.

"How did she seem when she left? Did she say where she was going?" asked Sullivan.

"Well, her bad mood had returned and she seemed a little hostile when she left. I think she felt guilty about having an affair, and she wanted to blame someone. Her father and I did our best for our children. They grew up belonging to a country club, and that's sure a lot better than we had it, honey, isn't it?" she said, looking at Miles, who nodded passively. "We put both our daughters through college, and then we offered to help Kathryn when she went to graduate school, although she insisted on borrowing all the money herself to finance her education. She was very stubborn. But on that morning, she left in a huff, like she usually did, and said she was going to the mall. Or, I guess she meant the mall. She said she was going shopping. And then she was going to have lunch with David and his father at the lodge."

"Mr. and Mrs. Faison, let me ask you again. Do you believe your daughter committed suicide by injecting herself with drugs?"

"Well, maybe she didn't mean to commit suicide. Maybe she was just going to use cocaine. I mean, she was found on a dirt road off the beaten track with cocaine next to her, wasn't she? Maybe she was just going to use cocaine and then she used too much." Mrs. Faison smiled sweetly. "Doesn't that happen, Detectives? I'm afraid I don't know much about drugs. I'm probably not even using the right language."

Detective Sullivan stared at her, without responding. He disliked women of any age trying to be seductive with him and playing the demure role when he was investigating a case. He knew he shouldn't take it personally. It was just the lady's style, and it had worked for women of her generation. But he still didn't like it.

"Do you believe your daughter used drugs?" Sullivan continued. "Wasn't she a Sunday school teacher and very involved in youth activities in the community? Was she a closet drug user? Did she have another personality no one knew about?"

"Well, Detective, things are not always what they seem, you know," Mrs. Faison said, cocking her head and lowering her voice as though she were telling him something in confidence. "Maybe she and her husband were involved in cocaine use in the privacy of their home. Who knows? That generation of baby boomers got into everything along the way, you know. That generation had it all, but they were never satisfied, and they blamed their parents for everything."

"What makes you think she and her husband may have used cocaine?"

"Just a suspicion I have. Mother's intuition, I guess. There's nothing I can really put my finger on. But, she was found with drug equipment around her, wasn't she?" Mrs. Faison paused, and what looked like an involuntary shudder came over her. "And as if it isn't enough to think your daughter committed suicide, it just gives me the creeps to think that the only other thing that could have happened is that someone close to her might have harmed her."

"Close to her? What do you mean? Who do you think might have harmed her who was close to her?"

Mrs. Faison shook her head theatrically and sighed. "I just don't even want to think that her husband might have been involved. But you know how things are, Detective. A lot of times things like this get down to what's happening between a man and a woman."

"Her husband? You think her husband might have harmed her? Weren't they happily married?"

She stared at him. "Well, Detective Sullivan, you never know what people's marriages are like on the inside, now do you?"

"Did you know her ex-husband, Mrs. Faison?"

"Oh, yes, we know him. Why, what did we pay, honey?" she asked her husband, "Was it ten thousand dollars for their wedding? And look what happened. It didn't even last a year. It's just a shame she couldn't have made that marriage work."

"What kind of relationship did she and her ex-husband, Mr. Galleria, have recently?"

"Well, like I told you before, she confided to me that they were having an affair. You know, he just came back into her life a year or so ago to strike up a relationship with David, and from what Kathryn confided to me, it sounds to me like she threw herself at him. Anyway, they started up a relationship, and I don't mean just a platonic one. Maybe her husband found out about it and went into a rage and killed her. Doesn't that happen sometimes, Detective?" she asked in a sugary voice.

"I thought Mr. Haddad was supposed to be rather mild mannered. Not really the type for rage. But is that what you think happened? I thought you said you thought it was possible that she committed suicide," probed Sullivan.

She shook her head and grinned. "Oh, I guess I'm trying to act like an amateur detective, John. Actually, I think both of those are possibilities. We know that another man was involved, so it might have been either way. Maybe she was so ashamed of herself that she took her life in a moment of weakness, or maybe her husband found out about it and killed her in the heat of the moment."

"I'm just curious. You and your daughter were pretty close, weren't you?"

"Yes."

"But you said earlier that your daughter didn't let the children come over here as much as they wanted to. How does that fit together, I mean, you two having a close relationship but her not letting the kids visit much?"

Mrs. Faison shook her head and looked weary. "That's a good question, Detective, and I see exactly where you're coming from. Our relationship with her was a struggle, and we had the best relationship we could, considering how eccentric and paranoid she was. We had to put up with a lot from her. She was so selfish with the children, and her father and I weren't able to maintain a relationship with those kids. She did things to spite us, Detective, like not letting us pay for them to join the country club and not letting the children get in with a good crowd of people. They're our only grandchildren, you know, and those boys are like the sons we never had. They just love coming over here, and we love them dearly, and we'd do anything for them. And, thank the Lord above, we're in the fortunate position of being able to provide many material comforts and a college education for them all, if we need to."

"Mr. Haddad must surely be planning on taking care of his children himself, don't you think?"

"Well, Detective, I can tell you that their grandfather and I consider it our sacred responsibility to make sure those children are in the best environment. We're from the old school, you know, Detective, and we don't go along with kids being raised by someone who's using drugs. Children need to be raised properly, and we're going to do whatever we have to do to make sure they're taken care of."

"Whatever you have to do? What does that mean?"

"Whatever we have to do," she replied flatly.

"Well, maybe you won't have to do anything, Mrs. Faison." He paused. "It is sad, isn't it, when little children are left without a mother?"

"Yes, but at least they have a grandmother," she smiled.

Detective Sullivan stood up and Detective Robbey followed suit.

"We certainly thank you for your help. Please accept our deepest sympathies about your daughter, ma'am, sir," Sullivan said, extending his hand to each of them.

"Oh, thank you, John, this has been so difficult for her father and me. But we appreciate your sympathy, and we also value all your hard work, not just on this case but all the time. You men do so much behind the scenes to keep us all safe, and you hardly ever get the praise you deserve," Mrs. Faison gushed. "We do appreciate our law enforcement officers, you know." She reached out her hand to stroke his arm. Sullivan pulled his arm away when he felt her touch.

"Thank you, Mrs. Faison. One more thing. We might need to talk with Sally. Can you tell us how we can get in touch with her?"

"She's out of the country."

"Doing what?"

"On her honeymoon," Mrs. Faison smiled.

"When's she coming back?"

"Maybe not for a few months."

Sullivan shrugged and grinned. "Long honeymoon. Well, thank you, ma'am. Now, you all have a nice day, and thank you for letting us invade your privacy like this."

Back in the car, John Sullivan and Nathan Robbey sat buckling their seat belts and arranging their papers. The Faisons' minimansion was outside the city limits on a paved road by itself. There were no other houses around. Nathan Robbey finally broke the silence when they reached the superhighway.

"Attractive woman," Nathan commented.

Sullivan stared ahead, then looked out his rearview mirror at the car passing. Then he looked quickly at Nathan before centering his gaze once more on the road ahead. "Yes, she is. Smart, too," Sullivan finally replied.

"What do you mean?" asked the rookie cop who had been assigned to Sullivan six months previously. Nathan Robbey had been thrilled to learn that he was assigned to apprentice with one of the state's most respected detectives in a new trainee program implemented by the sheriff's department. He knew John Sullivan had a reputation as a straight-arrow. From a rich family whose ancestors had come over on the *Mayflower* and lived in Macon, Georgia, for generations, Sullivan's grandfather had been a rich attorney and his father, after inheriting a fortune in real estate and other assets, had decided to use his law degree in public service. So his father had never practiced law; instead, he ran for district attorney and was elected in a close victory when he was in his mid-twenties. He never again experienced a close contest for district attorney. Rapidly he earned a reputation as "the only district attorney in the state money can't buy." Following in the footsteps of the grandfather and father couldn't have been easy, but John Sullivan had been cut from the same cloth and was determined to make his own way in the world and forge a reputation as a thoroughly honest man, the same as his dad. Although he'd inherited a small family fortune, primarily in real estate holdings, he'd carved out a career as a homicide detective and was respected nationally. Whatever John Sullivan said was worth listening to.

"She's full of smart insights about who might have killed her daughter or how she might have died," Sullivan said. "But she's a little on the cool side for a mother who's just buried a child."

"Aren't some people just more emotionally controlled than other people?"

"Yes. And we know they didn't have the best relationship in the world, anyway. Death doesn't change that."

"So what's next?"

"We'll keep asking questions. Let's go see Mrs. Haddad's best friend."

THIRTEEN

Mary opened the double doors of her redbrick, two-story home after the officers rang the bell twice. "Hello, officers," said an extremely attractive, trim, fortyish brunette with short hair parted in the middle. She was wearing jeans and a long sweater. "May I help with something?"

"We'd like to speak with Mary Deckle."

"I'm Mary Deckle," the woman replied with a curious look, as she searched their faces.

"Mrs. Deckle, I'm Detective John Sullivan and this is Detective Nathan Robbey. Could we come in for a few minutes? We'd like to ask you some questions about Kathryn Haddad."

Mary's face became visibly sad as she replied. "Yes, of course, come in, I'll help you all I can."

She showed them into the living room decorated in teal and raspberry, then excused herself and disappeared into the kitchen briefly to fetch iced tea. After she brought tea on a tray, she set a glass on a coaster in front of each of them.

"This is delicious, Mrs. Deckle. I haven't had iced tea in a long time. I'm going to have to ask my wife to keep a pitcher of this in the refrigerator," Sullivan said.

Mary smiled in appreciation of Detective Sullivan's compliment. When she smiled, Sullivan noticed how pretty she was. When a woman is that pretty in her forties, it's character and personality, not just physical looks, he'd learned from years of police work.

John Sullivan cleared his throat and then began. "Mrs. Deckle, we're looking for clues, to tell you the truth. We want you to tell us about Mrs. Haddad, as much as you know about her life and relationships."

"Has her death been ruled a suicide? That's what people say. But the media say an investigation is proceeding."

"The official autopsy hasn't been published yet, so we have to treat her death as a possible homicide for now. But let's start with your question, ma'am. Do you think she committed suicide, Mrs. Deckle? Would that have been in character for her?" John Sullivan asked.

"Absolutely not. She would never have done anything that would leave her children alone in the world without a mother. She used to tell me what her grandmother said about feeling especially sorry for little children who have to grow up without a mom. She was devoted to her kids, and she wouldn't have left them voluntarily. She was a very good person, Detective Sullivan." She paused. "It's funny, but I remembered yesterday how she once told me that she thought suicide was a permanent solution for a temporary problem. It just doesn't seem like something she would have done."

"Please tell us about her. How long had you known her?"

"About all my life. We met in junior high school and were good friends all through high school. She used to spend the night at my house a lot, and we were in the same activities, like honor society, and we were elected class officers and things like that. Then I went to the University of Georgia and she went off to London. And we basically went our separate ways. I became a school psychologist, got married, and started a family, and she went to college in London and worked there for a few years and traveled around the world, and then she went to Boston to the Harvard Business School."

"And she got married there, right?"

"Yes, she married Marcos Galleria. They went to Mexico after they married, but the marriage only lasted a few months. I actually met him when they came through Macon to get her furniture the summer after they got married. I was home visiting my mother when they came through. Then, a few months after she moved to Mexico, she came back for a visit and ended up staying, having a baby by herself, and becoming a single parent. She had it tough, but she had a great attitude about it. She worked so hard to make sure that she and David were a family. She was happy in spite of the circumstances."

"Circumstances? What do you mean?"

"I mean, she had to find a job when she was pregnant and separated. It had to have been very hard."

"Didn't her parents help her out during that period?"

Mary flashed them a smile that looked like a grimace. "Help her out? She'd have been better off if they hadn't helped so much."

"What do you mean?"

"I mean, they meddled, Vera meddled, in her first marriage. Her mother thought up the plan that she should leave Mexico shortly after she got there. People who meddle want their meddling to look like helping, but meddling is never helping. Generosity isn't generosity unless it's based on principle. Vera wasn't being helpful or generous. She was just plain meddling."

"Wasn't Mrs. Haddad unhappy in her first marriage?"

"Isn't everyone unhappy in marriage from time to time, especially in a cross-cultural marriage in the first year? Every marriage is fragile, and every relationship is vulnerable, Detective," replied Mary with a wry smile. "Kathryn was twenty-nine years old when she married. She could have married a dozen times before that if she'd wanted to. She was a beautiful and talented and independent woman who, I'm sure, must have been feeling very alone in Mexico. She wasn't a good fit with that culture, to begin with. She'd just graduated with an MBA, and she wasn't working, and she couldn't speak the language. Anyway, she was several months pregnant when her mother went to Mexico to help her pack her things and leave her husband, and the marriage broke up after that."

"So why'd she leave Mr. Galleria, then?" Sullivan probed.

"Oh, I'm sure they were having problems. I think there was a problem with tempers getting out of control. They were both hard chargers, I suppose. He had all his family there, and she had no one, and she must have suffered from major culture shock. But her mother took advantage of her confusion and unhappiness and led her in a plan that was sure to produce hatred and rejection on his end. I think what Kathryn wanted when she came back here was to let things cool down and get the communication going between them. But things went the other way. I was living in Atlanta when she came back for a visit, so I never knew anything about their divorce until I heard about Kathryn getting a job when she was pregnant and making plans to stay in Macon."

"You seem to blame her mother for the breakup of her marriage. Isn't it possible she was genuinely trying to help her daughter get out of a bad situation?"

"I have to admit it, Detective Sullivan. I don't like Mrs. Faison much." Mary Deckle paused, as though trying to choose her words carefully. "I've known Vera Faison a long time, and I watched her flaunt her infidelities in her daughter's face the whole time we were in junior high and high school. Mrs. Faison is the kind of person who wants everybody to see her doing a good deed, but in the privacy of her own home, in the background of her life, she's a tyrant. I dislike her sneaky ways of doing things. So, no, I don't think she was looking out for Kathryn's best interests—or her son-in-law's interests, or her grandchild's interests—when she helped a newly married pregnant woman leave her husband." Mrs. Deckle paused. "I'm in my forties now, Detective Sullivan. I have a son in college, and I'd never do anything in a capricious way to break up his new marriage, if he were married. So, no, I think it was malicious and treacherous. It was typical Vera. She wanted everyone to see her helping her daughter, when all she was doing was wrecking a marriage."

"Mrs. Faison couldn't have wrecked it all by herself, though, could she? Maybe you're being a little hard on the lady because you don't like her."

"No, she couldn't have wrecked it all by herself, but rocky marriages don't need much help to fall apart. It's hard enough to stay married, even without the in-laws trying to pull you apart. If married people are going to work out their problems, they have to be left alone and they have to stay together to work them out, not be separated by family meddling in their business. Anyway, newly married people don't know how to be married yet." Then she smiled impishly. "Not that the rest of us ever become experts on marriage, either, Detective."

"I'll agree with that, Mrs. Deckle," John Sullivan replied, flashing a boyish, toothy smile. Then the businesslike look reappeared on his face. "Was Mrs. Haddad close to her mother?"

"Are you kidding?" she replied, making a face that looked like she'd just eaten a sour pickle. "Kathryn wrestled with her relationship with her parents all her life. She put up with their domineering, bullying, abusive attitude toward her a lot longer than most people would have. But she was a religious person and a kind person. She was fun loving but she took seriously the idea of perfecting her character. She used to tell me that she thought the main evolutionary challenge facing the human was to perfect his character. I think she tried hard to make moral choices. That's another reason I know she wouldn't have committed suicide. She believed life was a gift from God, and she wouldn't have extinguished that life for any reason."

"When we spoke with Mrs. Faison, she said she and her daughter were close," Sullivan replied.

Mrs. Deckle shook her head slowly. "She's close to her other daughter, Sally, who's a carbon copy of her mother. But Vera and Kathryn have never been close. Why, Vera used Kathryn like a servant when she was a little girl. When I used to spend the night with her when we were girls, Kathryn had to get up at six-thirty on Saturday morning to clean her mother's house, with her mother screaming at her to clean better and faster. I don't think I saw Kathryn have a Saturday off when she was growing up. Vera's a control freak." Mary Deckle swallowed and her tone of voice was more mellow when she continued. "But you know what? Kathryn spent her whole life trying to earn her parents' love and working hard to forgive them for the abusive way they treated her."

"What about Kathryn's relationship with her ex-husband during the last fifteen years?"

"He wasn't a part of her life. He only called last year to say he wanted to develop a relationship with David and add something to his life, and Kathryn was very gracious about it. Most women wouldn't have gone along with it. But she felt it would be wrong to stand in the way of the love and enrichment the boy might gain from knowing his natural father. And Stefan was a gentleman about letting it all happen, too. They were a very together couple."

"If they were so together, why was she having an affair with her ex-husband?"

Mary sighed and looked down at the rug. "I don't quite know the answer to that, Detective Sullivan. A lot of my friends have had midlife crises of some sort, and usually those crises arise out of some unmet need for love and acceptance. And by the way, from what I've seen in private practice as a psychologist, that unmet need might not have anything to do with their marriage partner. It seems like people get a little restless at middle age. I think Kathryn just got derailed temporarily. She really loved her husband and her children and her life, but everything got out of focus for a brief period of time. And then it really went wrong after that."

"What do you mean?"

"Oh, I mean her death. I still can't believe she's dead. It just seems like when one wrong thing happens, like her affair with Marcos, then other things go wrong as a consequence."

"One thing leads to another?" said Sullivan.

"Yes, one thing leads to another," echoed Mary. "That's a lot like what happened in her first marriage, too, I guess. A bad decision led to all kinds of things she didn't expect, like divorce."

"On the matter of the drug overdose, have you ever known Kathryn to be involved in drug use?" asked Sullivan.

"No, no, no," Mary said, shaking her head vigorously. "I know she took a drink every now and then. But it's ridiculous to imagine that she had some secret lifestyle where she was using cocaine like I've heard some people gossiping about. For one thing, she was too busy to use drugs! She ran a business and had four children and was very active in the community . . ."

"Well, how do you think the drugs got into her then, and why were drugs found beside her?"

"I can't help you there, Detective. Maybe it was something bizarre. I don't know. It baffles me."

"Did she have enemies that you know of?"

Mary paused and shrugged her shoulders as she shook her head slowly. "No, not really. She was a very outspoken, hard-charging businesswoman, and some people may have found her too bold for their tastes, but she was a lovely, generous, and warm person underneath a brusque style. I think she only developed that style to protect herself. She grew up in an environment where you got used if you were a sensitive, giving person." Mary paused and seemed in thought for a moment. She nodded as she spoke. "She did have a rather brittle exterior at times, but it was the product of a childhood where the relationships were explosive and inconstant. Some people found her intimidating, but she didn't have any enemies. I can't think of anyone who would have harmed her."

"How about her ex-husband?"

"I don't know. I don't really know him. I only met him that once after they married, and I can't think of any reason he'd want to hurt her. I can't see how it would be to his advantage if she were out of the picture. And besides, he's a gentleman, he's a businessman, he's a refined kind of person from what I understand. I mean, he's not a killer."

"Maybe he wanted his son to live with him and she was standing in the way."

"I don't know. Kathryn told me he was just trying to add something to David's life, not take David from her. If he had a hidden agenda, I don't know anything about it."

"Will David live with his natural father now or with the father who's raised him?"

"I don't know," Mrs. Deckle said, looking Sullivan directly in the eyes.

"Mrs. Deckle, you said you're a school psychologist. And you have a small private practice, too, don't you?"

"Yes."

"Can you tell me something about suicide? I mean, why do people commit suicide?"

Mary Deckle sighed and took a deep breath before replying. "Well, there are various theories, Detective, and there can be different motivations for suicide. There are suicides that are romantic, like when someone is distraught over a lover. And there are suicides that occur when the victim is trying to punish someone or make someone feel guilty. I deal with a lot of teenagers who are suicidal, especially in my small private practice. And from what I've observed, the suicidal crisis arises when the victim has lost hope. It happens when someone is fearful of living in the future and dealing with the problems in the future. A lot of times people consider suicide when there's been a great change in a family relationship and that's produced stress. The suicidal adolescents I've helped often come from family environments in which there's intense hostility toward the child or an excessive pampering of the child. But even a family environment that's too pampering can be perceived as hostile to the child in that it thwarts the child's ability to gain independence. So, yes, I'd have to say that a hostile family environment of some sort is often a common denominator among the suicidal adolescents I see." She thought for a few seconds before continuing. "Suicide becomes a possibility for some people when there's an enormous feeling of helplessness and hopelessness."

"When did you last see Mrs. Haddad?"

"Several weeks ago."

"How did she seem?"

Mary was silent for a few seconds before answering. "She was depressed."

"Was she in any way what you might call suicidal?"

"Maybe." Mary paused, as though she were trying to find the words she was looking for. Then she continued. "I think Kathryn was caught all her life in some vicious cycle of emotional abuse that she couldn't get free of. She was a person with a very damaged self-concept because of the constant and vicious belittling by her parents. My favorite uncle told me once, 'It's not what you do, it's what you *don't* do when you're a parent, that's most important to your kids.' Her parents gave her lots of material things, but the verbal and nonverbal message they gave her was that she wasn't worthy of respect or friendship or love or protection unless she did exactly what they wanted her to do. Everything they did was designed to diminish her emotionally. Oh, they'd try to do lots of favors for her to keep her in their debt. That's what I've seen about emotional abuse. The abusers never want you to get out of debt to them. They injure you emotionally and make you feel that it was all your fault. And Kathryn was an idealist who was always trying to make things right, so she'd keep pushing to understand Vera and Miles and forgive them and turn the other cheek and do what they wanted her to. It was just pushy, pushy, pushy all the time. Kathryn used to tell me that it felt like smothering, not mothering. I read not long ago that parents tend to fall into two categories: they're either stepping stones or stumbling blocks. Hers were definitely stumbling blocks."

"What about her father? Her mother seems like the boss of the family."

Mary smiled. "Well, there's an old saying in the South that you've probably heard, Detective Sullivan. 'If mama ain't happy, ain't nobody happy.' My daddy told me once before he died that eventually the men just give in to the women to have peace at home," Mrs. Deckle said, smiling. "That's not true of every home, of course, but I think that's what Mr. Faison's done over time. He's grown more compliant and less capable of contradicting his stern, autocratic wife as he's gotten older. Mrs. Faison always has to be in control. That family is definitely a matriarchy."

"Well, Mrs. Deckle, I think that's all the information we need from you right now. If you think of anything you feel we should know about, please call the number on this business card."

Mary Deckle showed them to the door and, once they got in the car, they sat in her driveway buckling up.

"Where to next, boss?" asked Nathan.

"We're going to see her ex-husband."

FOURTEEN

They phoned ahead from the car telephone to make sure Mr. Galleria was going to be at the hotel when they came calling. He sounded cordial on the phone and invited them to come right over. He was reading the *Economist* and other international magazines, he told them, and they were welcome to come to his suite to talk with him.

Just one knock brought to the door an Hispanic gentleman wearing a red polo shirt and khaki pants with a smile on his face and an air of sophistication about him.

"I'm Detective John Sullivan and this here's Detective Nathan Robbey, Mr. Galleria."

He ushered the detectives into his spacious suite. "Come in, please. I originally checked into a small room thinking I'd be hunting all day and would only be sleeping here, but I decided to spend my last several nights in this suite. Because of the sad event, we're not doing any more hunting, so David comes to visit me here each day. We don't have the stomach for hunting now, you know?" he said, as he led them toward the living room. He was staying in a sunlit suite decorated in red and black that had a kitchen, living room, and adjoining bedroom. "Besides, when I saw these University of Georgia colors, I had to move here out of patriotism to the Bulldogs," he added, grinning. "I guess you gentlemen are probably Bulldog fans yourselves, no?"

"Oh, yes, sir," Nathan Robbey enthused, seeming instantly charmed by Galleria's cultured Spanish accent and by his interest in Robbey's favorite team. Robbey appeared awestruck by Galleria's genteel, stylish demeanor that looked clearly upper class to a country boy. Nathan Robbey hadn't been farther than Florida and Tennessee in his life. He looked at John Sullivan. John's face didn't reveal any clues as to what he thought of Galleria.

"Mr. Galleria, we'd like to ask you a few questions," Sullivan began.

"Of course, of course," Galleria said, sounding genuinely obliging. "Ask me whatever you want," he answered with a gracious smile. "I can't promise that I'll know all the answers, but please ask whatever you want."

"Very well. Let me begin here," Sullivan said. "Mrs. Haddad was your ex-wife, sir, is that correct?"

"Yes, and the mother of my son."

"Okay, well, let's actually start there then, sir, since you brought it up. Is it true that you made the acquaintance of your only son just recently, for the first time?"

"Yes, it's true." Galleria wasn't smiling. He looked directly at John Sullivan when he said it, but his face was devoid of the cheerfulness that had characterized it just a moment earlier.

"Would it be too personal, sir, if I asked why that was?"

"Is that what you came to ask me, Detective?" Galleria didn't sound antagonistic or angry. His voice simply had a lifeless, weary tone, as though some powerful emotion lay buried underneath.

"No, sir, but I don't quite know where we should start. Let me tell you that I came here to try to fit some pieces of a puzzle together, and I have to interview everyone who was close to her. So I'm not trying to pry, sir, into your personal business, but I need to know what your relationship with her was, and I need to understand it very well. I may end up knowing more than I need to know, but what you tell me may help me determine the exact cause of death."

"So you don't think she committed suicide?" Galleria looked surprised.

"We're still investigating, sir. Now, would you please tell me about your relationship with Mrs. Haddad?"

"Where do you want me to start?"

"Anywhere you like," replied Sullivan.

"Okay, well, I guess you want to know how we met and all that. We met and fell in love in graduate school, at the Harvard Business School. It was a turbulent relationship, mostly because of me, I guess, although she was headstrong and temperamental, too. To make a long story short, we married and went back to a Spanish-speaking country where, I can see now, in hindsight, she had too many relatives around, no friends, a husband who was too young and immature to understand her needs, and a mother who was all too willing to meddle in something that was not her business."

"How long were you married?"

"According to the records or actually? Actually we lived together as man and wife only seven or eight months. She abandoned me. Her mother flew to Mexico City and then she and Kathryn drove my car back to Georgia pretending she was going home to visit her family. What I found after she left was that she took with her the things that meant the most to her—her diaries, and so forth—so that's how I figured out she left me. And, when she got back to Georgia, she telephoned after a couple of weeks and read me a list of the behaviors I would have to change if I wanted her back. I was young and macho and hot-tempered and, even if those things needed changing, I didn't like her ultimatums, so I told her, don't come back. That's how it ended. Very immature, very childish. She was pregnant, but I didn't care about that first. All I could see was how she humiliated and shamed me in front of my family by leaving me, and I was around a lot of people who persuaded me that letting her go was the best thing long-range for me."

"And was it the best thing, Mr. Galleria?"

Nathan Robbey cast a searching look at his mentor. This kind of questioning was very personal and seemed unusual, but John Sullivan had to know what he was doing. He was fishing.

Galleria looked up at the ceiling, rolled his eyes, and moistened his lower lip nervously with his tongue. Then he looked Sullivan directly in the eyes as he spoke slowly. "Have you ever loved a woman, Detective Sullivan?"

"Yes, sir."

Galleria stared at Sullivan. "So have I. I loved Kathryn. I didn't realize how much I loved her then. I was selfish and immature, and she was temperamental and stubborn, and that led to some intense quarrels in our home. I had a bad temper, which I've learned to control, and she was hot-tempered and insecure herself, so a storm could blow up quickly at our house. All I could see when she left me was my own pain, but I can see now that she didn't feel safe and loved in the home we had together. So she sort of bolted, like a colt, you know? After she left, I was surrounded by machismo friends who convinced me that a headstrong Protestant gringa with no intention of honoring her marriage vows would never make a suitable wife and I'd better get out while I had a chance. So I guess I called her bluff and then turned my back on her. When she called me after the storm settled, I told her I didn't want her to come back. So she didn't." He paused. "It takes a strong man not to take back his pregnant wife, don't you think, Detective?" By the remorseful look on his face and the tone in his voice, they could see that Galleria was ridiculing his decision.

"If you say so, sir."

"No, actually the old saying, 'Never send a boy to do a man's job,' comes to mind. I was stupid and hurt and couldn't see beyond my frail, damaged ego. What I didn't see was that by letting her go, I would lose the woman I wanted to spend my life with. I wanted her by my side. She was my intellectual match. She was my soul mate. We were operating on so many different levels that there was bound to be friction, especially moving to a different culture where I was at home while she was in an alien land where she didn't understand the language." Galleria took a deep breath and shrugged his shoulders. "I've had many regrets, Detective."

"But you're remarried, right, sir?"

"Yes, and I have a lovely family. But you go into marriage the second time around with more experience and more knowledge of how to make things work. You know what they say in Spanish about the devil, don't you? They say the devil is the devil not because he's wicked, but because he has the experience. And do you know, with all his experience, what the devil figured out is the main tool he can use against man?"

"No, what is it?" asked Sullivan, looking intrigued.

"There's a Spanish legend that tells how the devil once called together his council of servants to consult about how they might cause a good man to sin. After rejecting many ideas like women, booze, and money, the devil finally heard the one he thought would work. One of his henchman said, 'I know how to make the good man sin. Let's discourage him.' I think there's some truth in that. At least, that's what happened to me and Kathryn. I got discouraged and traumatized by her leaving. And then she had our son alone, after we'd been separated for nearly five months, so obviously she was discouraged and traumatized. Then inertia set in, and it reached a point of no return. She was afraid to contact me and interest me in seeing my son, for fear that I might decide I didn't want her but wanted the child." He paused, as though momentarily prevented by emotion from speaking. He regained composure quickly and spoke again, this time with a touch of melancholy in his voice. "She lived all those years thinking that I never gave a damn, and that's the impression I wanted to give her. She humiliated me, and I turned my back on her. She trashed me in public, so I decided to trash her in public. I wasn't thinking with my brain or my heart. I was thinking with my wounded ego and pride. If I'd only known then what I know now, I would have gone to Georgia to bring her back to Mexico. It was the sort of dramatic gesture she would have liked." He smiled a smile that had a trace of wistful sadness in it. "I used to call her a 'drama queen.' But by the time she figured out what she'd done, I wouldn't take her back when she called to reconcile. In a way, we divorced over an argument. It sounds pretty stupid in retrospect, Detective Sullivan. You probably wouldn't believe that I run a multimillion-dollar international business, would you?" He paused and his voice had a reflective tone when he spoke again. "Life has taught me some things in the last fifteen years. You have to fight for your marriage. You have to fight against the relatives, the friends, the schedules that separate you, against temptation, against doubts, against a lot of things."

"On the practical side, Mr. Galleria, did you and your ex-wife argue over money or visitation or custody or anything?"

"No, we didn't argue about anything. After we both remarried, I saw so many divorced families where little children were pulled back and forth like meat with constant squabbling over everything, and I just decided that I couldn't do that to my son. So I decided I would leave him alone until he was a teenager. I knew he was growing up in a happy home because I heard reports of Kathryn." He paused. Then he spoke again, this time in a somber tone. "I was always happy David had a happy home to grow up in."

Sullivan assumed he was finished, but he resumed.

"So, no, Detective Sullivan, on the practical side, we didn't argue about anything because I wasn't in their lives. But I've paid a price for my decisions. If I had it to do over again, Detective, I'd do many things differently."

"Yes, sir. I know what that feels like myself," Sullivan answered, with a wry smile. "So you didn't hate your ex-wife, then?"

"Hate her? No," he smiled, shaking his head, "I didn't hate her."

"Where were you on the morning of her death?"

"She brought David over here to the hotel around four-thirty in the morning, as we'd arranged, so he and I could go turkey hunting. Kathryn was supposed to meet us at the lodge for lunch, but she never showed up. Didn't you find her car on a back road near the track that runners use?"

"Yes, that's where we found her car. So you and David were together the whole time?"

"Yes."

"What time was she supposed to show for lunch?"

"About eleven o'clock."

"Do you know anyone who would have wanted to harm your ex-wife?"

"No. I don't. But I really haven't been in her life for the last fifteen years."

"What kind of relationship did you and Mrs. Haddad have lately?"

There was silence. Then Galleria replied matter-of-factly. "A warm relationship."

"Warm?" asked Sullivan.

"Yes, warm. Even though we were no longer married, she'd always spoken well of me to my son and encouraged him to have a tender heart toward me. I admired her qualities. I admired her intelligence. I admired her."

"Were you having an affair with your ex-wife, Mr. Galleria?"

Galleria cleared his throat. "Yes."

"Does your wife know you were having an affair?"

"No."

"What's next between you and your son, Mr. Galleria?"

"What do you mean, what's next?"

"I mean, will you be seeking custody of him since you're his natural father?"

"Detective Sullivan, they say that 'experience is what you get when you don't get what you want.' And one thing I've learned from experience is that control doesn't work in human relationships. Love that's given freely is the only kind of love worth having. So I guess what I'm saying is that I would like for David to live with me and my family, but I wouldn't try to force him." He became silent for a moment. "He's my only son, you know."

"Yes, I know, sir."

Galleria got out of his sitting position on the couch and walked toward the picture window that looked out on the courtyard garden of the hotel. He stared down in silence at the crocuses and daffodils bursting through the hard ground below, signaling winter's end and heralding spring. When he spoke again, he seemed to be talking to himself, although his words were audible to the detectives a few feet from him. "That noncontrolling love is like the love that God gives us, you know. I finally figured out, after all these years as a Catholic, why God didn't make us like robots who would do anything he wanted. He doesn't force us to love him because that isn't love. In fact, love that is commanded gets closer to hate than to love. All we ever have is an invitation to come to God, not a command. Love isn't the product of demands and control. I figured that out after losing the woman I loved."

"But you might try to influence your son to live with you now, though, sir, isn't that right?"

"Yes. I probably will. I love him." He paused and his voice was soft when he spoke again. "He's very like his mother."

"With Mrs. Haddad out of the picture, that makes it easier for you to become a bigger part of the boy's life, doesn't it, sir?"

"Yes, you could look at it like that," Galleria replied.

"Mr. Galleria, when will you be leaving town, sir?"

"What's today? Thursday? I'm leaving on Saturday, as originally planned. I have to get back to work on Monday, and my family is missing me. I just thought, after Kathryn's death, that I'd stay around and help David cope with his mother's death."

"Yes, well, we'll be going now, sir, but do you have a business card, so we can have your number if there's anything else we need to ask you once you get back to Texas?"

"Yes, yes, let me get it."

Once the thank-yous and goodbyes were said and they were back in their car with Sullivan at the wheel, Robbey spoke first.

"What'd you think, John? You think he's being straight with us?"

"Possibly," Sullivan replied, with an almost condescending definiteness in his voice.

"There's no way he could have been involved in her death?"

"I didn't say that."

"But you believe he loved his ex-wife, don't you?"

"Yes. But lots of homicides involve people killing people they love."

"Well, maybe his wife found out about the affair. Maybe she arranged to have her husband's lover knocked off."

Sullivan looked at Robbey and laughed heartily. "You watch too many soap operas and television detective stories, Nathan. Stay close to me, son, and I'll show you how it works in the real world."

Nathan felt a little defensive. Sullivan was talking to him like he was a puppy or a "sonny boy" who didn't know the difference between detectives and detergent. "Okay, boss man," he said, sounding more defensive than aggressive, "what's your theory?"

"The theory evolves, Nathan. Right now we're just bloodhounds who have to take it step by step."

"So what's the next step?"

"Getting some sleep. It's past quitting time and we've had a full day. Let's go check the office. We'll figure out soon what the next step is. Tomorrow is Friday, isn't it?"

"Yeah, tomorrow's Friday."

Robbey followed Sullivan into Sullivan's office, where his desk was piled high with files. Sullivan grabbed the telephone messages from the middle of his desk. He read through the dozen or so messages and put all of them back except one. Then he walked around his desk and over to the window, apparently studying and rereading one of the notes. He looked up at his sidekick.

"We're going to have to get a search warrant, Nathan."

"Search warrant? For what? For who?"

"I just got a departmental order put on my desk today that says the sheriff wants a search conducted of Haddad's house. It'll be done tomorrow morning, and McCormick wants us riding herd on it."

"Why? I don't get it."

"Seems like the sheriff's office is getting some heat from the press. Apparently word is leaking out that the medical examiner in Athens isn't going along with the suicide theory. This internal memo says that a reporter in town is working on a story that will quote the Athens medical examiner as saying that the crime scene looked staged. The medical examiner in Athens is a very respected industry professional, so whatever she says gets taken pretty seriously. The official autopsy report hasn't been released, but now the pressure's on McCormick to find a murder suspect, or at least look like he's going through the motions of doing that."

"It seems like Sheriff McCormick is trying to sit in the driver's seat in this investigation."

"Yeah. But he's got election jitters, and he's got to perform for the peanut gallery. Go home and get a good night's rest, Robbey. We'll pick it back up in the morning, and we may push it hard and late tomorrow. Before you go, though, call the lab and order an analysis of what Mrs. Haddad ate for breakfast the morning of her death. And call the guys downstairs and find out whose prints were on Mrs. Haddad's car."

FIFTEEN

It was Friday. Stefan was in the family room helping Calvin write a civic oration speech he'd give to his class after spring break. David was helping his third-grade sister with math while Booth sat on the other side of him reading and asking his big brother for help in sounding out an occasional word. In ninth grade, David was a gentle and generous boy who'd been trained by his mother to lend a helping hand to his brothers and sister, whether in figuring out a topic for a science project, or retrieving an object too high for them to reach, or tying a shoe. Their week of spring break obviously hadn't gone as planned—a quiet holiday during which David went hunting with his other dad. The children were going back to school on Monday without a mom. It hurt.

Booth put his book down and walked over to the couch where Stefan was helping Calvin and climbed on his father's lap, looking glum. A brawny six-year-old, he was a handsome little fellow and, although no more loved than any of the other children, he was "the baby" of the family. Stefan put his arms around him and gave him a hug.

"Dad?"

"Yes, son?"

"Is Mommy in heaven?"

Stefan took a deep breath. Where was Kathryn when he needed

her most? She'd been the spiritual guide in the family. Kathryn was
the one who used to handle the spiritual and moral teaching of the
children in their family, as a Sunday school teacher and in routine
discussions at home. Now the children would turn to him, as Booth
was now. Although Kathryn had wanted him to attend church with
her and David right after they married, she'd never nagged or insisted.
Kathryn thought religion had to do with having a personal relationship with God, and she didn't believe in badgering him into perform-
ing the rituals. In fact, she had contempt for religion that was "all
show," although she felt strongly that God was a God who wanted his
creatures to gather together routinely to worship him. After Stefan
had fathered three children, he began to see for himself the wisdom
of bringing up the children in the church. The fact that she didn't nag
was probably one reason why he eventually began to join her and the
little Haddads at church for the eleven o'clock service. "A little child
shall lead them," the Scriptures say. Marketing professors at the
Harvard Business School would call it the "pull" strategy. He wasn't
pushed into going but was pulled into church by the children. He
could see the positive influence religious teaching had on the children, and he wanted to show support.

"Yes, son, I think your mom thought that God has a place in
heaven for everyone."

Stefan swallowed hard and looked at his littlest child. He and
Kathryn used to laugh at how Booth seemed like a "wise old man."
Stefan himself had been thinking a lot about the afterlife and about
religion, especially after those people from the church had come up
to him at her funeral saying her death was "God's will," as though
that might comfort him. He thought that was crap. He couldn't believe in a God who would program a human life to engineer a mother
dying like that. Kathryn had believed that he gave you free will and
the chance to make choices, and that God was always out there rescu-
ing people from the situations they got into because of their bad
choices. She used to say God gave humans the freedom to choose,
and that God could always take our bad choices along with the suffering those bad choices caused us and use them for a good purpose.
Somehow good could always enter the picture again, even after a lot

of bad stuff. But there's no way Stefan could ever worship a God who micromanaged people's lives and made bad things happen to good people, just so he could show he was the boss and had the power. If God is love, he wouldn't do that.

Stefan looked at his youngest child and resumed their conversation. "Jesus told his disciples after the resurrection that even though he had to leave them to go back into heaven, he would send the Holy Spirit to live inside us when he left. And he told his disciples that where he was going, they would also be going one day, because he was going to his Father's house to prepare a room for them. So, yes, I think your mom is up in heaven with Jesus and God."

"But I don't want her to be there yet. I want her to be here with me. Who's going to take me to karate?"

"I'll take you, son, don't worry about that. I'm going to be home when you get home from school, just like your mom was, and I'll get you everywhere you need to go."

Stefan remembered how he and Kathryn had argued about whether the other children should be allowed to ride with David after he got his license at age sixteen. Stefan had been opposed to it, and he'd told Kathryn that under no circumstances would his other children ride in a car David was driving for quite a few years. How quickly one's opinion can change. How would he possibly get everyone to and from ballet and soccer and football practice and everything else if David couldn't help with the driving? Kathryn had been right.

"Are you going to marry some other lady, Dad?" Booth asked.

"Son . . . no . . . ," muttered Stefan, aware that he didn't need to overreact to the childlike questions of a boy wondering what life was going to be like without his mom.

"Dad's not thinking about getting married again, Booth. How can you ask that?" blasted David.

"No, David, take it easy, son, everyone wonders about different things after someone's death. It's okay to ask all the questions you want to ask. You kids don't need to hold anything back. I may not know all the answers, but I want to know what you're thinking about."

Suddenly David cracked an impish smile. "Do you remember when Mom brought Booth home from the hospital? We were living in the other house then, and she brought him home and laid him on the floor, and we all crowded around. I was nine, and Calvin was four, and Veronica was almost two, and we thought he was the cutest thing in the whole world. Remember how you used to call me 'Da Do' when you couldn't say 'David,' Booth?"

Easygoing David was responding to his dad's wishes to be gentle with his littlest brother. Booth smiled appreciatively at his elder brother. He idolized David and thought he knew all the answers in life.

Then David aimed his stare at Calvin. "And remember how Mom and Dad used to crack up over what you said, Calvin?" David continued. "Remember when Mom and Dad were congratulating you on answering some question correctly when you were five years old and you told them, 'Well, I'm not as dumb as I look.' Remember how Mom used to laugh about that?"

Stefan smiled. Some of the happiest moments he'd shared with Kathryn were over the "childrenisms" of the four kids they raised together.

Calvin piped up. "Hey, remember how Mom cracked up when Booth came running in the door after his first day at kindergarten yelling, 'Guess what, Mom, I'm an American and I was born in the United States, and we're going to have a fun raiser . . .' and then he asked, 'Mom, what *is* a fun raiser?'"

"Oh, yeah, Mom really enjoyed those fund-raisers, didn't she?" added David, wrinkling his brow to emphasize he was talking tongue-in-cheek. "She used to say our family had forty-two fund-raisers a year when she counted Girl Scout cookies, Cub Scout popcorn, Boy Scout spaghetti, Rotary Club roses, the Methodist Women's bazaar, youth fellowship car washes, school book fairs, science club candy sales, debate club T-shirts, the sports teams' solicitations, and all the other stuff."

"Yeah, but she did something for every one of them, remember?" chimed in Stefan. Obviously the children were ventilating their longing for their mother, and they wanted to talk about her, not just think about her. He would encourage them to say her name and smile when they remembered her.

"She did," said David, "but she used to say having four kids kept her 'fund-raiser poor' all the time."

"Hey, what about that first-grade story Mom used to tell about you, David?" asked Calvin.

David's black bushy eyebrows furled up in a *V* as he shot a quizzical look at Calvin.

Calvin supplied the story David was trying to recall. "Remember? You were in first grade and your teacher was asking everyone what he wanted to be when he grew up . . ."

"She asked the *girls* in the class, too, you know," corrected Veronica grumpily. Calvin shot his sister a disgusted look, and Stefan had a flashback to the numerous times he'd ask Kathryn how Veronica's feminist training was coming along. Kathryn always had the same reply. "Just perfect, honey, thanks for asking," she would reply, in a greatly exaggerated form of her Southern accent.

"That's what 'he' means, stupid," replied Calvin condescendingly. "Pay attention in English class and you'll learn that 'he' can mean a 'he' or a 'she.' And, Dad, tell her to quit interrupting me!"

"Go ahead and finish what you were telling us," responded Stefan.

"Okay. Don't you remember how everyone else in David's first-grade class was telling the teacher that *he*," he emphasized, glaring at his sister, "wanted to be a fireman or policeman or something like that? Then she asked David what he wanted to be when he grew up, and David said, 'A paleontologist.' And Mom said when the teacher recovered from her shock, she asked what a paleontologist does, and David said, 'Oh, he digs up dinosaur bones.' "

Veronica burst out laughing and looked admiringly at David. Then she spoke with an impish smile, "And don't you remember what Mom told us about when David was getting potty trained?" She had the look of a little girl getting ready to tell a naughty joke.

"No, I don't remember," replied Booth, looking upset and left out. As the youngest, he was still being initiated into the family folklore.

"Well," Veronica began, looking extremely knowledgeable, "Mom said she was helping David pull up his underpants one day when he was getting potty trained, and he dripped on his underpants after he used the toilet, and when Mom asked him about how that happened, he said, 'Oh, I guess my penis is just too long.'" Calvin roared with laughter.

"Yeah," David said, blushing and looking slightly uncomfortable that his little sister was discussing his private parts, even if it was a story from childhood. "And what about when Calvin broke his collarbone?" he asked, changing the subject.

"Oh, yeah, let me tell that story," interrupted Calvin.

"No, I want to," insisted Veronica.

"Let Calvin tell it," mediated Stefan, "since it's about him. You can tell one about you next, Veronica."

They turned to look at Calvin, and he looked suddenly embarrassed. He began slowly. "Well, I was just over two years old, and Mom was getting ready to give birth to my nasty little sister any day." He paused to glare at Veronica. She glared back, unintimidated. "It was about six o'clock at night, and Mom and I were out on the front porch waiting for Dad to come home from work when the phone rang. I was walking around in some of her high heel shoes, and Mom said I must have fallen off the porch when she ran in to answer the phone. When she came back to say Dad would be late, I was whimpering. Anyway, the next morning we had to go stay with Grandma for three days 'cause Mom went in the hospital. When she came back, she let me climb up on a chair to help her make cookies, and she saw that I had to turn my whole body around to look at her when she called my name. Then she called Dad and took me to the doctor and found out I had a broken collarbone."

"And your mom never threw away the soft brace you had to wear for three months," added Stefan gently, remembering the toddler who had to wear the brace continuously for weeks so the clavicle would heal properly.

"Hey, Dad, remember how Mom liked the classical music story?" asked Calvin, with a mischievous smile on his face.

"Yeah, you go ahead and tell it. That's a good one," Stefan answered.

"Well," said Calvin, "we were driving down the street one day, just Mom and me, and she was listening to music and flipping from one station to another like she always did. Then she turned down the music and asked me, 'What kind of music do you like, Calvin?' And I said, 'Classical music.' And Mom was so happy! She said she figured she must be doing a great job as a mom if I liked classical music! Then she asked me what I meant by that and I said, 'Oh, you know, from the sixties and seventies.' So Mom used to say that her children thought she was from the classical era!"

"Now it's my turn," pouted Veronica, with a sour expression on her face, looking as though she'd been holding her breath until Calvin finished his second story.

"Okay, go ahead," smiled Stefan at his only daughter. Kathryn had loved that little girl so much. Once, though, after Veronica was born, Kathryn had confessed to him that, during that pregnancy, she'd been fearful of having a girl because she was afraid she would have the same jealous, hostile, and competitive relationship with her own daughter that her mother had with her. Thankfully, Kathryn's relationship with Veronica was nothing like Kathryn's relationship with Vera. Stefan looked adoringly at his daughter as he remembered a story about their mom.

"Remember when you were in the car with your mom when you were just two years old, and you looked over at her and shrugged your shoulders and smiled and said, 'Two girls!' And that became your and Mom's slogan, didn't it?"

"Yes, Dad," responded Veronica impatiently, gritting her teeth as though he was pushing her to her physical waiting limit, "but let me talk now."

"Go ahead, sorry I interrupted, but I just remembered that."

Then, as though she were preparing to give the stage performance of her life, Veronica took a deep breath and smiled sweetly at each one of her brothers and then at her dad, signifying that she was officially on the air. "Don't you remember how I was born dad's favorite color—purple?" As soon as she said it, she lifted her chin and tossed her long hair and made her face up into an expression reminiscent of Moses coming down from the mountaintop with all the answers. It was the little-miss-know-it-all face that drove her brothers crazy.

Stefan's mind raced back in time. These stories reminded him of the sweetest moments in his life, those times when his children were born or were very young. Calvin had been born about eighteen months after they married, and he was a joy to him, Kathryn, and David from the moment he was born. David was thrilled to have a little brother, and he used to sit in the child's rocking chair and give Calvin his bottle. Then Kathryn, who always got pregnant easily—he used to kid her that he could look at her wrong and she'd get pregnant—miscarried when she was three months pregnant. She miscarried at home and then went to the doctor's office to be cleaned out internally. Typical Vera, she'd shown up at the doctor's office to give Kathryn a lecture about how she was too old to be trying to have more children and that's what God was trying to tell her with the miscarriage. Then, right away, she got pregnant with Veronica. Until then, Kathryn had normal vaginal births, and they were expecting no problems on this one, either. Kathryn said later she should have realized that her tummy was in a different shape than with the other pregnancies, but the doctors never suspected a breech baby and Kathryn didn't know what a breech baby was until after Veronica was born.

"Go ahead, you can tell it," Stefan said to Veronica, as she was bumping up and down on the couch trying to get his attention so she'd be called on to continue the story.

"Okay, well," Veronica proceeded, "Mom said she went to the hospital, and then the lady doctor checked her over by putting her hand up inside Mom."

"Ooooh, gross!" screamed Booth, covering his head with one of the pillows from the couch.

Veronica shot him a look like the ice maiden trying to melt down a mortal enemy. "Be quiet, please," she commanded sternly, in a tone of voice that showed her annoyance of his immaturity. "Well, anyway, the lady doctor said to the nurse that she didn't feel the head! And Mom said she was thinking, *Well, I'm sure this baby must have a head*. And then Mom said the young lady doctor on call that night telephoned an older doctor, and he had to leave his dinner on Saturday night to come over to the hospital. The nurses and doctors were giving Mom shots to try to keep the baby from coming 'cause they said Mom was already 'an eight.'" She paused and looked searchingly at her dad. "Dad, what is 'an eight,' again?"

"Well, when you have a baby, the opening where the baby comes out has to get to ten centimeters, and Mom was already at eight centimeters, so they were trying to stop her from having the baby until they could see where the baby's head was."

"Oh, that's right," continued Veronica, "Mom said they were taking X-rays, and they finally got an X-ray that showed that I was feet first." She smiled the know-it-all smile again.

"Yeah," Stefan recalled with a grin, "Mom said you probably didn't want to mess up your hair by coming out head first, like most babies do."

"Dad, what's the big deal about being feet first?" asked Calvin, shooting Veronica a look that clearly communicated that he thought her story was pointless and irrelevant.

"Well, son, it turned out alright in Veronica's case because they had to rush your mom into the delivery room, and she only pushed twice and Veronica slid right out. But sometimes a breech baby might not be feet first. Sometimes a knee or an elbow can get caught on the baby's way out of the birth canal. Anyway, if the baby's head doesn't come out quickly and get oxygen to the brain, the baby can be born brain damaged. That's why most breech babies are born by what they call a cesarean section. That means they don't let the baby get born the regular way, but they cut a hole in the mom's tummy and lift the baby out."

"So, anyway, Dad," huffed Veronica, looking red in the face and sounding irritated, "as I was saying before I was interrupted, I slid right out of Mom, and Dad was even in the delivery room, although he *wasn't*," she emphasized, glaring at Calvin, "in the delivery room when the boys were born." Then she smiled sweetly and looked at her dad adoringly. "And Dad said he looked at me and I was purple— his favorite color!"

"So you weren't in the delivery room with Booth and me, right, Dad?" asked Calvin.

"No, son, I wasn't. I guess I was kind of old-fashioned. I thought the man should stand outside the delivery room with cigars. But when your sister was born, I went in with your mom because it looked like there might be a problem."

"Is that what happened to her? Is that how she got brain damaged?" Calvin smiled wickedly at his sister as he asked the question.

Veronica replied sarcastically, in the style of a country preacher delivering the truth. "No, Calvin, Mom said the pediatrician came to the hospital and checked me out and said I was a perfect ten! And what were you, Calvin," she asked contemptuously, "about a four?"

"Wait a minute, wait a minute," said Stefan, sensing that a quarrel was getting ready to erupt between the two middle children. They were the two always ready to argue with each other, whereas Booth would intelligently avoid a squabble, and David was a peacemaker.

"And then Mom said you gave out pink bubble gum cigars after I was born, right, Dad?"

"Did you give out any when I was born?" interrogated Calvin, who was always interested in making sure he received his share.

"Did you give out any for me?" added Booth.

"Yes, I gave out blue bubble gum cigars that Mom got for me when you two were born."

"Hey, what about the time Brownie got lost, and we got him back on Christmas Day at twelve noon? Remember how Mom said that little things happen in life that show you that God looks after each of us?" After David spoke, they sat in silence for a moment recalling the incident nearly three years ago when the mutt they'd had for over thirteen years got lost. He was David's dog, really, because Kathryn and David had brought Brownie home in a shoe box from the SPCA when David was almost three years old. A mongrel mix of terrier and cocker spaniel, Brownie got lost when they were building the new house. They'd left the dog in the fenced-in backyard at the old house while they built the fence at the new house. Kathryn had gone every day to feed him and knew he was lonely and unhappy, but he had to stay there while the fence got finished. When the fence was seven days from completion, Brownie, the doe-eyed terrier who'd grown older and weaker as the children grew stronger and taller, clawed his way under the fence, probably looking for his family. He was gone when they showed up to feed him.

It had been a real family crisis. Even Stefan, who pretended he wasn't all that attached to Brownie, felt sad to think of the animal

alone in the world, possibly dead, perhaps searching for them, probably without food and water, and very likely picked on by bigger dogs
roaming the city. Growing up in Montreal, he'd known dogs only as
guards and sentries, usually vicious animals who had to be locked up
when you went to someone's house, so he hadn't been keen when
Kathryn told him by phone before they married that she and David
had adopted a dog.

After Brownie got lost, just nine days before Christmas, Kathryn
and David littered their old neighborhood with poster bills, giving
the telephone number of the Chic Boutique. They checked every animal shelter. Days went by, Christmas came closer, and there was still
no sign of Brownie. Then, on Christmas Day, at eleven o'clock in the
morning, the phone rang and a lady with four little children, cooking
Christmas dinner, called to say she'd used the city directory to track
down the residence of the owner of the Chic Boutique because she
thought she saw a dog matching Brownie's description near their
church.

When Kathryn told the children that someone said she'd seen a
dog looking like Brownie near the church, David had replied, "At the
church? Well, he knew where to go to get help, didn't he?"

So two months after they moved into the new house, the seventh
member of their family was home again.

"Yeah, that's right, Mom said some things happen that just let
you know that God has a sense of humor, and that he looks out for
you in a personal way. That dog was like her baby," said Calvin.

"Well, that's different from what you said then, Calvin," responded David. "Don't you remember when Mom told you and
Veronica that Brownie was lost, expecting you to be all broken up
about it, all you said was, 'Well, can we get a cat?'"

Veronica and Calvin smiled broadly, remembering their goofy
response.

Suddenly their nostalgia was interrupted by the sound of the doorbell. It was the front door. David jumped up and said he'd take care of
it.

"Probably some kids on a fund-raiser," he joked, as he left the
family room.

They heard David talking in a low voice with an adult male, and then they heard the door close. David reappeared in the family room.

"Dad, I think you'd better come to the door. There are some people that want to see you." David had a solemn look on his face.

"Sure, son," Stefan said, rising from the couch after taking his littlest son off his lap and resettling him on the couch beside his big sister. "You two read for a minute. I'll see who's there."

When he opened the front door, he was surprised to find four uniformed officers and a rottweiler-looking dog, along with the two detectives Sullivan and Robbey, standing on his front porch. "Hello, Detective Sullivan," Stefan said, extending his hand, "what can I do for you gentlemen?"

"Mr. Haddad," replied John Sullivan, looking Stefan straight in the eyes and holding up the piece of paper he had in his hand, "we have a search warrant, and we've been instructed to search your house. We'd like to ask your cooperation, sir."

"Search warrant?" Stefan felt as though someone had shot him. "What on earth do you want to search my house for?"

"We're continuing our investigation into your wife's death, sir, and we have to conduct every kind of search possible so we get the answers we're looking for."

"Well, yes, of course, go ahead. I'm just so surprised. I mean, you don't need a search warrant. If you'd asked me if you could look around, I would have said yes, anyway." He put both his hands on top of his head and ran his fingers through his hair, as though in a daze. "Well, how does this work? Come in, please, Detectives, you can go wherever you want. Oh, wait, I need to tell my kids what's going on . . . and . . . are you bringing the dog inside, too?"

"Sir, we're going to use the dog to search the garage and the outside of the house."

"What are you looking for, I don't understand," said Stefan, sounding bewildered.

"Just let us get on with the search, sir. We'll try to get out of your way as soon as possible."

"Well, let me tell my kids what's happening. But, come on in. Why don't you start upstairs while I tell the children what you're doing."

"Would you mind opening the garage for these two officers, sir, while these other two officers come inside and start upstairs?" asked John Sullivan.

"Yes, I'll do that," Stefan said flatly, in a tone of voice that sounded like he was sedated.

After opening the garage, Stefan went back into the family room to find his children looking puzzled. "Hey, guys," he announced as cheerfully as he could, "some officers have come to search our house for any clues that will help them solve the mystery of your mother's death. I told them they can go wherever they want to in the house, and we'll just stay here and read or do something like that while they work."

It seemed a nice theory that the five of them would simply sit in the family room and chat and tell stories while the officers sifted through their most personal and intimate objects, but the mood had been too radically altered by the intruders for polite conversation to occur. The five of them sat in silence, listening to footsteps above as the officers searched the four bedrooms, storeroom closets, and game room. There was a grim air of suspense about the silent wait, as though they shared a common understanding that the intruders were not looking for good news. No one spoke of suspicion, but the air hung heavy with an ominous uncertainty. Nostalgia and laughter had been chased away by fear and dread.

"Detective Sullivan?" exclaimed a young officer coming into the family room from the garage. He looked excited, as though he'd just found the Holy Grail. Stefan looked at his young face and decided he couldn't have been more than twenty years old. Suddenly it hit him that there was less than a five-year difference between the young officer and David. He couldn't believe David was almost a man; it seemed like just a couple of years ago that he and Kathryn had married, and he'd taken on the job of being daddy to that little boy.

"I think Detective Sullivan is upstairs," Stefan said to the young officer.

"Thank you, sir," said the young man, politely nodding at Stefan as he passed them in the family room and went into the foyer to climb the stairs to the second floor.

Stefan heard voices talking upstairs, but he couldn't make out what they were saying. Then the officers came downstairs, through the family room, and disappeared past the kitchen into the hallway that led into the garage. Within five minutes Detective Sullivan reappeared in the family room and spoke to Stefan.

"Mr. Haddad, will you come with me for a moment, sir?" Sullivan asked.

"Of course," Stefan said, following him into the garage. Sullivan led him to the cubbyhole in the garage wall where he kept the family paints and paintbrushes.

"Do you know what this is, Mr. Haddad?" began Detective Sullivan.

"It looks like a mirror. And that bag looks like it has a white powder in it," answered Stefan.

"Do these belong to you?"

"No, I've never seen them before."

"What're they doing here, sir, if they're not yours?" continued Sullivan.

"I have no idea. I didn't know those things were there. I don't know who they belong to and how they got there. They're not mine." As he heard himself making the declarations, Stefan could hear how disjointed and lacking in self-confidence he sounded.

"Mr. Haddad, I think you'd better come down to the law enforcement center so we can ask you some questions. I'd like you to come with us now, sir, if you can find a neighbor to stay with the children. Is that possible?"

Stefan swallowed hard. It felt as though his human secretions were drying up, leaving him parched and barren. He'd never felt more alone. He'd always had Kathryn to turn to when he had a tough decision to make, or when he needed someone with a good head to help him think something through. She was smart and had the ability to become calm and focused in a crisis. Where was she now when he needed her? He felt numb and like he was just half a person without her. It felt like he was getting beat up but didn't know why they were pounding on him. It was the first time since Kathryn's death that he had felt really alone, all alone, in the world.

"Okay, ahmm, I guess I can ask my neighbor, June, to come in and stay with the kids for a couple of hours. David will be sixteen tomorrow and he could supervise everybody, but I think I'd like someone here with them." He went inside the house to call June. She said she'd noticed the patrol cars and was wondering what they were doing outside his house, and she'd be happy to be with the kids for a few hours. She said she'd cook dinner for them while she was there.

Down at the law enforcement center, Stefan had his rights read to him. He declined having a lawyer present. He didn't have a lawyer, anyway. He'd always functioned without an accountant or lawyer, since he had the education and analytical skills required to prepare his own taxes and even to create the legal documents related to incorporation for the Chic Boutique. Aside from a few guys in the Rotary Club, he wouldn't know who to call even if he needed a lawyer, which he didn't. If you haven't done anything wrong, he reasoned to himself, why would you need a lawyer?

The questions the detectives asked were curious. Had he and Kathryn ever used drugs? Did they use drugs recently? How did he explain the fact that the officers found a bag of cocaine and a mirror of the type often used in snorting coke in his paint cubbyhole? Had his wife been a closet druggie? Was he a closet druggie? How long had he known of his wife's affair with her ex-husband? How did he feel about that affair? Hadn't he felt angry and hostile toward her? What had prompted him to take out the special key-person insurance policy on his wife? How did it feel knowing that he was suddenly a multimillionaire upon his wife's death? Did he have a girlfriend on the side, by any chance? Where exactly had he been on the morning of her death?

"Well, what do you think?" Robbey asked Sullivan after Stefan Haddad left to go home after nearly four hours of questioning.

John Sullivan leaned back in his chair, worn-out mentally and physically from the four-hour conversation and the events that preceded it. He put his feet up on the long table where he, Robbey, and Haddad had been sitting just minutes before.

"Well," Sullivan began, as he looked at the notes Robbey had taken during the interrogation, "I think we learned something new. We now know that after she left the house early, she returned home about eight-thirty to bring a box filled with high school trophies and college yearbooks from her parents' house, and he thought she said she was going shopping. Then he drove off in his own car, to go running, at the same time she drove off." He was speaking slowly and deliberately, as though trying to make sure he recited perfectly the chronology of events Haddad had described.

"Why didn't he tell his story like that before? Why didn't he tell us previously that she came back home after visiting her parents early that morning?" asked the rookie.

"He said he just remembered it. He said when we questioned him before, he was groggy from a sleeping pill he'd taken the previous night."

"Yeah, I know that's what he said, but it seems like an odd thing to forget. It tarnishes his credibility a little, don't you think? So, now what do we do?"

"You go on home, Nathan. It's been a long day. I'll go upstairs to the office to make our official report on the search and on the questioning of Haddad. I'll see you in the morning. Let's meet at Cathy's Coffee Shop to have breakfast at seven o'clock, and then we'll come to the office to check in and figure out the day's agenda. That bag of cocaine and mirror have gone to the lab for analysis and fingerprints, so maybe they'll have some results by midmorning. We might get the official autopsy report tomorrow, too."

SIXTEEN

C athy's Coffee Shop on Highway 75 was a favorite with truckers and had been open since five o'clock when Robbey and Sullivan arrived. The fragrance of grits, sausage, egg, and coffee assaulted their senses as soon as they walked in. After breakfast, they went to the office. It had long been Sullivan's practice to drop by the office on Saturday morning to read his mail, and he'd made it a requirement years ago that the mail room deliver mail to his office six days a week. On top of his desk were what looked like two official reports and one note. One was the complete autopsy report signed by the medical examiner from Athens. Another was the report from the lab. Sullivan opened them both and read them. The note surprised him. He figured it must have been written late the previous evening or early that morning. An early riser, his young secretary had the habit of dropping by the office to tidy up on Saturday mornings before her visit to the spa, so maybe she'd been there that morning and intercepted a call.

JOHN,
CALL MCCORMICK RIGHT AWAY. HE'S HOT!
SARA

His funky young secretary from the Northeast had an electric way of communicating with her boss, but he liked the spirited twenty-eight-year-old whom he'd hired a year ago. She was different from the other women in the office, most of whom were lethargic, dull women who hadn't been out of the county in their lives. They hadn't expected to befriend the lithe, saucy Yankee from Connecticut who had a salty expression for nearly everything, but slowly the trim-figured girl from the Northeast won them over. What had begun as a frosty relationship had thawed recently, when the women in the office more or less adopted her after her boyfriend dumped her. Why was it, Sullivan wondered, people related better to the failures rather than the successes of other human beings? Why was it that success seemed to breed only resentment and jealousy? Anyway, when the culturally different, sassy, bright, and vivacious Sara was dumped unceremoniously by the guy for whom she'd moved South and who never deserved her in the first place, the girls in the office checked into Sara's life with a little Southern hospitality. Maybe it was just men dumping women that seemed to make women bond together. Anyway, there had a been a bonus for him in the fact that young Sara the transplant was cementing relationships around the office because it helped him get more securely connected into the informal information network. If you wanted to know what was happening, and what was getting ready to go down, you could forget reading the formal reports. Just ask the ladies in the office. They always knew which way the wind was going to blow.

"Is Sheriff McCormick in?" John asked the switchboard operator after he dialed the number.

"Who's calling?" she replied, in a tone that was sufficiently polite with a slight hint of condescension.

"John Sullivan returning his call."

"He's at home, but I can connect you. Just a moment," she commanded.

Within seconds Sheriff Matt McCormick picked up. "John, I hope you're close to identifying a suspect in that murder case of Kathryn Haddad." It sounded more like an order than a question.

"Sir, I wouldn't say we're real close. We're still investigating."

"Investigating, hell. You need to show some preliminary results of the investigation and name a suspect. Frankly, I can't believe that medical examiner wouldn't rule this a suicide. The medical examiner from Macon took a look at the body after it was shipped back from Athens, and he would've been willing to call it a suicide. I'd like to wrap this thing up and get on to something else. But that Athens examiner is a bitch, and I know she'll cause trouble for me if I don't make sure we're looking hard for a murderer."

"I just read the autopsy report she signed. Seems like she's making a lot of the fact that Mrs. Haddad had a suspicious bump on her head, which could indicate foul play, and then the examiner felt the death scene looked staged. She found it implausible that a lady without any track marks in her arm would shoot up with a mixture of heroine and cocaine."

"Yeah, I know, I read the damned thing," McCormick said, sounding disgusted. "The lady missed her calling. She should've been a homicide detective, not a medical examiner. She's a bitch. I've met that woman." McCormick paused, then continued. "But, if there is a murderer, it's pretty obvious who the most likely suspect is, from the reports you've written the past few days and especially the one you wrote yesterday, after the search." It was a matter of policy that detectives on homicide cases input a formal daily report.

"You've read them, sir?"

"Hell, yes, I've read them. As soon as you input your findings into our computer, I have access to them, even when I'm home. That's what that new information system is all about. Those damned county commissioners never understood that this new system gives them twenty-four-hour surveillance. And it gives them a twenty-four-hour-a-day sheriff. That's why I wanted it. Those idiots can turn anything into something political."

Sheriff McCormick was referring to the controversial new information system he'd ordered for the department. Word around town was that the department had overpaid by a lot for what it should have cost, and after the purchase there had been considerable discussion among the county commissioners about the fact that the system should have been put out for bid. But it hadn't happened that way. McCormick had simply picked one of his buddies in town, a big campaign contributor and a country club crony, as vendor for the system. The controversy had mysteriously died down for a while, and

Sullivan figured there must have been some backroom deal with the commissioners for them to suddenly drop it. But the controversy was continuing in the newspaper, with citizens writing letters to the editor demanding more details on how the money had been spent, and with an unflattering article written recently by a young reporter with a Jewish name who was obviously a Yankee transplant with no local loyalties. This was an election year for McCormick, so he was feeling some heat.

When the new communications system was installed, the sheriff had implemented a departmental policy that a report be provided daily by each detective, using the computer with modem he'd purchased for them. Even the patrol cars had been equipped with computers called mobile data terminals. Following policy, Sullivan had written his report of the Haddad search as soon as it was concluded, so McCormick had learned the night before about the cocaine and drug paraphernalia found there.

John had never liked Matt McCormick, and the feeling was clearly mutual. It seemed to Sullivan that it was a bit of a farce to call McCormick "sir," even though McCormick was a contemporary of his father. McCormick and Sullivan had more or less always known each other. McCormick and Sullivan's father had played football together on the high school team, played basketball on rival church teams, and, as early as junior high, had fallen into a natural adversarial relationship. Even in the junior high forensics club and then on the senior high debate team, they took completely opposite positions— Republican versus Democrat, conservative versus liberal, and so forth. From what his father had told him, there hadn't been any doubt in anyone's mind in high school what Matt McCormick's destiny was: he was going to enjoy daddy's money and take the easy way out. McCormick's father owned several businesses in town that he'd inherited from his father, and Matt McCormick ran his daddy's real estate company for several years. Then he decided that running for public office was how he should spend his forties. Sheriff was an elected position in the South, and the job attracted many candidates interested in power and control. In Macon, the successful candidate was usually some redneck with family money who could afford to run for the office and who would make whatever promises or deals he had to in order to win. McCormick had been elected for several terms and was full of self-importance. His management style was a no-manners approach, and he was particularly irritating to John Sullivan, who'd grown up in a family that exalted honest principles and scrupulous loyalty as the only way to operate in the public arena. McCormick was a loudmouth who had no style and no morals. Sullivan's dad used to say that "people get the government they deserve," but Sullivan wondered how any town could deserve a conniving con artist like Matt McCormick whose only advantage in politics was that he could buy any office he wanted. As a detective, John worked for him, and McCormick seemed to enjoy lording it over the gracious, well-heeled, and conscientious gentleman who came from a family respected for its decency and integrity, unlike McCormick's.

"We don't have a suspect yet, sir, but we're working hard to find the right one."

"I think the suspect is right in front of your face, John," McCormick sneered aggressively.

Sullivan didn't reply. He could hear McCormick breathing hard on the other phone, and he imagined McCormick talking on the speaker phone in his private library with his feet on the desk, as he sat barking commands at the county's leading homicide detective.

"Did you hear what I said, John?" asked the belligerent McCormick.

"Yes, sir, I did, but I'm not sure what you're talking about."

Nate Robbey was standing near John's desk listening to Sullivan's side of the conversation. He could see Sullivan was vexed. When Sullivan noticed out of the corner of his eye that Robbey was listening intently, he hit the button that made McCormick's voice come through on the speaker phone so Robbey could hear the other side.

"I'm talking about the cocaine and drug mirror you found in her husband's house. He's the only one who has a motive in this case. From the talk around town, she was having an affair, and he probably knew about it and killed her. Sometimes the answer you're looking for is right in front of your face, Sullivan. You just want to beat every bush before you face the facts. Don't be such a slug." Sullivan was accustomed to the sarcastic tone in McCormick's voice, but it still irritated him.

"Well, I agree that the cocaine and mirror cast some suspicion his way, but I don't think it necessarily makes him our murder suspect, Sheriff McCormick."

"Oh, you don't? If you look closely, you'll find you have a strong circumstantial case against the guy. Just look at it. This guy Haddad is basically an unknown. He's a damned naturalized citizen who probably married Kathryn Faison for her money and family connections. Look at how well he's made out. He snuffs his old lady, who was running around on him, and he suddenly comes out rich. He owns a business, he's the owner of a multimillion-dollar insurance policy, and he's rid of an unfaithful wife. From what I hear, he came to town just over ten years ago with nothing except the clothes on his back. He's no different from all the Cubans and Puerto Ricans and Haitians who get off the boat and strike it rich in the good ol' U.S. of A."

"He's seems like a nice guy and a family man. I don't think he killed his wife."

"Oh, hell," he sneered, "he wouldn't be the first nice guy who ever killed his wife, would he, Detective? And as a practical matter, although I realize you don't have to worry about practical matters," he said sarcastically, "I'm getting a lot of heat from the media to close in on some answers in this case. I can't keep telling them you're still investigating, but that you haven't come up with jackshit. You need to provide the name of the most likely suspect within thirty-six hours, Sullivan. You don't have to be sure. That's not your job to decide who did it. You're just supposed to collect the evidence. The grand jury will let the guy off if he didn't do it. I'll trust the grand jury to make the decision. You just get me a name." He paused. "Or I'll provide the name myself. I have to throw some meat to the media dogs. Those sons-of-bitches. I wish they'd get off my case about that communications system." He paused again. When he continued, it was in a tone of voice that was almost confessional. "The election is just a few months away, you know, and we have to take every opportunity to make the department look good. I'm going to use this case as a way of proving to the public that I had great insight when I bought this new information system ... I mean, that's how we've cracked this case so soon, isn't it, Sullivan? I'm going to bust the balls of those county commissioners."

McCormick abruptly hung up. His exit was always like that, rude and ill-mannered.

"What now, boss?" Robbey asked of his pensive-looking mentor.

Sullivan picked up the phone and dialed McCormick's home number. "Mrs. McCormick, I hope I'm not disturbing your breakfast. This is John Sullivan. May I speak to your husband again, please? We were just talking, and I remembered something I had to tell him."

"Sheriff McCormick? This is Sullivan again. I think we need to look a little further into the involvement of either the ex-husband or maybe a family member in her death. I just read a lab report and the autopsy report, and there are a couple of things that bother me. The ex-husband's prints were found on her car door, and Kathryn Haddad didn't have any breakfast in her stomach, even though her mother says she cooked her a big breakfast." As he was speaking, Sullivan pushed the button to turn the speaker phone on, so Robbey heard the blast of McCormick's response.

"Have you gone stark-raving mad, Sullivan? What a bunch of crap! What mystery novels have you been reading lately? You better be damned glad you told me about your so-called reservations, because there's no way I'm going to let you embarrass this department. The Faisons are well respected in this community, and it's common knowledge that they've done everything they could to help both their daughters. They've been model parents, and there's no way you're going off on some ignorant tangent, especially with the election coming up. That's all we need, is for you to make us look like a bunch of clowns. You could damned well be run out of this homicide department if you try to chase some loony theory like that." McCormick stopped barking threats and resumed talking in a more civilized, conciliatory tone. "Look, John, you have a husband and an ex-husband in this case. I don't give a damn if you nail the ex-husband. Just do it within thirty-six hours. The press already know that we're not calling it a suicide, so they're on my back for a suspect. One of them did it. Figure out which one. I'm going to announce the identity of our main suspect on the evening news tomorrow in a press conference, and if you don't supply a name different than Haddad, then I'm going to have him arrested for his wife's murder. We're not going for a jury conviction today, don't you understand, Sullivan? We're just trying to feed the press enough to make a meal. But I'm not going to allow you to humiliate Vera Faison. You're not going to add insult to the grief that family is already feeling."

When Sullivan heard McCormick hang up, he was visibly upset, more upset than Robbey had ever seen him.

"What do we do now?" asked Robbey in an almost inaudible voice. He wanted to ask the question out loud, so Sullivan would know he was there for him. He was proud to be John Sullivan's partner.

Sullivan shook his head, and a frustrated and melancholy look came over his face. "All the evidence so far points to a man who might not have done it."

"What should we do?" asked Robbey.

"We have to call Haddad. Better yet, I'll call him and tell him we're coming, and then we'll go see him."

There was a grim silence in the car ride to Haddad's house. It didn't seem like normal procedure, advising a murder suspect that the investigation was closing in on him, but Robbey asked no questions and Sullivan gave no lessons. It seemed Sullivan had a sense of foreboding.

"Come in, Detectives!" Haddad seemed genuinely glad to see them. Haddad had always been gracious and polite to them. Robbey felt a twinge of guilt as the kind man let them in the front door.

"Can we talk privately somewhere, sir?" asked Sullivan.

"Yes, of course, in the dining room. I'll let the children know you're here, and I'll ask them not to disturb us." Sullivan and Robbey heard the gentle-talking fellow from Canada tell Booth he'd be back shortly to finish solving the math problem they'd been working on. He asked Veronica to go upstairs to tidy her room, and he persuaded the two older boys to go into the garage to work on a science project Calvin had to present the following week. His mother had helped Calvin get the written paper done, but he had to go create more of the volcano and finish up the exhibit portion of the project.

"Okay, Detectives, everybody is taken care of. Now what can I do for you?" Haddad smiled when he came back into the room. "And how about some tea or a soft drink?"

"No, sir, we don't want any," said Sullivan, apparently making the decision for both of them. "I need to talk to you about something, Mr. Haddad." Sullivan took a breath and paused. He seemed nervous. Robbey had never seen him nervous.

"I have to tell you, sir, that at least for the moment, you appear to be emerging as the prime suspect in your wife's murder."

Stefan was seated in the chair at the head of the dining room table, where his wife used to sit. He appeared drained of emotion. Then he shook his head slowly.

"The nightmare continues," he said quietly and reflectively, as though talking to himself while he stared at the table. "This is just unreal. I can't fathom how or why anyone would think I would kill my wife."

"Well, sir, the department has sufficient evidence to name you as a possible suspect. It's a matter of record that you've been enriched by the insurance policy you bought two years before her death and, of course, you stand to inherit all the assets you both owned together. Her adultery will be viewed as your motivation. And then, there's the mirror and bag of cocaine found at your house during the search. The autopsy puts the time of her death somewhere between nine o'clock and eleven o'clock, which is about when you were outside the house yourself. It seems there is motive and opportunity sufficient to identify you as a suspect, sir."

"What are you saying, exactly?"

"What I'm saying, sir, is that I believe the sheriff is going to have you arrested for the murder of Kathryn Haddad."

SEVENTEEN

The following day, Sunday, during a live press conference on the six o'clock news, Sheriff McCormick reported that Stefan Haddad had been charged with the murder of his wife on the basis of evidence discovered during a legal search of his home, and he emphasized that his vision in procuring the new communications network for the law enforcement center had contributed to the speedy arrest of the alleged murderer. McCormick made sure that there was an air of carnival about the announcement, and photographs of Haddad being arrested at his home with handcuffs placed on him were made available to the print media. Broadcast reporters had obviously been alerted in advance of the arrest, because they were on site when the arrest was made at four o'clock that afternoon and obtained full photographic coverage for the six o'clock broadcast. The sheriff also announced to the reporters that Kathryn Haddad's children were being placed in the temporary court-ordered guardianship of their maternal grandparents. Mrs. Faison was interviewed by a reporter as a follow-up story to the sheriff's press conference.

"My husband and I hope very much that this will all be over with soon. We'll never have our older daughter with us anymore, but her children will always have a home with us, if they need it. It was my daughter's wish that her children live with their grandparents if anything happened to her. She left a handwritten will . . . ," Mrs. Faison said, and then she turned her head down to wipe tears away. Miles Faison put his arm around his wife's shoulders to comfort her. When Mrs. Faison was asked, after she composed herself, if she thought her son-in-law had killed his wife, she responded, "I'm going to let these fine officers and the grand jury do their jobs, and I'm not going to interfere or make predictions. I'm just going to do my job as a grand-mother. I trust in the Lord to see that justice is done."

"As you can see, ladies and gentlemen," the reporter said at the conclusion of the segment showing Mrs. Faison with the children clinging to her, "this is a very brave woman who is generously wel-coming these grandchildren into her home."

As soon as Haddad was arrested, and after the initial shock of his arrest wore off around town, there seemed to be a general acceptance and presumption of his guilt. That inclination to believe in his guilt was bolstered by a series of stories in the local paper along the lines of "how we caught the bad guy." The hero-supersleuth of those news-paper stories was the new information system and, of course, Sheriff McCormick, mastermind behind it all. Details of the circumstantial evidence incriminating Haddad were apparently generously released by the sheriff's public relations department. McCormick was hailed in the newspaper stories as an astute strategic planner, and he was congratulated by most people as having done a good job of finding the bad guy.

First thing on Monday, Sullivan and Robbey were assigned to another case involving a John Doe whose body had been found in the Ocmulgee River. As far as Sullivan and Robbey were concerned, the new case was a non-case, and it felt like they'd been assigned "busy work." When the new assignment came down in writing from the sheriff's office, the wording strongly implied that no more help would be needed on the Haddad case. The sheriff's special investigative unit and the grand jury would be handling it from then on.

When Sullivan returned to his office on Tuesday, after he and Robbey had just been through a particularly useless exercise trying to find homeless people in the community who might have known John Doe, he found a message on his desk that Mrs. Deckle had called ear-lier that day. He returned her call immediately.

"Detective Sullivan, I'm very upset about Stefan's being held and charged with Kathryn's death. Somebody told me that it's unlikely he'll get out on bail since he's been arrested for murder, and I hear they've frozen all his assets. Vera's got Kathryn's kids, and the gossip around town is that she's going to eventually put Sally in charge of the Chic Boutique. Kathryn must be turning over in her grave. Can't you do something? He didn't do what they're accusing him of, Detective Sullivan."

"I think you're right, Mrs. Deckle, but I'm officially off the case." Mentally, though, he had to admit, the case was still inside his head. *Maybe there is something I can do as a private citizen,* he thought to himself after he hung up the phone and said goodbye to Robbey for the day.

The county jail was a crowded place, as all jails are, but there was a large room in the new section of the building where prisoners could sit with their visitors. Not much privacy was afforded, but at least there were no bars between the people staring each other in the face. There were some children in the room, sitting on the laps of prisoners who were clearly family members. The common denominator in the room was that no one was smiling. It had the feeling of a roomful of people without hope or dignity.

Stefan Haddad looked shell-shocked when he came out from behind the door that opened into the waiting room. He looked glad to see Sullivan and shook his hand. Then he sat down glumly at the end of the long table next to Sullivan.

"Detective Sullivan, what am I doing in here?"

"Hasn't your lawyer briefed you on the facts so far?"

"I'm still trying to dig up a lawyer. You know, this isn't the greatest town for criminal lawyers, and every one I've called so far seems to be a family friend of the Faisons and doesn't want to talk to me. The Faisons talked to a judge who's a friend of theirs, and he gave them power of attorney over the business and all our liquid assets, so I can't even get to any money to pay an attorney. I may have to accept the representation of the public defender. I still don't know what I'm doing in here, and I miss my kids so much. Have you seen them lately?"

Sullivan stared at the man facing him in prison garb. Even in the humblest clothing, Haddad had an air of gentility about him, and he looked distinctly out of place in a room filled with lawbreakers. Slim and nearly six feet tall with an olive complexion capped off by short, graying, salt-and-pepper hair, Haddad had an air of refinement about him along with the educated style and bearing of a doctor, lawyer, or minister.

"The court has appointed their grandparents as legal guardians. I haven't seen them."

Sullivan realized that his visiting a murder suspect whom he'd helped to put behind bars was a first in his career. Here he was, a tough veteran detective, responding more like a family friend than a law enforcement officer. He wasn't on duty during this visit, he told Haddad. He'd been reassigned. Stripped of responsibility for this case. What he didn't tell Haddad was that he strongly felt the case had taken a wrong turn, and he felt responsible, like the guy on the basketball team who was supposed to put up the game-clinching shot when, all of a sudden, the ball got stolen and the other team came from behind to take a surprise win. It wasn't comfortable to see Stefan Haddad in this place. Years of experience had given him instincts about who was guilty. All his instincts told him Haddad didn't belong here, and he couldn't shake the feeling that somehow, for some strange reason that didn't seem logical, part of the responsibility for helping this man get a fair shake lay with him.

"Listen," Sullivan continued, "I came to see you more as a courtesy than anything else. It's not official business. But even though I've been taken off the case, I just wanted to know if there's anyone you wanted me to call. Is there anyone who can help you?"

Haddad shook his head. "No, I really don't have anyone I can call. My parents are both deceased. My mom was an orphan, so I have no family on that side. I only have a few relatives, just some distant cousins on my father's side, and they're not even in this country. My kids are all the family I have now. And I just wish they didn't have to worry."

"Well, sir, it's probably beyond the don't-worry stage. You know, the story made the national evening news last night. They're describing you as a jealous husband who allegedly went into a momentary rage over his wife's infidelity."

"So that means my kids know about their mom's infidelity? Everybody knows?"

"Yes. I guess sex sells everything, including the evening news. They made it sound pretty glamorous about all of you being together at the Harvard Business School and all that. They're trying to make it into an elite Ivy League multicultural love triangle gone bad."

Haddad shook his head as he stared sadly down at the table in front of him. "I wonder what my kids are thinking. My poor children. I can't believe they have to even consider for a second the possibility that I harmed their mother." For a man facing a murder charge, Haddad looked remarkably calm, and Sullivan wondered how he could live so gracefully with such fear and dejection as he must have felt. "The only thing I can think about is my children having to suffer through all this. And how could they possibly have any evidence connecting me to her death, since I didn't do it?"

"Well, sir, it's all circumstantial at this point, but the forensics people have been told by the sheriff's office to help put together a "probable cause" theory about your involvement. They have hair taken from your wife that's definitely your hair. The fact that you were going to become a multimillionaire as a result of her death points the finger at you, and you've even admitted that you were on the property somewhere near her car on the morning of her death. It's circumstantial, but it looks like motive and opportunity. The press is making you and your wife out to be closet druggies. You know, upstanding citizens in public and party types behind the scenes."

"We weren't party types at all."

"So you and your wife didn't use cocaine?"

"Never."

"Maybe she used it on the side when you weren't looking, sir. Wives do sometimes have secrets from their husbands, you know."

"Absolutely not," protested Haddad emotionally. "Kathryn would enjoy a drink every now and then, but I hardly ever drink, except maybe having a couple at a cocktail party. Never had a taste for it. It seems odd about that bag of cocaine and mirror you found in my house. It almost seems as though they were put there recently, because I don't think they've always been in the paint cubbyhole. Why,

I would've found the bag and mirror last summer when I had some touch-up painting done. And Kathryn would've seen that stuff, too, because she used to warehouse Christmas presents in that cubbyhole before taking them to her regular hiding place at the office."

"But who would've put those things there? And why?"

"I don't know. I don't know how they got there. But . . . on that part about my hair being on Kathryn . . . don't you think that's ridiculous? I mean, I'm her husband. My hair would have been all over the car, since it was our car, and all over her clothes. And what else did they find? Did they find my semen in her, too? Is that a crime to go to bed with your wife?"

"Yes, sir, they did find your semen inside her."

"So what else am I accused of? Marital rape?"

"No, sir. Just murder."

"Sorry, Detective, . . . I didn't really mean to be sarcastic with you. I know you're trying to help." The pain, frustration, and helplessness he felt were etched on his face.

"Call me John," Sullivan said, pushing a stick of gum across the table at him.

Haddad raised his head erect and sat up straight in the chair as he reached over to accept the gum. "I can't believe this is happening. You know, I'm a very logical person, and I tend to think most things come to a logical conclusion in life. But, this isn't logical. And all I want is to be with my kids. They need me so much now. Their mother just got taken away from them, and now this cruel blow . . . it's like my poor children have lost both parents."

"Yes, sir, I know. Is there anything I can do to help you, or anyone I could contact for you?"

"I can't even think right now, but I know I have to. I just wish I had Kathryn here. She was always the one who could think clearly in a crisis."

EIGHTEEN

The following day, Wednesday, a guard came to Stefan's cell to tell him he had a visitor. Stefan felt his heart practically leap into his throat. His kids! How he'd longed to see them! And they were here, at last, to visit him! He felt like running into the reception area, but he settled for walking as fast as he could. When he opened the door into the room where he'd sat with Sullivan the day before, he didn't see any children. Instead, he saw a tall, tanned man whom he recognized after a few seconds. It was Kathryn's uncle, Billy James. He'd been Kathryn's favorite uncle and the relative who seemed to care about her most.

"Hey there, partner," Billy began, in his Tennessee twang and with an obvious attempt at joviality. "How're you doing, there, buddy?" He walked over and gave him what they called a "bear hug" in Tennessee.

"Not great, Billy," Stefan replied, "but it's great to see you. What're you doing in town?"

Billy was the only brother of Mrs. Faison. It was Billy's mother, Kathryn's grandmother, who had largely raised Kathryn and with whom Kathryn spent every summer of her life. As he stared at Billy, Stefan remembered what Kathryn said when her grandmother died: "Well, she waited until I was a real grown-up woman before she died. She waited 'til I didn't need her anymore." Stefan knew that Mrs. Faison and Billy didn't get along. Apparently, Billy had resented Vera's domineering style toward his feeble and elderly mother, and that had caused bad feelings toward his only sister. Kathryn had told Stefan a few months ago that her uncle and mother never spoke anymore unless one of them had to tell the other about a funeral of someone in Tennessee. According to Kathryn, Billy was a loving and supportive uncle who had taken her side on several occasions when her father had cursed and slapped her when she was a girl. Hot-tempered, Miles would get stirred up over something trivial, and Billy James had sometimes stepped in to help Miles control his anger and restrain him from hitting his daughter.

"I've come to see you. I couldn't believe it when I heard they had you in jail. I saw it on the evening news. Vera didn't even call me. I know Kathryn wouldn't want you in here, and I want you to tell me what you're doing here."

For the next thirty minutes, Haddad chronicled the events of the last few months. Billy listened intently, without interrupting once, and he watched carefully as Stefan told the story.

"Well," Billy began when Haddad finished the story, "I sure am going to miss Kathryn. I never imagined that, when I went home last week after her funeral, I'd be coming back up here a week later to see you in jail." He paused and looked reflective. "I was barely a teenager when Vera got married, so I was home with Mama during those early years when Kathryn practically lived with Mama and Daddy. It used to tear Mama up when Vera and Miles would come back to get their daughter. They'd pick her up like a piece of property that belonged to them, like a dog or something else they owned that they thought they'd take home for a while, and Kathryn used to cry her eyes out when they'd come to take her away. She even called her grandmother "Mama," you know. And Mama really was the only mother she ever had. For some reason, Vera and Miles were hard on that child, I don't know why. Mama and Daddy and I felt bad about it, but we couldn't do much except love her ourselves."

"But aren't they supposed to be good Christians? It just seems so illogical. Kathryn was brought up in the church, and I was never taken to church as a child. But inside her family are more diseased emotions than I ever saw in mine."

"Yeah, well, that's right, and that's a good way to put it—diseased emotions. That's what the ministers say when they talk about original sin." Uncle Billy paused and, in the silence of that pause, Stefan remembered how Kathryn used to describe her Uncle Billy. She said he was a God-centered man whose simple faith focused him on the act of continuously and obediently humbling himself to God's will. Kathryn had respected and trusted him, because what he said and what he did were the same thing. Billy continued. "We inherit diseased emotions and a tendency to be led by lust and greed and selfishness. But we always have a choice. We can go to God and he can strengthen and purify and heal us. Some religions say we can go to God through Jesus, his son. That's how I was brought up. Believing in Jesus as God's son. Now, my Jewish friends don't believe in the divinity of Jesus, but they still believe in the healing grace of God. But we have to go to God for more than blessings and forgiveness. If we want forgiveness, we have to truly repent. We have to really turn away from the bad that we're doing and not do it anymore. But I guess the reason I'm here now is that I feel like Kathryn became victimized somehow. And now, you and the kids have wound up as victims."

"Yeah, I guess that's how I feel. I feel like a victim. But what can we do?"

"We have to get you out of here. And I have to work on the assumption now that my sister and her husband aren't going to lend you a helping hand."

"But why? They can't believe that I killed their daughter, Billy James, could they?"

"Well, it's hard to imagine."

"Have you seen my kids?"

"Yes, I saw them this morning when I visited Vera and Miles. They were off from school because of some kind of teacher workday."

"Why didn't you bring them with you?"

Billy took his time before responding. "They want to see you real bad, Stefan, but Vera thinks it wouldn't be good for them emotionally right now. The two littlest ones look like they're in bad shape. You know, Vera is partial to David and she always has been."

"So that's why she tells me they're not at home when I call on the phone."

"Yeah, probably. Well, anyway, the main thing we have to do is get you out of here. You need a good defense attorney. You need the best criminal attorney money can buy."

"I don't have any money. Or not any that I can get hold of, it seems. A court order gave the Faisons control over everything I have."

"Well, I happen to know someone who wants to pop for your legal expenses."

"You do? Who?"

Billy had a serious look on his face when he replied. "Marcos Galleria."

In his characteristic low-key, laid-back manner, Haddad showed little reaction except that one bushy eyebrow shot up in a *V*. "Marcos? What do you mean? Is that a joke? Do you know him? What are you talking about?"

"I'm very serious about this. I've come to know him through Kathryn. After NAFTA passed, one of my Tennessee farming buddies and I wanted to see about doing some soybean exporting from Tennessee into Mexico, and I knew Kathryn had an amicable relationship with her ex. So I asked if she'd introduce me to him by phone a few months ago so I could pick his brain about Mexican infrastructure and import-export policies. Anyway, I've gotten to know him, and he's a pretty nice guy. He feels bad about a lot of things, like the way he handled things with her, but one thing he feels good about is you. He's appreciative of the fact that you raised his son, and he wants to show his respect for you."

"I see. So Marcos comes along as a good Samaritan? The minister at the church hasn't visited me once since I've been in jail, but the guy who had an affair with my wife is offering to help me with my legal expenses? Life really isn't too logical, is it?"

"Well, buddy, that's how the good Samaritan story is told by Jesus, isn't it? The priest walked by, but the passerby stopped to help the victim. Life is full of surprises, isn't it?" Billy asked, with a rueful smile on his face. Stefan could see why he'd been Kathryn's favorite uncle.

Then Stefan felt his anger boil up from deep inside. "What makes you think I'd take a dime from him, anyway, after what he's done to my family? He's in large measure to blame for all this."

"I think he feels guilty about his part in all this, Stefan. But I think his motivation is to help you and your family now. And it's going to be expensive. Somehow you've been endplayed here. You have no money, no access to power, no anything. You need to take the help that's offered here, I think, and try not to focus on the source. Just try to concentrate on doing whatever's best for your family."

Haddad made no response, but he stared directly into Billy's eyes, as though trying to see behind whatever facade was there.

"Maybe murder makes strange bedfellows," Billy continued, staring into Stefan's eyes while he reached over to put his hand on one of Stefan's shoulders, to give it a quick squeeze, like a doting uncle. "I think his motivation is just to help you and the kids, and he expected that you would feel hatred toward him and feel like rejecting his offer. That's why he asked me to come. He's told me a couple of times over business dinners in San Antonio that he feels very appreciative, man to man, of how gentlemanly you've been toward him and how you've encouraged his son's relationship with him. I think he admires you and feels he owes you a debt." Billy paused again, then resumed. "And he does owe you a debt. Take the help, Stefan." There was a firmness in his voice at the end.

"I resent having to accept money from him. I feel like a major pawn in a chess game that has nothing to do with me," Stefan said in a voice that sounded angry.

"I can see how you'd feel that way. But listen, buddy, we just have to do whatever we can to get you out of here, right? Now before I go, can we say a prayer together?"

Stefan felt a little embarrassed as Billy reached across the table and held his hand down on the table as he bowed his head. The prisoners nearby with their visitors quietened and stared. Stefan bowed his head, too, as much in embarrassment as in worship. Then he heard Billy's prayer, and he tried to feel a reverent connection to his Maker.

"Dear God, we know that all things are possible for you. Help us to be obedient to your will. Give us the wisdom to see your will working in things we don't understand. Thank you for your saving grace and bless Stefan and his children, Father. We praise you for every-thing, Lord. Amen."

Stefan looked puzzled. The prayer Billy prayed certainly sounded like the indirect approach.

"Why didn't you pray for my release?"

Billy stood up and put his arm around his shoulder. "It says in the sixth chapter of Matthew that our Father knows what we need before we ask him. That's when he taught us to pray that famous prayer:

> *Our Father who is in heaven,*
> *Holy is your name.*
> *May your kingdom come,*
> *May your will be done,*
> *On earth as it is in heaven.*
> *Please satisfy our needs today,*
> *And forgive us of our sins,*
> *As we forgive the sins of others;*
> *And do not lead us into temptation,*
> *But deliver us from evil."*

"I've always liked that prayer," Stefan said reverently.

"Yes, and you see how it ends. We can depend on God to rescue us from evil, and he always will, if we only turn to him and turn the problems over to him and let him solve them. We get into a lot of trouble when we don't remain obediently humbled, with God in the driver's seat in our life." He heaved a deep sigh, and a look of remorse crossed his face. "Maybe something like that was what happened to Kathryn."

Stefan's downcast expression showed he, too, was thinking of his deceased partner in life. Billy gave him a hug as he stood up to leave.

"Oh, by the way," Billy said, as the guard was opening the door to let him out of the visitors' area, "someone named Hugh Saxton will be contacting you tomorrow."

NINETEEN

At three o'clock sharp the next day, Thursday, the guard came to Stefan's cell and announced he had a visitor. When Stefan walked into the reception area, the first thing he saw was the cowboy hat on the table. It was next to a large man in his early fifties who was wearing an expensive suit with designer sunglasses perched on the end of his nose. He was sitting at the end of one of the long tables in the room. On the table lay what looked to be an ostrich-leather briefcase. An impeccably dressed, slim, preppy-looking young man wearing wire reading glasses sat near him. The young one was listening to the senior gentleman and taking notes on a legal pad. They stood up as soon as Stefan entered the room, and the large man thrust out his hand. Stefan guessed the large man to be about six-foot-three, and he had a broad, boyish smile.

"Are you Mr. Haddad?" he said jovially. He flashed a smile that made him look like Mr. Hollywood Cowboy. Maybe it was the designer sunglasses.

"Yes," Stefan answered, shaking the hand he extended.

"I was going to call, but I decided to call in person rather than on the phone," the man declared in a loud, booming voice that signaled he was someone who was accustomed to taking charge. He took off his sunglasses, and Stefan looked into steely, crystal blue eyes that had a touch of warmth buried somewhere way far back. He had the look of a man who was used to a rich lifestyle and lush surroundings. He looked distinctly out of place in this linoleum-lined, colorless room that was the jail's reception area.

"My name's Hugh Saxton," he continued, "and this here's my slave, Russell Kapstein. We're from San Antonio. We're here for Mr. Galleria."

"Are you a lawyer?" asked Stefan. If he was a lawyer, this Hugh Saxton looked too "big city" to be his lawyer. Stefan had a bad feeling this wasn't going to work out. He'd seen out-of-town lawyers come into Macon and other Southern towns and be totally ineffective because they were perceived as Yankee carpetbaggers coming to take advantage of and outsmart the locals, just like the real carpetbaggers had done after the Civil War. Decades later, those Southern boys still didn't like Yankees or big-mouthed Texans, and they relished every opportunity they got to settle the score when the Northerners and Texans ended up on Southern soil. If the lawyers didn't make mincemeat of them, the judges ate them for lunch. It just never worked, with out-of-town, slick lawyers taking on local cases.

"Well, yes, you could say that. I am an attorney, licensed to practice in Georgia, too," he said, smiling at Stefan. He looked too slick and plastic. Mr. San Antonio. How could a lawyer like Mr. Urban Cowboy possibly help him in this Southern-grits town?

"Are you a criminal attorney?" Stefan continued.

"Why don't you sit down, Mr. Haddad," the man ordered suddenly, in a blunt and imperious tone.

Stefan had grown accustomed to doing as he was told. That was part of what jail was all about. Go here. Sit there. Do this. Stop that. It went on like that all day. He sat down.

"I want to be very straight with you, Mr. Haddad. Mr. Galleria hired me to get you out of the mess you're in. Yes, I'm an attorney, I'm a criminal attorney. But the reason he sent me here is because I'm a son-of-a-bitch, and he knows that a son-of-a-bitch is what you need more than you need a lawyer." He paused and the corners of his mouth went up in what appeared to be a smile. Then the corners of his mouth dropped suddenly. It hadn't been a smile after all. It had been an artifice, something that looked like a smile. He folded his arms on the table and leaned his head over until his face was closer to Stefan's face than Stefan was comfortable with. The man called Saxton looked at him in a deliberate hybrid of a glare and a stare.

"Mr. Galleria is a son-of-a-bitch himself. We work together on import-export business between Mexico and the U.S., where everyone in the chain expects to get a commission for his part in moving the goods. He has to have ass kissers and ass kickers to help him move the goods across the border without getting his pocket picked, so that's where I come in. I'm his chief executive ass kicker." He smiled his plastic smile again that wasn't really a smile at all. "Sweet talking doesn't work on everyone, you know." For some reason, in spite of himself, Stefan found him likable, man to man, even though he was sure he'd be hopeless on his case. He could see the flinty determination in Mr. San Antonio, and he admired such grit.

"Well, I appreciate your coming here," Stefan replied kindly, "but this isn't Mexico, and I'm in a Southern jail charged with killing my wife. I don't quite see how some tough international lawyer is going to help me here. It's a style thing, you know what I mean?"

Saxton smiled. This time the smile was real. At least some warmth crept into the handsome, well-lined face of this supremely confident lawyer.

"You make a good point, Mr. Haddad. I can see you're an intelligent man with a very logical way of looking at things. But you don't really need a lawyer as much as you need someone who can kick ass. A lawyer would try to help you get justice from the legal system. But the legal system has put you here, and the legal system is the friend of the people who put you here. All the legal system is going to do is close in around you and tighten the circumstantial case they already have. Grand juries are handpicked by the prosecution, and they return an indictment more than 90 percent of the time. So it's definitely moving in the wrong direction, and time isn't on your side, either. The longer you stay in here, the more they think you probably did it, and the more they forget you're here. And you especially ought to forget about the innocent-'til-proven-guilty stuff, Haddad. You're a damned immigrant who just got off the boat, compared to people whose relatives came over on the *Mayflower*. You're a nobody, you have no damned rights in this Southern town, and the worst thing you could do is depend on Southern justice to set you free."

"I'm a naturalized American citizen, you know."

"I know," he replied impatiently, as he unzipped and flipped open his ostrich briefcase to retrieve a pen. Then he leaned back in his chair and crossed his hands behind his head as he positioned himself to stare at Haddad. "But these damned rednecks never wanted to join the Union anyway, remember? You need to face facts. You're a Princeton-educated guy. You're smart. You have to be in here because some influential people want you here so they can sit on the outside and further develop the case they have against you."

"I didn't do it," Stefan replied coolly and matter-of-factly.

Saxton shrugged his shoulders, as though Haddad was making a point that was irrelevant. "You've heard the old saying, 'Nice guys finish last,' haven't you?"

Stefan looked thoughtful. He thought of Kathryn and remembered how practical she was and how she would undoubtedly want him to take help from any source if it was in the best interests of the children and their family. Stefan would have to swallow some pride, but he'd take Galleria's help. When he broke the silence to speak, his tone was polite and resolute. "I don't understand what you're going to do, but I'll take help in whatever form it comes if it can get me back to my children. You've heard the old saying, 'Beggars can't be choosers,' haven't you?"

Saxton smiled one of his real smiles. "Galleria said you were a real nice guy. Smart, too, I see." He picked up his briefcase to peer inside, pulled a piece of paper out, and then laid the paper down in front of him. "Look, nobody likes to see the bad guys beat the good guys, and that seems to be what's going on here. We're just going to try to make sure the bad guys don't win."

There was silence for several seconds. Then Saxton spoke again.

"Okay, let's break the ice a little. Let's get to know each other better."

Apparently that was code language because, as if on cue, the young attorney introduced as Russell Kapstein took out a tape recorder and placed it on the table. Then he repositioned his yellow legal tablet and adjusted his sitting position for serious note taking.

"So you're a nice guy, Haddad, right? Maybe a little too nice, huh?"

"What do you mean?"

"Well, your old lady was sleeping around on you, right?"

"So I hear." There was cold anger in Haddad's eyes.

"Did you kill her?"

Haddad looked hard at Saxton. "No, I didn't kill my wife. I loved my wife." The cold anger mixed with pain and sadness stayed in Haddad's eyes as he spoke.

"Look, I'm just curious. It doesn't have anything to do with my getting you out of this mess. Personally, I don't give a damn if you're guilty or innocent. I'd do this job the same way and aim for the same result. I just want to know if you really killed her."

"No."

"So you loved your wife even though she had an affair with an old flame and got you into the mess you're in? What are you, a masochist? A glutton for punishment?"

The words stung, but there was a calculating way Saxton was interrogating him that made Stefan sense there was gamesmanship here, as though some test of ego or endurance were being conducted. Saxton was measuring something, and the tool he was using was provocative and inflammatory language. So, although the words stung, Haddad maintained the self-control he was known for. "My wife was basically a good woman. She was a good mother. She was a religious person. And she was a wonderful, loving wife. Anyway, I didn't know she was having an affair until after her death, so I certainly couldn't have killed her for that, could I?"

"Well, maybe you suspected it. And it probably wasn't the first time she slept around, right? Was this one of many affairs for her?"

"No. Like I said, my wife was a good woman and a good wife."

Saxton laughed heartily. "Now that's some framework you got there, Mr. Haddad. But I guess we all cling to whatever beliefs give us support." He paused, then looked Haddad straight in the eyes. "I don't think I ever loved a woman that much. You know, to keep loving her after she screwed around on me and got me put in jail and ruined my life."

That feeling came over Stefan again, and he shook his head. This just wasn't going to work. Here was some slick big-city lawyer who said he wanted to help, but all he was doing was busting his balls. He felt exasperated. "Let me just ask you this. Why is Galleria doing this? Why is he trying to help me? He knows I have no damned respect for him. He's as much to blame for Kathryn's death as anyone, as far as I'm concerned." There was deep anger in Stefan's voice.

"You're a family man, and you're David's father, too. This is about control, who gets control of your family, and Galleria thinks your wife's parents shouldn't have control of the kids. The family is the most important thing, and his machismo philosophy dictates that the man should be in control." Saxton paused. "And besides," he smiled broadly, "he doesn't like bossy women."

"You know, it's funny, but I thought Marcos might cause me trouble over custody of David when all this happened. He could probably get custody if he wanted to, since he's the natural father. And whether he went for custody or not, he could probably convince David to come and live with him."

"Well, I can't promise he won't give you trouble in that area, Haddad. That may be a separate issue for him," Saxton replied, matter-of-factly. "I wouldn't assume that Galleria won't try to persuade his son to come to live with him, but he's not going to steal him from you while you're in jail defenseless. That's not Galleria's style. Winning something that way wouldn't give him any pleasure. But David is his only son, you know, and the Latins are very possessive of their wife and children. They're more or less property, if you know what I mean. He's actually married to his job. It was a marriage arranged by his father when he was just a child, and the corporation is his partner for life, 'til death do them part. Women and children are a secondary activity." Saxton paused. "Knowing Galleria, this help he's offering you has a lot to do with wanting the best thing for his son, and he knows you're a good father. Latins are very big on punishment, too, and I guess this is 'round two' between him and Mrs. Faison. He hates scheming women who try to outdo men, and he probably feels his son would be better off raised by either you or him than by the grandparents. The Faisons are trying to take things that don't belong to them, and I think Galleria feels it would do them good to lose this battle in public."

"I don't feel totally comfortable with that either," Stefan replied. "I mean, they are the kids' grandparents."

"Yeah, but you've heard the old saying, 'War is hell.' Just don't worry too much right now about who gets humiliated in public as long as it isn't you and your kids, okay? Can we adopt that philosophy? That's why, as a matter of tradition, gentlemen often don't fight their own fights. When there's a street fight to take care of, they need a street fighter to send in. You're a refined gentleman, Haddad. Not a street fighter."

"Well, I have a feeling I'm going to learn a lot of old sayings from you, Mr. Saxton, but I'm still wondering what you're going to do for me legally."

"I'm not going to do anything legally for you, Haddad. Like I said before, the legal system isn't going to let you out of here. The legal system is closing in around you. What we're going to have to do is to use a strategy that doesn't have anything to do with courtroom maneuvers."

"You're not going to do anything legally?" Stefan sounded disgusted. He should have known that anything coming from Marcos wouldn't be real help. All he did was send Mr. San Antonio Bullshit.

"Oh, sure, I'm going to pretend that I'm doing something legally. I'm going to get my name in the paper, and I'm going to allow myself to be used as a decoy. These country lawyers would like nothing better than to take a big-city lawyer and teach him how things get done in Hicksville. So I'm going to let them think they're giving me a lesson or two in lawyering. But, like I said, what I'm here for is to be a decoy." His eyes narrowed and his eyes bore into Haddad. "Now that's just for your information, you understand, not for anyone else's ears."

"Unfortunately, I don't have anyone to tell," he replied. Stefan had been totally alone, stranded in jail and isolated, since the day he got there. None of the people he thought would visit had visited. Like Mary and Dr. Kotler. And apparently his own kids were prevented from visiting. How he missed seeing them, and they had to miss him, too. "So what's our strategy then?"

"You know the old saying, 'Two heads are better than one,'"

Saxton said, as his eyes met Stefan's. Then Saxton continued. "I like dealing with smart clients, and I'm going to need your help."

"What do you want me to do?"

"I need your help in one area especially. We're going to have to find a country boy we can trust who'll get some information for us."

Stefan nodded his head as though he was thinking. Then he changed the subject. "What do you think really happened to my wife, Mr. Saxton?"

Saxton took a deep breath. "There seem to me to be two main theories so far, that is, if we can rule both you and Mr. Galleria out as suspects."

"You can rule me out," Stefan said.

Saxton continued. "No matter what the medical examiner says, this may be a suicide." Saxton looked hard at Stefan as he spoke. "Your wife was three months pregnant, right?"

Stefan nodded.

"What if she was carrying Galleria's child and flipped out? Wasn't your wife a temperamental and impulsive type? Maybe she saw a major problem there appeared no solution for and she acted hastily, in a moment of weakness, and took her life."

"I don't think so, Mr. Saxton. She was a strong woman and a woman of faith. We'd just come back from a second honeymoon in Jamaica, and she seemed very happy recently. She'd been a little depressed for several weeks before that, but something dramatically changed while we were in Jamaica. It was like she had an ailment that got cured on that trip."

"Okay. You say the suicide theory is out. Let's go back for a minute to the theory that everyone seems willing to believe. That's the theory that says that we have a classic situation of a jealous, suspicious husband with a strong case of possessive love and without a strong alibi. Nobody'll believe you didn't know she was running around. If this is a setup, I wish they'd thought up something more original. It's like connecting the bloody dots! You were running on a track that goes right past the parking lot where she was found—maybe you ran into her and some violent argument ensued. Who knows, who cares? It's a little dull for my tastes, but it'll work on a jury. It's plausible. Juries like simple explanations. And if the jury has any doubt, they're not going to put a daddy who killed his wife back with his young kids."

"I thought it was innocent 'til proven guilty."

"Like I told you before, don't be such a nice guy, Haddad," Saxton said, cocking his head and staring at him as though he should be ashamed for making a comment of such limited intelligence. "You grew up in a big city, so you're no stranger to political intrigue. You know how life is. Didn't you grow up seeing the greed and corruption that rules the world? I need you to think in a very clearheaded way if we're going to get you out of this. Everyone is already closing rank around you, and I can do just so much. I can only pull off a charade that I'm a big city goofball ready to be taught valuable lessons by the country bumpkins. Now, help me here. What we need is to develop other theories if we don't like the ones we have. So, like I told you before, I need somebody who talks Southern. A real Southern grit."

Haddad thought for a moment. He thought of Mary, but he didn't think she'd do it. She wouldn't want to get involved. All he knew was that the only two people who'd visited him in jail had been Kathryn's uncle and John Sullivan. "Well, I can think of one person. His name is John Sullivan. He's an honest person, and he's the chief homicide detective here in town. He came to see me after they put me in here, and he acts like he wants to help me and the kids."

"Fine. Can you get in touch with Sullivan? From what I've read in the newspaper, he's off the case. Doing some work on the side on your case would almost certainly be against departmental policy, so that might put his career and reputation in jeopardy. Do you think he'd do that?"

"I don't know, Mr. Saxton. I can ask."

"No, I'll tell you what. I'll call Sullivan and arrange to meet him away from here. They're probably monitoring your phone calls, so it'll be better if I contact him and talk to him." He paused. "Oh, there's one more thing. You're going to be in here for the duration, I'm afraid. I really tried to work out a bail situation, even if it's in the millions of dollars, because Galleria could post it discreetly and you could get out of here and assist in the fact-finding. But they're hanging tough on the murder charge. Georgia law will allow bail if you're arrested on first-degree murder, but it's unusual and I don't think it'll happen for you. Sorry. They were very careful when they put you in here to make sure you wouldn't get out until the grand jury chews you up. But don't worry," Saxton said with a wry smile, "I'll try to make sure you don't rot in here for the rest of your life." His dry wit would have been amusing if the subject matter of the joke hadn't been Stefan's life or death.

"Well, let's do whatever we have to do to figure out the real murderer in the fastest way."

"Whoever it is, is smart, and knows how to cover his tracks."

TWENTY

A s the pilot announced their descent into San Antonio International Airport, John Sullivan reflected on the events of the last few days. The Haddad case was as full of surprises as any case he'd handled, not the least of which had been the surprise phone call from the San Antonio lawyer Hugh Saxton asking to meet with him confidentially. Sullivan had suggested a diner a couple of miles outside the city limits.

He had been in the middle of a second cup of coffee when the tall Texan and his prim Jewish assistant walked in the door. Sullivan had picked an out-of-the-way spot to talk. The diner was a place where working stiffs could get generous portions of real food at honest prices three times a day, but, at three o'clock, the working stiffs were at least an hour away from clocking out, so they had the diner to themselves. That turned out fortunate, because the Texan even had a loud whisper, and what he'd talked about was something that required utmost confidentiality. The Texan had told him that Stefan Haddad had given his blessing to the idea of asking Sullivan if he'd conduct some undercover work related to the Haddad case, with all expenses paid by the ex-husband of the dead woman.

"Why is Mr. Galleria offering to pay for all this?" Sullivan had asked Saxton.

"He's trying to show some support for Mr. Haddad. He doesn't think Mr. Haddad killed his wife, and he feels an obligation to make sure justice is done."

Sullivan stared into Saxton's eyes and scrutinized his expression. "From the research I've done so far on the case, I know something of Mr. Galleria's reputation as a shrewd businessman, and I have a hard time seeing him as a good Samaritan or as someone on a crusade for justice. So the first question I need an answer to is, Why's he doing this? At least level with me about what's in it for him." Then he narrowed his eyes, and his stare bore into Saxton. "I don't like people trying to play me like a pawn on a chessboard."

As Saxton shrugged his huge shoulders, a hostile look crossed his face, and he looked as though he wanted to tell Sullivan that he was getting into an area that was none of his business. "He's willing to pay five thousand dollars a week, plus expenses," he said flatly, staring at Sullivan in a no-nonsense, take-it-or-leave-it way.

It took Sullivan only a few seconds to decide.

"I'll do it. I'll ask for a two-week leave of absence at work. I don't think they'll object, since all they've got me assigned to is scooping up dead drifters around town. I've been taken off the Haddad case. I believe the sheriff and his special investigative unit are handling the case now. The homicide detectives have been told that our services are no longer needed on that case." Sullivan paused. "I don't think Haddad did it."

"Neither does Mr. Galleria." Then Saxton smiled at the detective. "So you're going to accept the five thousand dollars weekly he's offering? Galleria didn't think you'd take the money. He thought you were too much of an Honest John." Saxton made no attempt to disguise the ridicule in his voice.

Sullivan stared at Saxton without smiling back. "I learned long ago that people don't value what they get for free. And the more they pay, the more they respect your opinions. So, yes, I'll definitely accept the money, and you might want to tell him that he's getting a bargain." He shrugged. "Anyway, there are a few questions I've been wanting to ask Mr. Galleria, and I like the idea of being on his payroll when I question him." This time he smiled at Saxton, but Saxton didn't return the smile. "There is one place I'd like to start in this investigation, Mr. Saxton."

"Where's that?"

"I want to fly to San Antonio to interview Mr. Galleria."

"Why's that?" Saxton looked uncomfortable.

"You've heard the expression, 'Beware of Greeks bearing gifts,' haven't you?"

Saxton didn't reply.

Sullivan continued. "When something looks too good to be true, it usually is. I want to start with interviewing Marcos Galleria at length about his relationship with Mrs. Haddad and about his whereabouts on the morning of her death."

"He's very busy right now. We have a major import-export deal going down worth millions, and I don't think he's got any time available."

"It's the only way I'm doing it," Sullivan replied.

"Just a moment, then. Let me go to the car phone and see if I can get up with him and see what he wants to do."

While Saxton was outside in the car talking for nearly ten minutes, Sullivan and Kapstein struck up a conversation about sports. Sullivan learned that Kapstein was a nice young man with whom he had something in common: they both liked the Boston Celtics and the Dallas Cowboys.

Saxton barged back through the front door of the diner, and the door slammed behind him. He looked flustered. "Okay. He said okay. But it'll have to be in the next few days."

That conversation had taken place two days previously, and that was how Sullivan happened to be on a flight to San Antonio. As he walked through the breezeway leading into the main terminal, he saw two Latin gentlemen dressed in suits in the area filled with people waiting for arriving passengers. The men stood out, because everyone else looked like a mother, father, brother, or sister expectantly awaiting a family member. Somehow, by sight or instinct, the duo identified Sullivan as the passenger they were expecting, and they locomoted through the congestion to meet him.

"Hello, sir," one of them said, extending his hand. "Welcome to San Antonio. We have a car waiting for you, and we'll drive you to Mr. Galleria's office."

The meeting took place at the Galleria Corporation's gleaming San Antonio headquarters, a fifteen-story building with a gold-looking veneer and with windows that looked black from a distance. Probably some kind of sun shield to reflect this hot Texas sun, Sullivan thought, as he was driven up to the entrance of the opulent structure. Galleria's office was on the top floor of the building, and Sullivan was shown into a palatial apartment that adjoined a balcony. The cheerful room decorated in yellow and white looked like a place where business got conducted in an informal fashion. On the tables were business magazines, and on selected tables in the room there were frames that contained photographs of a woman and two children. Sullivan imagined them to be Galleria's wife and daughters.

"Oh, hello, Detective Sullivan," Galleria said warmly, as he breezed into the room about twenty minutes after Sullivan arrived. "Sorry to keep you waiting. Please, freshen up in the bathroom, if you haven't already. We have a saying in Spanish, *'Mi casa es su casa.'* There's a shower you're welcome to use if you like, and I'm having some food sent up to us soon."

The bathroom Sullivan was invited to use was a massive place with double marble sinks, sunken Jacuzzi, sky lights, shower, and large walk-in closet with built-in shelves on which shirts and other garments were neatly placed. Sullivan had the feeling that he was in some kind of executive suite used by traveling business people.

"Nice bathroom, sir," Sullivan said, as he emerged.

"Thank you, Detective," Galleria responded. "I spend a lot of time here, you know. This is home away from home, and I told the architect that I wanted it to feel more like an apartment than a business suite. We built on some prime property in San Antonio. I'm very proud of this building." Galleria walked over to the picture window and stared outside. "My father would have been proud of it, too. He founded this company years ago, and I just wish he could see how it's grown." There was a wistful tone in his voice.

"Yes, I know how that feels. My own father died of a heart attack about ten years ago, and I still miss him," Sullivan said warmly, as he walked over to the picture window and stood beside Galleria, staring out at the beautiful Texas sky and landscape. "Well, sir, as you know,

I have an evening flight out of here, so I think we'd better get down to the business I came here for. I'd like to ask you some questions."

"Fine, fine," Galleria said, ushering him to the plush, yellow leather sofas surrounded by state-of-the-art telephone and computer equipment.

"Okay, sir," Sullivan began, "I'd like to ask straight out why you're spending money to assist Mr. Haddad."

"I can see why you'd ask that, Detective Sullivan. I feel I owe Stefan a debt. He raised my son during the years when I wasn't in David's life, and I want to show my support and respect for him."

"So you don't feel he killed his wife?"

"No. He's not the type."

"Well, in all my years of detective work, I have to tell you that I haven't discovered any certain type of person who is clearly a murderer. A passion or rage that explodes suddenly is frequently the cause of a crime, and as a detective I've learned that most of us are capable of most anything, given the right circumstances."

"Yes, I'm sure you're right philosophically. But I don't think Stefan Haddad would do something like that because it would hurt his family. I just don't see it."

"May I ask you, sir, what you plan to do with regard to your son?"

"My son? I plan on asking him to live with me."

"So, you do plan on taking him away from Mr. Haddad?"

"I plan on asking David if he'd like to live in San Antonio with me, now that his mother's dead. And I'm sure that Stefan will see that as my taking David away from him, but, yes, I'm going to do it anyway. He is my son, and I intend to make up for lost years with him and groom him to take over this business one day, if he wants to. So, yes, I'm planning on getting into that difficult area once all this is sorted out."

Sullivan leaned back against the couch and rolled his eyes toward the ceiling. "So you're helping Mr. Haddad now, but you're planning on taking one of his children from him soon." Then he looked back toward Galleria. "Is that right, sir?"

"That's right. You wanted it straight, Detective Sullivan, and I'm giving it to you straight. Now, of course, I haven't asked David yet.

The timing hasn't been right, and he hasn't said yes, yet. But I am planning on launching a major campaign to have my son come to live with me. I'm telling you straight out."

"Well, why not leave Haddad in jail then? Why are you helping now?"

"Those are separate issues, Detective Sullivan, my helping Haddad beat a murder charge and my wanting my son to live with me. And there's some family pride here, I guess. I don't want people to think my son was raised by a murderer. It wouldn't look right in the family tree."

Looking as though he was picking up steam, Sullivan pressed forward with his questioning. "On the report from the ID technician who examined Mrs. Haddad's car after her death, it says your fingerprints were on her car door."

Galleria didn't reply for a moment. "Yes, when she brought David to the motel for our first day of hunting, I walked her out to her car. I opened the car door for her when she got into the driver's side, so, yes, my prints would have been on the driver's door."

Sullivan stared at Galleria. "Mr. Galleria, let me explain something. I've only got a short time, working on your dime, to get to the bottom of some things. Please don't hold anything back. I'm going to find out the truth about this case, and I already know some things that have aroused my suspicion. That's why I'm here. Now let me be straight with you, sir. I got an anonymous phone call from someone who works at the lodge who told me that he saw you leaving the lodge that morning after you and David came in from hunting. The caller said David watched television in the lounge while you went outside for about forty-five minutes." He paused and stared at the smooth, enigmatic Hispanic gentleman facing him. "Where were you, Mr. Galleria? Don't play games with me, sir. I don't care who's footing the bill here, I'm going to find out the truth."

Galleria sighed. "You're right. Yes, I did see her that morning. Twice. But only one time alive. She was very distraught when I walked her to her car after she dropped David at the room about four-thirty that morning. She told me she was pregnant, and she thought it was our baby. I tried to soothe her, but she was crying, so I asked if we could meet to discuss it further, and she suggested that I meet her in that parking lot near the lodge so we could talk for thirty minutes prior to joining David for lunch and decide what she should do. So," he said, pausing momentarily to catch his breath and shaking his head, "I did walk out to the lot, and I saw her slumped against the car seat. I opened the car door and felt her pulse and realized that she was dead. I probably didn't handle it right, but I just walked away and left her there. There was nothing I could do, and I didn't want to get involved." He sighed again.

"What time was it when you saw her lifeless in the car?"

"About ten-thirty."

"So what else haven't you told me, Mr. Galleria?"

There was a sad tone in Galleria's voice when he spoke. "She was very distressed about the pregnancy. And she was talking about a lot of things at the same time. She said she was finished with fake families and plastic relationships. She was talking out of her head, you know?" He shook his head. "I didn't tell you this before because I knew how it would sound, that it would incriminate me."

"From what you're saying, Mrs. Haddad might have been suicidal that day. I mean, she had a big problem on her hands, didn't she?"

"Yes. But that's not all she said. She said she'd been thinking about our affair and had to break it off. She said she knew it wasn't right. She told me there are feelings more compelling than the love between a man and a woman at certain times in life, like the commitment to your children. She said the commitment she'd made to her children came first. She said she had to be a moral example to her children."

"That must have come as sad news to you, sir."

He shrugged. "It wasn't unexpected. That was her character. But that's what makes me know for sure that she didn't commit suicide." Sullivan thought he saw Galleria's eyes water, as though tears were welling up. "She didn't kill herself. And I didn't kill her, Detective Sullivan. I loved her."

"Was Mrs. Galleria aware of your involvement with Mrs. Haddad?"

Galleria rolled his eyes. "Not until that evening news show that reported the Ivy League love triangle that resulted in the murder of a Harvard Business School graduate." He shook his head, despairingly. "She's gone into something like toxic mourning since it happened. She's very active in Catholic charities, and she thinks she's fallen from grace a bit in society's eyes since I've been branded as an adulterer." He paused. "She's not real happy with me, Detective. I'm paying for it big time. Actually, you're sitting in my doghouse at the moment."

"I may need to interview her at some point, Mr. Galleria."

"You can interview her anytime you like. If you're looking for someone who wants to put me away for a very long time, that's the mood she's in. And if my current conditions continue, being in jail with a bunch of thieves and rogues would seem like a carnival atmosphere compared to the sullen contempt with which I'm being treated at home." Galleria folded his arms across his chest. "I may look like I've come out of this unscarred, but I've paid a heavy price in terms of my reputation and home life. I have no peace at home now."

There was a knock on the door and an army of waiters entered as soon as Galleria said, "Come in."

"What's next, Detective Sullivan?" Galleria asked, as they prepared to dine on a full-course dinner of Duck l'Orange.

"I leave on the flight back to Macon in about two hours, and then tomorrow I'm going to try to catch the scent."

On the flight back to Macon, Sullivan pondered their conversation. What was Galleria's ulterior motive in helping Haddad? Was Galleria figuring that no one would suspect him of murdering his ex-wife if he hired a lawyer to defend the husband who'd been fingered for the crime? Could Galleria have murdered his ex-wife in a blind rage? Maybe he wanted her back, and she wanted to break it off with him. Maybe he didn't want her back and the unexpected pregnancy lit his fuse. Obviously they'd had an explosive relationship in the past. Galleria was controlled and accustomed to having everybody do what he wanted. Was he on the payroll of the murderer? Did Galleria have something he was trying to hide behind this cloak of generosity?

TWENTY-ONE

"Mrs. Beaut?" Sullivan asked the sixtyish woman who answered the door.

"Yes, Detective Sullivan," the lady replied. "Come in, I've been expecting you."

Sullivan had called earlier that morning to ask if he could talk with Mrs. Beaut. She was apparently a family friend of the Faisons and had known Kathryn all her life.

"Thanks for seeing me, ma'am," Sullivan said, taking a seat on the couch in her living room as she sat in an adjacent chair. "I'd like to ask you some questions about Kathryn Haddad."

A stern look appeared on her face as he said the dead woman's name.

"Did you know her very well, Mrs. Beaut?"

"I've known her, or I guess I should say, I had known her, practically since she was born."

"What was she like, Mrs. Beaut?"

Mrs. Beaut made no response at first, then spoke as though choosing her words carefully. "I don't like spitting on the dead, Detective, but she was a hard person. Very hard on her mother. She just wouldn't forgive people for anything, and she had a very hard heart. Even if she is dead, that's the truth."

"Tell me about that. What do you mean?"

"She thought she was better than her parents. She was brought up with all the advantages, she had all the material possessions a girl could want, but from the time she was very little, she acted like she was better than everybody else in her family. She went off to fancy schools, like that one in London, and then to Harvard, and she thought she was above the rest of them."

"Why did she think she was better than them?"

"I have no idea."

"Did she and her parents have a good relationship?"

"As good as it could be, given her contrary personality. She just wanted everything her way, and she didn't give her parents the respect they deserved, especially her mother."

"What's her mother like?"

"Her mother is an angel. She would do anything for you. She'd give you the shirt off her back, if you needed it."

"Have you known Mrs. Faison a long time?"

Mrs. Beaut squirmed in her chair and readjusted her sitting position. She fiddled with the cross hanging on her necklace as she replied. "Yes, since we were in our twenties."

"What kind of relationship did you have in your twenties?"

"Oh, a little fun loving, I suppose. I was married to a man who never liked to go anywhere, and Vera's husband was frequently out of town. So I used to go over to her house to keep her company." A smile involuntarily crossed Mrs. Beaut's face, as though she were remembering happy times.

"What's Mr. Faison like?"

Mrs. Beaut pursed her lips. "He's alright. He's mellowed somewhat in his old age, but he was a hard and difficult man in his younger years. Vera could have done much better than him, I think. She's the best thing that ever happened to Miles. He would have been an ignorant country boy cleaning cow manure out of barns if it hadn't been for her and her ambition."

"So Mrs. Faison is an ambitious woman?"

"Very ambitious, and very smart. She can do anything she sets her mind to. She's very active in the church and is on the board of several local organizations. Why, if Vera had had the advantages

Kathryn had, and the chance to go to college, she might be president of the United States by now!"

"Do you know Stefan Haddad?"

"I've met him on several occasions. He seems nice enough, but they were both loners. They just stayed to themselves and didn't belong to anything, as far as I know, except their church."

"Did they seem like they had a happy marriage?"

"Who knows? What is a happy marriage?" In her voice he heard cynicism and bitterness.

Sullivan smiled. "You ask hard questions, Mrs. Beaut. What I'm trying to figure out is whether Mr. Haddad might have killed his wife, and whether you ever saw anything in him that might have indicated that he had such a rage like that inside him."

"I don't know. All I can say is that Kathryn couldn't have been an easy person to live with. She was so opinionated. Anybody who doesn't treat her mother the right way, Detective, just isn't a very nice person. How do you know she didn't kill herself, anyway?"

"We don't know that. But let me ask you this. You said a moment ago that Kathryn didn't forgive her mother. Forgive her for what? What did you mean?"

Mrs. Beaut looked uncomfortable and began moving one of her feet back and forth as she sat in the chair thinking. "Vera got married when she was just seventeen and became a mother shortly afterward. She hadn't been able to do anything in life by the time her first baby came along. And Vera was a fun-loving girl who liked to have a good time. She loved meeting people and having them over to the house to talk, and Kathryn seemed to have a lot of resentment toward Vera for some things in her childhood. Maybe Vera wasn't a perfect mother. But who is a perfect mother, Detective? Vera certainly didn't have a perfect mother herself, and neither did I. And, believe me, Kathryn wasn't any perfect daughter. So I don't know where the younger generation gets off thinking that they should have everything perfect. We never had everything perfect. Why should they think it's going to be perfect for them?"

"Is there anything else you can tell me about the relationship Kathryn had with her family or with her husband?"

"No, not really. Just that she wasn't a very nice daughter." She paused. "You can tell a lot about somebody's character by the way they treat their parents, you know."

After he thanked Mrs. Beaut and was backing out of her driveway, he picked up the car phone and telephoned Mrs. Deckle. He just needed to get a firm handle on the dead lady's personality and chemistry so that he could know which direction to take. He knew Mrs. Deckle would paint an opposite picture of Kathryn Haddad, but, sometimes, it wasn't the lines spoken, but the way one read between the lines, that provided the most clues in a case.

Mary Deckle was taking a walk with a friend in the neighborhood when he arrived, her daughter said when she greeted him at the door, but he was expected and was welcome to come in and wait. He was a few minutes early. It was a beautiful spring day outside. The dogwood trees and azaleas were blooming, the purple plum trees were in brilliant foliage, and the town was ablaze with breathtaking color. Taking a walk in Macon at this time of year was a spiritual experience, it was so beautiful.

"Oh, hello, Detective," Mary said cheerfully, after she came in the front door and found him in the living room. "It's nice to see you again so soon. Sorry I wasn't home when you got here. I didn't expect you quite this early."

"I just got here, ma'am. Thanks for seeing me on such short notice."

"Oh, that's no problem. It's an early release day, so I have a half day off."

"Mrs. Deckle, I'd like to ask you to search your memory again to help us identify any people who might have hated Kathryn Haddad enough to want her dead. But let me ask you this first." Sullivan paused. "Do you think Stefan Haddad could have killed his wife?"

"Absolutely not," she said immediately and vehemently. "He was a devoted husband and father, and he would never harm his family. He loved Kathryn! They had a good marriage."

"Well, you know from the newspaper stories that circumstantial pieces of evidence collected during a search of his house point to him, Mrs. Deckle. He ended up enriched by her death materially. He suddenly became an insurance millionaire and the owner of a profitable business that they were getting ready to franchise. And, on the face of it, he got rid of a wife who was cheating on him and, who knows, may have been planning to leave him and the family."

"No," she protested vigorously, "that's not the way it could have been. But why did they reject the suicide theory?"

"The medical examiner from Athens wouldn't give her blessings to the suicide theory. What looks probable from the autopsy is that she was struck on the head, then possibly driven to the site where she was found, and then the cocaine-heroin mixture was administered to her, or maybe it was administered to her first, and then she was driven to the site. The medical examiner thought the suicide looked faked, and that's when they turned to Haddad as a suspect."

Mary Deckle sighed and looked down at the floor and stared at her tennis shoes.

"No, not Stefan. But it's hard to believe that anyone killed her. Who could have possibly wanted to kill her?"

"That's what I want you to help with. You knew her. You knew her innermost thoughts. She trusted you. Who had she had a strong disagreement with lately?"

"Well," she began slowly, "she always had her strongest disagreements with her parents. I know she'd had a falling out lately with them, but that wasn't abnormal. They were always picking at her over something." She paused, then continued. "They didn't beat her up physically. They were too smart for that. But they definitely beat her up emotionally, all her life. And that leaves scars, too, you know? Scars that can't be seen. She told me on the phone a few weeks ago when I called her—I think it was right after she came back from Jamaica— that she wasn't going to take it anymore."

"What was it she couldn't take anymore?"

"Detective Sullivan, I told you the other day when we talked that I'm a school psychologist. I have a very small private practice on the side, too. Well, I've done a bit of research through the years to try to understand Kathryn's particular kind of dysfunctional family."

"What do you mean, dysfunctional?"

She sighed as she began. "What I've learned through the years,

Detective, is that a lot of people come from families that are dysfunctional, and a lot of people get traumatized in childhood by some family dysfunction." Mrs. Deckle spoke slowly, as though attempting to be very sure of each word. "But, in Kathryn's family, the dysfunction seemed to escalate as she got older and more successful. Even though I'm a psychologist, I've never been able to understand the escalating cruelty of her parents. Kathryn loved them and wanted them to love her, but they'd always find new and creative ways to victimize her and reduce her to less than what she was. Lately, she felt they were trying to turn her own children against her. It didn't work, but that still lit Kathryn's hot Irish temper. And you know there's no outrage like the outrage a mother feels when she's trying to protect her children."

"I don't understand, Mrs. Deckle. It seemed like Mrs. Haddad would have been the perfect daughter."

Mary Deckle smiled. "Yes, everyone would say that, except her parents. The one thing they couldn't do was rule her, and that's what they wanted. A lot of strong passions and hot tempers run in that family, Detective, and their relationship was one storm after another. I don't think either of her parents ever loved Kathryn the way a parent normally loves a child. That's strange to say, but I think that's at the root of the matter. Her mother was always chasing some new stimulation, and her father traveled all the time and had his women on the side, and Kathryn got neglected. She was always a good student, and she never got in any trouble, so she pretty much raised herself. They never got to know her, as strange as that sounds. Kathryn spent her summers in Tennessee and, when she was home, she was a house servant. Besides housecleaning, she had the job of looking after her little sister, and she really loved Sally. But she figured out after she had her own children that it wasn't her responsibility to raise her grown sister anymore, and Mrs. Faison held that against her. The relationships among all of them got more angry and twisted as they got older. The baby sister hasn't amounted to anything. She turned out weak and dependent, the perfect product of her upbringing. Mr. and Mrs. Faison love her but despise her weakness, whereas they loved Kathryn's strength but hated her independence from them. And they seemed to hate her, too, most of the time. Mrs. Faison told Kathryn once that they wouldn't have anything to do with her if it weren't for the grandchildren. She's a mean and hateful woman. Vera resented Kathryn because of the problems Sally caused them. It's an odd transference that really makes no sense, but I guess that's what dysfunction is all about."

"So Kathryn was the strong one?"

"Yes, the strong one, the accomplished one, and the keeper of the family secrets. Maybe that's what Vera really resented. The fact that Kathryn knew all her secrets. When Kathryn was a child, she had to keep her mother's secrets about who her boyfriend was that month, and they all had to step on eggshells around her father's violent temper. You know how some families have scapegoats? Kathryn was theirs. It's odd and twisted, really. Kathryn loved her sister and parents, but she was a very smart woman, and she refused to let them treat her as a scapegoat for the rest of her life." Mary Deckle paused. "Kathryn tried to be a Christian about the way she handled things with them, too, you know. She told me she wrestled with the problem of how to honor her parents and obey that commandment, even though they were cruel in their treatment of her."

"But why would they have made her the scapegoat?" Sullivan asked. "I took a psychology course in college, and I thought parents made a scapegoat out of the troublemaker or the difficult child or the good-for-nothing kid."

"No, a scapegoat has to be strong to take the abuse of several family members. And don't you see? Kathryn got it all. That's how her mother saw it. Kathryn grew up in the same house with Sally, but Kathryn got it all, while her little sister only caught on to the adultery and manipulation. No matter how hard they tried to pamper and privilege their baby, what they did was teach their favorite daughter how to use people. If you ask me, Vera Faison is a bitter and jealous old woman who resented Kathryn's good character and tried to twist everything so Kathryn would look bad. The Faisons were a very quarrelsome couple when Kathryn was little, and they seemed to team up against Kathryn after she got to be an adult. Mr. Faison gives me the creeps, to tell you the truth. There was always an undercurrent of violence and intimidation with Mr. Faison. Why, he barged into Kathryn's house one day when Kathryn was a single parent and beat up a man who was visiting her and David. He literally knocked several of the guy's teeth out just because he was sitting in Kathryn's den with her and David! The guy was going to press charges against Mr. Faison, but he felt sorry for her and the baby and decided not to. And I know they were bitterly opposed to Kathryn's marrying Stefan—I don't think they wanted her to be happy—and rudely didn't go to the wedding at the last minute. I think Kathryn was getting very tired of them lately, and I think she figured out that their disapproving attitude toward her was ridiculous. They just ran the parental authority thing into the ground."

"So some families single out one of the kids and mistreat that one?"

"Yes, psychology is full of research about that, and the scapegoats are usually the best and brightest in the family. The abusive family members want to destroy anything they can't have, and the strength of the victims attracts and angers them. Family scapegoats have to take punishing abuse from multiple family members, so they have to be very strong. And the scapegoats are often in some kind of role reversal, where the child is expected to parent the adult. So scapegoats have to be strong to survive the continuous abuse, at the same time that they're expected to nurture the others." Mary Deckle paused. "The scapegoat is usually the sensitive, tenderhearted one who's always trying to do the right thing toward the others. A callous parent loves to see the look of pain on the scapegoat's face, and it's quite a power trip to know that the scapegoat will almost never choose to give up her family, no matter how despicably that family treats her." Mary Deckle sighed and shook her head. "Abuse always imprisons the victim and makes her feel responsible for keeping the family intact."

"You make the Faisons sound obnoxious, Mrs. Deckle."

"Oh, now, they go to church, and they're well connected in the community. You're going to find people who will say nice things about them. They give money to the right causes, but they are nasty and manipulative and conniving people who mistreated their firstborn daughter throughout her life. And she bore it with grace and dignity."

She paused. "I've known Kathryn since junior high, and Vera was always confiding in her little girl that she was going to leave her husband. She turned Kathryn into her confidante and accomplice in her adulteries, and that's an abusive thing to do to a child. It was never a mother-daughter relationship. It was something else. It was a kind of perversion of a mother-daughter relationship, because it was just a relationship that was there to serve Vera's purpose. As Kathryn got older and stronger, Vera and Miles seemed to invent a family mythology that, if only Kathryn hadn't been such a difficult daughter, they would have had a happy marriage, or Sally would have turned out better, or they would have had a better relationship with the grandchildren. As they got older, they chose Kathryn as their target for displacing all their hatred, bitterness, anger, and disappointment. Kathryn wasn't the problem at all, but they made her the problem in their vindictiveness."

"Vindictiveness? Do you think they would have been vindictive toward Kathryn?"

"Well, there's the old saying, 'Hell hath no fury like a woman scorned,' and I think it could be as true of parents. There was something definitely hateful and violent about their attitude toward her."

"Do you think her parents would have been capable of harming Kathryn?"

Mary licked her bottom lip with her tongue thoughtfully before she answered. "I think they're mean enough to do anything. Underneath her independent veneer, I think Kathryn was scared of them."

TWENTY-TWO

A few days later, a guard came to Stefan's cell to tell him he had visitors. He felt his heart jump when he realized it might be his children! He yearned to see them, to hug them, and to reach out his arms and offer his lap to the two littlest ones. Stefan called his in-laws' house every time he had an opportunity to use the pay phone, but every time, Vera, Miles, or Sally would pick up the phone and tell him the same thing. The kids were outside playing, or busy doing homework, or out shopping. His children had been kidnapped right under his nose. At least that's how it seemed. He knew they had to be in pain, and he felt sick to his stomach when he thought of not being there for them because he'd unwittingly fallen into a trap.

Walking into the reception room, he felt his stomach tighten as he saw that the children weren't there. At the far end of the room he saw Saxton with his sidekick Kapstein.

"Hello, Mr. Saxton, Mr. Kapstein," Stefan said, nodding to each of them and extending his hand for a handshake to both of them.

"Oh, don't be so formal. Call me Hugh, and he's Russell, Stefan. It's nice to see you," Saxton greeted him warmly. "Please sit down. We have some interesting news for you," smiled Saxton, as he shook his hand vigorously and then motioned to him to sit down in a chair beside them at the long table. After he took a seat, Saxton continued, "I think we've found some weak spots."

"You have?"

"Yes. Oh, it's all just bits and pieces right now, but eventually all the bits and pieces will fit together into a picture. It will all cohere pretty soon now, I hope. Just be patient. How're you holding up in this horrible place, anyway?" Saxton was obviously making an attempt to be friendly toward him. And he was, after all, the only friend he had at the moment, except for Sullivan, who was operating under-cover. Actually, he seemed a congenial fellow. Stefan couldn't resist liking this plainspoken, bold Texan.

"I miss my children, Hugh, and my mother-in-law doesn't want them to talk to me. I know they miss me terribly, too, because we spend so much time together, but I can't seem to break through the wall the Faisons have built to keep me away from them."

"Well, let's hope it won't be too much longer. Let me tell you what we're finding. It seems Detective Sullivan is getting a lot of people to talk to him. Even though he tells them he's not on official business, they think a detective is asking and they tell him whatever they know. His family's well respected and so is he, so he can open any door in town he wants to. Anyway, everybody has enemies, and Sullivan's been talking with people who have grudges against the Faisons and who've known them a long time. The only way we can get you out of here is to break up the 'house of secrets.' You know the old saying, 'A house divided against itself cannot stand.' So we have to divide the Faisons and drive a wedge between them. If they fall apart, one of them will break and the truth will come out. And I think it's going to be the husband. Women are always the toughest and crustiest, you know. That's why they live longer than men."

"You think so?"

"Oh, without a doubt, men are the weaker sex. Women go in one of two directions in life. They either get stronger and meaner, or stronger and nicer, as they get older, but they definitely get stronger. I'm talking about mentally here. Men, they get weaker. Especially if men are married, they eventually just give in to the women. That's the only way men can have any peace. So, I think we can bring Mr. Faison to the breaking point."

"What's Sullivan finding out?"

"Well, Kapstein and I have been questioning Mr. Faison. Actually, I had to depose him to force him to talk with us. I didn't want Sullivan talking to the Faisons because McCormick would find out that he's involved in the background. You know the Faisons have a tight relationship with the sheriff. Anyway, we've been learning a lot about Mr. Faison. Seems he's a typical self-made man who never wants to let anybody forget it. People say he was quite a punk and a bully in his younger days. Real hot-tempered and foulmouthed, and pretty hard on his wife and kids. But you know something, Haddad? There's one thing I've learned over the past twenty years. The punks turn weak in the end. Weakness in character eventually shows through, and the bullies and punks don't have the firepower when they get older. The old man did have a mistress, somebody he really loved, according to the gossip, for several years, and she's been willing to talk to Sullivan. Seems she hung on for years thinking the two of them would really get together, but Mrs. Faison let him know he'd be leaving with nothing financially except the clothes on his back if he humiliated her by leaving for another woman, so he stayed. Mrs. Faison controlled her old man by holding his affair over his head—threatening to tell the children and all that—so he stayed home like a good boy." Saxton paused, then cracked a half smile. "It would have been a shame to break up such a happy family, don't you think?" Stefan returned Saxton's smile and then Hugh Saxton continued. "Oh, I'm sure there's some bitterness and regret doing some of the talking, but the ex-girlfriend says Vera Faison is a real bitch, for whatever that's worth, which probably isn't much. Also, according to the ex-girlfriend, there was some confirmed bad chemistry between your wife and her mother. She says the old man said his wife bragged to him in private about how she more or less put her foot out and tripped her daughter when her first marriage fell apart. She thought the girl might benefit from a good lesson in hardship and humility. Mrs. Faison has some pretty interesting child-rearing techniques, don't you think? Nice family you married into, Stefan!"

Stefan shook his head slowly. "The only thing I can think about is that she has my children with her now." Stefan squirmed in his chair and then switched subjects. "But, to tell you the truth, I don't know if you've found out much. I mean, it's not like it's a big secret that the two women didn't get along."

"That's well put, Stefan. You're right. So far, we've just found out more about things we already knew. But I do think we're getting close to something now. I'm an old bloodhound, and I can smell it. And here's an interesting new fact. It seems that baby sister Sally was snorting cocaine with some buddies at the country club on the night of her recent wedding, and one of the waitresses turned in a bag of white stuff to the general manager, who then turned it over to the sheriff, who was there that night. And you know what the sheriff did with the bag?"

"No, what?"

"He gave it to Mrs. Faison."

"He did?"

"Yeah, he did. The general manager was stunned when he saw the sheriff do it but, apparently, the sheriff took the GM aside and tried to handle it kind of man to man. He told him he and Vera had an affair a long time ago, and he said Mrs. Faison knows 'where all the bodies are buried' in his life, so he didn't really want to make any trouble for her—or for Sally on her special day. Seems like Mrs. Faison made an A in her blackmail techniques course, huh?"

"So what did the general manager do?"

"What could he do? He couldn't exactly make a citizen's arrest of the sheriff, could he? And if he reported it, he'd probably lose his job because the sheriff's on the board of the country club. So he blinked and swallowed hard."

"So that could explain how Vera got hold of a bag of cocaine."

"Yep."

"How did that mirror and cocaine get in my paint cubbyhole?"

"Not sure. The old lady probably put it there during the week of the funeral. She had lots of opportunities during the days when your house was overrun with people. And she knew she could pressure McCormick into forcing a search of your place. I know Mrs. Faison's type. She's a powermonger. With some people, that's what really turns them on, not sex or even money, but using their power to control other people's lives. And she had the power to orchestrate a lot of things behind the scenes. A lot of people were in her debt, apparently."

"But I still don't see how these links lead anywhere. It's nice information, but there's no bottom-line result."

"I think we're weakening Mr. Faison. We're questioning him about his extramarital involvement with this lady I've told you about, and he gets real weak-kneed and teary when he hears her name. If we can push him to the wall, he'll see what an ugly situation he's in, and he may confess what happened."

"You seem so sure he's got something to confess."

"He's got something to confess," Saxton said, nodding his head. "I can see it in his eyes. He's scared and remorseful about something. We have to push him hard in areas he thought were confidential, so that he thinks it's just a matter of time before we know all his secrets anyway. Then we'll break him, I guarantee it. The weak ones always break under hard questioning. It's funny, the bullies who like to push people around are the ones who can least withstand someone else their own size pushing them. They turn into little, crying, whining dogs." Saxton made a face like he'd just tasted sour milk to show his contempt for the old man's weakness and spinelessness.

"That's too bad. I wish he didn't have to be going through this."

There was silence. Then Stefan spoke again.

"You're not questioning her? You could depose Mrs. Faison, too, couldn't you?"

"Mrs. Faison?" Saxton smiled and shook his head. "What's the point? She's made out of shoe leather and steel. She'd never break. She'd lie. She'd manipulate. She'd try to seduce. She'd slander. But she'd never, never break. I know her type. They get stronger as they get older. And as their conflicts and secrets increase in number and complexity, they create elaborate stories to explain the contradictions. So, no, we're not even interviewing her. Part of the skill in battle is sizing up your enemy, you know, and she's a formidable one."

"The newspaper is making you out to be a buffoon. An article yesterday poked fun at the Harvard-trained San Antonio lawyer who took two hours to find the courthouse because he couldn't figure out the one-way streets around the law enforcement center."

"Yeah, that's what they said. Actually, I was enjoying my round-about journey because I was checking out the sweet little Southern prostitutes who line the city streets around the law enforcement center and downtown. Now, that's what *I* call law enforcement!"

Stefan smiled. Mr. San Antonio had insightfully nailed one of the city's public relations problems. It was a standing joke at Rotary Club the way the law enforcement center was right in the middle of the strip joints and topless bars and other night spots. Rumor had it that several prominent families, including McCormick's, owned the seedy downtown properties, and that's why they were never closed down, although there was overwhelming public sentiment to do so. A few people in a back room somewhere were controlling things.

"Anyway, don't you remember I said I was coming to town like a circus clown, to put on a show for the Southern boys?" Saxton asked. "What these Southern boys don't understand is that the game we're playing is 'catch me if you can.' That keeps Sullivan obscure. He's not supposed to be interviewing these people. He had to take official leave, you know, just to do it, and if people find out, he may be called up for disciplinary action."

"Hugh, can you arrange it so I can make a phone call out of the country?" Saxton looked into Haddad's face. There was a plaintive, searching look in his eyes.

"Who do you want to call?"

"Kathryn and I went to Jamaica on a second honeymoon in March, a couple of weeks before she got killed. I want to talk to a lady named Pearl Haddad. Kathryn spent some time with her while I played golf with Pearl's husband. I don't know what they talked about, but Kathryn came back renewed after her talk with Pearl. I've got to understand what they talked about."

"Chances are she won't tell you anything because of client privilege," Saxton said.

"Don't worry about that. Just find a way for me to make the call, will you?"

"Okay, I'll take care of it. Give me the number, or tell me how to find it, and I'll place the call so it comes through on one of these pay phones."

TWENTY-THREE

"Pearl?"

"Stefan!" It was heartwarming to hear Pearl's refined, gracious English accent. "We've been so worried about you. I've called your home so many times, and Kahlil offered his legal help to you through your father-in-law when we phoned them, but we just get the cold shoulder from them. It's been hard for us to know what to do to help you since we're at such a distance. But Kahlil was planning on a business trip to Georgia to see you in a week, if we couldn't get anyone to tell us what's going on there."

"Pearl, I need to ask you something."

"Of course, dear."

"I need to know what you talked about during those days when you and Kathryn were alone in March. Something like a miracle took place during the three days she spent with you."

There was silence on the other end.

"Hello? Are you there?"

"Yes, yes, I'm here, Stefan. It's just that I have a duty to respect the privacy of my interactions with clients. In fact, I'm legally bound to do so."

"I understand, Pearl. And I want to thank you deeply for what you did for Kathryn. She was a new woman when you got through with her."

"Oh, you're welcome, darling. I got your sweet thank-you note."
She paused.

"Pearl, the reason I called is that there may be something you two
talked about that could clear up a loose end and help us make a connection to the circumstances of her death. I've got to get out of here,
and I've got to get my children back. I have to ask you to tell me what
you can."

He could hear Pearl take a deep breath on the other end of the
phone. "Okay, I'll tell you. I'm always in trouble with my profession,
anyway, because I believe morality rather than what they euphemis-
tically call 'professional ethics' should be our guide." She paused and
he could hear her take another deep breath. "Am I being taped? Am I
being deposed?"

"No. It's just me asking right now, Pearl. I'm trying to understand
my wife a little better."

"Okay, Stefan. I'll do it out of love for you and Kathryn, God bless
her. Let me ask you, have you ever heard of the Oedipus complex?"

"Isn't it something from mythology where a boy kills his parents?"

"You're on the right track. Freud used Oedipus complex to describe the multiple emotions a child feels toward his parents. The story
of Oedipus is horrifying, actually. Oedipus was born to a queen and
king who'd been warned they were going to have a son who would
murder his father and marry his mother. So they maimed their own
baby and sent him away to be killed."

"Sounds about as comforting as Hansel and Gretel. Kathryn always said that was the one fairy tale she could never read to the kids."

"Yes, I agree. Well, anyway, Oedipus was rescued and raised by
another king and queen as their son. When he was a young man, the
boy was told about the prediction that he would murder his pop and
marry his mum, so he left his home to protect the people he thought
were his real parents. He came across a man in another country, whom
he killed, and then he married the man's wife. It turned out the man
was his real father and the woman his birth mother. When he found
out the truth, he blinded himself and his birth mother committed
suicide."

"Great bedtime story," Stefan commented dryly.

"Yes, it is a terrifying story, but we psychiatrists think it reveals some bitter truths about life, one of which is that Oedipus started out in life utterly rejected and mistreated by his parents. We think the myth also illustrates the damaging effect of secrets on a person's life, and psychiatrists use the myth to warn people that buried secrets and unconscious rages can lead to emotional catastrophe."

Stefan breathed hard and tried to find polite words to tell Pearl he needed something more than academic theory. "That sounds very 'touchy-feely,' Pearl, as we used to say at the Harvard Business School, but what does that have to do with Kathryn?"

"Kathryn and Oedipus were alike in one way, and that is in the way early childhood shaped their personality."

Stefan felt frustrated. Maybe this wasn't going to lead anywhere. Why was it, he wondered, that academics always seemed to tell us things we already know? "But that should come as no surprise to any of us that childhood shapes our personality to some degree, right, Pearl?"

Pearl ignored his unbelief and went right on explaining. "Freud believed that all adult fears and phobias have their root in childhood."

"If you're saying Kathryn had fears and phobias, I'll agree. She handled it in a dignified way, but she lived with demons and monsters from her childhood."

"Dignified? Do you mean she repressed the fears and phobias? She rarely talked about them? Is that what you mean by dignified? That she rarely bothered you with them?"

He did not respond for several seconds. "Maybe that is what I mean. She didn't talk about them, but I knew they haunted her."

"Well, when you two visited us in March on your second honeymoon, she went through a very significant rebirth, in a way. She became quite transformed, in my opinion, Stefan."

"Yes, Pearl, I felt it, too. When we went to Port Antonio after she saw you, she was a new person."

"She wanted me to put her under hypnosis when she was here. I agreed to do it, and she went through the unraveling of some important repressions under hypnosis. I know she found it frightening, like a plunge into the abyss of the unconscious. She was very brave, though, and she had a great desire to confront her neurotic conflicts. She was desperately afraid she would lose you and her marriage if she didn't get in touch with the fearful child still inside her."

"What do you mean?"

"For one thing, she wanted to forgive her parents for their harsh and dictatorial attitudes toward her. And she wanted to be permanently free of their manipulation. They'd been emotionally blackmailing her for years, withholding love and respect because she didn't cater to their whims."

"Let me ask you something, Pearl. Don't you think people can focus too much on their childhood pain? Don't you just have to make a decision to give it up after a while? Doesn't everybody get bruised in childhood?"

"I understand your point, Stefan, and the reality is that few of us graduate from childhood without picking up some neurotic conflicts. A child is often failed by his parents just like they were failed by the people on whom they were dependent for love and support. One generation fails the next, and there's no forgiveness between generations, you know. Forgiveness comes easier among countries and races than within families and between generations. A lot of times people are doing their best, but their best just isn't close to good enough." Pearl paused. "But then, of course, there are a few people who wound and damage their children on purpose. People who make a deliberate attempt to damage their child's ego and self-concept. People who treat their children like property that exists to serve their whims."

"What you say is interesting, Pearl, but what does this have to do with Kathryn?"

"Well, Kathryn was bruised in childhood. It started with physical abuse, things like harsh whippings when she was a baby and little girl. Then the physical abuse changed to emotional battering when she got older. Psychiatry says the main defense we use to deal with unhappy experiences is repression, and that's what Kathryn used. The main goal of psychiatry, though, Stefan, is to help the person look behind the inhibitions and repressions that are restricting the personality from achieving its greatest potential."

"Well, what did you find when you talked with Kathryn? I mean, when we got on the plane to come back home, she was like a new person. So you must have gotten to the root of something when you talked with her. Didn't you?"

"Yes. I felt strongly when I spent those days with her that she was suffering from post-traumatic stress disorder. We refer to it as PTSD."

"I've heard of it, but what is it exactly? Isn't that what some Vietnam veterans have?"

"Yes, PTSD occurs when there's a significant trauma in one's life that more or less gets reexperienced, over and over, in a cyclical way. Kathryn had all the signs of PTSD. She was reexperiencing a trauma that had occurred years ago. She was reacting by burying memories of the trauma and trying to ignore feelings resulting from the trauma. She was going through a cycle in which she'd involuntarily recall incidents when she'd been traumatized, and that would be followed by attempts to repress the memories and numb her emotions. And that cycle was actually making her quite physically ill, as you know, Stefan."

"Yes, she was very weak and discouraged when we first saw you. That's why I wanted to bring her on holiday. So what was the trauma she was reexperiencing? Was this some trauma related to her divorce years ago?"

"No, Stefan, I don't think so. I think she exhibited signs of PTSD for the first time shortly after she married David's father, and I think she went a little crazy in her first marriage."

"What do you mean?"

"I mean, from what I learned when she went under hypnosis, she experienced PTSD for the first time when she married and went to Mexico. She found herself in an intimidating situation that immobilized and disabled her and, to put it in layman's terms, I suppose you'd say she blew a fuse. Powerful memories of her traumatic childhood surfaced and tormented her, and she became traumatized by the neurosis that her marriage was going to be like her childhood. In the modern vernacular, one would say she freaked out during her first marriage. She felt she was in a life-threatening situation, and that caused her to feel terror, and she did what psychiatrists call 'fight-or-flight.' Her body was remembering childhood pain, and her mind believed what the body was telling it. She'd grown up in a hostile family, and she felt like she was back in another hostile family. And she wanted to escape."

"I think I understand what you mean, but tell me more."

"Kathryn was a trauma survivor from her childhood, and she felt herself to be back in that traumatic situation after she married her first husband. From what she told me, she nearly completely abandoned her reasoning and reverted to a childlike state of learned helplessness and turned for help to the parent who'd always devalued and dominated her."

"So she told you about her childhood." There was a touch of bitter sarcasm in his voice. "Did she also tell you she was having an affair with her ex-husband?"

"Yes, she did tell me, Stefan," Pearl answered softly. "Kathryn was a person who didn't feel good about herself at the core most of her life, you know. She'd suffered a lot of callous treatment by her family. She'd been trained to think of herself as someone who should serve them, and if she didn't meet their expectations, they punished her with emotional coldness and mental cruelty." Pearl paused. "Her parents were not the people I was speaking of earlier who try to do their best but their best isn't good enough. Her parents weren't content with anything except ruling her. Not everybody gets a good family to grow up in, Stefan. She didn't."

"Everything you say is true, but Kathryn still made her choices where the infidelity was concerned. They certainly weren't responsible for her affair."

"No, they weren't responsible for her making that choice, but they have some responsibility for the grief they deliberately inflicted on her in childhood and in adulthood. It's very difficult for a child when a parent is abusive, because there's a taboo against expressing anger at one's parents. People call it 'parent bashing,' and certainly it can be carried too far since all of us fail each other unwittingly. But the power is always on the side of the parents, because there's such a strong cultural and religious feeling that one should honor parents, and that code makes it difficult for abused children to deal with perfectly legitimate anger toward them. But both religion and psychiatry are in agreement on this important principle: each person should be permitted to unlock his or her fullest human potential. And if bogey-men from childhood haunt us and keep us from doing that, then the bogeymen have to be exorcised. What psychiatry tries to do is get rid of the 'ghosts' and repressions that keep trauma from reoccurring. 'Making unexpected house calls' is how we used to describe the on-slaught of PTSD when we were in med school. PTSD is like having a tyrant boss that can pop up anytime and make life more miserable than it ought to be."

"Why did Kathryn's family dislike her?"

"We don't know why some families single out one person as a target for mistreatment. In Kathryn's case, the family members de-meaned her and exploited her resources in whatever ways they could. Abuse survivors are trained to do favors for the family, and they're programmed to feel that they owe everything to the family, yet the family makes the victim feel that she never does enough. Those kinds of families are continually revictimizing. I mean, it doesn't just hap-pen in childhood, but it goes on and on. And it's very difficult to live near such a family because they invent new ways to traumatize and humiliate. When Kathryn was growing up, only her father, who was quite a violent man, was permitted to express his anger, and he did so cruelly and in a way that instilled fear. The mother took out her anger toward the father by having a string of relationships with other men, and Kathryn had to be a child in a situation in which she was expected to nurture the adults and meet their expectations. She was never al-lowed to express her anger. Everything had to be repressed, yet she had to project a perfect image to the outside world. She lived in a shell that she came out of for public performances from time to time. They battered her socially when she was a single parent by trying to isolate her and control her public interactions. They failed, of course, be-cause Kathryn was so strong. She was made out of steel, just like them. Abusers always try to control the victim and cut them off from other people and from relationships that will help them see that abuse is not normal. Her mother wanted to be the only one to have an adult relationship with Kathryn, so she'd have control, but Kathryn rejected her. So the mother retaliated with psychological warfare. So the first time Kathryn experienced PTSD was when she married the first time.

Basically, she flipped out and, not uncommonly for abused children who are always trying to get things right with their abusers, she turned to her parents for guidance, and they led her on a destructive path. She experienced PTSD again recently when she ran into her first husband. Seeing him again stirred up some deep hurts, and she became overwhelmed with emotion and sentiment."

Stefan did not speak when he heard her pause. When she heard him breathing ponderously into the phone, she continued.

"There's also something we see frequently in psychiatry, Stefan, that a psychiatrist named Betsy Cohen called the Snow White syndrome. That's the name for a mother-daughter relationship where a self-centered mother envies her daughter the opportunities and fun she never had. Kathryn's mother envied her, and she trained the sister to envy her. I believe Kathryn's sister became a very damaged person under the brute force of the strong egos in that house. Kathryn never did anything to deserve their envy except be talented and beautiful and successful."

"So where does all this lead us?"

"There's something else nearly all psychiatrists agree on, and religion is in agreement, too. And that is that the greatest crime you can commit against a child is to instill a dishonest and hypocritical philosophy of life. That, I think, is what caused most of Kathryn's childhood neuroses. They taught dishonesty and hypocrisy by the way they mixed church work with adultery, and by the way they dished out cruelty and kindness in a completely random fashion. Even as a child, Kathryn was intelligent and knew her birth parents didn't have the integrity or morality to be her teachers, but she repressed her feelings. Kathryn was lucky that she had grandparents who taught her about morality and values, and who also taught her that she was special. The problem was that even when she was an adult her parents kept insisting on their right to be her authorities. When we get to be adults, we try to forget our childhoods, and we think we do forget, but then our body remembers. Repression is so harmful because it's like a wall between experience and intelligence that makes us act blindly, and we often don't figure out the reasons for our destructive behavior until it's too late. That's why PTSD occurs, because the body is remembering even though we've trained the mind to ignore the painful images. The only way we can really stop ourselves from hurting over and over is to break the cycle, and we can only do that by actually confronting our repressions."

"Well, it didn't do Kathryn much good to confront her repressions, did it?" There was sadness and some anger in his voice.

Pearl responded aggressively and passionately. "Kathryn couldn't have continued living as she was living. It's terribly sad that she's dead, but I truly believe her soul was cured of its sickness before she died. Freud believed that 'the truth shall make you free.' And freeing people to have abundant life was what Jesus was all about, too, you know."

He breathed into the phone for a few seconds, wondering what to ask. He felt suddenly discouraged and weary and very aware in a new way that the woman he loved was dead. His question, when he finally asked it, was halfhearted and intended more as a polite rejoinder than anything else. Actually, he felt his mind wandering back to memories of Kathryn and him and the children together. "So religion and psychiatry have the same goals, Pearl?"

"In many ways, they do, Stefan. Freud thought of himself as a physician of the soul and he was concerned with the same problems as theologians and philosophers: curing the soul of its torments. He believed mental sickness couldn't be understood apart from moral problems. Freud believed we can make ourselves sick by ignoring the demands of the soul." She paused. "And there's another belief religion and psychiatry have in common."

"What's that?"

"Well, psychiatry subscribes to a belief that many great religious leaders and philosophers have shared. People like Buddha, Isaiah, Jesus Christ, and Socrates. They all believed in holding up love as the true test of moral righteousness. Remember how the Bible says, 'By their fruits you shall know them.' If we see people such as parents encourage growth, strength, freedom, and happiness, we see the fruits of love. If we see people who try to constrict or dominate human potential and harness it for their own use, those people cannot be motivated by love. Love is from God. Lying and deception and manipulation are from the evil one. Truth is the basic aim of psychoanalysis and of religion, and the enemies of both psychoanalysis and religion are deception and dissimulation and deceit. There is neither truth nor love in the liar, you know."

"Well, I appreciate your talking to me, Pearl. They're motioning to me that I need to get off the phone. I don't know if I've solved any mystery here, but I think I understand my wife a little better." He paused. "Better late than never, I guess. It's ironic that I waited until she died to try to understand her soul, don't you think?"

"I don't know how Kathryn died, Stefan, but I know her soul was at peace when she died. You said yourself she was a new person after we spoke. I *know* her soul was at peace." She paused, then continued. "And I've lived long enough to know this, too, Stefan: nothing ever happens that God can't use for a good purpose. I don't think he causes bad things like this to happen, but I think he can always make something good from something bad and always make something positive from something negative."

"Thanks, Pearl."

"Take care of yourself, darling. We want to see you and the kids soon."

TWENTY-FOUR

There was a big smile on the guard's face as he unlocked the cell. Stefan wondered who his visitor could be. Then the guard announced with a smile, "Looks like you're a free man, sir."

"What? What do you mean?"

"Your father-in-law just confessed. Seems like the mother and daughter were in the middle of it, somehow. I just got a call saying the official paperwork will be coming momentarily to release you, sir."

At that moment another guard came down the hall, walking quickly. He stopped beside Haddad's cell.

"Visitor, Mr. Haddad. I think it's that homicide detective, sir."

Sullivan greeted him in the reception room with an embrace. He hugged Haddad and kissed first, one cheek, and then, the other. It was the way his Middle Eastern relatives embraced and kissed him when he was in the Caribbean.

"You're free."

"What happened?"

"The old man cracked. We didn't even have to push all that hard. I mean, we did and we didn't," he said, cocking his head. "Like so many things in life, it's more a matter of technique than strength, if you know what I mean. I'm not even sure we should claim credit. The old man had such guilt that he got some relief by becoming an honest man."

"I can't believe all this," Stefan said, standing up and looking out the window with bars on the outside that faced the prison parking lot. He was a free man, but he wasn't the same man as he'd been three weeks ago. Then he turned to face the detective, seated at a table near the window.

"Tell me what happened."

"According to your father-in-law, she went to her parents' house on the morning of her death. Actually, she went twice. She went to tell them that she was completely breaking off her relationship with them. The first time she went was real early in the morning, and she picked up some of her old books and trophies and took them back home. That's when you saw her that morning, just as you were going out to run. Then she went back the second time, sometime after nine o'clock, and when she went back, she and her mother got into a nasty quarrel. There was a lot of name calling, apparently. Then the baby sister showed up on the scene and joined in on mommy's team. There was a bitter argument. Mr. Faison said your wife was ranting and raving like a crazy woman and said a lot of things that were uncomplimentary, and what she said inflamed them. I think your wife was playing with fire there, because she was around some pretty volatile personalities. I remember once in catechism class I had to memorize what the Book of James says about our tongue, that 'the tongue is a fire setting on fire the cycle of nature and set on fire by hell.' I guess that just means that the tongue is the most violent weapon we ever have in our house. Anyway, what she said stirred up the fires of hell. The younger daughter was there, drugged up, and came up from behind and hit her sister with a baton they'd argued over in childhood, and then your wife fell down a flight of steps. The blow and the fall knocked her unconscious. The parents moved her to one of the couches downstairs, thinking she might have a minor concussion. When the mother and father weren't looking, the sister administered a mixture of cocaine and heroine to Kathryn while she was unconscious. Mr. Faison has protested that his baby daughter just intended it as a joke and had no idea that the dosage she gave your wife was so potent that she'd go into a coma and be brain dead in five minutes. But, when the parents checked on her a little later, they saw that

Kathryn was dead. So, then, Mrs. Faison figured they had to protect their baby daughter. Your wife had told them she was meeting David and Galleria for lunch at the lodge, so Mrs. Faison thought that driving her to the parking lot near the lodge would be a good solution. They knew the sheriff was responsible for all homicides outside the county, and they knew McCormick would swallow the suicide explanation. What happened, though, is that the body got autopsied that Easter weekend in Athens instead of in Macon, where the medical examiner would have signed whatever McCormick told him to sign, and the medical examiner from Athens didn't buy suicide. Framing you for her murder was an afterthought, you know. By the time I interviewed the Faisons after their daughter's funeral, the sheriff had already told them that it looked like there was going to be a homicide investigation because the Athens examiner felt there had been foul play. That's when Mrs. Faison decided you had to take the fall so she could protect her middle-aged baby."

"Did the sheriff help them cover up the real murderer?"

"No," Sullivan said, rolling his eyes, "McCormick is basically just a big dumb jock, and Mrs. Faison's been leading him around by the nose for years. He's in her stable of debtors, apparently."

"So they drove Kathryn to the parking lot and left her there?"

"Yes. The mother and daughter had the old man put Kathryn in her car and drive her to that deserted lane where, actually, Mr. Faison had been caught one time with his lady friend by Mrs. Faison. Anyway, they were leaving Kathryn there so Galleria could find her, or so you could stumble upon her when you went running. Vera Faison followed her husband in her own car, a BMW, and then he got in the car with her and the three of them went back home. Just one big happy family. Yes, sir, that's what we need in this world, don't we? More family values!" Sullivan grew quiet and stared at Stefan in silence for a couple of minutes before he continued. "The old man insists that Sally didn't mean to kill her sister. It was an accident, and she just meant to play a trick on her. But I heard through Saxton that the Faisons' lawyer is preparing a pretty good defense based on the fact that their baby suffered from 'intermittent explosive disorder' when she hit your wife with the baton. The defense will contend that your wife provoked them, and Sally was overcome by a rare condition characterized by episodes in which a person cannot control violent impulses. They'll use Mr. Faison's violent history of punching out people who worked for him and that kind of stuff to prove their point. I guess that's some kind of meanness-runs-in-the-family defense. And you know how the legal system is these days, Stefan. Nobody's responsible for anything anymore. There's just one fancy condition after another that causes human behavior. Nobody is really responsible for his or her choices in our society. Ours is the age of hypocrisy, I'm afraid, Stefan. Nobody's personally to blame."

"So Mr. Faison told you everything?"

"Oh, yes, he broke down crying like a baby. He was protesting that Kathryn was always so difficult temperamentally. She caused the scene and drove her sister to it, according to the old man. But I don't think deep down even he believes it. I think he felt relieved when he confessed. Now, he doesn't have to keep the secret. And he doesn't have to live in a pretend world raising the kids of a daughter murdered by the family."

"Did Mrs. Faison admit that she tried to sabotage the investigation?"

Sullivan cocked his head. "No. I think she knows she's caught in a net, but she's cunning. She claims that her husband is out of his head. She denies what he said and says he's gone temporarily insane because of the enormous pressure we put on him." Then Saxton's face grew taut. "But she looked pretty sad to me when I saw her earlier today at the sheriff's department. She looks like a woman who's full of regrets."

"How do families get so screwed up?"

Sullivan sighed and shook his head, as though he'd been asked a question too hard to answer. Then a look came over his face as though he'd figured it out, and he broke the silence.

"Choices is what it comes down to in life, I guess. The theologians tell us that we can be forgiven and get cleaned up from anything, no matter what we do. But it's not quite as simple as that. There are immutable laws of the universe that govern us, and, no matter what the theologians tell us about forgiveness, we really do reap what

we sow. We probably need to listen to the philosophers as much as
the theologians, but we don't like what the philosophers say. They
tell us that we end up being the sum total of our choices in life, and
it's our choices rather than our circumstances that bring inner peace
or inner torment. I guess that's what happened to the Faisons. They
became embittered by their choices and had no peace. They tried to
demand love and respect from your wife, but it doesn't work like that,
so they turned on her and she became a scapegoat for all their unhappiness and regrets." He paused. "And you know what the Jews used
to do with scapegoats, don't you?"

"No."

"Well, everybody in the community would put all their sins onto
the goat, and then they'd kill the goat, and that was supposed to make
their sins go away."

"If Kathryn just hadn't gone over there . . ."

"Yeah, that's right. Apparently that's the riskiest time in an abusive relationship, when the victim is trying to break away from the
abusers. That's when the possessive, violent rage often breaks out. A
lot of people end up dead right at that point when they try to leave the
relationship."

"I still wonder why she did it."

"You mean, Mrs. Faison?"

"No. I mean Kathryn. Part of the mystery still remains for me.
We had a good marriage. And she was a good Christian woman, I
mean, really good, not a hypocrite. Why did she have the affair? It all
started with that, didn't it? Maybe there's something I should have
done differently in our marriage."

"Ah, I thought you were going to ask me an easy question, like
where are the kids, and when can you actually get out of here, and
how do you get your hands on your insurance money. Now you're
asking something only God can answer."

Stefan shot him a look that implied his surprise at Sullivan's talking about the Creator.

The intelligent detective saw the look in his eyes. "I was brought
up by good parents who taught me about Christianity. Actually, I
almost became a minister. I really thought about it. I don't think there's

anything wrong with Christianity, it's just that people don't do Christianity very well."

"What do you mean?"

"There's a lot of self-denial and discipline in religion, if you do it right. But I don't think most people want to do it right. They want religion to be something else. Something that makes them feel good, and forgiven, and loved, and valued. The obedience part of Christianity, that's the part people don't get right. I think I know the way it has to be done, but it's very difficult to do over a lifetime. There's too much sacrifice involved. And life is very tricky on occasion."

"But Kathryn was always good at the discipline and sacrifice part of religion. I still don't understand."

Sullivan looked at the tall, thin, handsome French Canadian standing beside the window facing the parking lot. He'd grown thinner in jail and he'd sprouted a beard. He'd have a hard life for a while being a single parent of four children, but he was a strong, resilient, honorable person who attracted good people, and he'd have no trouble finding another woman when the time came. Sullivan took a deep breath and leaned back in the chair, his hands folded behind his head.

"Maybe we try to make religion too complicated. Jesus Christ said that all the laws of God boil down to two main ones. Put God first above everyone and everything, and treat others as you would like to be treated. But I guess we don't do a good job of applying those religious principles in our relationships. Most of us just can't make our human relationships work out like we want them to. Everything else in life is easier than the human relationships part. And we all go around more vulnerable and needy than we want to admit. We want to love and be loved, we want to fix our broken relationships, we want intimacy, we want to feel alive. We want to chase a dream, and have a dream chase us back." Sullivan paused, then continued. "We're all weak and defective, and more in need of mercy than judgment in our relationships. Maybe that's why Jesus said we have to forgive over and over, and he called on us to perfect our character and be peacemakers. Forgiveness, Stefan. That's what we need more of in this world. Because all of us mess up big time and are in great need of forgiveness at many points along the way." Sullivan's face took on a cheerful look, and he sounded reverent and respectful when he spoke again. "You know, everything we heard about your wife was very complimentary. She was a talented and beautiful woman and a great mother and wife. You were lucky to have her."

Stefan looked at Sullivan. No emotion showed in his face. "You think I should feel lucky right now, John?"

"No, I don't think you should feel lucky at this moment, that's not what I meant. But you loved her, and she loved you, and you had four beautiful children who take part of her with them, and you were alive with her in such a vital way, for a moment in time. That's not nothing, you know. Not everybody gets that out of life. So many people sit around never taking the risk of relationship because they know it'll hurt too much to fail. And even if you don't fail, love breaks your heart a time or two. But then, if you don't take the risk, you never live, I mean, really live." Sullivan paused. "We're all defective, you know. That's what original sin is all about. We just don't want to follow the commandments that are designed to protect us, and we rebel. And our disobedience brings shame and punishment, and we suffer because of our sins. God gave Adam and Eve a choice of being obedient or disobedient, and they didn't control their greed and lust any more than we do. Jesus Christ said we should follow the commandments out of love for God. He said we should have the commandments written on our hearts and just do them out of love. That sounds like pretty good advice when we're in Sunday school but, when nobody's looking, we want to taste the forbidden fruit. We just want to take one little bite. That's all Adam and Eve really wanted, you know—just one bite. The problem is that one bite leads to so much more than we expect it to. And we just don't want to live in submission and obedience to the rule of God all the time. We don't want to give up having a bite every now and then. I always liked the way the Apostle Paul put it in Romans. He said that his good nature was continually at war with his bad nature, and even when he wanted to do the right thing, he often ended up doing the wrong thing."

"So we're destined to fail anyway, because of our weak and defective mortal nature, is that right? What's the damned point, then, if the carnal part is always going to beat out the spiritual part?"

Sullivan smiled a wry smile. "Logical to the end, aren't you, Stefan? Well, like most people, I'm better at telling someone how to do it than doing it myself, but the theory is that we're called to a process of continuously perfecting our character. We have a way of being saved from temptations if we want to be saved from them, but most of us want to enjoy the temptations first and get saved later. We just don't see that God gave us the commandments to protect us from falling into deep pits of trouble. The commandments are like road signs for living a happy life that God has given his human children. But we have to learn the hard way that disobedience never brings happiness. We trade off the long-term and throw away all our peace of mind for a short, sweet taste of the apple. All of us do it, you know, so we can't sit in judgment of others."

There was silence between Stefan and Hugh for what seemed like minutes. Then Stefan spoke. "What about you and McCormick? Are you in trouble for working on the case behind the scenes?"

"Are you kidding? I'm a hero!" He lowered his voice and added, "Seriously, McCormick is appreciative. I broke the case, you know, although he's still trying to figure out how to give some credit to his new information system. Saxton has become known as the buffoon who's still trying to figure out how to get through the long legs of those Southern prostitutes to the law enforcement center, but I'm a hero. Sheriff McCormick is begging me to come for photo sessions with him so he can use the pictures in his reelection campaign."

"What about my kids?"

"Well, funny you should ask, but they just happen to be coming into this room at this very moment. I just saw your oldest boy's face pressed up against the wall."

A second later, four children pushed the door open with a guard coming close behind them, and they nearly fell over each other getting to their father. All four grabbed a piece of him to hug. After bending down to receive his children, Haddad sat down to let his daughter and littlest son sit on his lap.

"Are we going home, Daddy?" asked Veronica.

"Yes, my darlings, we are going home," he answered.

Another guard brought some paperwork in for Haddad and

Sullivan to sign. Then the guard informed Haddad that he could pick up his keys and personal belongings from the front desk and change clothes.

After he picked up his personal items, Stefan, his children, and Sullivan walked outside where photographers swarmed around them.

"How's it feel to be free, Mr. Haddad?"

"It feels great to be with my children again. I just wish my wife were here with us, too. But we're a family, and we're going home."

Haddad convinced the photographers that he was too tired to answer questions, but he said he'd let them interview him by phone the next day. Mercifully, the reporters and photographers deferred to the obvious needs of the children to have their father alone, especially since Sullivan said he'd stay and hold a press conference to answer their questions.

Hugh Saxton was outside with a rented luxury car, and he insisted on giving them a ride home.

Once they pulled up in front of the driveway, Stefan gave David the house keys. He asked the kids to go on inside and said he'd follow.

"Are you going back to San Antonio tonight?" Stefan asked.

"Yes, actually in about an hour. I have a flight booked and my job here is done, happily," he smiled.

"I appreciate it, Hugh," Stefan said, extending his hand to receive the Texan's strong handshake. Then his voice changed and became colder and businesslike. "Tell Marcos thank-you for me, will you?"

"I'll tell him."

Stefan didn't disembark so Hugh knew more conversation was coming.

"Let me ask you something, Hugh."

"Shoot."

"It was love, wasn't it? That he felt for her, I mean. All this wasn't just about lust, was it?"

Saxton didn't reply for a few seconds. "That's outside my area, Stefan. I have no idea."

Stefan lingered for another minute, looking somberly out the car window. Then they both jumped as they heard a thump on the car door on Stefan's side.

"Come on, Dad," Calvin said impatiently. "Let's play some football." The ten-year-old had a football in his hands and his brothers and sister were running on the front lawn, waiting for their dad to join in the familiar family football ritual.

After Stefan closed the car door and waved goodbye, Saxton rolled slowly out of the fashionable suburb. When he reached the intersection at the main road, he calculated his route out of town and, after doing so, picked up the car phone as he increased the speed at which he was cruising along the town's major highway.

"Is Galleria in, Linda?"

"Oh, just a moment, Mr. Saxton," said the youthful and gracious Mexican voice. "He will be glad to talk to you."

"Hola, Marcos, this is Hugh. The mission has been accomplished, the good guy is out of jail, the bad guys are trying to talk their way out of it, and I just delivered the merchandise to the Haddad home. The Beverly hillbillies are together again, home alone, safe at last. I'm on my way out of town. The flight for San Antonio leaves in an hour. I've got the soybean import agreement you faxed me, and I'll look it over on the plane. My preliminary reading is that we can squeeze them some more." He paused, then continued in a softer tone of voice. "Oh, one more thing," he said, as he made an abrupt turn into a cemetery, "I've got the five dozen red roses in the trunk, and I'll put them on her grave on my way out of town, like you asked me to."

ABOUT THE AUTHOR

PATTY SLEEM was born in North
Carolina. She holds an MBA from the
Harvard Business School and a BA in
English from the University of North
Carolina at Chapel Hill. She is the author
of *Back In Time,* and her writings have
appeared in a wide variety of publications.
She has lived in London, San Francisco,
Boston, and Washington, D.C. Currently
she resides in North Carolina.

PREP PUBLISHING is a subsidiary of PREP, Inc., a communications company founded in 1981, which owns the world's largest resume-by-mail service. Writers with substantial business backgrounds as well as military translation specialists are the backbone of PREP's writing team, which prepares professional resumes, cover letters, job and school applications, business proposals, speeches, and other written products. For information on PREP's professional writing and editing services, call 910-483-6611 or write PREP, Box 66, Fayetteville, NC 28302.